RIP TIDE

A Ripple Effect Cozy Mystery
Book Two

Jeanne Glidewell

Cover and Book design by eBook Prep
www.ebookprep.com

January, 2016
ISBN: 978-1-61417-821-7

ePublishing Works!
www.epublishingworks.com

DEDICATION

This story takes place in Rockport, Rip and Rapella Ripple's hometown on the Coastal Bend (Gulf Coast) in south Texas. My husband Bob, Dolly, the best traveling cat we've ever owned, and I, spend much of our time there, too, in our waterfront condo on Key Allegro Island. Heaven to me is relaxing on our back deck with a cup of coffee, after a successful day of wade-fishing, and enjoying a beautiful sunset from our hard-to-beat viewpoint on Little Bay. I thought it would be appropriate to dedicate this book to a few of my most beloved Rockport friends: Cheri Sheets, Barb Harrison, Cindy Colmer, and Sue Hale. These ladies not only support me in my writing career, but they're also a lot of fun to hang out with, go fishing with, and just spend time with doing all sorts of amusing and entertaining things. They play no small part in why Rockport, Texas, is my favorite place in the entire world. Thanks for all the great times we've had, ladies! And here's to many, many more in the future!

ACKNOWLEDGEMENTS

I would like to thank my editors, Alice Duncan of Roswell, New Mexico, and Judy Beatty of Madison, Alabama, who take very good care of my manuscripts. I'd also like to thank Nina and Brian Paules, of eBook Prep and ePublishing Works, who take very good care of my books after Alice and Judy are through with them. All four are very special people and incredible to work with.

I'd also like to thank two women I met through messages they sent me via my website, www.jeanneglidewell.com, whom I now consider friends. They are Yvonne Pineiro, of Centereach, New York, and Shirley Worley of Shawnee, Kansas. My thanks to Yvonne, an incredibly talented artist, for her random acts of kindness and for providing me with inspiration. Using a photo she took off my Facebook page of baby elephants I'd photographed while on a Kenya Safari, Yvonne sent me a beautiful framed print she'd drawn of it. Her breathtaking drawing hangs proudly in the entryway of our Kansas home now. You can see and/or purchase some of Yvonne's amazing work via her online store http://www.amazon.com/handmade/studioyp

I also greatly appreciate Shirley, an author in her own right, for her proofreading skills. Having completed her debut novel, *Easy Money*, she is currently writing a sequel. It's nice to have Shirley's sharp eye to catch obscure and occasionally bizarre errors *before* the books are released. The ones she doesn't catch—that's all on me.

CHARACTER LIST

Rapella Ripple—A spunky senior citizen and full-time RVer who's determined to track down the killer of her son-in-law's best friend and business partner when Milo lands on the top of the suspect list. Despite being miffed when her daughter, Regina, refers to her parents as "rednecks," nothing says "Get 'er done" quite like Rapella.

Clyde "Rip" Ripple—When a murder is committed in the county where he once served as Sheriff, the other half of this sixty-eight-year old couple is miffed when he's banned from the police station by the man he'd groomed to replace him. Sheriff Joe Peabody considers Rip's involvement a "conflict of interest."

Regina Ripple—The Ripple's fifty-year-old daughter is miffed when her husband won't consent to buying her a new high-dollar vehicle. Perhaps she's unaware of the true reason Milo is denying her this luxury she feels she so greatly deserves. Much to Rapella's chagrin, Reggie and her mother are polar opposites when it comes to money.

Milo Ripple—A nasty bar brawl ensues after Milo becomes miffed at his best friend when Cooper Claypool's poor judgment threatens the future of their co-owned business. Having no verifiable alibi and a perceived motive to kill, Milo is considered a good candidate for the title of "killer." His boneheaded and tight-fisted tendencies frustrate Rip, who is trying to clear his son-in-law's name. Are all of Milo's in-laws' efforts in vain?

Cooper Claypool—This victim of a gruesome death is found floating, spear-side up in the Gulf of Mexico. Miffed at being blindsided by his best friend's ire the previous day, he had opted to go spear-fishing alone. Perhaps he needed to give his mind and heart a chance to cool off. But being shot dead with one's own spear-gun is just plain cold-hearted.

Big Bob—Big Bob is miffed when he feels as though he's being stalked by a determined senior citizen. Could this large gap-toothed man be someone other than who Rapella thinks he is?

Dr. Patrick O'Keefe—Newly divorced, this general practitioner is miffed that his ex-wife, Avery Curry, is fighting him for custody of Liz, while she's shacking up with the murder victim. And Rapella's habit of cooling him off doesn't unmiff him any, either. Could his most recent "operation" have been an ominous plan carried out to eliminate the competition?

Avery Curry—The victim's current live-in girlfriend is more panicked than miffed when she's asked to cook up something she doesn't have a clue how to prepare. Her miffedness subsides when an unexpected Master Chef steps in and tries to help pull her backside out of the fire. But was her professed love for Cooper Claypool sincere?

The Schillings—Both Mack and Trey are miffed when MC Hammerhead Construction Company fails to hold up their end of the deal. How far will the father-and-son team go to get even?

Julio Sarcova—A local barber and former customer of Milo and Cooper's who becomes miffed when his young son's health is compromised by MC Hammerhead's less than professional standards. Did Julio find time between protests to exact justice on his son's behalf?

"Captain Hook"—An unidentified menace who's determined to recoup the funds owed his boss. This dude stays miffed. But without a lofty level of miffedness he couldn't intimidate debtors over the phone as effectively. The Ripples suspect Captain Hook is a moniker for the real killer and could possibly be someone they're already investigating as a potential perpetrator. Is this dude miffed enough to actually eliminate debtors who don't cave into the pressure?

Philip Bean, a.k.a. "Pinto"—A local fisherman who's miffed that the over-harvesting of oysters was forcing him to stretch every dollar to the max just to eke out a living. After all, he has to pay the crew even when the day's booty ain't worth a hill of *beans*. It's said killers often return to the scene of the crime. Is this adage true in this crime?

The Willis Brothers—Billy and Spider are miffed because their court-ordered AA meetings were cutting into their drinking time. Fortunately for these two rummies, Pinto can't afford to be too particular about who he hires as deckhands. These two siblings have set the bar low for their stations in life. But could they have had another objective in mind?

FROM THE DESK OF
JEANNE GLIDEWELL

Dear Reader,

As a cozy mystery writer, every one of my novels should begin with the same nine words. *Make yourself comfortable while I tell you a story.* Because that's what I am; a storyteller. I'm not a wordsmith, a grammar professor, or even a fifth-grade spelling bee champion. I'm just a storyteller who's always happy to spin a yarn for the entertainment of others.

Please do not feel compelled to look up questionable words in this novel that my wonderful editors reluctantly let slide (while gritting their teeth). I grew up winning a good deal of Scrabble games by making up words (with believable definitions too bizarre and specific to have been made up) and I'm not above making them up now on those occasions when no word recognized by Funk & Wagnalls quite fits the bill. "Miffedness" is not the result of one of those occasions, by the way, but I won't vouch for "unmiff." I suppose my novels should come with the warning: "Do not try this at school."

Also, keep in mind, *Rip Tide* is a work of fiction, and I have freely used the creative license that comes with it; such as a few specific non-facts about the Rockport area, local business names and places, specifics about spear-fishing (which, like the majority of readers, I've experienced exactly zero times), and other random acts of total fabrication that are merely products of my imagination. I try to be as factual as possible, but when that option's not feasible, I just reach in and pull something out of my bag of tricks. And it's a very deep and crowded bag.

I'd also like to apologize in advance for the fact I can't seem to quit my bad habit of blathering—something Alice Duncan chides me for every time she edits one of my books. (I've tried patches, pills, even hypnotism—but nothing seems to work.) *Rip Tide* might have been more aptly titled *Blathering Heights*. With all that in mind, I hope you enjoy this tale involving one of my favorite pastimes: fishing while wintering in our Rockport, Texas, vacation home.

Happy Reading,
Jeanne

CHAPTER 1

"Fishy, fishy in the brook, come and get on daddy's hook," my husband, Clyde "Rip" Ripple, sang as he pretended to cast a heavy duty fishing rod inside Tackle Town, a popular sporting goods store in our hometown of Rockport, Texas. I don't think he had any idea how ridiculous he looked when he set the invisible hook on an imaginary fish. When Rip began pretending to reel in a large catch, which was clearly putting up quite a fight, I had to walk away so it wasn't obvious to other shoppers that he was my husband.

Satisfied with the fishing rod's performance, after apparently landing the "whopper" successfully, he walked over and placed two identical rod and reel combos in our basket.

"I can't wait to catch a big redfish," he said excitedly.

"Oh, wasn't that what you just caught in the bait bucket aisle? I didn't see you measure it, honey. Just how large was that thing? By the tussle it gave you, I have to assume it was a dandy."

"Oh, good grief! I almost forgot I need to get a couple of those stick-on measuring tapes to adhere to the sides of our poles. Thanks for reminding me." He turned on his heels to head back in the direction from which he'd just come.

"Seriously? I can't wait to see what a $117.29 fish looks like!" I exclaimed, speaking to his backside.

"What are you talking about?" He turned back around to ask.

"We're buying fishing licenses, expensive rods and reels—"

"I wouldn't want a trophy red to get away because we were using inferior equipment."

"Hand-held nets and neoprene waders—"

"Milo said they like to get out and wade for redfish in the shallows of Aransas and Copano Bays, and we wouldn't want to have to sit in the boat feeding bait to the crabs while Milo and Cooper are catching keeper fish right and left."

"And fishing line, nets, stringers, life jackets, pliers—"

"Duh."

"And why do we need all those four-and five-dollar plastic lures when Milo said we'll be using live bait? Mullet and shrimp, I think he said."

"Well, dear, it's because I need something to fill my new tackle box. There's no sense having a big tackle box if it's not fully stocked with tackle. And I had to have something to keep my steel leaders, sinkers, hooks and all in. It'd be embarrassing to have to keep my fishing gear in a Ziploc bag. I'd look like a kid fishing with a Mickey Mouse fishing pole. Besides, that way we'll be prepared if the reds aren't biting and the guys decide to 'throw some plastic' for speckled trout, as Milo put it," Rip said in defense of his power-shopping spree.

"Okay, I get it, Mr. Trump! My point is that Milo said we were each allowed to keep three redfish per day. If we both limit out we'll have a total of six fish. Divide six by what this basket-full of stuff's gonna cost us, and by my account we'll have about $117.29 invested in each redfish we catch. And that's not including the bait we'll still have to buy!"

"Just be thankful we didn't have to buy the boat, too," Rip said. "We might catch our limits in trout, sheepshead, flounder and/or black drum, too, you know. Besides, you can ask any fisherman and they'll tell you they can buy fish at the grocery store much cheaper than they can go out and catch them themselves. But that's of no significance. One doesn't fish to save money on their grocery bill. They do it for the pure enjoyment of the sport and the excitement of catching that trophy fish. The same thing goes for hunting, sweetheart."

Not interested in any response I might have to his explanation, Rip walked away to check out a rack of Guy Harvey merchandise: t-shirts, belts, jackets, and ball caps, with depictions of trout, redfish, sailfish, tarpon, and other game fish on them. I assumed the fish needed to see which particular fish you were hoping to catch before they decided whether or not to bite down on your bait. Judging by the cap Rip brought back and tossed in the basket, he was hoping to land a hammerhead shark.

"I'm putting my chest waders back if we're going to be out there wading amongst sharks," I said.

"Actually, Milo told me we were more in danger of a dolphin grabbing hold of the fish on our stringer than being attacked by a shark. But he did say a fisherman pulled a five-hundred-pound bull shark out of Aransas Bay a few years ago."

"Thank you, honey. That makes me feel so much better about wading now!" I said with a dramatic shudder. Rip shrugged and turned to head toward a rack of Columbia fishing shirts with mesh backs covered by cape-like material. Air vents, I assumed. "Don't tell me that to have a successful day of fishing we have to dress like Harold Ensley, too."

For years, Rip tuned in weekly to watch Harold Ensley's show, *The Sportsmen's Friend*, to see what the fishing legend would reel in on that episode. Even though we resided in a fishing community, Rip's career had kept him too busy to participate in the locally popular activity. But learning the art of angling had been on his bucket list since he retired from law enforcement. I really was happy to see him enthusiastic about the upcoming fishing excursion, just appalled at the chunk the trip would take out of our checking account.

As I watched Rip select a pale blue shirt from the rack, I wondered if the fish might not take me seriously if I had on the stained Texas Rangers shirt I was planning to wear. They'd been handing the t-shirts out free at the admissions gate when we attended one of the Rangers' baseball games nearly twenty years ago. And if something's free, I'm all over it whether I need it or not.

I was much more financially conservative than my husband of nearly fifty years, as was abundantly clear by the over-flowing basket of merchandise he was now pushing toward the check-out counter. All I'd added to the cart was a two-dollar tube of lip balm with SPF-30 sun protection in it. I was more concerned about getting blisters on my lip than I was about catching fish.

Rip and I had sold our home in Rockport five years ago when we were sixty-three, and bought a thirty-foot travel trailer. We, or more accurately, I, nicknamed it the "Chartreuse Caboose" after we'd painted the trailer that color to amuse ourselves on a slow afternoon. Rip would classify the phrase "we painted" as a misnomer because he was neither amused by the work, nor in favor of the paint job to begin with. It might have been the yellow and brown sunflowers I'd added to give our trailer a little extra pop that had turned Rip off. Fortunately, a lengthy foot massage was his weakness and in exchange for one, I could have gotten him to paint all the *SpongeBob* characters down the sides of the trailer, too.

Rip's idea of amusing himself on a slow afternoon was being stretched out on the couch with a Crown and Coke in one hand and the TV clicker in the other. It was often up to me to keep Rip busy, or even mobile, at times. My restlessness was the primary reason we were now full-time RVers, traveling the country and living a more active lifestyle.

Occasionally, we'd stay in an RV park for several months and help out the campground owners for free rent and occasionally a little cash, to boot. Other times we'd drive from place to place just enjoying the scenery and the open road. We had a tendency to follow the sun like a field of sunflowers. Hence, the reason I added a few of them to our trailer's paint job. And here, you probably thought it was an odd decision on my part.

We were spending this entire winter back in our south Texas hometown on the Gulf so we could spend some time with our fifty-year-old daughter, Regina, and get to know her husband a little better. Also, we felt it would give Rip, with his new artificial hip, some much-needed time to recoup and recover in the warmer climate.

Dolly, our plump grey and white tabby, traveled with us. Her belly didn't drag the ground when she walked yet, but she seemed to have set her sights on that attainable goal. Her favorite place to take a cat nap was stretched out on the back of the couch with the sun glaring through the window, roasting her fur. Dolly was actually hot to the touch sometimes. We nearly had to use hot pads to pick her up at times. But like a pig on a spit, Dolly turned over on occasion to ensure she roasted evenly and didn't get too done on one side or the other.

We'd found a nice site in a newer RV park only a matter of blocks from Regina and Milo's home. Reggie, as we most often call her, and her husband, Milo Moore, were still newlyweds. They worked as a team, buying up properties that needed a little TLC, work they frequently hired out, and then selling the houses for a profit. They called it "flipping houses."

Cooper Claypool was an old friend and business partner of Milo's. He'd been responsible for getting Milo involved in the house-flipping business, and they co-owned MC Hammerheads Construction Company. Cooper had offered to take the three of us out on a fishing trip the following day while Reggie spent the day having her hair done and getting a manicure and pedicure at a local nail salon. Have I mentioned that Reggie is what I like to refer to as high-maintenance?

Reggie worked as a realtor for a small agency in town and listed the houses that Milo and Cooper had refurbished. I was certain she was very successful at her job. As a child, she could sell dandelions to the neighborhood kids for a quarter. Reggie once persuaded a young boy to give her his new bicycle in exchange for an old ragged, sodden, and basically eligible, copy of *Playboy Magazine* she'd found on the ground outside a local convenience store. When I'd learned of the trade, I'd called the boy's mother. Charlie got his bike back and, like my daughter, probably two weeks of hard labor.

I glanced over at Rip as he withdrew his Mastercard from his wallet. He was standing in line behind a young couple who were purchasing out-of-state fishing licenses. Their joyful banter and laughter was contagious, and I could feel myself getting pumped as well.

Despite the "bite" the fishing equipment would take out of our budget, I was now actually looking forward to the fishing excursion. Milo said we'd be launching the boat at the Little Bay boat ramp by Rockport Beach, and crossing the Intercoastal Waterway to fish in the shallow areas along a narrow piece of land called St. Jo Island, which was about six-and-a-half miles across the ship channel from Rockport. The island separated Aransas Bay from the Gulf of Mexico. I'd been over there a number of times throughout the years, but only on pleasure cruises with friends.

I joined Rip at the check-out counter. I had resigned myself to the fact that even though our fishing excursion wouldn't come cheap, it would no doubt be a memorable adventure. I was even getting excited at the prospect of landing a trophy fish that I could brag about at the Bunko party I was planning to attend Tuesday evening..

As I approached Rip, his cell phone rang. After a few brief one-word responses to the caller, he ended the call and turned to me. He said, "We need to head straight to Reggie's house when we leave here. She's so riled up, I can't even make out what she's trying to tell me. I'm not sure what, but something has happened to upset her."

CHAPTER 2

"Our daughter is a first-class drama queen," Rip whispered to me as we stood in the entryway of Regina and Milo's luxurious home.

"I know," I quietly replied.

Reggie was in the early stages of a temper tantrum when we'd arrived on her doorstep Saturday afternoon. She was now in the midst of a total meltdown, entirely unaware Rip and I were conversing with each other about her over-the-top behavior.

I'd been a young mother—only eighteen when I'd given birth to Reggie—but had done my very best to raise a responsible and mature child. I was standing there next to my stoic husband, thinking, *Is this ranting and raving a result of her upbringing? Have I let my only child down in some way to make her behave so childishly? Is this outlandish display she's putting on due to those eleven or twelve Lucky Strikes I'd smoked during my first trimester?*

"I can't believe Milo won't let me buy a new Mercedes," Reggie lamented as the three of us made our way into the living room. "I should have known better than to marry such a tightwad! Milo's walking on thin ice where I'm concerned, let me tell you. I'm a real estate agent, for goodness' sake. I have to drive clients around in my vehicle and it's downright embarrassing hauling them around in a two-year old car that doesn't even have a sunroof!"

"It's still an impressive car, honey," Rip said, trying to calm her down. "In fact, your vehicle looks like it just rolled off the assembly line. It's a hybrid SUV, which I know are not cheap. That car had to set you back at least forty grand."

"Fifty-two, actually."

"Good grief, girl!" Rip exclaimed. "How much more lavish does it need to be to transport clients? It can't have more than thirty thousand miles on—"

"Twenty-four," Reggie corrected him with a dramatic sniffle.

"Only twenty-four thousand?' Rip asked incredulously.

"Hundred. Twenty-four hundred. Rockport is a small town so I hardly ever drive over ten miles at a time. Any farther than that, I drive Milo's Beemer."

"Beemer?" I asked. "What's that?"

"It's a BMW. Welcome to the twenty-first century, Mom," she replied with a hint of annoyance in her voice. The annoyance quickly changed to contempt as she added, "Milo's car is brand new, of course! As is his company truck, a three-quarter ton Dodge Ram with all the bells and whistles. His truck even has seat warmers. My car doesn't. On a cold day, Milo can press a button and have his tight ass on fire in less than a minute."

"I see. So, are we to presume your clients need to have their asses set on fire before they'll consider purchasing a piece of property with you as their agent?"

Reggie totally blew off her father's scathing question, and stated, "So, the way I see it, I deserve a brand new vehicle too."

"Are you completely bonkers, Reggie?" I had to get my two cents in because I was in as much disbelief as Rip was. "I have a bottle of Worcestershire sauce in our fridge that's probably twice as old as your current vehicle."

"Then maybe you should bite the bullet and spend a couple bucks on a new bottle," she replied spitefully. "And I realize that's not a tremendous number of miles for a car, but the point is that it's nearly two years old now."

Rip shook his head and said, "It's the condition of the vehicle, not its age, that matters. Honey, our truck had sixty thousand on it when we bought it. It has one-hundred and fifty-five thousand on it now and still runs like a champ."

"You're not a realtor dealing with well-to-do clients, Dad! You can get by driving an ancient piece of dilapidated junk that should have been laid to rest a hundred-thousand miles ago. I can't!"

I saw the steely look in Rip's eyes. I knew he'd taken offense to his trustworthy and beloved Chevy being referred to in such an offensive fashion. He'd always taken pride in keeping it in top-notch condition.

"Why would you want to throw away hard-earned money on an expensive vehicle when you have a perfectly good one already?" I asked before Rip could respond to Reggie's insulting remarks. My daughter didn't have the sense God gave a Milk Dud when it came to finances. I've been accused of using clichés too often, but I felt compelled to say, "Money doesn't grow on trees, you know!"

"Humph," Reggie replied in disgust before clenching her fists and exclaiming, "I should have known you'd both take Milo's side. You two just don't get it! And neither does he!"

In a fit of fury, Reggie furiously brushed a coaster, an empty water bottle, and a paperback book off the end table with a swipe of her arm. Rip leaned toward me and said under his breath, "She's got that part right. I don't 'get' it at all. Milo must be rolling in it. Flipping houses must be more lucrative than I'd ever imagined it could be."

"Milo must have the patience of Job, as well," I whispered back.

Then to his daughter, Rip said more loudly, "We aren't

taking anyone's side, Regina. We're just not accustomed to throwing good money out the window. You do know that as soon as you drive that new Mercedes off the lot, it will depreciate quite a bit in value, don't you? And even though your car isn't even broken in yet, you'll also take a huge hit on its trade-in value."

"I don't care!" Reggie was pouting like a five-year-old who wasn't allowed to add a candy bar to the grocery cart in the check-out line. She went on to say, "Besides, the Mercedes is a convertible, and I negotiated a really good deal on it, Dad. I'd look like a very successful realtor driving around in this car, which you should realize could only be advantageous to me in obtaining new clients. It's really a sweet ride, too."

Reggie had calmed down, but I knew her mood could swing wildly in the other direction at any moment. I'd witnessed her tantrums many times as she was growing up. She'd be blissfully up in the clouds one minute and lying flat on the floor wailing and stomping her feet the next. I'd hoped she'd grow out of this behavior before she hit twenty, but she'd passed that mark three decades ago and nothing had changed.

"I'm afraid to even ask how much this new car would cost," Rip said to Reggie as he shook his head in disgust.

"Well, that's what's so awesome about the deal. It's worth over two-hundred but I got the dealer down to one-seventy-five. So there goes your stupid depreciation theory, huh, Dad?"

"One hundred and seventy-five thousand? Are you for real? For goodness sakes, Regina Louise! Use your head!" Rip said, his voice rising in anger. I thought for a second he might fall to the floor, wail, and stomp his feet just as Reggie used to.

It was apparent to both Reggie and me that Rip was totally fed-up. The use of Reggie's full name was reserved for when he was so irritated with her he couldn't see straight. I'd noticed he'd been using my middle name, Ann, more and more in recent years, but surely that was just out of habit, not annoyance.

Reggie and Milo owned a ritzy waterfront home on the exclusive island of Key Allegro. They had a boat-lift, Jet Ski lift, and a fish cleaning station on their dock. There was a fancy-pants in-ground pool in the backyard, as well, with a concrete dolphin statue that spewed re-circulated water back into the swallow end. I felt the pool was indulgent, but admit I enjoyed using it on occasion to exercise my arm and leg muscles.

Having lived in Rockport for many years before becoming a full-time RVer, I knew many of the homes on Key Allegro Island were nothing but million-dollar vacation retreats; tax write-offs, no doubt. There were only a few other full-time residents on the street the Moores lived on. But some of the older homes on the north end of the island were still affordable for the only moderately affluent folks, and more of those homes were lived in year-round.

Reggie had what I was sure were crocodile tears in her eyes now as she whined. "But we can afford it. I work hard and earn my share of our income and should have just as much access to our bank account as Milo. But no! He insists on handling all the finances himself and it's just not fair!"

"Thank God for that!" Rip muttered.

Reggie and Milo had more money invested in their marble countertops than we had in our thirty-foot travel trailer and pickup truck combined. It made me want to slap our enraged daughter and say, "Grow up and get over it, girl!"

Fortunately, Rip stepped in before I could carry out an instinctive reaction I'd later regret. He said, "Look around you, Regina. Do you know how fortunate you are to have all of these luxury items that normal folk could never imagine owning? Your mother and I couldn't even afford that rather pointless bronze statue in the corner over there."

Reggie glanced where Rip was pointing and repeated

her incensed, "Humph!"

I asked, "What's it supposed to be, anyway? A pelican? Whooping crane? A dolphin, maybe?"

"I'm pretty sure it's a swordfish," Rip said, turning to me.

"Oh, good grief! You two beat anything I've ever seen! It's a damn flamingo, for God's sake! Get it? Like Flamingo Road, the street Milo and I live on. Get it? Jeez."

"Was the artist smoking that wacky weed when he was sculpting it? If that's a flamingo, he certainly used a creative license to create it. I could have thrown together something that at least resembled a bird." I should have kept my opinion to myself but it would have taken more self-restraint than I possess. "That thing could be a bust of Abraham Lincoln for all anyone could tell."

"Wacky weed? Good Lord, Mother. You guys are so backwoods, it's almost embarrassing to introduce you to my friends. Rednecks plum to the bone! I think Larry the Cable Guy should use you two as an inspiration for his stand-up comedy." Reggie was livid, practically foaming at the mouth. I'd been right to anticipate the mood pendulum would swing back rapidly in the "incensed" direction.

I have to admit that "redneck" barb stung, even though most people would agree it was a fairly accurate description of Rip and me. I flinched before saying, "I'm sorry if you're ashamed of us, Reggie. We certainly never meant to be an embarrassment to you. Maybe we should be going now."

Reggie shook her head and stormed out of the room. I was beginning to believe she really did need to be slapped to put an end to her hysteria before she needed to breathe into a paper bag. Rip took my hand, and said, "Let's get out of here and let her cool down. My guess is she needs to be on some kind of medication, or seek counseling for anger management."

Rip had forgotten that when he wasn't wearing his

hearing aids, which was the majority of the time, he had a tendency to speak louder than normal. Reggie screamed from the kitchen, "I don't need medicine or counseling! I need a husband who treats me like an equal and parents who understand what I'm going through!"

Rip led me to the door. Before we exited the house, I yelled, "And, by the way, there ain't no 'damn' flamingos here in south Texas!"

"I never said there were!" Reggie shouted back in a rage. I heard her holler a very profane expletive just as her front door was closing behind us. There's no way I'd take the blame for her potty mouth or her impertinent attitude. I'd raised her better than that. Even those few ill-advised cigarettes I'd smoked during my pregnancy could not account for her current irrational behavior. At five-nine, Reggie was taller than both her father and me, so they hadn't stunted her growth, either.

Rip and I both walked to the truck in stunned dismay. Even the Chevy appeared disappointed when it failed to start on the first two attempts. *Perhaps the old girl overheard Regina's description of her*, I thought.

I hated having such a hurtful confrontation with my only child. I worried about the state of her marriage, and also the ripple effect the argument might have on our relationship with her. It saddened me and I felt terrible about the nasty spat. However, I really didn't believe Rip or I had done or said anything we should repent for, so didn't feel compelled to offer our daughter what would have been an insincere apology.

"So how are you enjoying being home for the holidays so far, sweetheart?" Rip asked ruefully after he pulled away from the curb.

"Not so much! And do you know what really ticks me off?"

"What?"

"That we just spent over six-hundred bucks on a fishing trip that ain't likely to take place now."

Rip didn't reply. This time I didn't think it was due to

his hearing loss but more to his despondency about the quarrel with Reggie. I'd wanted to suggest that we head straight back to Tackle Town to return all the items we'd just purchased, but the poignant look on his face and moisture in his eyes persuaded me to remain silent.

CHAPTER 3

To my surprise, Milo called early Sunday morning to ask if we were ready to head out on our fishing excursion. Rip, a glass-half-full kind of guy, had already laid all the gear we'd need on the sofa in our trailer. This was one of those times I wished we had a larger trailer, with a slide-out or two, to give us extra space for things like a huge pile of expensive fishing equipment we'd probably never use again. The pile of useless crap would no doubt take up valuable storage space for years until Rip finally broke down and pitched it all in some campground's dumpster one day.

We had no place to store the stuff; even the extra space under the bed was already jammed full. But Rip had assured me he'd make room for it in the storage compartment under the trailer's chassis. I wasn't sure I wanted to know what he planned to throw out to open up extra space. I just knew it better not be my pressure cooker and two cases of empty canning jars I had every intention of utilizing again someday. Finding a place to grow a garden might prove challenging for a full-time RVer, but despite that, I'd steadfastly refused to remove gardening from my bucket list. And until I came to my senses, the canning jars and pressure cooker were going to remain in storage.

While speaking with Rip on the phone, Milo told him it'd just be the three of us because he hadn't been able to get in touch with Cooper Claypool. Milo explained the other man was not home when he drove by his house the previous night or again that morning. Together, the two men had originally planned for the four of us to go out in Cooper's boat. According to Rip, Milo had sounded annoyed his friend wasn't adhering to the arrangement they'd agreed on. I had to wonder about the comment Rip told me Milo had muttered under his breath: "I figured he'd hold a grudge."

As Rip was sorting through his new tackle box, I was mentally going over all the items we'd purchased and trying to figure out which of them we might still be able to return to the tackle store after one day of use. I could make a ten-year-old skillet look unused, even untouched, if that's what it took to get my money refunded. Of course, it was merely wishful thinking that Rip would let me return any of the merchandise to begin with. It would, no doubt, all take up residence in our storage compartments until Rip developed a new fascination in another pastime.

When asked, Rip explained why he'd been expecting Milo's call. "Today is Sunday and Milo has the day off. Which would you prefer to do if you were him? Take your in-laws out on a fishing trip or stay home and listen to our daughter throwing a hissy-fit?"

"Good point!"

"Get dressed, dear. Milo will be here to pick us up in a few minutes."

Suddenly a sense of dread seeped through me. *Why do I have this overwhelming premonition that this will not be a day I'll look back at with joy?* I asked myself as I donned my ratty Texas Rangers shirt and a pair of my oldest holey blue jeans. If Rip hadn't appeared so elated, I'd have suggested we cancel the trip.

Sitting in the back seat of Milo's Dodge Ram, I watched as Rip helped Milo with the boat. Milo had backed the boat down the ramp into the water, and Rip was going to park the truck and trailer in the parking lot. After floating his boat off the trailer, Milo had tied the boat up to a wooden pole beside the concrete bulkhead, waiting for us to climb aboard. With his light green eyes, well-trimmed mustache, and medium-length sandy-colored hair, held in place by an embroidered *Seaworthy Marine* ball cap, my six-foot-three, lanky son-in-law looked like a natural mariner to me. He was definitely easy on the eyes but I wasn't sure yet how I felt about his personality. Or if he even had one.

If one were to judge Milo by his boat, one could only surmise the guy liked to be the center of attention. The shallow-hulled fishing boat had a custom paint job and a black bimini top to shade the passengers. It was painted bright purple with loud orange and red flames down both sides of the hull, and had a decal depicting a pastel yellow skull on each side at the bow of the boat. "Maverick" was painted across the aft in a glittery gold color. Milo's fishing vessel was quite gaudy, but definitely an eye catcher. Of course, who am I to talk? Our self-painted travel trailer could hardly be classified as inconspicuous either.

While we'd been traveling next to the banks of Little Bay in Milo's truck on our way to Rockport Beach, he'd told us the free boat ramp at Rockport Beach was the closest, most convenient place to launch the boat. As I mentioned before, I'm always game for anything that's free, whether I have a use for it or not. But in this instance, it was the only thing Rip and I didn't have to pay for all morning.

Earlier, at the Fleming Bait Shop, we'd paid for forty-two bucks worth of bait; two quarts of live shrimp, and three dozen finger mullet, along with a ten-dollar "bubbler" and batteries to supply the necessary oxygen to keep them alive. Milo had explained the aerator in the boat's bait well was not working properly and he hadn't had time to have it repaired.

After acquiring the bait, Milo had pulled the truck and boat trailer alongside a Valero gas station pump to fill the boat's fuel tank. At his request, I'd gone inside to purchase two large bags of ice to keep the fish we caught fresh in the large cooler under the bench seat in front of the helm. Not surprisingly, the boat's live well was not working properly either. Milo had also asked me to pick up two six-packs of beer to quench our thirst out on the water. On each occasion, he had suddenly needed to use the john or make an important phone call, and was already occupied when it came time to pay for anything.

Rip shrugged his shoulders and told me, "I guess it's only fair we pay for the bait and supplies. After all, we're using his boat."

Although I found Milo's vanishing acts a bit irksome, I figured we'd already spent hundreds of dollars for our gear. What was another seventy clams? I was discovering more and more about the high price of being an avid angler.

As I placed the ice and beer in the boat's cooler, which also served as a seat, Milo was holding the gas nozzle while filling the fuel tank. I heard him gasp. I turned to watch him, with his hand on his empty back pocket, say, "Gosh dang it! I left my wallet on the kitchen table."

I whispered to Rip, "Tell him we aren't in any hurry and don't mind taking the time to go back to his house to get it."

Rip shook his head and grumbled to me, "I have a hunch this station is not going to accept moths as a form of payment. I think we'll just have to accept this as one of those live and learn situations. Besides, as I said before, we *are* using his boat."

Live and learn, my sagging behind! I thought, as I watched the numbers on the gas pump mounting so rapidly I couldn't keep up with the total. Finally I asked Milo, "How much gas does this thing hold?"

"Sixty gallons," he replied without batting an eye.

Good grief! I thought. Who'd have ever thought a boat could hold twice as much fuel as the vehicle you towed it with. Is there anything involved in angling that isn't detrimental to one's net worth?

"You do know the definition of 'boat', don't you?" Rip asked me as Milo instructed the attendant to include a bottle of fuel additive on the bill. When I shook my head, Rip continued. "It's a hole in the water in which you pour money."

I'd have laughed if the escalating expense wasn't so painful. I would have at least responded had Milo's next comment not taken the breath out of me. "I guess I better fill up the truck too, or we'll be driving on fumes before we get to the boat launch."

Eighty-seven gallons and almost two-hundred dollars later, Rip, with a barely discernible amount of steam coming out of his ears, leaned over and grudgingly told me, "I'll have to use the credit card, Rapella. I used the last of my cash at the bait stand."

I bit my tongue until it nearly bled to keep from making a spiteful remark. We hadn't even got a hook wet yet, and the already exorbitant cost of a grilled redfish steak had just increased substantially. Rip began to walk away from me, then stopped and turned to make another cutting remark.

"At least Milo filled up at a gas station instead of the marina, where the price of fuel is even higher. If he hadn't, we could have had to cough up another Ben Franklin."

"Gee. How thoughtful of him."

"Rapella!" Milo hollered. He was guiding the boat, Rip was standing next to him at the helm, and I was sitting on a cushioned cooler on the bow of the twenty-four foot bay boat. "Throw the anchor out for me!"

I did as requested and then joined the men, who were stepping into their chest waders. A few seconds later, Milo turned to me and asked, "Why are we drifting? Didn't you throw the anchor out?"

"Yes, of course, I did. Right after you asked me to."

"You did tie the rope to the boat before you pitched

the anchor into the water, didn't you?"

"Oops!" I replied in embarrassment. "Sorry, Milo. I guess I assumed it was already tied to the boat. After all, you said, 'Throw the anchor out,' not 'Tie off the anchor and throw it out.'"

"Oh, don't worry about it," Milo said with a chuckle. "I'll wade over and retrieve it later. For now we can lower my new power pole. It buries itself in the sand and mud and keeps the boat in place."

I wondered why he didn't just use the power pole in the first place. The electronic device obviously cost a great deal more than the anchor. And if it didn't *work* better than the anchor, why would anyone pay to put one on his boat? It seemed clear to me at that point that neither Reggie nor her husband had a lick of sense when it came to spending money.

I followed the men into the water by ungraciously swinging my butt and legs over the side of the boat and sliding off. Rip attached the nylon cord from the bait bucket to a metal loop on my wading belt. The belt had been a last-minute purchase he'd felt driven to buy for each of us at the tackle store, as if we needed one more cumbersome accessory.

The bottom was soft, and my wading boots sank several inches with each step, making me ungainly and a little uneasy. I tripped and fell to my knees at one point, and it wasn't an easy task to get back up to my feet. I was on edge, thinking any given step could land me in a quicksand-type hole that'd have me up to my eyebrows in water before I knew it.

Propelling my body through the thick grass in the water was a chore. Milo, wading beside me, appeared unfazed by the thick underwater foliage and mucky bottom. In comparison to me, he looked like a kid running through a field of clover. After I regained my foothold following my fall, he was courteous enough to help me restore my balance and get my bearings before letting go of my arm. He warned me to be more cautious, as if I were rushing recklessly through the muddy and grassy water to get to my fishing spot as rapidly as possible. In actuality, I was doing nothing more than doing my dangest to keep putting one foot in front of the other without doing a face plant into the muck.

"You need to tread slowly, Rapella," he said. If I moved any slower I'd be drifting backward and be back at the boat before the men reached their fishing hole. "There are potholes out here where there's no grass, and it's hard to tell how deep they are. Those potholes are a great place to catch a redfish that's waiting for a bait fish to swim by in the clearing. But they can also be deadly if they're deeper than you anticipated."

"How so?" I asked, not sure I really wanted to know. I felt anxious enough as it was, scanning the surface of the water constantly for menacing dorsal fins moving on a direct path toward me. I swear I saw at least two humongous bull sharks swim by about thirty yards out. When I anxiously pointed them out, Milo laughed. I let him know I wasn't amused and he promised me all I'd seen were a couple of large bait fish. They were skimming the surface, occasionally flying out of the water like tiny sailfish, as if fleeing a larger fish hunting for its breakfast.

Milo explained. "Those are mullet, just like we'll be using today for bait, only larger. Keep an eye out and you'll probably see another one breaching the surface soon."

I watched for a few moments until I spotted another mullet, probably a foot long, flying in and out of the water five times as it scooted swiftly away. It was like watching a shiny rock being skipped across the top of the water.

"Don't forget what I told you earlier," Milo said, after the bait fish had at last submerged and not resurfaced. "If you were to accidentally step into a pothole over your head, your waders would instantly fill up with so much water you likely wouldn't be able to surface. There aren't too many really deep ones in this area, but there are a few scattered out there, so it's always a possibility. And it seems like at least one wade-fisherman drowns out in these bays every year."

"Oh, swell. Thanks for bringing my anxiety level down a notch. You're making wade-fishing sound like more and more fun with every comment you make."

"You'll be okay, Rapella. Just be careful and walk slowly. You'll feel more at ease as you get accustomed to wading," Milo assured me. Rip was already twenty feet ahead of us, not a care in the world. "Soon you'll be perfectly at ease out here. And trust me, if you fish for any length of time at all, it will get into your blood."

After Milo felt confident I could get along by myself, he picked up speed and was soon wading side-by-side with Rip, who had forged ahead as Milo assisted me. I was carrying a fishing pole, and had a hand net, a bait bucket, and a stringer to put the fish on, attached to the fishing belt. I felt weighed down by all the pricey but, according to Rip, necessary, wade-fishing accessories I was dragging around.

A few minutes later, I was in water up to the top of my thighs. I had absolutely no desire to get into even deeper water, so I decided to tack in a different direction. I was hoping to find shallower water which, thankfully, I quickly did.

When I arrived at the general location Milo had pointed to, he hollered loudly enough I could just make out what he was saying. "Right there's a good place to start! Make sure you scoot your feet as you wade around in the water so you don't surprise a stingray and get stung. They have sharp barbs on their stingers and are difficult and painful to get out of your leg."

Seriously? Now you tell me that? I was beginning to feel a sense of dread, as my mind filled with visions of Steve Irwin, the Crocodile Hunter, who'd died from a stingray's barb imbedded in his chest. Rip and I had always assumed it'd be a huge croc that'd take him out.

Instead of responding with the first caustic remark that came to mind, I tried to still my jumpy nerves and shouted back, "Swell. Now please stop pointing out every conceivable way I could get injured—or worse— today. Just tell me what I need to do next."

"Bait your hook and cast it out toward one of those light greenish areas. Those are the potholes I was telling you about. If you feel a tug, wait a few seconds and pull the rod back forcefully enough to set the hook. I already sat the drag on your reel, so just fight the fish, reel it in, net it, and put it on your stringer. That's all there is to it!" Milo's voice reverberated across the surface of the water, which had small ripples due to a slight breeze. I had to admit it was a beautiful day to be outside.

My first order of business was to bait my hook, Milo had said. So I opened up my bait bucket and saw a dozen slimy mullet about five inches long, and an even larger number of medium-sized shrimp darting here and there. When I opened the lid of the bait bucket, two of the shrimp flew out unexpectedly, nearly causing me to lose my balance again. I couldn't decide which of my two choices seemed less icky to handle. Since the leaping shrimp had startled me and looked more menacing with their pointed snouts and black beady eyes, I chose the mullet.

It took me at least forty-five seconds to snag a mullet. They swam faster than I could move my hand around in the bucket and were able to evade being caught until I finally trapped one against the bottom. I pulled it out and reached for my hook. As soon as I grasped my line, the slimy mullet slivered out of my hand into the water. I swear it sneered at me as it scurried away.

It took thirty more seconds to capture another elusive mullet, only to have it spring free from my hand, as well. Finally, on the third attempt, I squeezed one of the little buggers so tightly its eyes were about to pop out of its head. I wasn't sure where to shove the hook in him and couldn't bear to watch such cruelty. So I just shut my eyes and forced it in. Opening my eyes, I discovered I'd hooked him squarely in the tail fin. I figured that'd work as well as any other place, and I didn't want to torture the poor thing any further. I couldn't bear to look the little feller in the eyes for fear I'd see the agony I'd inflicted.

Now to cast. It was a complicated-looking reel, for sure. I recalled Rip instructing me to open the bail before I cast, allowing the line to fly freely out over the water. On my first attempt, the bail closed as soon as I began to cast the line out. My hook and lead weight splashed down and sank to the bottom about two feet in front of me, but not before my mullet broke loose and sailed another fifty to sixty feet through the air.

Poor little critter. And I'd thought I was having a bad day. Crap! Now I have to start this whole ordeal over again. I baited the hook and tried again. The mullet landed on the sandy shore behind me. After many disastrous attempts, and spending at least an hour untangling the rat's nest of fishing line that resulted from an errant cast, I managed to land a mullet within a foot or two of the pothole. It was close enough that I wasn't going to mess with it again unless I had a bite.

The next hour-and-a-half seemed to last a full week. My back was already beginning to ache from the awkward position I'd assumed in order to maintain my balance in the undulating water as I waited impatiently for a tug on my line. I set the hook on more than one imaginary fish, not exactly sure how it'd feel if I got a bite. When each of those imaginary fish failed to take off in a frantic attempt to shake the hook, I let my bait lie where it had landed after my spastic yank.

Finally, I decided it was time to check my bait, only to find the mullet was long gone. It occurred to me then I might have spent the last four hours fishing with no bait. Apparently one of those earlier bites had not been just a figment after all.

After another taxing effort to bait and cast my line, it hit the water at least a city block from the closest pothole. Although no one could hear me, even the brown pelicans a hundred yards away pounding the top of the water for fish to consume, I shouted out a long string of profanities. I cussed the "fish gods" for the suffering I was enduring. I was beginning to understand the old saying, "swear like a sailor."

Later, I nearly fell into a coma from standing in the same place for yet another two hours with my boots buried six inches in the muck beneath me. I wondered exactly how much time it usually took for fishing to "get in one's blood," as Milo had assured me it would. The way I felt just then, I didn't think I'd live long enough for that to happen.

I hoped Rip was having better luck and a better time than me, which wouldn't take a heck of a lot. The bar had been set extremely low on my end of this fishing experience. I finally decided my back couldn't take much more abuse. I told myself if I didn't get a bite in the next ten minutes, I'd head back to the boat, which now looked like a speck on the horizon from where I stood. Any energy I'd started out with was long gone. I feared returning to the boat would require more oomph than I could scrounge up. I almost prayed for a dorsal fin to emerge behind me when I headed back, giving me the adrenalin rush I'd need to reach the boat.

After checking my bait, only to find it gone again, I mindlessly cast out and finally landed a lively mullet just inside the edge of a large pothole. I began cheering out loud, as if I'd won the lottery, which was virtually impossible because I was too cheap to buy a ticket.

To while away the allotted ten minutes before giving up, I mentally made a list of groceries I needed to pick up at H.E.B. and debated about what to cook for supper. Fresh redfish was most likely no longer an option. I had glanced toward where Milo and Rip were fishing on occasion and hadn't seen any sign of yanking going on.

I then pondered how much longer my hair and nails had gotten since I'd flopped myself out of the boat what seemed like a month and a half earlier. Suddenly, I was jerked from my reverie by a solid tug on my line that nearly pulled the rod out of my hands. I'd been instructed by Rip to resist yanking so hard and fast that I'd reel in nothing but a pair of fish lips. But he'd also said there was a fine line between yanking too early and waiting so long I'd give the fish a chance to swallow the hook. He'd said, "Milo told me they're tough to get out when they swallow it. And if you're unlucky enough to catch a hardhead, don't let it prick you with its dorsal fin, or it'll burn like crazy for a good twenty minutes."

"What's a hardhead?" I'd asked, thrilled to learn there was yet another hazard I'd have to be prepared for.

"It looks like a little catfish, but is nothing more than a nuisance down here, a trash fish Milo called it, and the fin contains some kind of poison. It serves as a natural defense for the hardheads," Rip had explained.

"Oh, okay. Good to know." And then, because I just couldn't resist, I'd added, "And here all this time I thought a hardhead was a roly-poly retired police officer who wouldn't get his throbbing, aching hip joint replaced until an unexpected accident left him no option."

"Being a smart ass will get you nowhere," he had returned with a smirk.

However, exasperating as it was, I couldn't dwell on Rip's stubbornness now. I had what felt like a blue whale on the end of my line. It was pulling away with a strong steady tug. When I yanked on my pole to set the hook, there was a second of stillness before the fish took off so fast I could hear the whirring of my line streaming out a mile-a-minute.

I tussled with that fish for quite a long spell, cranking the reel's handle whenever the fish took a break to get a second wind and the line began to go slack. But before long the monster would be on the run again and unwinding my line faster than I could crank it back in. This back and forth struggle went on for a good thirty minutes. Looking back later, I'd realize it was actually more like five or six minutes, but my story would forever remain unchanged. Truthfully, I knew it probably *would* change in time, growing even more astonishing with each telling, but I wouldn't be the first fisherman to exaggerate their fish tale. It was practically expected of dedicated anglers.

Could this fish possibly be a state record? I wondered, still fighting Moby Dick with all the strength I could muster. I was having the time of my life trying to land my admirable opponent. It'd be the first fish I'd caught in my entire life if I could get him in my net.

I'd even forgotten that my back had been throbbing in rhythm with the waves slapping the banks of St. Jo Island, which was not far from where I stood knee-deep in water that was brackish from recent heavy rainfall.

I was so wound up I nearly peed in my waders, not only from the excitement of fighting the fish, but also because I'd been foolish enough to drink two cups of coffee that morning. I'd had to hold it for hours and it was beginning to get painful.

It was to the point I felt my bladder had to be stretched as tight as my friend, Mabel Hick's, girdle. Unlike the men, I couldn't just slide my waders down and take a leak in the water. Still, despite my discomfort, I had a fish on the end of my line, and this was the first time I thought all the expense entailed in this adventure was worth every dime.

While I watched line peeling off my reel once again, I was visualizing the pride I'd have in showing my Bunko club a photo of me holding my trophy fish. Of course, Gracie Parker would be at the party too, and she'd probably one-up me as she always did all of us girls. I could just see her reaching into her brassiere and pulling out a faded Polaroid snapshot of a young Gracie at sixteen, holding up a tarpon the size of a Volkswagen.

Oh, well. At the rate I was going, my trophy fish would die of old age before I got him reeled in close enough to net, anyway.

When I finally got the thrashing fish within a few feet of me, I reached for my net only to discover it was tangled up with the braided nylon cord attached to my bait bucket. Both cords had wrapped around me several times due to the motion of the waves. Before I could unwind myself from the entire conglomeration, the fish swam between my legs and started to circle me. I spun around and around like a carousel at a carnival. *This blasted fish is just playing with me now*, I thought. *But we'll see who gets the last laugh.*

Frustrated, I was starting to get dizzy and was gasping for breath like an asthmatic having an attack. I was ready to throw in the towel when the fish, which appeared to be as exhausted as I was by this time, swam directly into the net. Apparently it had thrown in the towel just seconds before I could. I held the net up so I could admire the huge fish and was relieved to see it wasn't a hardhead. Shining in the sun's glare, it was a beautiful shade of red and had the distinctive black dot on its tail that Milo had explained would indicate it was a redfish.

My next realization was I'd waited too long before setting the hook. The redfish had swallowed it nearly to its tail, it seemed. I could have cared less about retrieving the hook, though. I was heading straight back to the boat with my incredible catch. After the guys admired my fish and congratulated me on my remarkable angling skills, one of them could worry about the hook.

I cut the line with my pliers and with the hook still embedded in the fish's belly, I put the redfish on my stringer to ensure it didn't get away. If I'd thought all the cords, net, bait bucket and fishing line were a mess before, I knew it'd now take me a good half hour to get everything untangled when I got back to the boat. At this point, I was wrapped up like a mummy in an Egyptian antiquities museum. I scooted an inch or two at a time, in fear of being stung by a stingray as I was sinking to the bottom of a ten-foot-deep pot hole. With no shark sighting to provide motivation, it took me twice as long to get back to the boat as it had taken me to get from the boat to the spot where I'd been mired in the mud for hours.

"Pretty, isn't it?" Milo asked as he held my redfish up for Rip and me to admire. Within seconds he'd removed the hook with a pair of long needle nose pliers, slapped the fish down on a measuring table along the rim of his boat, and let it slide over the side back into the water. In one fluid motion my fish was gone. Like an apparition, it disappeared from sight in a flash.

"What the hell?" I exclaimed in surprise, and then repeated louder, in anger. "What the hell? You just tossed my trophy redfish overboard! You pitched it out like it was chopped liver!"

"Yeah, it's called 'catch and release,'" he replied. "Besides, a redfish has to be at least twenty inches long to be a keeper. It'd be illegal to not release your nineteen and three-quarter incher, and the penalties are steep if you get caught with an undersized game fish."

I couldn't catch my breath for a few seconds as I struggled to come to grips with the fact my fish was probably a mile away from the boat by then, and Rip hadn't even had time to use his phone to take a photo of me proudly displaying it.

No fish, no photo. All I had left was a bladder about to explode like a water balloon thrown from a third-story balcony.

When I finally calmed down and accepted the fact my redfish wasn't as remarkable a catch as I'd imagined, I turned to the men and asked, "So, how many keepers did you guys catch?"

"Not a bite all day," Rip responded, obviously more

than a little disappointed. "Well, except for when Milo hooked what he thought was a stingray by the way it fought. Fortunately, the line got cut when the fish steered it into a small reef of oyster shells, so he didn't have to mess with getting it off the hook."

"Oh, so my thousand-dollar fish was the best catch of the day," I boasted.

"Yeah, I guess so. But Milo's going to take us a ways out into the Gulf, where he and Cooper go spear-fishing for red snapper. They fish right by an oil rig where the snapper tend to hang out. He said we'd give it an hour or so using cut bait and head home if we don't have any luck there."

"Oh, jeez. Another hour out here?" My tone made it clear I wasn't thrilled about the prospect. My bladder was even less thrilled.

"You had fun catching that redfish didn't you, honey?" Rip asked, as Milo stored a few loose items in storage compartments so they wouldn't blow out of the boat.

"Of course I did, Rip," I replied. "But that fifteen minutes of fun was swallowed up by another five hours worth of mind-numbing boredom. Fishing's not for me. Besides, if we took this sport up as a hobby, before we knew it we'd be standing at busy intersections, holding up a sign. 'Will work for bait. God Bless You.'"

Rip smiled, rolled his eyes at me, and said, "At least you're not going to get melodramatic about it."

"I have to pee too. And there's no way I can hold it another hour."

Milo had retrieved the anchor I'd accidentally flung out earlier and raised the power pole. After learning of my dilemma, he pulled the boat as close to shore as he could and helped me out. Peeling wet, chest-high neoprene waders off and crouching behind a palm tree in an area full of ants and sand burrs was not as much fun as it sounds. However, the relief I felt afterward made it all worthwhile.

After I'd rejoined the men in the boat, Milo fired up

the motor and soon we were moving along the shore line at a rapid clip. I sat up front enjoying the passing scenery, the wind in my hair, abundant flora and fauna, a pod of dolphins in a feeding frenzy, and, most of all, an empty bladder. We could have just cruised around like that all day and I'd have been happy as a tornado in a trailer park. And, in case you're wondering, tornadoes don't turn their noses up at RV parks either.

Another mile or so down the coast, we passed two whooping cranes; a mating pair from the nearby wintering flock of the endangered species. One was searching for small crabs while the other one served as sentry, keeping a trained eye on us as we sailed by. Soon after that, Milo reined back the throttle to point out a flock of the pink-colored roseate spoonbills up close to the bank. They were beautiful creatures that paid no heed to us as their platypus-looking bills swayed back and forth in the water. Milo explained that their main source of food was shrimp and, like those 'damn' flamingos', it was the iodine in the shrimp that gave them their pink color.

I was very much enjoying the cruise and the view when the motor abruptly shut down and the boat's forward motion ceased. Lost in the moment of pure pleasure, I was caught off-guard by the sudden stop, and pitched forward off the padded cooler. My first thought was the motor had stalled. My second thought was that I was too old to be flung across the bow of a bay boat and would be sporting a battery of fresh bruises the following morning.

Then I looked in the direction Milo was pointing and spotted a passenger-free boat rocking back and forth in the waves. It had a very similar design as Milo's boat, but much less flashy. At least that one didn't nearly glow in the dark like the *Maverick*.

"I'm almost positive that's Cooper's boat," he said, sounding shaken. "It's too far from shore to be anchored." Is it the fact that Cooper came out here without us, disregarding the plans he and his friend had previously agreed upon, that has Milo so disturbed? I wondered. Or is it something even more disconcerting?

By Milo's expression, I felt certain it was the latter. It didn't take long for me to realize that if the boat was adrift without Cooper aboard, there was little doubt something was off beam. With a trembling voice, Milo instructed us. "Start scanning the surface of the water to see if we can locate him. The tide is rising and he may be so focused on fishing, he isn't aware his boat has drifted away."

"Are you sure that's what's happened?" Rip asked, clearly aware of Milo's concern. "You were telling me about spear-fishing earlier. Didn't you say you usually exit the boat in your snorkeling gear out in the open water, like Cooper's boat is now?"

"Yes, but only in shallow water where the anchor can reach the bottom. Often we tie our boats to oil rigs so we can fish in deeper water."

"Do they actually let boats tie up to the oil rigs in this day and age when terrorism is always a potential threat?" Rip asked, dubiously.

"Well, um, not exactly, but, um, well, we—"

"Never mind, son. I'm pretty certain the USCG doesn't allow boats to tie up to any offshore platform, but that's neither here nor there right now. Go on with what you were saying." Rip's tone was sharp and disapproving.

"All right. Cooper's pretty careless at times," Milo began. "Still, it's crazy for him to not keep a closer eye on the tide, his boat, and, for that matter, his entire surroundings. I'm afraid something more ominous may have happened to him. He's been drinking so much recently, there's always the chance he fell overboard. And, to answer your question, Rip, no, I'm not sure what's happened, but this is not normal."

"In that case, shouldn't we alert the Coast Guard?" Rip asked.

"Not quite yet. I guarantee you he doesn't want the Coast

Guard alerted unless absolutely necessary. Keep scanning the surface of the water, Rip. It's possible he might be treading water and in immediate need of rescuing," Milo instructed. With a great deal of trepidation in his voice, he added, "Rapella, why don't you try to focus on the shore line. He's got to be out here somewhere."

Even though I was wearing my eyeglasses, I was way past due for a new prescription. I hadn't felt as if I'd gotten my four-hundred dollars' worth out of my current pair yet. I could barely make out the shore line, the east bank of St. Jo Island, so I doubted I could distinguish between a man waving desperately for help and a palm tree swaying in the breeze. But I squinted and concentrated as best I could, anxious to help any way I could.

We cruised around in circles for over two hours. My eyes watered profusely from not blinking enough in the increasing wind. Rip and I were becoming as concerned for Milo's friend as he was. Darkness came early in mid-November, and the dwindling light would become an issue before much more time had passed. Despite the fact we'd spent a big chunk of my entire Social Security check on fuel, I was relieved we'd filled the tank up. We'd crossed the Intercoastal Waterway, gone around the island, and sailed a significant distance out into the Gulf. There was the chance we might have been adrift soon too had we not had sufficient fuel on board.

Gravely concerned now, Milo asked us to keep searching while he contacted the Coast Guard with his marine radio. It didn't take long before we spotted two Coast Guard vessels trolling about, skimming the water's surface with a high-powered spotlight. Soon we heard the familiar sound of a chopper circling overhead. We were accustomed to the sound because helicopters frequently flew out to oil rigs and back in to the small Aransas County Airport. As the sun slipped below the horizon, the Coast Guard radioed us, forty-five minutes into their search, to let us know they would have to call off the search soon and resume at first light. They advised us to do the same before total darkness overtook us. I knew that meant the "search and rescue" mission had most likely just transformed into a "search and *recover*" operation to be conducted the following day. The realization was sobering.

This fact was not lost on Milo, either, and naturally he was hesitant to stop trying to locate his friend and business partner. But he was an experienced mariner and knew that within minutes, he'd have no other choice but to turn and head for home.

Milo claimed that with money tight, he'd been putting off buying a GPS system for his boat. He didn't even have a rudimentary flashlight on board to assist us back to Key Allegro, much less a spotlight that would enhance our view of obstacles in front of us. Without GPS we had no way of knowing where the channel markers, gas wells, or other odds and ends protruding from the water were located. Even the barges proceeded so quietly down the ship channel they could be hard to detect in the dark over the din of one's own boat's motor.

These factors meant waiting too long to head home could be risky. As desperately as he wanted to bring his friend home safely, Milo probably felt some degree of responsibility for our welfare, too. Or at least one would hope so.

In a trembling voice, Milo said, "I'm going to put the boat on the lift at our dock so I can head back out as soon as I'm able in the morning. I usually keep it there until I need to take on fuel, which we did this morning. But just to be safe I should probably top off the tank before going out tomorrow, anyway."

"I'll go with you in the morning, son," Rip volunteered. "If you haven't got the funds right now, I'll cover the fuel. Again."

I'm not sure if Milo noticed the faint hint of sarcasm in Rip's final word, but I did. After Milo had trimmed down the motor and thrust the throttle forward, the boat came up on plane in a split second. I looked to my left to judge the amount of daylight remaining in the sky and saw a ray of sunshine glint off a speck of red floating on top of the water two or three hundred yards away from us. I quickly tapped Milo and pointed in that direction. He swallowed hard, nodded, and sped full throttle toward the object.

Milo's face paled more and more the closer we got to what even I could now identify as a body. He nearly fainted when it became apparent it was the body of Cooper Claypool. He explained to us. "I recognize his red inflatable life belt because I have an identical one. We both always wear a safety belt when we go spear-fishing, in case we find ourselves in trouble underwater. They have a manual CO_2 inflation system. But it looks to me as if there's something embedded in his chest. Perhaps that's a good sign."

"And just how could that ever be a good sign?" Rip asked.

"Well, I wasn't referring to the 'something embedded in his chest' part. I just thought he may have passed out and was still aware enough to inflate his life belt when he started feeling faint. He could just be unconscious, maybe stayed out in the sun too long. I know too much sun exposure makes me light-headed sometimes."

It was apparent to both Rip and me that Milo's rationalization was more wishful thinking than a realistic probability. Milo was trying hard to convince himself that Cooper Claypool was still alive as he navigated the boat toward his bobbing buddy. I'm pretty sure all three of us already knew mere unconsciousness wasn't the case. And that fact became blatantly obvious when we drew up beside the body, which was encased in a scuba diving wet suit. Cooper was floating face up, and he did indeed have something protruding from his chest. It was a spear, as if another spear-fisherman had mistaken him for a large grouper.

There appeared to be a dark greenish bruise on the man's left cheek that contrasted with his pale, blue-tinted face. His eyes were open and his cornea had a cloudy, opaque appearance that I found extremely creepy. I had to look away when bile rose in my throat.

"Oh, my God!" Milo cried out. "Coop's been shot with a spear-gun. His own, most likely. How could this happen? Who would do such a cruel thing to him? I can't imagine why anyone would want to do that to another person, much less a guy like Cooper."

"What makes you automatically assume the spear was fired from Cooper's own gun?" Rip asked, after he and Milo had hoisted the body aboard the boat. He was already in detective mode, accessing Cooper's body for evidence. "That would indicate his assailant had been close enough to Cooper to gain control of his spear-gun."

"Yeah, I guess you're right. Coop and me, as well as another fishing buddy, Pinto, all bought new spear-guns at a hunting and fishing expo in Corpus a few months ago. The only difference was that Pinto and I bought top of the line pneumatic models with reels and a lot of power. But Cooper told us he was a bit short on funds, and he bought a cheaper model with only a nineteen-inch barrel. It does have strong bands, but is very hard to load."

"How do you load a spear-gun?" Rip asked curiously.

"You hold the butt of the gun up against your chest. I use a chest loading vest, but Cooper didn't. He'd have bruises on his chest from the impact sometimes, but still wouldn't break down and buy a vest."

"Stick to the basics." Rip was getting impatient. I remained silent.

"Okay, so anyway, with the butt against your chest, you use both hands to pull the first band toward you and hook the wishbone into the front notch. Then you pull back the second band and hook it in the rear notch."

"Sounds easy enough."

"It is, once you got it down pat. It's more a matter of technique than strength."

"I see." Sometimes Rip had the attention span of a blade of grass. I could tell he was losing interest fast in

Milo's detailed descriptions.

"You always load the guns in the water and keep the safety on until you're ready to fire, or it can be very dangerous."

"I see."

"Coop wasn't much on following safety procedures, but I never met anyone who could hold his breath as long as he could. I'd have to surface three times before he surfaced once. Pinto, who's older than us, would have to come up for air even more frequently. Cooper had unbelievable lung power for a guy who used to smoke."

"That's nice," Rip replied absentmindedly.

"I'm glad I bought the more expensive gun, even though sometimes, with a new model, the manufacturers haven't had time to get the bugs worked out."

"That's nice," Rip repeated. He clearly was not paying attention to Milo's babbling.

"One drawback of the cheap gun Coop bought is that the trigger mechanism was sensitive and had a habit of jamming when you tried to fire at a fish. Still, all-in-all, we were all pleased with our purchases. Because we all bought one at the same time, we were given a thirty percent discount."

"I totally agree," Rip mumbled. Milo's rambling remarks had not registered. The exchange between them sounded like it was on auto pilot and neither man was paying a lick of attention to what the other was saying.

When Milo's chattering ceased, Rip cocked his head in puzzlement, and asked, "So, what I still don't understand is what led you to instantly think the spear in Cooper's chest was fired from his own personal gun?"

"I dunno. Just a gut feeling, I guess," Milo answered awkwardly, refusing to make eye contact with either Rip or me.

Rip held up the frayed end of the line attached to the spear, and asked, "Is this spear designed specifically for the nineteen-inch model Cooper purchased? Or is it basically the same used on every gun? And how about the line attached to the spear? Is it generic or custom? This line's been severed, presumably so the killer could take the spear-gun, or in this case, the murder weapon, with him."

"I dunno," Milo repeated. He shook his head, donning the expression of someone being backed into a corner with no escape route in sight. "I really have no idea."

I began listening more intently to the discussion between the two men, and started to feel uncomfortable. But not as uncomfortable as Milo appeared to be. He started babbling once again, about red snapper recipes, spear-gun fishing techniques, and a new brand of fish fry batter he wanted to try. Milo chattered nervously about anything and everything but the spear in Cooper's chest and the line that connected the spear to the gun, which allowed the fisherman to retrieve a fish once it had been speared.

When the cat finally grabbed a hold of Milo's tongue, he turned his back to us and ran his sleeve across his eyes. He was blotting tears with the fabric of his shirt, I was certain. I could sense Milo was not only on edge about Rip's questioning, but also embarrassed to show his emotional side to his in-laws.

Meanwhile, Rip was performing another cursory inspection of the body lying across the forward casting deck. "He's got abrasions on his left knuckles, but taking into account they've nearly healed, I'd estimate they're at least four or five days old."

I didn't bother to respond because it was evident to me Rip was talking to himself, not Milo or me. He turned Cooper's body on its side. Rigor mortis had already set in, so it was like turning a mannequin over, or, more aptly, a tuna that'd been chilling on ice for an hour or two. I listened as Rip continued to voice his observations. "He's got a three-to four-inch laceration on the back of his skull, but has already had metal staples applied to close the wound."

Without thinking, I said, "So his attacker hit him with

something before he shot him with the spear-gun?"

Rip graced me with his oft-used "duh" expression, and said, "The fact he'd already received medical attention for the wound makes it clear it had no bearing on his death, dear. Did you really think the attacker whacked him on the head, closed the wound with a suturing staple gun he just happened to have on him, and then proceeded to shoot him dead with a spear?"

Without even waiting for my response to his sarcastic, rhetorical question, he continued, "But I do think the odds are good that whoever caused this wound came out here in the middle of no-man's land to finish the job. The killer would have known there'd be a slim chance of the murder being witnessed by anyone out here."

He then turned to Milo, and asked, "Know anything about this head wound?"

After a brief interlude, Milo slowly shook his head. His hesitancy made me think he knew more about the laceration than he cared to share. But given the circumstances, I could understand Milo's reluctance to own up to any knowledge about anything at all.

"Do you think your other fishing buddy might have gone out with him on his fishing trip?" Rip then asked. "What'd you say his name was again?"

"Pinto; and no, I can guarantee you that he wasn't out here with Coop."

"Why are you so sure?" Rip asked. Before Milo replied, he exhaled loudly and slowly. He then looked up briefly, as if asking God for guidance before speaking.

"Pinto doesn't have time to fish right now. He's out on his boat working daybreak to dusk this time of year. I'm almost positive he didn't accompany Cooper," Milo said. His expression was that of remorse, more than sorrow. "I doubt Pinto even knew Coop was out here. If he did know, he wouldn't have been happy about it. But that doesn't mean someone else didn't come out fishing with him."

"Any idea who else might have accompanied him?" Rip asked.

"No, not really. But I know it wasn't Pinto." Milo seemed intent on making sure his friend, Pinto, was not suspected of Cooper's death. Almost too intent in my opinion.

"Pinto's sure an odd name," I said.

"Everyone calls him that because of his last name. His first name is actually Philip, but—"

"All right, folks. We need to get a move on," Rip cut in. I could tell Rip would have liked to continue his Q and A session with Milo, but knew time was of the essence. His years of experience in dealing with emergency situations had taken over. "Get back on the radio, Milo, and notify the Coast Guard of our discovery. Then ask them to advise us."

Milo contacted the Coast Guard once more to report the finding of his friend while Rip and I held on tightly to Cooper. It was as if we were afraid the body would unexpectedly come back to life and take flight, forcing us to begin searching for it again. I listened to Milo as he conversed with another man over the marine radio. The great despair in Milo's tone saddened me. His responses to Rip had indicated he might have had some prior knowledge of Claypool's death, but now his voice and demeanor said differently. Milo's contradictory reactions confused me.

The man on the other end was relieved to hear we'd retrieved Cooper's body and asked that we bring it in with us. With a lot of square miles to search, it might have taken many hours to locate the body in the morning, the man said. Was the Coast Guard rescue team truly afraid we'd just dump Cooper's carcass back in the water and let them try to track it down the following day? But then I realized these men had probably dealt with a number of dim-witted morons in the past and didn't want to risk us being three more. Nor did they want us to attempt to intercept them to transfer the body to their vessel, which was already many miles away from us. Locating another boat in the dark would have been a big challenge. The deep voice on the radio commented that a rip tide had probably been what caused Cooper's body to drift so far from the abandoned boat.

"Oh, no!" Milo exclaimed, shaking his head. "I forgot all about Cooper's boat. We need to find it and tow it in behind this one. I was only concentrating on locating him at the time."

Rip put his arm around Milo's shoulders to comfort him and said, "The boat is of no major significance right now, son. We could be out here all night trying to locate it again. We best let it go and head in before we lose what little light we have left. As it is, we'll be lucky to get home before its pitch black out here. I'm sure the Coast Guard will eventually be able to locate the boat. As a career law enforcer, I know that because there's a homicide involved here they'll need to process his boat for any DNA evidence, signs of a struggle, and so forth. But, as far as we're concerned, getting Cooper and ourselves back to shore takes precedence right now."

After more discussion with the Coast Guardsman, it was clear he agreed with Rip. He instructed Milo to come straight in to the boat ramp at Rockport Beach. They'd meet us there to pick up the corpse and transfer it to the morgue.

"Oh, my God; oh, my God; oh, my God," Milo muttered, his head in his hands. The word "corpse" spoken with total lack of emotion seemed to bring the finality of the situation home to him. After a moment or two, he turned to Rip and me and said, "I have this terrible feeling something horrible is about to happen."

"Really?" I asked in astonishment. "Your best friend and business partner was just viciously murdered, Milo. I'm thinking the 'something horrible' ship has already sailed. Or, more appropriately in this case, the 'something horrible' boat has already floated away with the rip tide."

CHAPTER 4

After I tentatively knocked on Reggie and Milo's front door Monday afternoon, I asked Rip, "What kind of welcome do you think we'll get from our daughter today?"

"I don't care if we get a warm reception or not," Rip replied. "We aren't here to speak to her anyway. We're here because Milo asked us to come over, which is good because I wanted to talk to him before the detectives got hold of him. Besides, you should be accustomed to Reggie's wild mood swings by now. Let it go in one ear and out the other."

Easy for him to say, I thought. Rip was always quick to put incidents like our spat with Reggie behind him. I, on the other hand, tended to brood about them for days. I certainly wasn't going to attempt to pacify her just because she was acting like a spoiled brat, and I hoped Rip wouldn't cave in and pander to her, either.

"Hey there! Good morning, Mom and Dad," Reggie greeted us with a cheery disposition and a broad smile that revealed entirely too many of her bright white and perfectly aligned teeth. However, having invested several thousand bucks on that dazzling smile during Reggie's teen years, I was pleased to see her utilizing it.

She gave us each a quick hug and invited us inside.

For a few seconds I wondered if the woman standing on Reggie's doorstep was an imposter, as flashbacks from Saturday afternoon flitted through my mind. With another brilliant smile, she said, "Milo's on the phone, but he'll be with us in a few minutes. Mom, your hair looks gorgeous."

"Well, I guess I did comb it this morning." My hair looked exactly as it had the last twenty-thousand times she'd seen me: shoulder-length and naturally curly, with a few gnarly strands that had a mind of their own and stuck out at unnatural angles. The color is best described as that of a grey squirrel's tail: a mixture of grey and brown, with a few white and black hairs thrown in for good measure. At sixty-eight, I was at that stage in life when my original dark brown hair knew it was time to turn into a lighter color but was fighting the transition every step of the way. Personally, I could care less about it changing, even though, if I had my druthers, it would turn a pretty shade of white rather than mousey grey.

"Well, it's a very good style for you, Mom," Reggie said. "It highlights your beautiful blue eyes."

I didn't know how my mop of multi-colored hair could highlight my denim-blue eyes, but I had to agree my eyes were one of my most becoming features. I knew this was Reggie's way of apologizing for the way she'd treated us on Saturday. Despite my valiant efforts to teach her, she had never learned to pronounce the words, "I'm sorry." It must have been the double "R" that stymied her.

"At least she still *has* some hair," my nearly bald husband quipped.

"Ha, ha. You're so funny, Dad. You're one of those men who still look like a young handsome stud, even without hair." It seemed that Reggie's father was on the receiving line of Reggie's sweet-talking attempt for forgiveness as well. *Young, handsome stud? Rip?* I thought. *Wow! Reggie's really on a roll.* I watched as

Rip straightened his shoulders and sucked in his belly roll, grinning like he'd just been awarded his own star on Hollywood's walk of fame.

"You really think so?" Rip asked, oblivious to the actual motive behind his daughter's flattery.

"Well, yeah. For an old guy, that is." After that reply, I could actually hear Rip's ego deflating, like air whooshing out of an over-inflated tire. Even Reggie realized she'd just stepped in it because she continued with, "I meant that in a good way, of course. Seriously, Dad, you've got it going on."

"Yeah, right," Rip replied, no doubt wondering how one could be called an old guy in a good way. Before she could put her foot in her mouth again, Reggie became the thoughtful hostess.

"I'm sorry. You two must be very thirsty. Can I get you something to drink while we wait for Milo? How about a diet cranberry and pomegranate green tea? Or, perhaps a Monster energy drink? We've got Red Bull, also."

You've got what? Reggie already believed her parents still lingered in the Stone Age, so I just shook my head and replied, "I'm good. Thanks, anyway."

"Got any plain old black coffee?" Rip asked. With their single cup brewer, it felt like only a matter of seconds before Reggie returned with a steaming cup of dark coffee. She knew her dad liked his coffee hot and robust.

"Oh, and I made a pan of those double chocolate brownies you love so much," Reggie said lovingly to Rip. She was practically fawning over her father now, and had been so friendly and overly polite to me that I was beginning to get concerned about the nature of this pow-wow with her and Milo. I knew nothing good could come of this over-the-top reception we were receiving.

"Thanks, babe. They'd go great with this coffee." Rip smiled at his beaming daughter, who then virtually skipped out of the room on her way back to the kitchen to retrieve a plate of brownies. Rip was a pushover when it came to sweets. You could lead him to hell and back if you dangled an apple fritter in front of his face.

After she'd left the living room, Rip turned to me and said, "I wonder if Reggie and Milo know there's a stranger in their kitchen. I don't know who that woman is, but I like her. I hope her brownies are as good as Reggie's."

"You're not beginning to get at least a little apprehensive?"

"Yes, I admit it's scary, but how bad could it be? I'm sure the reason Milo asked us over has to do with Cooper's death, but I haven't been able to connect the dots yet."

"Maybe that's because visions of brownies are dancing in your head. Speaking about Reggie's most recent mood swing, it sure doesn't seem as if she's very upset about her husband's best friend and business partner's brutal death, does it? Surely Milo has told her about it, wouldn't you think?"

Reggie reentered the room before Rip could respond. She placed the plate on the coffee table directly in front of Rip and calmly asked, "Can I get you anything else, Dad? How about you, Mom? I've got some fresh grapefruit from the valley."

Rip shook his head, and I replied for both of us, "This is more than enough for us, sweetheart. Have a seat and relax. How are you holding up with Cooper's death, and all?"

"I'm fine. Never cared much for him to begin with, Mom." Reggie's quick response made it clear she wouldn't be losing too much sleep over Cooper Claypool's grim demise. I listened as she elaborated. "It seemed like Milo and Cooper had been disagreeing on every single business decision the last several months. It's kept Milo so uptight that he's been hard to live with at times. Recently, he's been upset so much of the time and wigging out over the tiniest things. When he's stressed out, he's not much fun to be around. Sure you guys don't need anything else?"

"I'm good," we both replied in stereo. It was evident Reggie didn't want to go into details about the business decisions behind the frequent disputes between the two men, so I let the subject drop. It occurred to me she might not even know what the problematic issues were.

"Okay. Just checking, in case you changed your mind about trying some of my green tea."

"No, but thank you, sweetheart." And, by the way, dear. Your diet cranberry and pomegranate green tea sounds absolutely god-awful.

"Hey, Dad. Did I tell you we decided against buying a new car?"

"Oh, really? How come?" I asked. I was curious if her "we decided" might be more a matter of "Milo decided for us."

Her next remark sounded stilted and rehearsed but I was relieved to hear it. "My car is still in like-new condition and—"

"That's what I tried to tell—umph—" Rip exhaled loudly as I elbowed him in the ribs. He spat out a morsel of brownie he hadn't swallowed yet.

Ignoring her father, Reggie added, "I don't really need a new one right now, anyway. Maybe in a couple of years or so we'll reconsider getting a new one."

"That's nice. I'm sure that's probably the best decision." I tried to be as nonchalant as I could, as if their decision to put off buying a new vehicle didn't matter to me one way or the other. Rip, however, tends to be a little less subtle.

"Damn straight!" He exclaimed. "Buying a new car right now would be downright foolish. We tried to tell you umpteen times that—umpth—"

I elbowed him in the sweet spot again before he could say any more. It caused him to choke a little on the brownie he'd just stuffed into his mouth, but it effectively shut him up. "Zip it," I said under my breath.

I didn't want him to say anything that might provoke Regina's evil twin sister to re-emerge. As he'd been speaking, I could see Reggie's ire building with each word. I swear I saw a tiny smoke ring drift out of her left ear. No sense fanning the fire after we'd almost distinguished it.

With perfect timing, Milo walked into the room and took a seat in a recliner. He looked exhausted, as if he hadn't slept at all the previous night. His discomfort was also apparent. His eyes darted around the room, never settling on any one spot for more than a few seconds or making contact with anyone else's in the room. Finally, after taking a deep breath, Milo spoke. "You've probably heard the Coast Guard located Coop's boat this morning and towed it in to the marina for processing."

Rip nodded, but made no comment.

"Um, well, uh, I want..." Milo seemed unable to form a full sentence. He looked around the room.

Impatient, Rip asked, "What is it, son? What do you want?"

Is Rip thinking the same thing I am? I wondered, my entire body tensing. Could Milo be preparing to turn himself in to the authorities for murdering his best friend? He'd appeared sincere in his grief yesterday. Could he be a better actor than we gave him credit for? I watched as he tried to speak coherently.

"Um, well, you see. I, um, wanted to thank you for coming over this afternoon. I honestly know nothing about what happened to Coop and need to ask a favor of you, Rip," Milo said.

Phew! I let out an audible sigh of relief at his remark. I'd been dreading a confession of guilt.

"Anything," Rip answered. I felt a shiver run up my back. That one-word response had come back to bite us in the keister more times than I could count.

"Well, you were the former sheriff of the police department here."

"Yes, I was aware of that," Rip replied dryly.

Without skipping a beat, Milo continued, "For what? About fifteen years?"

"Ten. But I was in law enforcement here in Aransas County for thirty-seven."

"I'm assuming you still know a lot of the detectives here."

"Yes, of course I do."

"And you're probably familiar with at least a few of them who'll be working on this case."

"Yes, I am."

"And I imagine you still have a lot of pull with the—"

"Not necessarily," Rip interrupted. And with an impatient, drawn-out sigh, he added, "Cut to the chase, son. What do you want from me?"

"Well, I just, um, just want, you know, to maybe get a copy of the autopsy report when it's available. After all, I was not only his best friend and business partner, but I'm also the person who discovered his body. Or...you, Rapella, and I found it, I should say."

"This is a homicide case we're talking about here. The authorities don't just pass out copies of the autopsy report to any Tom, Dick, or Larry who walks in the—"

"Harry," I corrected.

With an expression of annoyance, Rip turned to me and asked, "What? Harry? Who's that?"

"You just used the phrase Tom, Dick, or Larry, and it's—"

"Whatever," Rip replied before dismissing me with an exasperated wave of his hand. As soon as the words had left my mouth, I sensed Rip wouldn't appreciate being corrected, even though he was the one who often accused me of using every cliché in the book. *At least I use them correctly*, I thought with a huff.

Rip turned back to Milo and continued. "It's already available; the medical examiner completed the autopsy early this morning. But I have no way to access a copy of the report. Nor do you. Particularly since you are probably high on their list of possible suspects."

"What?" Milo and Reggie exclaimed in stereo. Milo looked as if he'd just been informed he had an inoperable ovarian cyst. "How do you know that?"

"I stopped by the station on the way here and spoke with Branson Reeves, the lead detective on the case. He's an old buddy of mine. He's been on the force almost as long as I was. Branson told me the medical examiner determined Cooper's death most likely took place somewhere between four and six on Saturday afternoon. He'd noted that the postmortem rigidity was already beginning to dissipate and the body was regaining flexibility by the time it arrived at the morgue last night. That led him to believe Cooper's death had occurred at least twenty-four hours before the three of us located his body. As we were already aware, he told Branson that along with the fatal wound caused by the spear-gun, there were abrasions on the victim's hands and face and a gash on the back of his head. Both of the latter injuries were prior to the mortal spear wound, as we already knew."

Milo paused for a moment to wipe away a tear before he said, "That's awful, but why would they suspect me of killing him? Coop was my best friend, from way back in high school, not to mention my business partner."

"Exactly! You just explained why you're a suspect, son," Rip explained. "It's *because* you were Cooper Claypool's best friend and business partner. That automatically makes you a suspect, just like a murder victim's spouse or significant other is always evaluated for motives and alibis. The vast majority of homicides involve people who are closely associated. Seldom is a murder committed by a random stranger. And, of those who knew their assailant, something like thirty percent were family members. You'd fall into the other seventy percent of that category, which are murders perpetrated by acquaintances. Incidentally, men are responsible for over ninety percent of the murders committed in the United States."

I could see that Rip was veering off into a litany of statistics about victims and killers, and I wanted to redirect him back to the subject at hand. "Speaking of cutting to the chase, dear, could you please practice what you preach?"

"Oh, yeah, sorry," Rip replied. "As I was saying, Branson spoke to Cooper's live-in girlfriend this morning and—"

"Avery Curry?" Milo asked. "Tall, willowy blonde?"

"Did Cooper have more than one live-in girlfriend?" Rip asked pointedly. Milo looked down as if he'd been chastised.

"My point is, there's no way you could not have landed a spot on the suspect list," Rip continued. "Especially given the fact there were witnesses who put you at Crabby Joe's Saloon on Saturday afternoon. That list of witnesses includes over a dozen saloon customers, as well as Avery Curry, who claims to have accompanied Cooper to the bar and grill on Saturday, and was present when you entered the establishment."

Milo's entire body went rigid, his face drained of color. Reggie stepped in to defend her husband. "Milo had been working hard all morning and went to grab lunch at one of his and Cooper's favorite hangouts. Not surprising that they ran into each other, is it? What does that prove?" Reggie was indignant. "How can having lunch with a guy make you a prime suspect for his death later on in the day?"

Rip turned toward Milo and asked, "Would you like to tell her, or should I?"

By the tone of the seasoned law officer's voice, it was clear the latter choice would not bode well for the younger man. Milo looked down at his lap and said, "It's not quite that simple, Regina. I didn't exactly 'have lunch' with Cooper on Saturday. And you see, babe, unfortunately it might prove difficult to come up with an alibi for that afternoon."

Reggie was gawking at her husband of less than six months like he had morphed into the Pillsbury dough boy. I could tell she was in utter shock. She shook her head and directed her comments to Milo, whose face flushed as he squirmed around in his seat. "What? That's impossible! You were at the house on Cactus Street in Fulton working with the electrician and flooring crew from eight in the morning until six or so that evening. I remember you saying you couldn't believe you got them all to work on a Saturday. Surely you can account for every hour that day, and the subcontractors can vouch for your whereabouts, too, if necessary."

"Um, well. Um, you see, dear, I, I, um…" Milo stammered, looking flustered as he tried to come up with the best way to explain his whereabouts on the day in question.

"Yes?" Reggie was on the edge of her seat, staring at Milo intensely. Truthfully, I was on the edge of the couch also, anxious to hear his response.

"Okay, here's what happened. I'm sorry, Reg. I guess I just forgot to tell you. I went to the job site in the morning and got all the subcontractors lined out for the day. At around eleven, I decided to go to Crabby Joe's to grab a bite to eat and ran into Cooper. A couple days earlier he'd told me he couldn't supervise the remodeling project at the Church Street four-plex on Saturday because he'd be visiting a sick uncle in San Antonio all weekend. I'd met his Uncle Charlie and knew he was fighting pancreatic cancer, so I completely understood Coop's desire to spend some time with him. I'd been planning to cover for him by stopping by that job site after lunch. It was no big deal that Coop didn't actually go to San Antonio, but it irritated me that he lied about it." Milo stopped talking, his gaze fixed on his folded hands resting on his lap. "Gosh, if he'd only just been upfront with me—"

"Okay. So, I don't understand, Dad. Why would it matter that witnesses put him at the bar and grill Saturday?" Reggie asked, after placing her right hand on her distraught husband's knee. "He should have workers at both work sites and at Crabby's who could vouch for his whereabouts the entire day."

"There's more, Reggie. A security camera in their parking lot identified Milo's presence there at eleven-thirty," Rip responded. "The investigators accessed the video after speaking to Cooper's girlfriend this morning. It didn't paint a pretty picture. It's quite incriminating, in fact."

At the exact same second Milo looked up in alarm, Regina spat out, "You...you...you did something horrid in the parking lot? Son-of-a—"

Cutting her off, Rip turned to Milo and asked, "Once again, would you like to tell her, or should I?"

For the second time, Milo considered his options for a few seconds and then faced his wife. "As you know, Regina, Coop and I have been buddies since we were sophomores in high school. We played on the football team together and even shared a locker our senior year. But when you become business partners, opinions, goals and work ethics often come into play. When your livelihood is at stake, like ours was, these issues can take a toll on a friendship. Disagreements happen on occasion. They just do. It's the nature of the beast when you're working together almost 24/7. I understand now why people always say you shouldn't do business with friends."

"I've noticed you've been uptight recently about Cooper's business decisions. So, Milo, tell me the truth. What happened in the parking lot?" Reggie asked. She looked disoriented, as if someone had just whacked her upside the head with a Louisville Slugger. I wondered if she was doubting her husband's innocence in his friend's death, as I was. And Rip too, I'm sure.

"Relax, Reg. It's not as bad as you're imagining," Milo replied.

"It's not?" Rip asked. By the derisive tone in his voice, I was even more anxious to hear the accounting of what the security camera had recorded. I hadn't had time to discuss with Rip what he'd found out at the police station earlier in the day.

Looking as if it just dawned on him he'd crapped in his own Easter basket, Milo took a deep breath, and began to explain. "When I ran into Coop at Crabby's on Saturday, I asked him why he wasn't at his Uncle Charlie's in San Antonio. Yes, I was angry. But who wouldn't be in my shoes?"

Milo ceased talking. It was clear he'd hoped that was all the clarification required to justify what occurred afterward. At Rip's impatient gesture to continue, Milo sighed again and went on. "We got into a heated argument, which turned into a scuffle out in the parking lot. It was not a big deal. We've had dust-ups before, including a recent disagreement about some inaccuracies in our company's bank account. But we've always patched up our relationship within a couple of days, just as we would've done this time had he not been—"

Milo choked up and was unable to finish the sentence. No one spoke for an uncomfortable period of time. To break the silence, I said, "I don't think you have anything to worry about. Scraps like that happen between male friends occasionally. Boys will be boys, you know. That doesn't mean you murdered him. After all, like Reggie said, you should be able to account for your whereabouts all day Saturday."

"It was a bit more than a dust-up or scrap, wouldn't you say, Milo?" Rip asked. "Seems to me, when you break a beer bottle over a guy's head your intentions are to cause serious harm to the fellow. That bottle should have never left the bar to begin with. But it explains the head wound and abrasions on his left knuckles. Why didn't you tell me about this before, Milo?"

Milo shook his head and remained silent. He appeared to have nothing to say. Unfortunately for him, however, Rip had plenty and was just getting started.

"Is there anything else you aren't telling me? I find it quite telling that you chose to hide this incident from me. I can assure you it'd be in your best interest to tell me the absolute truth right this minute. I can't help you if I'm armed with only lies, evasive details, and innuendos. In fact, without the complete story—every stinking detail you can recall—I won't get involved in the case at all. You'll be entirely on your own to dig yourself out of whatever hole you've dug for yourself. Is that what you want, son?"

"No," Milo said, eyes wide and beginning to water. Rip had become an intense interrogator. He had his "suspect" squirming nervously in his seat and sweating profusely. You could have wrung Milo out like a sopping rag mop.

"So, where did you go when you left Crabby's? The security tape shows you getting in your truck and peeling out of the parking lot, leaving your *best* friend bleeding and struggling to get to his feet." Rip enunciated the word "best" in the most ironic manner possible.

I realized Rip was in his element and didn't want to be interrupted, but I couldn't resist making a snide remark of my own. "Holy crapola, boy! If that's how you treat your closest friends, I'd hate to see what you'd do to an enemy."

"I was pissed off, I'll admit. But I wouldn't have left the premises if I'd thought Coop was seriously injured. I'm not that cold-hearted, I swear. In fact, I tried to get in touch with him late Saturday evening to apologize but he didn't answer his phone. Sadly, now I know why." Milo glanced at Reggie, waiting for her to vouch for her husband. When she didn't, he slowly reverted his gaze back to Rip who, unfortunately for Milo, did have a response that was anything but supportive.

"It appears to me, as well as to the homicide investigators, your actions Saturday afternoon *were* cold-hearted, to the nth-degree. You surely saw the mark that bottle left. Yet you didn't consider a three-inch gash caused by the blunt end of a beer bottle a serious wound?"

"Well, okay. But he didn't act like he was all that

injured. In fact, he hadn't even gotten in a punch or laid a hand on me, yet he wanted to go another round. That's why I left, by the way. Didn't want him to get seriously injured, you know."

"It's called *adrenalin*. Ever heard of it?" When Rip began making cutting remarks, it was a sign he was approaching the end of his rope. "Was there blood gushing out of his head at that point, Milo?"

"Um, well, yeah. I guess there was quite a lot of it pooling on the pavement."

"And that wasn't a clue he was seriously injured? Was Cooper in the habit of having blood gush from his head? Was this an everyday occurrence with your buddy, or should I say 'your victim?'"

"Well, no, of course not. But I didn't think he was going to bleed to death, if that's what you mean," Milo replied in obvious distress. I think Rip's deliberate use of the phrase '*your* victim' had had the effect he'd intended. *No wonder he'd been so respected as a law enforcer throughout his career*, I thought. *He's actually kind of hot when he's grilling someone this way. As long as that someone's not me, of course.*

Rip was downright impressive in this environment. Talk about bringing sexy back. The last time he'd had what few hormones I had left working overtime was when I caught him vacuuming the living room carpet in his boxers.

Now he was leaning forward, arms on his thighs. The fingers on his right hand were tapping his kneecap impatiently.

Milo swallowed hard before speaking. "I really didn't think I hit him hard enough to cause a concussion or anything."

"The bottle was shattered, Milo. That takes a significant degree of blunt force. And, naturally, there were shards of glass on the ground where the assault occurred."

"Assault?" Milo asked in alarm.

"Yes. Assault. Assault with a deadly weapon, to be more exact. That makes it aggravated assault, a felony offense. You'll be lucky to get the charge reduced to a Class A misdemeanor and only get a four-thousand dollar fine."

"Damn, man!" Milo replied. "We don't have four grand right now."

"Would you rather sit behind bars for a year? There's always that option if you'd prefer."

"No, not at all! That sounds terrible!"

"Duh," Rip said, echoing my own thoughts. "It *is* terrible! Worse than terrible, in fact! And not only that, in the homicide detectives' eyes, you had compelling motive!"

"Will this make them think I might be the one who killed him?"

Duh, I said to myself again. I thought Milo had asked a moronic question, and apparently his interrogator did too.

"Seriously? What do you think?" Rip asked incredulously. "If you were a detective on the case, wouldn't you consider the possibility that this violent scene, captured on tape, no less, might have led to a more serious confrontation a few hours later?"

Without replying, Milo put his head in his hands and began to sob. *Is he crying about the loss of his dear friend, or at the notion of how Cooper's death might affect him personally?* I wondered.

Reggie sat as still as the hideous flamingo statue in the corner of the living room. Her mouth agape, she stared at her husband as if he'd just declared he enjoyed trying on her negligees when she wasn't around. She seemed to be debating whether to console him, fear him, or detest him. If I'd been in her shoes, I'd be calling a divorce attorney, getting a restraining order, calling a locksmith, tossing all my husband's clothes into a lawn and leaf Glad bag, and advising him not to let the door hit him in the rear end on his way out. In that precise order!

What most concerned me just then was whether or not a marital spat might lead to a serious threat to Reggie's safety. Milo Moore had proven with the parking lot incident he could have a violent temper. Was that what Reggie was thinking? I was worried about her well-being and wondering if her father was too.

Like Regina, I was pretty much cemented into place. I felt a bit sorry for my son-in-law, even though I now had more serious doubts about his innocence. I'd rarely witnessed Rip in his element, as he was at that moment. Unmoved, the unyielding lawman stared silently at the recipient of his brutal interrogation. The look in his eyes was menacing when he leaned forward again and asked, "I want the truth right now, son. Did you kill Cooper Claypool? Were you involved in his death in any way at all? Damn it, boy! I can't help you if you don't tell me the truth. Shooting blanks is not going to get us anywhere in trying to convince the investigating team of your innocence. I have no intention of looking like a fool trying to help you if I don't know the facts. Tell me the truth right now, or you're on your own to fend for yourself! One call by me and the detectives will be here within minutes to haul you down to the station and book you on murder charges."

Rip's voice had risen so that he was nearly yelling. Visions of Jack Nicholson were floating around in my mind. I half expected Milo to jump on the couch and scream, "You can't handle the truth!"

Milo stared at Rip with trepidation. I had never seen such rugged resolve in my husband's eyes, and it was unnerving to me, too.

I think I'd have confessed to killing Jimmy Hoffa and tossing his body in the alligator-infested pond at the Aransas National Wildlife Refuge if Rip had directed that intimidating glare at me. Along with Rip and Reggie, I waited nervously for Milo's response.

It was a good fifteen uncomfortable seconds later when Milo looked up and said through his tears, "I swear to you I didn't kill him, sir. I promise I had nothing to do with his death. In fact, I felt really bad after I left the scene. When I went by his house around three to make amends he was gone, as was his boat. I assumed that in order to cool off, he'd gone fishing or taken his boat to the car wash to wash the salt off it. You know, down here on the coast, the salty air can—"

"Don't try to distract me, boy. I lived here for more years than you've been alive. I know all about salt."

"Yes, sir. Sorry, sir."

Rip barely took a breath before continuing his questioning. "When Cooper wasn't home when you stopped by Saturday afternoon, did it occur to you he might have had to go get his head stitched up?"

"Um, no, not really."

"Well, he did!" Rip said forcefully. "Gaping head wounds normally require attention, as someone your age should know. According to Detective Reeves, records indicate he was treated at the Care Regional Medical Center in Aransas Pass by a Dr. Rinehart on Saturday afternoon from twelve-oh-five to three fifty-five. Not only did he require sixteen stitches to sew up the gash, Cooper was also treated for a severe concussion and held there in the ER several hours for observation."

"I'm sorry," Milo muttered. "I really didn't know I'd hurt him that badly."

I was appalled. Would he show the same lack of concern if our daughter were to sustain an injury of that magnitude? In a venomous tone I couldn't contain, I lashed into Milo. "You didn't think to check on your so-called best friend directly afterward? You know, like to inquire about his injuries to make sure you didn't give him permanent brain damage or something? I find your actions and apathetic attitude deplorable. Should I be concerned about my daughter's welfare if she suffers a similar injury?"

Milo's wide-open eyes were trained on me, as if the fight or flight response was kicking in, and he had only seconds to flee before I pounced on him like a mama bear whose cub he'd chased up a tree.

Before Milo could choose an option, Rip shot me a look that said, "Sit back, shut up, and leave the questioning to me."

I'll admit the hair on the back of my neck bristled at Rip's unspoken remark, and you can be sure he'd hear about it later. After nearly fifty years of marriage, he was accustomed to being in the doghouse for things he didn't say but I knew damn well he was thinking. However, I was also aware the current situation was in Rip's wheelhouse, not mine, so I reluctantly sat back, shut up, and concentrated on Milo's next remarks.

"Oh, man! What did I do? I could have killed him. Oh, man!" Milo repeated, as a tear escaped and ran down his left cheek. Then, as if the gravity of the matter had just sunk in, he sat up straight and with a quivering voice, said, "I didn't kill Coop, Rip! I'd swear on a stack of bibles I didn't see him after I drove away from the bar following our tussle in the parking lot. Or, at least not until we found him floating in the Gulf."

"Are you a religious man, Milo?"

"Well, no, not really."

"Do you attend church on Sundays—or on any other day, for that matter?"

"Well, no, not really," Milo repeated, looking ill-at-ease. At that moment, I believe Milo would have sacrificed his left testicle to have attended at least a few church services in the previous couple of months so he could have truthfully replied affirmatively to Rip's question.

"In that case, you swearing on a stack of bibles means about as much to me as you swearing on a stack of Bugs Bunny comic books. Maybe you *should* consider joining a church. I don't think a little spiritual guidance would hurt you at this stage of your life. And Rockport has a number of fine houses of worship to choose from. So, Milo, what did you do after you couldn't locate Cooper at his home?"

"I drove over to Tin Can Point to sit on a rock and try to cool off. I was still a little hot under the collar, you see."

"And then?" Rip wasn't going to let Milo off that easy. He wanted an accounting of every single minute of Milo's whereabouts on Saturday afternoon.

"When I couldn't find him at home, I took my own boat out to see if I might catch him out at our most productive floundering area. That's why we had to get fuel before the three of us went out yesterday."

"Why that particular area?" Rip asked, not interested in the empty gas tank.

"On Friday, Cooper suggested we go out and try to catch some flounder with these Carolina rigs he'd bought, since gigging's not allowed in November."

I had no clue what a "Carolina rig" was, and I doubted Rip did either. But Rip wasn't interested in insignificant details, anyway. He wanted locations and possible individuals who could substantiate Milo's claims. He needed a verifiable alibi for Milo if he had any hope of convincing the investigating team his son-in-law could not have murdered his friend. "Go on. But stick to the basic facts, outlining your whereabouts that afternoon. I don't need to know what kind of fishing lures you use."

"Sorry, sir. So, anyway, I still wanted to apologize and try to work things out between us, but he wasn't at our floundering hole, nor did I see his boat anywhere else I checked. But I couldn't cover the entire bay, you know."

I thought Milo's description of his encounter with Cooper—"little tussle"—was a gross understatement. However, from his demeanor, I thought Milo might be telling the truth. I was certain Rip did too, because his manner softened as he said, "Go on. What happened next? That detail won't help your alibi much, I'm afraid."

"Why?" I asked. It sounded to me like a fortuitous detail. "Surely, someone saw him leave in his boat and can attest to his whereabouts at the time. His subcontractors could also verify his presence at the project after he left Crabby's and returned to work. It would take a good deal of time to go out in the Gulf, kill Cooper, and make it back to shore, all before returning to his job."

"Yes, dear, that's true. But he didn't return to work. Isn't that right, Milo?" Rip didn't pause for a response from our shell-shocked son-in-law. "And it's his whereabouts at the time that's going to further incriminate him."

"Oh," was all I could say.

Rip directed his next comments to Regina and me. "As you're aware, Milo's boat is unique. Kitschy, but unique. And, you're absolutely right, Rapella. Several witnesses at the boat ramp, as well as on the beach, did see him leave in his boat. But the witnesses all told the detectives the *Maverick* was headed directly toward the area where Cooper Claypool's body was found. That doesn't exactly scream 'innocent' to the detectives, I'm afraid."

"Oh, dear God," Milo muttered. "I hadn't thought of that. First, I was going to check to see if he was spear-fishing out there, but changed my mind. Now I wish I'd stuck to my original plan. I may have been able to thwart the murder somehow. But it's crazy to go spear-fishing out in the deeper water alone, and I couldn't imagine that even Cooper would do something that foolish. I decided our flounder hole was more likely and changed directions just before I cleared the island, already out of view of the beach goers and people launching their boats at the ramp. I went back into Allyn's Bight instead of heading on out to the Gulf. You see, I was low on fuel already and was hesitant to venture out that far. Oh, dear Lord. What am I going to do?"

"Son, I think you need to report to the police station forthwith and give a full and detailed statement. A completely honest one. Spare no details. Tell the detectives exactly what you told me and anything else you can recall. That would bode much better for you than to force the detectives to confront you, which, according to Branson Reeves, is on their agenda for this afternoon. You don't want to look like you have something to hide. And I wouldn't dally if I were you. Squad cars could be pulling into your driveway at any second."

Three sets of eyes were trained on Milo. He sat quietly, in deep thought. I wondered what was going through his mind as we all waited for him to respond.

"Okay, I will. I'll head over there right now," Milo finally said, looking as if he'd rather be reporting to the front lines of an attack on an ISIS training camp with only a pocketknife for protection. The reticent expression worn by Milo, who was just shy of fifty-two, resembled that of a grade-schooler who'd been sent to the principal's office for peeking under a girl's skirt on the playground as he asked, "Will you come with me, sir?"

"It's Rip, not sir, Milo. In fact, I'd be fine if you called me Dad, Pappy, or even my given name, Clyde. Anything but sir. And of course I'll go with you. Mind you, there's not much I can do to help you other than be there for moral support. My former position as the sheriff here won't influence the investigating team to turn a blind eye to any involvement you might have had in this crime. In this case, it's not *who I* know, but *what you* know."

Suddenly, I wished we'd never returned to our south Texas hometown of Rockport. Home may truly be where the heart is, but my heart was doing flip-flops as it raced toward what felt like an impending cardiac arrest. However, a few minutes later my heart melted when my daughter walked over and stepped into my open arms for a long and loving embrace. She laid her head on my shoulder and wept softly.

This mess might turn into a disaster. It doesn't sound promising for Milo. I don't know what Regina will do if

Milo goes to jail for assaulting Cooper with a deadly weapon, I thought. *It appears to me Reggie is worried about it, too. What can I possibly say to alleviate her fears?*

It sounded lame and unconvincing, but it was all I could come up with, when I said, "It will all work out okay, sweetheart. I promise."

I had never reneged on a promise to my only child in the past, and I prayed this wouldn't be the first time I'd be unable to deliver on my word.

CHAPTER 5

"Your son-in-law is a blooming idiot," wasn't the first thing I'd hoped to hear when Rip walked in the door a couple of hours later. "It's all taken care of and Milo's off the hook for killing Cooper Claypool," or, "They've arrested the real killer," would have been preferable. His next comment was even more disconcerting.

"He'll be lucky if he doesn't get the needle."

Reggie walked into the room just in time to catch Rip's last words. In unison, she and I gasped. Then I asked, "The needle? Oh, good Lord. What's going on?"

"I'm not entirely sure. He was still in the interrogation room when I left. On the way to the station I stressed to him how important transparency was. I told Milo he needed to tell the detectives everything he knew and exactly what happened at Crabby Joe's on Saturday, even though the truth wouldn't compliment his character any. He needed to give them no reason to doubt his word or believe he had anything to hide."

"And?" I asked when Rip stopped talking.

"First thing the knucklehead said when Detective Reeves walked in the room to question him was, 'I want to see my attorney.'"

"He did?" Reggie asked. "Why does he think he needs

an attorney when he's innocent? Dad, do you think there's a chance Milo really did have something to do with the murder? He never mentioned a word to me about the fight with Cooper before today. Could he be lying to all of us? As you already know, he'd never have mentioned the fight if not for being outed by the restaurant's security tape."

"I really don't know, honey. I honestly believed he had nothing to do with killing Cooper. At least until he immediately lawyered up in the interrogation room. I guess all we can do now is wait and see what happens," Rip replied with a long sigh as he plopped down into the closest recliner.

The wait took less than two minutes. Rip had gone out to the back deck to take a call on his cell phone. He walked back into the house after a very brief conversation with the caller and, with no preamble, said, "They've booked him on aggravated assault charges, as I was afraid they might. The judge granted a bond order. Judge Martin's a friend of mine, or it might have cost me even more to bail the fool out."

I knew my daughter was a nervous wreck. She sat on the sofa sniffling, and her trembling hands continuously messed with the fine tufts of hair hanging down on her forehead like wispy bangs. That had always been a tell-tale sign she was troubled about something she had no control over.

"Sweetheart, don't worry. I promised you this would turn out all right, and I meant it," I said to comfort her. When Rip turned to stare at me, I shrugged my shoulders and added, "Your father and I will do some looking into the matter on our own and see if we can't find some answers. After all, your daddy being the sheriff for so many years ought to make our pursuit much easier."

As it turned out, "ought to" were the defining words in my reassuring statement.

* * *

"I'm having blackened amberjack. What are you having?" Rip asked.

"I'm not sure yet," I replied, flipping through the menu. "I thought I might try the garlic shrimp skewer and grilled vegetables. Either that or the seafood platter. No, that's just too much food, and I'm not paying that much money for something that will go half-uneaten. You know what they say: waste not, want not."

"It wouldn't go uneaten. Trust me," Rip said. I knew he'd clean up the leftovers, but I still couldn't bring myself to pay for the platter of mahi-mahi, shrimp, oysters, and mussels when there were a number of other things on the menu that were cheaper.

"The grouper fillet sounds good. Maybe I'll—"

Rip interrupted me with a touch of exasperation in his voice. "Really? Do we need to go through this every single time we go out for supper? It's the same routine over and over, nearly word for word, in fact. Who do you think you're kidding?"

"Whatever do you mean?"

"We both know you're going to end up ordering the $10.95 grilled chicken breast, because it's the cheapest entree on—"

"And quite tasty," I remarked, cutting him off just as he had me. "And, yes, I believe that's exactly what I'm going to have. Thank you for suggesting it."

Rip shook his head before looking up at our waitress, Casey, who was ready to take our drink orders. We had decided to treat ourselves to an evening meal at our favorite restaurant, located in Fulton Harbor just minutes from the RV park. They were throwing a pot luck supper at the campground, but Rip had always refused to attend such events. "How do we know how clean all these other ladies' kitchens are? Even ours scares me sometimes," he'd always say with a wink, before getting walloped on the top of the head with the closest non-lethal weapon.

We were chatting about Milo and Regina when I

asked, "Seriously, Rip. What do you believe the chances are that Milo is truly innocent and wasn't, at least to some degree, responsible for his friend's death?"

"I honestly don't know what to think, honey. He appears to be sincere, and I want to believe he had nothing to do with it. But it's hard to ignore all the evidence that point straight to him as the perpetrator. I know if I was the lead detective on this case, I'd be on Milo like stink on—"

"Shush," I told my husband, whose low, resonating voice tended to carry clear across a crowded room, especially when he wasn't wearing his hearing aids. I never had any problem tracking him down at a party for just that reason. "Keep your voice down. Milo's headed down the crapper fast enough without your help."

Silently, Rip turned toward the window looking out over Fulton's fleet of oyster and shrimp boats resting in their slips in the harbor's marina. I realized I'd probably offended him, but I didn't want to be the source of any rumors that could possibly incriminate our son-in-law.

I still wanted to believe Milo was innocent, to the point I was willing to stick my neck out and, with Rip's assistance, do a little investigating. We'd been successful in proving our friend, Lexie Starr, wasn't guilty of murder in late August. Who was to say we couldn't be just as successful this time? After all, not only was Milo's future in jeopardy, our daughter's future was at stake as well.

As I was ruminating on how to best launch into this impromptu investigation, my thoughts were interrupted by a boisterous group of four men who were seated at the table behind us. I listened as they ordered a round of drinks. The man with a ponytail asked for a rum and Coke, a short stocky guy requested a Miller Lite, the tall redhead with his back to me ordered a Guinness Black Lager, and the Hispanic man chose a dry martini. I never could quite figure out how any beverage could be served dry, but that's beside the point.

I was most intrigued by the redhead. His voice had a very strong Irish Brogue to it. When I overheard the waitress ask him where his practice was located, he replied with what sounded like, "Terty-tude and Turd Stweet."

Due to his finely tailored suit and sophisticated air, it didn't surprise me to discover he had a "practice" and was probably a physician or an attorney. Maybe it's just me, but when I have a legal or medical issue that's troubling me, I don't want an individual who's still practicing. I want someone who has his professional skills down pat.

When the four men began to discuss the tragic death of the local construction superintendent, I had to wonder if he might be the lawyer Milo asked to see in the interrogation room. Even more so after I heard him say with his thick accent, "This case is bound to be a feather in any attorney's cap. By the way, has anyone heard if they've caught the killer yet?"

After the others responded in the negative, the dapper dude went on to say, "Ten-to-one it's Milo Moore, that dingbat partner of Claypool's. Not that I wouldn't like to pin a medal on him now. Moore's a total loser himself. Still, I feel like I owe him a beer at the very least for getting Claypool out of my hair."

He laughed along with the rest of the men before the bald-headed Hispanic guy facing us from across the table replied, "Yeah, that's a no-brainer. Beat you to it, didn't he, Pat?"

I wasn't eavesdropping, I'll have you know, but the men were sitting so close to us their voices were impossible to ignore. I was disappointed that due to some clamor across the room, I'd missed the Irish fellow's response to the bald dude's question. The redhead was sitting with his left side to me, facing in the opposite direction. I could have back-handed him, and briefly considered it. But just then, Casey arrived with our drinks.

I hadn't appreciated the way the Irish fellow had characterized my son-in-law. Even so, I swear it was entirely accidental when my hand twitched ever so slightly as Casey handed me the glass of water. With the ill-timed twitch, my drink toppled, and the water rained down on the Irishman's lap just before the glass fell to the floor and shattered.

The rude man jumped up at the shock of the ice cold water saturating his nether regions and I nearly laughed out loud. Rip shot me his "What the hell?" look as the sodden gentleman glanced at me in disgust before giving the poor innocent waitress a tongue-lashing. I felt bad for Casey. She was not responsible for the mishap but apologized profusely to the over-bearing jerk nonetheless.

I felt even worse about the incident when the flush-faced young lady apologized to me. She assured me she'd be back with a fresh glass of water after she cleaned up the spill and shards of glass before someone accidentally stepped on one. As Casey walked away, a clearly annoyed Rip whispered across the table, "Are you happy now? What was that all about, anyway? And *you* told *me* to keep it down?"

"Didn't you hear what he called Milo?" I hissed back.

"Yeah, I did. But frankly, at the moment, I'm not sure his description of our son-in-law wasn't spot-on. Besides, it doesn't mean he deserved a cold-water drenching, does it?"

"Well, in my opinion, he—"

"Here's your water, ma'am," Casey interrupted me as she sat the replacement glass of water on the table. "Again, I'm so sorry for the mess. I hope you didn't get too wet."

"Oh, no, I'm fine, dear. The gentleman behind me took the brunt of it," I responded, with a polite smile, hoping it didn't look like a self-satisfied smirk.

"I know, but—"

"Don't worry about it, sweetie. Accidents happen," I

graciously replied. "No harm done."

Casey flashed me an appreciative smile, walking away as Rip shook his head and said, "No harm done to you, anyway. Shouldn't you at least offer to have the man's suit cleaned?"

I shrugged, but made no such offer to the redhead. After all, his suit was wet, not dirty. Rip, still annoyed, turned back toward the window to idly watch bulky burlap bags of oysters being pitched onto the bulkhead from the aft of an old and dilapidated boat. I was getting the cold shoulder, but it's not like I hadn't gotten it from him before. In fact, the current episode was the third time that day alone. We'd be celebrating our golden wedding anniversary in May. No couple reaches that milestone without having learned which battles were worth fighting, and which should be left unchallenged. If Rip and I squabbled over every minor disagreement, we'd more aptly be known as the Bickersons than the Ripples.

Just then, a deep voice from the table behind us caught my attention, and I'm sure Rip's as well. "Is Avery still demanding full custody of Elizabeth?"

"Yeah, but I'm going to fight for joint custody." Responding to the question was the man I'd accidentally given a crotch dousing.

"Well, of course. I would too," the other man laughed and replied in what seemed to me as inappropriate amusement. "She's as much yours as she is Avery's. I don't blame you for wanting your share of time with Elizabeth."

I didn't know how common the name Avery was, but had to wonder if he was referring to Avery Curry, Cooper's live-in girlfriend. Could the dripping redhead be her ex-husband? That might explain why this high-faluting dude had a bone to pick with Cooper Claypool, and why his friend implied he'd have liked to whack him himself if someone else hadn't done it before him. Also, the Irishman had claimed earlier he'd wager ten-to-one that "someone else" was Milo.

I admit I was purposely eavesdropping at that point, but only because the men's discussion was relevant to an active murder investigation. I tried to catch the response to the man's comments. The noise level in the room had increased substantially, as one would expect during the dinner hour in a popular eating establishment. I was forced to scoot back within an inch of the redhead's chair to hear him say, "As you guys know, I could care less about spending time with Liz. I'm pressing the custody deal just to tick Avery off more than anything."

I was disturbed by the cold, calculated way he spoke about Elizabeth, evidently his and Avery's daughter. It seemed to me he only wanted to use the child as a pawn in his divorce proceeding. My stomach roiled at the man's callousness. My heart went out to poor Elizabeth.

Just then, Casey set our plates down in front of us. If I hadn't been so hungry and already had an irked dinner partner, I might have considered trying for an encore with my plate of chicken, linguini and grilled veggies. But prompting another ass-chewing for Casey from the hotheaded bloke behind me would have been inconsiderate to such a gracious hostess, so I'm glad I didn't attempt to upset her tray of food. As Casey walked away, Rip signaled me silently with his fork to eat, and, by his mannerisms, to extract my nose from the heartless man's business.

Suddenly it occurred to me. I now had a starting point for an investigation. It might take a lengthy foot massage to get Rip to agree to assist in my quest to clear our son-in-law's name, but it'd be worth my while.

CHAPTER 6

After we finished our supper and debated about how much of a tip we thought Casey deserved for her service, we decided to take a relaxing drive along the coastline. For the record, Rip won the battle with the line, "And just how pathetic a tip would you have left a waitress whom you *hadn't* used as a weapon against a diner at another table, and whom you also forced to clean up a mess she didn't create?"

We drove down Fulton Beach Road toward Copano Bay Bridge, admiring the view and abundant waterfowl, including two blue herons, a snowy egret, and a flock of white pelicans being fed fish carcasses by a fisherman who'd apparently just finished filleting his day's catch at the nearby fish-cleaning station.

We continued on down to a sandy beach area called Tin Can Point, where Milo had claimed he went to cool off after his "dust-up" with Cooper. We could hear the clatter of construction taking placing on the Copano Bay Bridge adjacent to us.

We sat on the tailgate of the truck, watching with amusement as several brown pelicans plunged head-first into the water after their suppers. Chuckling, we observed one successful pelican struggle with a small but uncooperative sheepshead, an odd-looking fish that had teeth very similar to those of humans and a sharp prickly dorsal fin. The diving bird fought to get his catch situated correctly in his pouch to swallow it headfirst while a flock of seagulls were dive-bombing him in an attempt to steal his meal. The pelican's efforts finally paid off as it tipped its head back to drain the water from its pouch and consume the sheepshead. The gulls flew off to try their luck somewhere else.

I stopped laughing when, after Rip's raucous guffaw, he said, "That reminds me of you trying to eat a hotdog when you don't have your dentures in."

My laughter made a comeback when I caught Rip by surprise with a mighty shove that dislodged him from his perch on the tailgate and left him butt down on a saturated mound of sand. *That will teach him*, I thought smugly. *He never even saw it coming.*

When I saw him grimace, I instantly felt bad. What had I been thinking? Not only was Rip sixty-eight, he also had a new artificial hip joint. Panicking, I helped him to his feet, "Oh, goodness! I'm so sorry, honey. Are you all right?"

"Yes. I'm fine, dear," he replied with an impish grin. "Just keep in mind what they say about paybacks."

Half an hour later, we pulled through the entrance gate of the packed-to-the-gills RV park. We drove past a large flock of snowbirds shooting the you-know-what around an enormous fire pit, following the scheduled pot luck supper they'd all just attended. Actually, down here folks refer to them as "Winter Texans"; it sounds more welcoming, you see. "Snowbirds" kind of has a game animal ring to it, as if there was a season on them.

I'm sure each of the clusters of senior citizens was involved in a chat fest about every ailment known to man, except perhaps diaper rash. A large percentage of them were comparing their daily cocktail of medications. Now that I think about it, diaper rash might actually have been a popular topic of discussion among a few of the attendees, who appeared to be born somewhere around the turn of the century. Not this last turn, of course.

"How many different versions of potato salad do you reckon they've just sampled?" Rip asked, jokingly.

"My guess—fourteen. That's the average, if I recall correctly. And among them, they've no doubt downed enough hard-boiled eggs that, if left un-deviled, could have staged an Easter egg hunt for the entire Rockport elementary school."

"Have I thanked you recently for not dragging me to pot luck dinners and bingo parlors? They're just not my cup of tea," Rip said. "I love you dearly, Rapella, and you know I'd do anything for you. But I have to draw the line somewhere."

"No worries. Not my cup of tea either."

"Thank God for that! What do you feel like doing this evening? I thought I might sit back with a stiff drink and look for a good movie on cable."

"You just saw *Fifty Shades of Grey* around the fire pit," I replied. "Why don't we go for a walk instead? It's a beautiful evening for it, and you need the exercise for your new hip. Especially after that unfortunate tumble you took onto the sand at Tin Can Point. We both could stand to walk off a few of the calories we just consumed."

"Oh, all right," was Rip's unenthusiastic agreement.

After a long walk, circling the entire campground several times, we were back in the Chartreuse Caboose, our cramped but comfy home on wheels. Rip had indeed found a movie on the television he was interested in watching, at least for five or six minutes until he fell fast asleep on the couch. Dolly had climbed down from her customary perch on top of the back cushions of the couch and was snuggled up on his chest with a paw resting on his chin.

I made myself a hot cup of chamomile tea and sat down

at the kitchen table, which also served as a makeshift bed, an office, a hobby room, and Rip's personal nest. On any given day he could amass an entire mound of dirty clothes, sorted-through mail, trash of every fashion, dirty dishes, candy wrappers, personal effects, and an ever-changing collection of odds and ends on the table. I couldn't complain, however. I had a nest of my own on the table next to the recliner.

After a couple of soothing sips from my tea cup, I opened up the iPad Regina had gifted us with the previous Christmas. When we'd attended a surprise birthday party at Lexie Starr and Stone Van Patten's, B&B, the Alexandria Inn, in August, I'd been given an eight-week course in tablet training in the space of a mere forty-five minutes. Much of the technical lingo went over my head like a rapidly-moving cloud. And I don't mean the "cloud" my instructor, Mattie Hill, had told me I could store my files in. I not only had no idea where to find this mystical cloud, I also had no clue how to stuff files into it if I did.

But I am proud to say I'd managed to learn how to obtain information on the Internet, how to play games like Scrabble and Mahjong, and, last but not least, how to ask some lady named *Siri* ridiculous questions. Her responses often provided free entertainment for Rip and me.

Rip's favorite question to date was "What should I be for Halloween?" Siri's response, "Dishes. Girls loving doing dishes." Who knew a technical device could have her chip in the gutter? Funny though, when I asked her to talk dirty to *me* she told me my carpet needed cleaning. Now, how entertaining is that? Who needed to sit around a campfire discussing their maladies with strangers when they had Siri to converse with?

Before I began nodding off at the table, I attempted to Google "Pat Rockport, Texas Attorney" and "Pat Rockport, Texas Physician" and came up with so many hits I decided my best option was to drive to 32 Third Street the following day. With any luck at all, I could locate this red-headed Irishman named Pat there.

CHAPTER 7

"Willow J. Bradford OB/GYN, Patrick R. O'Keefe GP, R. G. Patel MD, and James Carney ENT," read the bronze-plated plaque on the door. I was standing on the front steps of a walk-in health clinic at 32 Third Street, a recent local addition I hadn't known existed before that moment. Thankfully, I'd also learned to utilize the GPS on the truck's dashboard last summer while staying at the Alexandria Inn.

So, the Irishman was a physician. A general practitioner, to be more precise. I'd have wagered on the other option if I'd had to make a guess, because he'd practically oozed attorney vibes. I could think of at least a dozen lawyer jokes that exemplified this particular carrot-topped doctor.

Suddenly, out of nowhere, I felt a slight twitch in my right shoulder. It was probably connected to the twitch in my hand I'd experienced at the restaurant the night before. Although I'm relatively certain it was a fluke nerve tic, you just can't be too careful these days. I decided it would probably be prudent of me to go into the clinic and request a professional opinion in the event it was an issue that might worsen and plague me in the future. That was my story and I had every intention of sticking to it.

I filled out the necessary paperwork while the

receptionist scanned my Medicare and insurance supplement cards. Then I sat in a chair next to an end table that had a stack of magazines and pamphlets piled on it. I sifted through a recent edition of *Arthritis Today* while I waited to be seen, along with a dozen other patients in the clinic's lobby. The magazine wasn't particularly relevant to my condition, but chances were good it could be in the future. These old bones weren't getting any younger, you know, and I'd put a lot of miles on them.

After scanning through several other health-related pamphlets, including one regarding the importance of routine prostate testing, I made a mental note to hound Rip about this recommendation at a later date. An hour and fifteen minutes later, a nurse called my name and led me back through a maze of hallways to a room in the rear of the building. She took my vital signs and entered the results into a laptop computer on a rolling cart she'd brought into the room with her.

The I.D. tag hanging around the nurse's neck indicated her name was Becky Winslow. Becky was quite chunky for a young woman of short stature. She'd weigh in at around two-hundred and fifty pounds, I estimated. For a woman who chose the medical field as a vocation, she didn't seem to be overly concerned about her own health risks.

I had to bite my tongue to stop myself from reminding Becky about the pot calling the kettle black when she chided, "You really should speak to the doctor about your border-line hypertension. And speaking of which, have you had a lipid profile test performed lately? I'd guess you're overdue for an EKG and chest x-ray, too."

Obviously, I had no way of knowing this young, but entirely too plump, nurse's actual blood pressure and cholesterol levels, but would have put mine up against hers in a heartbeat. No pun intended.

It was probably fortunate that a medium-height Indian gentleman with a stethoscope around his neck walked in before I could respond to the nurse with a snarky comment of my own. After the long wait to be seen, I wasn't in the mood to be lectured by a nurse who'd be lucky to make it to my age at the rate she was going.

The well-groomed physician who'd just entered the room introduced himself, and said, "Feel free to call me R.G., Ms. Ripple."

"Nice to meet you, Dr. Patel," I said politely, because I felt even freer not to reply so intimately to a man I'd just met. Using his initials felt too personal for my liking, particularly after he'd just addressed me by my surname. Having read his I.D. tag, however, I completely understood why he went by R.G. in lieu of his given name, Ramakant Gurcharan Patel, MD.

"What have we got going today?" He asked with a toothy smile.

"Me, shortly," I wanted to say, disappointed I'd drawn the short straw and wasn't being seen by the physician I'd hoped to get an audience with. But I realized I couldn't just walk out of the room without an explanation, so I explained my current malady. "I've had this twitch in my shoulder that's bothersome."

He immediately began to probe my shoulder, stimulating the nerves and muscles in an attempt to find out where the unusual twitch originated. He advised me to let him know when he touched a sore spot. "Does this hurt?"

"No."

"How about here?"

"No, not that spot either." If I indicated he'd found the root of my problem, he'd give me some advice on how to eliminate the issue and the appointment would be over before I had a chance to question him on how, when, and where I could meet his colleague. "No, a little to the left. No, that's not it. Maybe a little more left. Just keep searching and I'll let you know when you hit the exact area that's bothering me."

Dr. Patel began massaging my shoulder with a firm touch, still trying to locate the area I was concerned about. If I hadn't been so intent on my mission, I'd have enjoyed the deep-muscle massage. He asked, "How long have you been experiencing this 'twitch' you're referring to? And how often does it occur?"

To myself I answered, *just once, on the clinic's doorstep*, aware that even the single incident might have been an opportunistic figment of my imagination. Out loud, I evasively replied, "Enough that I felt I needed to come to the clinic to speak with a physician about it."

"Hmmm. How about here?" He asked, pushing hard on my right clavicle. I shook my head then and after each probe that followed. As Dr. Patel increased the pressure with which he was prodding me, it actually did begin to hurt everywhere he touched. I'd be lucky if I didn't wake up black and blue the next day.

"Not there, either," I answered, stifling a groan. Although I had no specific strategy in mind, I decided I better not waste any more time. So I plunged right in. "And, by the way, you're not the physician I was expecting to see."

"Excuse me?" Dr. Patel look confused at first, and after my comment registered, his expression changed into one of indignation. I must say, the tall, dark and handsome doctor had the sexiest hint of a dimple in his left cheek when he frowned. So adorable, in fact, I briefly considered trying to offend him again.

I gave myself a mental slap. Reminding myself I was there with a specific objective, I swiftly came to my senses. I made a feeble attempt to clarify my remark. "Not that you're not exceptional, Dr. Patel. It's just that a good friend of mine's husband practices at this clinic, too. I figured since he's a general practitioner, he'd be the logical physician I'd be assigned to for treatment today."

"Oh, yes, I see. You're referring to Dr. O'Keefe, who's off this morning due to an unexpected family obligation." He smiled broadly, revealing sparkling pearly whites that contrasted so beautifully with his dark complexion. "I'm covering for him until he reports at noon. As I'm sure you noticed, I'm swamped as a result, which is why your wait was longer than usual. My apologies for any inconvenience it might have caused you."

"No big rip," I said, using my husband's favorite saying, which should come as no surprise to anyone. I wanted to give some kind of indication I really was acquainted with Dr. O'Keefe and his ex, so I added, "Too bad about the divorce, isn't it? I'm sure you're every bit as competent as Pat. And, for the record, much easier on the eyes too, if you know what I mean."

Dr. Patel's hands flew off my shoulder as if his skin had been singed. The wink I'd bestowed upon him at the end of my comment might have come across a little more lecherous than I'd intended. The doctor looked kind of like a condemned man having a noose placed around his neck.

The doctor clearly viewed his oddball patient as a cougar on the prowl now, for he was easily three decades younger than I. Here was a woman who initially felt it would be too forward to use his first name suddenly turning into a wanton seductress—what's not to understand?

"Nothing personal, of course," I felt compelled to add before he threw up in the soiled-gown hamper. "I just meant to say you're a very handsome young man as well as an extremely accomplished physician."

The tense doctor relaxed and beamed at my clarification. The relieved smile made the cute little dimple reappear and deepen. I'd have to find a way to make him smile again before I left, I decided. I'd always been a sucker for a man with dimples, and Rip's cheeks were too plump to give a dimple a fair chance. And, although this may sound a bit like too much information, that goes for both sets of cheeks in his case.

"So you're tight with Avery, huh?" The doctor inquired politely, as he resumed applying pressure to my shoulder, clavicle, upper arm, and embarrassingly damp arm pit. Lying did that to me, you see. I would sweat buckets if I were ever to perjure myself in a court of law. The bailiff would have to pass out flotation devices to everyone in the court room by the time I finished testifying. And, to be honest, having multiple parts of my body stimulated by this young sexy physician might have contributed to the excessive perspiration, too.

It suddenly occurred to me the doctor's hands had stilled and he was staring at me. My hesitation had concerned him, and I knew he was waiting for a response to his query about my relationship with the ex-wife of a fellow physician who practiced at the same health clinic.

"Well, describing our relationship as 'tight' might be a little much." *It also might qualify as the most flagrant fabrication of my entire life*, I thought. Even though I could feel a drop of moisture slithering between my breasts and down my abdomen, I decided to wing it with whatever white lies I felt necessary. I chose what I thought was the safest explanation. "Actually, we're co-workers."

I'd already had to fork over a thirty-five dollar co-payment for an imaginary health concern, and by now you know how deeply that went against my grain. I came to the conclusion I might as well get my money's worth and try to extract as much useful information out of young Ramakant Gurcharan Patel, MD, as I could before I left the clinic.

"Really? You work at Jugs 'n Mugs in Corpus Christi?" The dazed doctor asked.

I have to admit I was taken aback by his response. Way, way back, in fact. If Jugs 'n Mugs was the topless bar and grill I'd read about in the *Times*, I knew I might have just stepped in a tall pile of poo.

"You really work at Jugs 'n Mugs in Corpus Christi?" The doctor repeated when I failed to respond.

"Yes, I do. Why is that so hard to believe?"

"Are you sure you don't mean the Pottery Barn? If I

remember right, Avery worked there for a while, too."

After I shook my head, he slapped his knee, and as if he'd just solved a perplexing riddle, he chuckled and added, "Oh, as a cook at Jugs 'n Mugs, I assume."

"You assume wrong, Doctor Patel. I'm a waitress there."

I immediately regretted my snippy reply, made impulsively because I'd felt insulted by his assumption I could only have been hired as a cook at a topless joint. I tried not to blush as he gave me the once-over and shook his head in obvious disbelief before resuming his manipulation of my shoulder. Apparently, he'd not been overly impressed with the age and quality of the servers Jugs 'n Mugs was employing these days. Still, I was pleased to discover where I might possibly be able to locate Avery Curry, which might assist us in our investigation.

"Sad how Avery and Patrick are fighting over custody of Elizabeth," I said in an attempt to segue into a discussion of the couple's relationship before I was forced to fabricate further about my job at Jugs 'n Mugs. I felt both Avery, the victim's girlfriend, and Dr. O'Keefe, her ex-husband, had potential motive to want Cooper Claypool out of the picture. I wanted to explore that potentiality a bit more if at all possible.

"Silly, isn't it?" Dr. Patel replied. "It's ridiculous to make such a to-do over something so insignificant. What difference does it make who gets custody of Liz? Frankly, I'd be thrilled to be relieved of the responsibility if I were Pat, er, I mean Dr. O'Keefe. I'd turn that thing over to Avery in a heartbeat."

Insignificant? That thing? Oh, goodness! Poor little girl, I thought. No one seemed to give a fig about Elizabeth or how her parents' divorce and custody battle would affect her, their own child. Dr. Patel's cold-blooded comments about Elizabeth were disheartening, as well. Was Elizabeth a responsibility made greater by a handicap? If so, his attitude was even more despicable.

I was tempted to give the doctor an earful when he pulled away from kneading my shoulder, and said, "Well, Mrs. Ripple. I can't seem to find the precise area that's causing you pain."

I extended my arm out and rotated it, swung it back and forth several times, folded my arm and lifted my elbow up, moving it from front to back, and finally replied, "Amazing! Great job, Doc! I believe it's just fine now. As good as new, as a matter of fact. Your therapeutic manipulations must have resolved the problem. I feel absolutely no pain now. Thank you so much! I'll be sure to tell all the girls in my bunko club about you."

Tell them you're a heartless pig, that is, I wanted to add. My opinion of Dr. Patel had plummeted after his callous remarks about Dr. O'Keefe's daughter.

At the restaurant the previous evening, O'Keefe had looked to be about the same age as Reggie and Milo, early fifties or so. Reggie's children from her first marriage were in their mid to late twenties. In which case, it stood to reason Liz was likely in the same age bracket, and if still living at home, there was a reasonable probability she was afflicted with some kind of disability that prevented her from venturing out into the world on her own.

I was appalled that two doctors who'd pledged to 'do no harm" would speak about a potentially handicapped individual the way I'd witnessed them both do. With that in mind, I sneered at Patel and hopped off the examining table. I bolted out of the room like I'd just spotted a one-hundred-dollar bill on the sidewalk and wanted to snatch it up before the wind blew it across the parking lot.

As I brushed past the doctor, his mouth was gaping and his head shaking in wonder. Evidently he didn't know quite what to make of me, a now wringing wet anomaly who had wandered into his health clinic with a worrisome figment of her imagination.

* * *

"Where have you been?" Rip asked as I entered the trailer. "I thought you were just going to run to the pharmacy and pick me up some hearing aid batteries."

"And I did. See, they're right here." I had stopped by the pharmacy on my way to the clinic. I swung the small plastic bag in front of his face and sat it down on the counter, hoping to end the conversation. As usual, it didn't work.

"It surely didn't take you two hours to drive to Walgreens and back. It's no more than five minutes from here."

"Yes, I realize that. But you should have seen how packed the store was this morning. There must have been some kind of special sale today."

"You don't say!" A disbelieving Rip remarked.

"Yes. In fact, I'm sure that's what was going on. And speaking of batteries, I saw a pack of two nine-volts on a rack for only three dollars. Three bucks for two name brand nine-volts? That's just unbelievable, when they're usually—"

"You've got the 'unbelievable' part right. So, tell me. Where is the bag of these unbelievably-priced batteries you purchased?"

"Um, well. I didn't, um, I didn't actually say I bought any of the nine-volts. I just picked up some batteries for your hearing aids, as you requested." I stuttered, knowing he was on to me. He stood there in his know-it-all stance; hands on hips, glaring at me over the top of his reading glasses. Still, I was too stubborn to give in that easily.

"Come on, Rapella. You know as well as I do you'd have bought some of the nine-volt batteries if you'd found them that cheap. Not only bought some, you'd probably have brought home a lifetime supply of them so you'd never be forced to pay full price for—"

"Oh, all right." I surrendered grudgingly. "I had to make another stop on my way home. Are you happy now?"

"By 'another stop,' do you mean the walk-in health clinic on Third Street, by any chance?"

"Uh, well, yeah. Yeah, that's the place."

"Break an arm in the band-aid aisle at the pharmacy?" He asked, his voice dripping with sarcasm. "Trip over a gum wrapper in the parking lot?"

"Mockery does not look good on you, buster!" I said, annoyed by his ridicule.

"So I've been told," Rip quipped. He added, "Let me use my psychic powers. On the way home from the pharmacy, you experienced one of those dreaded shoulder twitches and feared you might need immediate surgery. You feared putting off seeing a doctor might result in having to have the entire arm amputated at a later date."

"Okay, okay, smartass. I truly did experience a troublesome twitch and needed to have the shoulder looked at, you see. And then a spur-of-the-moment inspiration, you might even call it an epiphany, made me decide to see if I could obtain some useful information pertaining to the murder case. You know, since I was there anyway."

"Wow! An epiphany, no less!"

"That's what I said," I replied haughtily. "And, by the way, my shoulder didn't twitch on the way home. It happened as I was entering the clinic."

"But of course! My bad! Makes perfect sense to me why you'd stop at the clinic, knowing a horrific 'twitch,' as you called it, might conceivably occur at any second. Woman's intuition, I think it's called. And lo and behold, your sixth-sense was well-founded!"

I silently glared at Rip, unable to come up with a reason I'd stop for treatment *before* the twitch occurred. Regrettably, this gave him another opportunity to rag me unmercifully.

I gritted my false teeth, fed up with his condescending attitude. Rather than this unrelenting dressing-down treatment, I really wish he'd just yell and scream at me when I've upset him and get it over with. I began to seethe as he continued his scornful remarks. "So, you say, you experienced one of those annoying instances when you felt perfectly fine getting out of your vehicle at an emergency clinic, but developed an acute health issue by the time you got through their door. Don't you just hate when that happens?"

"Can you give me some kind of guesstimate how long I can expect this charade to go on? I haven't got all day. And just how did you know I went there?" I asked. "Did you have one of your cop buddies tail me? Am I on twenty-four-hour surveillance now for some reason? I want to know why I'm being followed! Let me guess: the homicide detectives think I had something to do with the murder and are keeping me under observation in case I decide to flee. We aren't that far from the border, you know. If I thumb a ride out on the Interstate, I could easily be in Matamoras by suppertime."

"Don't be melodramatic, sweetheart. It's tiresome and it doesn't suit you."

Noticing my woeful expression, which was only used as a last resort, Rip backed off abruptly and his voice mellowed. Unfortunately, it "un-mellowed" more and more with each word he spoke. "The receptionist at the clinic called to inform you she'd forgotten to give you back your insurance cards. Naturally, I was concerned about why you were there requesting medical attention in the first place, so the gal explained your life-threatening health crisis. She went on to say you'd been treated by Dr. Patel and the issue seemed to resolve itself. Imagine that! It must have been a miracle brought forth by the doctor's magical healing powers. You can't imagine how relieved I was. Here I was, visualizing the Jaws of Life being utilized to extract you from burning wreckage on some side street between here and Walgreens and—"

"Cut the crap," I interrupted, disappointed his softer side had surfaced for less than a nanosecond. "All right.

I'll tell you why I concocted a fictional health concern to give me a reason to stop by the clinic."

Once again, Rip put his hands on his hips and looked at me over his glasses as he waited for my explanation, one I knew would sound weak, even to me.

"I remembered the address where that rude red-headed dude told the waitress his practice was. I'm sure you recall the man I accidentally spilt water on last night. So I decided to drive by there and see what kind of 'practice' he was referring to. Just out of curiosity, you know." Rip had rolled his eyes at my use of the word "accidentally" and then again when I mentioned it was pure curiosity that had tempted me to drive to 32 Third Street. I truly hoped his eyes would stick in that position next time he rolled them. Kind of like my momma always warned me would happen if I crossed my eyes too often.

I told Rip exactly what had happened and then went on to tell him why I thought it was important to do our own detective work in order to help clear our son-in-law of murder charges. Okay, let me back up. "Exactly" might have been an over-statement. I should probably have said, "I told him exactly what I wanted him to know about what had occurred."

I pleaded with Rip, prepared to pull out the never-failing foot massage offer if everything else I threw at him landed like a lead balloon. "We went to great lengths to exonerate Lexie, and she was merely a good friend. Milo is family, for goodness sakes!"

Rip was unmoved. Even with several more persuasive appeals, he remained stoic; unconvinced we should put everything on the line for a grown man who was behaving like a full-blown idiot. I had to admit Rip had a point. Even so, I persisted.

The plea that finally hit pay dirt was, "Think about it, Rip. If Milo goes to prison, what's going to happen to Regina? Do you want to risk being forced to sell this trailer and buy another home here in Rockport so she can move back in with us?"

"Just tell me what you want me to do, and I'm all over it," he replied zealously after he quit choking. "I'm not sure why, but all of a sudden I agree with your assessment of the matter. I even approve of your health clinic visit this morning."

"Good. I'm glad to hear you say that, because my stomach is beginning to cramp and I'm feeling a wee bit nauseated. I probably should return to the clinic at noon to see if Dr. O'Keefe can make certain I haven't contracted some nasty bug going around."

Rip shrugged and said, "Whatever it takes! Remember to pick up your insurance cards while you're there."

With that, he turned, picked his truck keys up off the counter, and opened the trailer door to leave. He looked like a man on a mission.

"Where are you going?" I asked.

"Down to the station to speak with Detective Reeves again. You were absolutely right, sweetheart. We need to beat every bush until we flush out the real killer, even if, God forbid, it turns out to be our son-in-law. It's imperative we do whatever we can to clear Milo of the charges, provided he's not deserving of them that is. Just do me a favor and keep me in the loop next time. I'll be back in time for you to return to the clinic, even though I think you're barking up the wrong tree when it comes to O'Keefe. There's no evidence whatsoever indicating your Irish doctor has killed, been in contact with, or even been anywhere in the vicinity of the victim in the recent past."

"We'll see," I said, reluctant to quit barking up that particular tree until I was convinced O'Keefe had nothing to do with the murder of Cooper Claypool. "Has he been at least questioned by the investigating team? Has he even provided them with an alibi to prove his whereabouts at the time of the death? For that matter, what about Avery Curry? Has she been interrogated? How can we be certain *she* wasn't somehow involved in her so-called boyfriend's death? I know where she works, and I think we should drive to Corpus for supper tonight. I want to get some answers out of her so I can cross her off my suspect list if she passes our scrutiny."

Rip's expression said it all. He was asking himself why he'd agreed to assist me and trying to convince himself that having Regina live with us for an indeterminate period of time would be a rewarding experience. With all the voices in Rip's head at that moment, I can guarantee you there was a very lively and uncomfortable conversation going on in there. He shook his head again, as if to still the voices, before exiting the trailer.

The noise from the door shutting roused Dolly from her nap. She'd been atop the couch, curled up and soaking in the sun. After yawning a couple of times, she jumped to the floor and, out of pure habit, strolled over to her empty food bowl. Searching and unable to locate a single kibble or bit, she looked up at me with pleading eyes.

This was an oft-used ploy to evoke sympathy so I'd break down and feed her. That tactic always worked for Rip when he was sure he was on the verge of dying of starvation, and it worked for Dolly the majority of the time, too. Rip often accused me of lowering our beloved pet's life expectancy by feeding her every time she begged for food. He had yet to realize I was probably lowering his in the exact same manner.

I poured a dab of dry food in the cat bowl and picked up the iPad. I was content to exercise my brain with a game or two of Scrabble while I waited for Rip to return with the truck and whatever news he was able to garner at the police station.

CHAPTER 8

I could sense Rip was seething internally when he walked in the door thirty minutes later. He laid his old *Rockport Police* ball cap on the table, and said, "Might as well pitch this out with the leftover scraps from breakfast."

"What's wrong, honey?" I asked in concern. I knew he wasn't merely upset; he was hurt. I'd rarely seen him looking vulnerable or emotional, and he was clearly both at that moment. The look in his eyes scared me. I hadn't seen that look since he'd been forced to shoot a fifteen-year old boy. He'd stumbled across the troubled teenager, who was selling methamphetamines behind the old abandoned Wal-Mart store late one night. The young man pulled a gun out of the waistband of his baggy jeans and fired twice at Rip, intent on killing the county sheriff. The shots missed their mark, but Rip's aim was true when he returned fire before the boy could shoot again. Even high on meth, the kid could have hit his intended target on a subsequent attempt. That disturbing experience had been the final straw that ended my husband's career in law enforcement. He put in for retirement the morning after the incident.

I watched now as Rip exhaled forcefully and sat down

on the couch. He leaned his head back, staring aimlessly at the ceiling. I sat down beside him and put my hand on top of his, willing to wait quietly until he was ready to talk. Finally, he said, "I bailed out Milo. I don't think they have any concrete evidence to merit charging him with murder, but I guarantee you they're doing their damnedest to come up with something. And he still has the assault charges to deal with."

"Is that what's bothering you?" I asked.

"No," he said. "That was exactly what I expected to happen."

"So, what is it?"

"I went in to discuss the case with Sheriff Peabody with whom, as you know, I worked side-by-side for years. Mind you, I wasn't trying to interfere with the murder investigation in any way, or requesting to use any of the department's resources in order to insert myself into the homicide case. I only wanted to offer my services and detective skills honed from a lifetime of experience in law enforcement. Not only to help close the case, but also, of course, to clear my son-in-law's name, who I contended was not guilty of murder. And, after all, I have an inside track on the matter, having been present when the body was discovered."

"The investigating team should have been overjoyed to have you onboard."

"You'd think," he replied dryly. "Instead, I was informed that I was to keep my nose out of the case. Joe explained that any involvement from me would be an egregious conflict of interest. In fact, he had already demanded I be barred from the station during the course of the investigation. He had the balls to say, 'You know yourself you shouldn't be here.'"

"Wow! Joe said that to you? And even banned you from the station? Has he forgotten that you're the former sheriff and the primary reason he's in that position now?"

"Yes. Exactly my point! I'm the one who convinced

Joe to apply to the police academy and then groomed him the next six years to take my place when I retired. Now he's banning me from the station I spent over half my life working in while putting my neck on the line to keep Rockport a safe place to live. How's that for a kick in the teeth?"

"I'm sure it wasn't a personal decision on his part, honey." I was trying to soothe his wounded pride. I knew Joe Peabody's respect for Rip was unmatched. He'd said more than once how much he'd appreciated the way Rip had taken him under his wing and helped him become the person and lawman he was today. I reminded Rip of that, and then said, "He's probably only following protocol, like you always did. In fact, I remember you preaching to the men on the force the importance of always going by the book in order to avoid giving a criminal a loophole in which to walk free and avoid punishment."

"I know, I know," Rip relented. "You're right. I don't blame Joe. I'd have probably done the same thing if our roles were reversed. I just feel useless. I guess my feelings were bruised. It was mighty humiliating, too, being thrown out of the station like a door-to-door encyclopedia salesman."

"I know, honey. It's only natural you'd feel the way you do. After all, you've always treated Joe as if he was your own son, and I know it's hard to accept those words coming from him. But put yourself in his place. If he'd welcomed you into the case with open arms, knowing full well standard procedure classified you as having a conflict of interest—and the fact you're just a citizen now—what would be your opinion of him? I'm sure Joe wants you to respect him as the new sheriff, not make you wonder if grooming him to replace you had been a mistake."

"Yes, I guess you're right. Joe was actually pretty kind and considerate about it. And he did have his arm around my shoulders as he escorted me out of the station. I'm sure I'm just over-reacting to the situation. But after talking to Milo on the ride home from the station, I really do believe he is innocent. And I've always been a good judge of character, you know. Of course, you might have been that rare exception but—"

He laughed and I joined him, knowing he was only kidding me. I was giddy in relief that Rip's mood had lightened. He quickly turned serious again when he said, "They might be able to ban me from the station, by God, but they can't stop me from looking into the murder on my own."

"Our own," I corrected him.

He glanced at me with a blank expression. He clearly was not overly confident of my detective prowess, and I didn't believe it was the proper time to remind him of my crucial role in helping exonerate our friend, Lexie Starr. After a few long seconds, he nodded and said, "You look pale, my dear. Could you be coming down with something?"

I smiled broadly, delighted to have his consent to return to the health clinic. This time I'd request to be seen by Dr. Patrick O'Keefe. I'd be danged if I was going to shell out another co-pay for no good purpose.

By the time I pulled the truck into the clinic's parking lot for the second time that day, I was actually beginning to feel a little queasy. I'm not sure if I was really falling prey to a virus, just reacting to an overabundance of jittery nerves, or perhaps being reprimanded by God for my deceitful actions. I chose the middle option.

"You again?" The receptionist asked as I approached the check-in counter.

"Been one of those days," I replied. "I think I've contracted a bug. Maybe that twenty-four hour flu that's going around."

"Oh, that's too bad." I could tell her insincere response was out of habit from speaking to dozens of ill patients every day.

"To be honest," I replied, being anything but honest. "I'm thinking I might have picked it up in the waiting room when I was here earlier. That Asian fellow sitting next to me looked feverish, didn't you think? If I recall correctly, he coughed several times and blew his nose once or twice, as well."

"Mr. Nguyen was here to have a broken finger set."

"Doesn't mean he couldn't also have a virus, does it?"

"Okay, ma'am. Whatever you say." It irked me that this snooty lady clearly didn't agree with me. Granted, it was a total cock-and-bull story. But it's still rude to infer a patient is lying about her ailment. She told me to have a seat in the waiting room "once again," and said, "A doctor will see you soon, ma'am. Dr. Patel is just finishing up with his previous patient and—"

"I'd prefer to see Dr. O'Keefe, even if it means I have to wait a spell."

"But you saw Dr. Patel just a couple of hours ago. Did you have a problem with him?" She looked befuddled at my request.

I winked at her as if it was apparent we shared a bad opinion of the Indian physician, and whispered, even though there was only the two of us in the room. "Well, let's just say we didn't exactly see eye-to-eye on the diagnosis."

Not knowing what to make of my response, she stared at me blankly and said, "Please take a seat *once again* and the nurse will call you when Dr. O'Keefe is available."

I picked up one of the pamphlets I'd already thumbed through on my first visit. Pretending to be absorbed in an article about the importance of dietary fiber, I made sure to cough and sniffle in convincing intervals. I'm allergic to dust mites and was pleased with an unfeigned sneeze just as the tubby nurse, Becky Winslow, opened the door and said, "Mrs. Ripple, the doctor is ready to see you now."

Becky's statement that "the doctor was ready to see me

now" was a gross exaggeration. It was a good forty-five minutes later before there was a light knock on the door. Without even allowing me enough time to put back a stethoscope I shouldn't have been messing with, the red-headed doctor opened the door and strolled into the room. He held my personal health folder in his left hand; a folder rapidly growing thicker. I was a little edgy about how warm a welcome I'd get from a guy I'd showered with ice water the previous evening, so was relieved when he simply extended his right hand for the customary shake. "Good afternoon. I'm Dr. O'Keefe."

"Nice to meet you. I'm Rapella Ripple." As I introduced myself, he gazed at me quizzically. He stared at me for several long seconds. *Uh-oh*, I thought. *Any moment now, the realization of who I am is going to hit him like a bolt of lightning.*

"Do I know you?" He asked at last.

"No, I don't believe so," I replied without hesitation.

"You look so familiar. Are you a teller at the NavyArmy Credit Union, by any chance?"

"No, I'm not."

"Oh, I know. I bet you're a checker at H.E.B? The express lane, right?"

"No, afraid not." How many Guinness Black Lagers had he downed last night before we arrived at the restaurant? I wondered.

"Wal-Mart?" At the negative shake of my head, he tried to place me again. "Do you have a shop in the Rockport Gallery? I spent a lot of time there last summer when we were decorating the clinic."

"No. Not there either. At this rate, we're apt to be here all day. I'm almost positive you've never run into me in town before. Or anywhere else, for that matter." I was tiring quickly of the guessing game, but relieved he hadn't immediately recognized me.

"Hmmm. I just know I've seen you somewhere."

Well, crapola!! Why hadn't I just owned up to being a greeter at Wal-Mart? I asked myself. O'Keefe was determined not to let this puzzle go unsolved. Suddenly, out of the blue, I thought of how I could induce him to drop the subject and get on with the matter at hand.

"Oh, wait a second," I said. "I think I've figured out where you've probably seen me. Do you ever watch any hard-core porn?"

That effectively put an end to the inquisition. Dr. O'Keefe now looked from his black shiny shoes, to the reclining examination table, to the two chairs, to nearly everything else in the room besides his patient. He avoided making eye contact when he asked, "What brings you here today, Ms. Ripple?"

I briefly described my imaginary symptoms as the physician went through his customary regimen; checking my blood pressure, listening to my heart and lungs, taking my temperature, and peering into my nose and mouth with his tiny flashlight. He looked baffled, which was understandable. I'm sure my vital signs were as good as, or better than, his. At this point, I was not even making an effort to appear under the weather.

I knew my window for questioning him was limited, so I decided it was time to dive right in. "Speaking of porn, do you know my friend, Avery Curry?"

Have you ever seen someone a split second after they'd been walloped in the face with a croquet mallet? The good doctor wore that same expression. Guess he didn't like thinking his ex-wife might have some connection with an aging porn star. I'd already raised his blood pressure with my 'hard-core porn' question, and was certain his heart rate was off the chart now, too.

No longer avoiding eye contact, he now stared at me in astonishment. O'Keefe took a few moments to recover and, with eyes as wide as bottle caps, he eventually responded. "Um, yeah, um, yeah I do. She's my soon-to-be ex-wife. How do you know Avery? She's never mentioned you that I can recall."

"We're co-workers." Considering the stir I'd created with Dr. Patel, I should have taken a moment to think before using the same explanation of my relationship with Avery.

"You are?" Spoken in the same tone he'd have used if I'd told him I was here today to take a pregnancy test.

Crapola, again! He'd dangled the Rockport Gallery right in front of me. Why hadn't I just latched on and gone with that? I could have pretended to be an artist. It's not like he'd have asked me to draw a portrait of him to prove it.

"You're co-workers? Seriously?" His outright disbelief made the hair on my arms stand on end. Afraid to embellish on my employment at this point, I merely nodded. Why was he so surprised I worked at a topless joint, anyway? Hadn't I just insinuated I was not only a porn star, but a hard-core one, at that?

"So, I assume you're a cook at Jugs 'n Mugs instead of a waitress like Avery." Just like that, the inquisition had reignited.

"No," I answered. I'd learned my lesson when I didn't take the easy way out and claim to be an express-line checker at H.E.B. So, wouldn't you think I'd just go along with being a cook this time? Yes, you would. But unfortunately, I didn't. I'd found his stunned expression insulting. And having both doctors "assume" I was a cook rather than a topless waitress irked me, too. So, instead of using some sense and taking the easy route this go-round, I replied arrogantly, "I'm a waitress there, Doctor O'Keefe. And you do know what 'assume' stands for, don't you? It stands for 'make an ass out of you and–'"

He cut me off as he looked me up and down, shook his head uncertainly, and asked, "You're a server at Jugs 'n Mugs? No kidding? I'd have thought being a server at somewhere like Ken's Diner would be more to your liking."

"As a matter of fact, I did work as a waitress at Ken's Diner, and ironically, a cafe called Zen's Diner in Missouri." I didn't add that my employment at Zen's didn't span an entire breakfast shift, and my career at Ken's hadn't lasted much longer.

"Well, that I can believe. But Jugs 'n Mugs?"

If you read between the lines like I did, you'd know he was actually saying, "You're too frigging old and frumpy to be flaunting those saggy boobs in a place like Jugs 'n Mugs. Or any other public place, for that matter."

I decided to get in a jab of my own. And, why not? I hadn't planned on sending him a Facebook friend request, or adding him to my Christmas card list. "You know, I'm not surprised Avery's giving you the boot."

The barb hit home. The doctor's reaction to my remark was frightening. I could see that he could be very intimidating when riled. He retorted with a lame attempt to get under my skin, "And I'm not surprised she's never told me she was a friend of yours. She was probably too embarrassed to admit it."

I wondered if he was surprised she'd never told him she was involved in pornography either? Was he thinking, "Has Avery been making porn movies behind my back, or is this old lady in my office certifiably bat-crap crazy?"

I laughed and added, "I'm sure she *would* have been too embarrassed to tell you something that shocking. And, actually, I really shouldn't discuss our relationship. It's kind of personal and probably something she'd rather keep hidden away in the closet, if you know what I mean." Naturally, I ended my last remark with a seductive wink.

Dr. O'Keefe could not have looked any more staggered than if he'd walked into his grandfather's bedroom and caught granddad wearing grandma's brassiere and panties. And by now I had him deliberating over the possibility Avery was bi-sexual and attracted to some whacked-out geriatric of the female variety.

I realized I was having way too much fun agitating the doctor. But, much like blathering, I just couldn't seem to quit. O'Keefe stood silently studying me like a medical abnormality, his mouth quivering. I decided to take advantage of his inability to think straight or form a full sentence. "Yes, and Avery told me about the custody battle over Elizabeth."

"Oh, well, yes, um, I guess we, um—" The bewildered doctor nodded, still unable to come up with the words to express himself.

"Shame to put the child through such a tug-of-war. I'm sure you know, it's always hardest on the—"

"Child? What child?" The doctor asked, suddenly able to speak not only coherently, but remarkably loud and angrily.

"What do you mean 'what child?' Are you so disinterested in your own daughter you can't even recall her name? Shame on you! That poor girl." I shook my head in disgust and practically hissed when I said in clarification, "I'm referring to Elizabeth, Dr. O'Keefe. Your daughter! Remember her?"

"What? Are you nuts?" He exclaimed. "Elizabeth's not a child. She's a pet lizard!"

"A pet lizard?" Embarrassed, my voice was much more subdued when I asked. "You named a lizard Elizabeth?"

"Actually, Avery named her. We usually call her Liz. You know, Liz, as in *liz*ard. I'm surprised Avery never mentioned her to such a close friend." It probably goes without saying that the words "close friend" were spat out sarcastically.

"Oh." Now I was the one at a loss for words. The steaming doctor was probably not far off when he asked if I was nuts. I was thankful he was able to calm down before he continued with his explanation.

"Liz is a chuckwalla that originally came from the Mohave Desert. She was Avery's pet before we got married. But now I'm fighting for joint custody, anyway."

"Oh, I see. You've understandably grown attached to

Liz over the course of your marriage." I spoke with insincere sincerity, in a lame attempt to atone for my own errant assumption.

"Oh, hell no!" He looked at me as if I'd implied he'd grown fond of a hairy wart on the tip of his nose. "Did you not hear what I just said? It's a lizard, for God's sakes! I can barely stand to look at the ugly thing."

"Huh? So why are you—"

"Fighting for joint custody of a big, repulsive reptile?" He broke in, finishing my question for me. "The truth is I think that kind of arrangement would be beneficial to my future relationship with Avery. For starters, joint custody would ensure we stayed in con—"

Dr. O'Keefe stopped speaking abruptly. It no doubt had suddenly occurred to him that he should not be discussing his divorce or revealing too much information about his covert intentions to his estranged wife's friend. A friend of such questionable affiliation with her, no less.

He trembled anxiously as he picked the folder up off the counter that held bottles of Q-tips and cotton balls, along with several boxes of different sized latex gloves. He opened the door to signal it was time for me to go. As I stood up to leave, he said, "I see no obvious signs of a virus, but you can pick up a script for antibiotics on your way out."

"Thank you." I'd pick up the prescription along with my insurance cards at the check-out desk so as not to look like an imposter, but had no intention of filling it.

"By the way," Dr. O'Keefe added. "The doctor/patient confidentiality clause works both ways. I expect you to keep our conversation to yourself. I'm having a rough enough time dealing with Avery as it is. Because of her, I had to go give a statement at the police station this morning."

There was no need to ask why he'd been called to the station. It was in regards to the murder of Cooper Claypool, not his dissolving marriage, I was certain. His last remarks also explained what "unexpected family obligation" had caused him to be a late arrival at work that day. But, most importantly, the red-headed doctor with the strong Irish brogue had presented me with a motive that put him high on my list of murder suspects.

CHAPTER 9

"I haven't been resting on my laurels either," Rip said, after I told him about my health clinic visit. "I was limited to what I could do to further our progress without wheels, since you needed to take the truck. But after you called me from the clinic's parking lot, I managed to speak with the manager at Jugs 'n Mugs. He told me Avery was off on Saturday, a normal working day for her, and took off again Sunday and Monday on bereavement leave. But she's expected to report for the evening shift later on this afternoon. I don't know about you, but I'm craving some hot wings."

"Me too! Let's go out for supper tonight. I'd planned on cooking liver and onions, but—"

"Liver and onions? Then it's most definitely a date, my dear!" He quipped playfully. Fixing liver and onions was an inside joke. Knowing Rip despised liver, I used the liver-and-onions ruse on the rare occasions I wanted to go out for supper.

I was tickled to see his morning funk had dissipated and he was looking forward to our dinner date as much as I was. But I had to wonder if Rip's enthusiasm was based on the possibility of obtaining useful investigative information from Avery Curry, snarfing down a boatload of hot wings, or being served by some young topless broad with bazookas the size of coconuts.

At five that evening, Rip and I were sitting at the bar holding a pager to notify us when a table was available. We'd been warned it'd be a good forty-five minutes before we would be seated in the dining area. Normally, we wouldn't wait ten minutes when there were other restaurants around that weren't as crowded. But this was not a normal situation. Besides, a mixed drink or two sounded very appealing to both of us, since we'd missed our usual afternoon highball.

The rough-hewn bar was straight out of an old John Wayne movie. Both the bar area and the kitchen had double swinging doors like the saloons often depicted in western movies. There was even an old leather gun belt with an empty holster hanging over the corner of the large mirror behind the bartender. I liked the old West ambiance the place embodied.

The only detail that seemed out of place was the dozen or so televisions lining the wall, all with different pro-basketball games being broadcast on them. At least they'd keep Rip occupied while we waited. With Rip riveted to the television screens, I opted to use this time to consider what I might say to Avery should I get the opportunity to speak to her.

I ordered a Tequila Sunrise and Rip requested a dark beer they had on tap. It was a quarter to five according to the clock on the wall, cleverly crafted using a mirror fit snugly into a horse collar.

We were accustomed to eating early, and on this night it was especially necessary if I were to get to my bunko party on time. Anything we ate after six was an open invitation to heartburn during the night. The refreshments at the party would result in enough acid reflux to choke the horse the aforementioned collar had belonged to without a heavy dinner added to the mix.

I was hoping Mabel Hicks had made her to-die-for

cocoa and caramel cookies to offer us that evening. I'd asked her for the recipe every single time she served them in the past, but so far the old hen hadn't cut loose with it. Mabel was sitting on that egg so tight, it'd never hatch. Even still, I knew I'd give it another shot if the cookies were on the refreshment menu tonight. I reckon it's on the order of asking a fisherman where he caught his nice mess of fish. Around here, anglers most often replied, "In the mouth."

While Rip waited for our drinks to be served, all the time eyeing the busty brunette behind the bar, I decided to go back to the reception area and question the young lady taking names at a podium. Her black clothing and fingernails, along with unnaturally jet black hair, were unnerving. She wore enough black makeup to seal the parking lot. I'd heard about the gothic subculture before, and figured she must be one of those spooks.

I told Rip I'd be right back. He nodded without taking his eyes off the stunning barmaid. Before I departed, I whispered, "Be careful, dear. You don't know where those 'jugs' have been."

As I approached the freak of nature at the check-in stand, I said, "Excuse me, miss. I meant to ask you earlier if Avery Curry was on duty this evening."

The eerie lady was struggling to keep up as people poured in the door faster than she could take their names. Handing a customer a pager, and without even turning to look at me, she replied, "Yes. Our head cook called in sick and Avery talked Archie into letting her cover in the kitchen tonight. According to Avery, she was just too upset to face customers."

"Why's that?" I knew why, of course, but was happy to hear Avery was emotionally affected by her recent loss. Sincere sorrow indicated to me she wasn't likely to have been involved in Cooper's death.

Blackie continued to work as she replied, "Someone just iced her boyfriend." She said this as dispassionately as if she were telling me one of Avery's goldfish had jumped out of the fish bowl and been consumed by her cat.

"Oh, my! Poor thing. Well, thanks for your help." The stoic young gal merely nodded in response as she asked another customer for his name.

Dang it, I thought. *That definitely makes this harder. But I've faced and conquered challenging tasks before and, by Jove, I'll find a way to do it again.*

As I made my way back to the bar, I wondered briefly if the lady in black sacrificed goats in her basement on slow days. With nothing to do but wait, I sat back down on the barstool and sipped my drink while I mentally chewed on how I could get into the bar and grill's kitchen. Finally, when I realized I wouldn't be chewing on anything else for a good long while, I decided I might as well spend the waiting time usefully.

I figured the best approach was to just walk into the kitchen like I owned the place. I've used that tactic successfully numerous times in the past. When you march in somewhere you have no right to be as if you have every right to be there, people tend to take for granted you *are* supposed to be there.

I set my empty glass on the bar while Rip was being handed his second beer. As he was busy thanking the bartender, I said, "I'll be back in a few minutes."

Leaving no time for Rip to impede my departure, I walked out of the bar area and straight into the kitchen.

"Oh, thank God you're here! Get in here and help me get caught up." A blond-haired gal I assumed was Avery exclaimed. At a respectable height of five-eight, I still had to look up to make eye contact with her. She had to be nearly six-feet tall, and her long thick mane hung below her belt. She was a striking woman. It was no small wonder Cooper Claypool had snatched up this knockout following her divorce from the fair doctor.

I'd anticipated the likelihood of being thrown out of the kitchen, but I'd never imagined someone would so eagerly welcome me back there. I smiled as she enlightened me. "Archie told me he'd called in extra help for me, but I didn't expect you to arrive so soon. I'm Avery, by the way. I saw some clean aprons hanging on a hook behind the walk-in freezer."

This was a fortuitous and well-timed opportunity to converse with Avery, and I jumped right on it. A little reluctant to introduce myself, I was relieved when she hastily pulled an extra hairnet out of her apron and handed it to me. It made the hairs on my arm stand on end when she said, "I hope you know more about cooking than I do. They offer a lot of oddball dishes here I've never heard of before, but I'm anxious to learn, and I just couldn't wait tables tonight."

She didn't elaborate on why she'd rather attempt something with which she had no experience than perform her normal duties. I already knew why, of course, but didn't want to show my hand that quickly. I also hated to inform her I probably had even less of a clue about cooking in a restaurant than she did, so I didn't. I thought I could fake it long enough to get her to divulge some valuable information. To quell her fears, I replied, "Oh, poo! Don't give it another thought. I've been working in kitchens all my life."

I didn't add those kitchens I referred to included my own, Lexie Starr's while she was wrongly incarcerated, and my daughter's.

"Oh, cool. I am so, so, so relieved to hear that you're an old pro at this." I smiled and nodded at Avery, thinking, *Well, you're half right. I am old, at least compared to your forty-some years.*

The next off-the-cuff statement I made was not well thought out. It was a misfortunate and highly fallacious claim. "Went to culinary school, you see."

"Really?" Avery's ears perked up, as did her mood. She'd appeared extremely gloomy up until then. "Which one?"

"Which one you ask? Um, well, you know, that famous one in Paris. Can't recall the name at the moment."

"Le Cordon Bleu?"

"Yes. Yes, that's the one." I should have left it at that, having already foolishly over-played the fictional "seasoned chef" card. As if it wasn't bad enough already, my next remark approached moronic. "Worked at Maxim's for a spell, honing my skills, as a matter of fact." *Or not*, I thought. *More like a matter of fiction, actually.* But I was mentally patting myself on the back for being able to come up with the name of a famous Parisian restaurant at the drop of a hat. Truthfully, it wasn't all that remarkable, since we'd watched a segment about Maxim's on the Food Channel only a week ago. But Avery Curry, an impressionable wanna-be culinary expert, didn't know that.

"Cool!"

"Do you happen to know of a certain young chef named Wolfgang Puck? He worked there too." Or so the recently aired documentary claimed.

"Wow! Did you get to meet him?" I could see in Avery's eyes her respect for me had just ratcheted up several notches.

"You bet! Puckie and I are old cronies now," I boasted. Good Lord, Rapella. Put a dinner roll in your pie-hole and quit talking, for God's sakes, before you claim to have had an affair with the dude! I chided myself. It was as if I physically could not stop telling one mind-boggling lie after another. I would have slapped some sense into myself if I weren't afraid Avery would get on her cell phone and call for the men in the white coats.

"Oh, man! That's so awesome! The Le Cordon Culinary School is my dream. I'd like to learn enough I can one day move on from waiting tables. Schlepping food and drinks around to often rude and demanding customers is just not my thing. Particularly when I'm half-naked like they require the waitresses to be here."

"Been there, done that, young lady." Like her ex-husband, she gave me the once-over and shook her head, not quite able to picture me waiting tables half-nude. I scanned the room for a fire extinguisher. If I told one more lie I'd probably need one to extinguish my Levi's. *Liar, liar...*

"I hope you'll teach me some tips and tricks while you're here, ma'am. Anything to help me improve my skills."

Uh-oh. I wondered if she already knew how to butter toast because that was about the extent of the culinary skills I could muster up under pressure. Just when I thought it couldn't get any worse, it did! The boss, named Archie I presumed, came rushing in the door, all aflutter. He looked curiously at me for a few seconds and then apparently realized he didn't have time to even inquire who I was.

"I need an order of 'Blooming Barramundi' – yesterday!" He exclaimed breathlessly. Archie was nearly hyperventilating. "I can't afford to keep this lady waiting. I want the absolute best one you've ever made and it needs to be served with flair."

He glanced at Avery for a split second and then turned to speak directly to me. He must have known Avery didn't have the training to handle it and assumed, because I was a senior citizen, I must have had decades of experience.

"Flair?" I asked.

"You know, parsley, slice of orange, that kind of fancy-shmancy presentation. We have a food critic in the house who's a columnist for the *Corpus Christi Times*. We don't want to give her any reason to give Jugs 'n Mugs a bad review in the paper. Just a derogatory comment or two in her weekly article, and the owner of this place will tie a rope around my neck and hang me out to dry."

He raced out of the kitchen as quickly as he'd raced in. Before he disappeared from sight, he voiced a resounding "Chop, chop, ladies!"

Avery looked at me expectedly. I knew I had no choice but to tackle the problem and try to create a presentable meal in a short amount of time. Where was the World Wide Web when I needed it? Rip would never give up his flip-top model with the huge numbers and keypad, but maybe it was time I invest in a smart phone for myself. Of course, I'd also have to adopt a five-year old child to teach me how to use it. The snowball-effect of upgrading to a more sophisticated cell phone could get pricey for some of us senior citizens who weren't born with an electronic device in our hands.

So now what? I asked myself. Could the critic not have judged the restaurant on their chili dogs, or even some dish in the fowl department? I could whip out a mean blackened chicken breast in a matter of minutes.

But a Blooming Barramundi? No matter what meat it entailed, I could almost guarantee it would end up in the "foul" department, too. For starters, what in the world was a barramundi? I'd have to find out somehow without appearing to be dumber than the spatula I was holding in my hand. I turned to Avery with an air of superiority and asked, "So, let's get to it, my dear. I assume we have some barramundi on hand. Can you grab it for me?"

Avery rushed to the large freezer and came out with a frozen package of something I couldn't recognize. I asked her, "How can we unthaw that thing in a flash and serve it in the allotted time, which according to Archie, was yesterday? Haven't we got one that's fresh, or at least thawed already?"

"I don't think so, but I saw a fresh mahi-mahi fillet in the refrigerator. Will that work?"

Okay, good. Now I knew barramundi was a fish. That was a good beginning for winging my way through this. All thought of questioning Avery about her dead boyfriend had flown out the window. I felt obligated to stick around and help as best I could with this challenge facing the two of us. I certainly didn't want to get the lady fired. "It will have to work."

I imagined most people were like me and couldn't tell

a tilapia fillet from a grouper. One fillet of fresh fish looked very similar to most other fillets, so how could they taste all that different from one another once they'd been doused in seasoning spices? *Oh, dear. What now?* I wondered. "Who'd you tell me was the head chef here?"

"I don't think I did, but it's Bobbi Jo Jons."

"Just to make certain I fix it the way it's usually served here, rather than the way I usually do when serving the rich and famous, does Bobbi Jo bake, broil, or fry it?"

"She grills it."

"Perfect! That's my go-to choice, too. And just to make sure we're consistent, which seasonings does she put on it?"

"I'm not sure," Avery replied. "But I know for certain she isn't a Le Cordon graduate, or have any culinary school training at all. So it'd probably be tastier if you use your own recipe, anyway."

Don't bet on it, sweetheart. Rip was a meat and potatoes kind of guy. That blackened chicken breast I mentioned, served with a green bean casserole, was about as complicated as supper got in my kitchen. Since I was a "three-ingredients-or-less" kind of cook, even that meal was on the upper limits of my culinary repertoire and was reserved for special occasions only.

"Yes, of course, Avery. I see your point. It's probably best I use my own recipe if we want to make an impression on the food critic." I slapped the fillet on the hot grill.

We'll make an impression on her, all right. I just hope I'm not around when it happens. If Avery knew what was good for her, she'd probably skedaddle, too, I thought. So, under pressure to deliver the meal quickly, and with no clue how to prepare it whatsoever, I grabbed the closest spice bottles and seasoned the already browning fillet. Afterward, I glanced at the labels, something that would have been wise to do before I liberally sprinkled them across the already browning fillet. I didn't know how the combination of cinnamon, curry, and ground habanera, a.k.a. the 'ass kickin' seasoning from hell,' would taste. But I was almost positive I didn't want to sample it.

Avery shot me a look that had "are you nuts?" written all over it. She swallowed hard, and said, "I'm pretty sure Bobbi Jo uses garlic and onion powder, and maybe celery salt, instead of your unique variation of the recipe."

"Of course she does," I assured her. *Oops!* "As do I, *after* the other spices crucial for making this barramundi dish extra special. This highly-regarded recipe I'm preparing has a very specific mixture of seasonings that, as my ol' buddy Puckie would say, 'treats the palate with a delightful surprise'." *Heavy on the surprise part,* I wanted to add. As Avery handed me the spices she'd mentioned, I applied twice as much of them as I had the first three spices. I was hoping to cancel out the original flavor I'd created. Or, at the very least, tame it down with heavy doses of the proper spices.

"Okay. If you say so," Avery relented, clearly skeptical about delighting anyone's palate with this conglomeration of spices. "I'm sure you know best, ma'am."

I don't know squat, I said under my breath. To Avery I said, "I can guarantee you, young lady, the critic will want to know what's in Maxim's secret recipe once she's sampled this Blooming Barramundi."

"You think?" Avery asked with a curious expression.

Of course, dear. She'll need to know those kinds of details when she files her lawsuit against this bar and grill. A potential outcome, but not one I wanted to share with Avery Curry. I was really glad I hadn't formally introduced myself to her or anyone else in this joint.

"No worries. Wolfgang let me in on it, but I had to promise Puckie I'd keep it to myself. In other words, mum's the word," I said with a wink. I'd made up such sensational lies already, I couldn't see any real advantage to stop. "More importantly, dear, if this secret recipe were to get out, every restaurant in the Coastal Bend area would add this dish to their menus. And we can't have that, can we? Trust me; every great chef keeps his masterpiece creations to himself. I only shared this with you so you could soak up some really worthwhile knowledge."

Avery looked pleased and honored at my remarks. As the fish was browning, I thought I needed to get a few questions in, knowing it'd be my only opportunity. I'd be making haste a split second after this order was ready to serve.

"See, you've learned something already, Avery," I said in a cocky manner, as I watched the young lady scribbling notes on the back of a deposit slip. Then my tone turned to one of deep concern. "Say, sweetie. When I first came in the kitchen, I noticed you looked kind of down. Why so glum, chum?"

"I lost my boyfriend Saturday."

"Oh, goodness, dear. Have you found him yet?" My attempt at humor failed miserably, as Avery's eyes began to mist over.

"No, ma'am, I meant he's really gone." Sniffle, sniffle.

"Oh, I see. That's a rotten deal, all right. Did the rat bastard dump you for some big-breasted bimbo like my first husband did me?" I asked. Of course I lied about having an ex-husband, but desperate times call for desperate measures. And my Levi's were already smoking, anyway. Besides, one more falsehood wasn't going to make a whole lot of difference once I departed.

"Well, er, no." Avery gave me a judgmental glance and began to sniffle even more profusely. She pulled a wadded-up Kleenex from a pocket on the front of her apron and blew her nose. She sputtered as she continued. "I meant...somebody killed him."

"Oh, my, my, my! That's downright awful! Are you referring to that Cooper Claypool dude someone shot an arrow into?"

"A spear, actually. But yes. It seems like the grapevine

is in full operating mode, cuz that's all everyone in the entire county's talking about."

"Word travels fast around here. The murder of a Rockport resident is a big deal because it just doesn't happen every day."

"Yeah, I know. But you never think it could actually happen to someone you love, like I loved Cooper. I don't care what anyone says, I loved him for himself. More than I've ever loved anyone before. And I don't think I'll ever find a guy again who I'll love the way I did him. My ex-husband couldn't even begin to compare to Cooper."

Were a lot of people claiming you didn't love Cooper for himself? I wanted to ask. *What else would you love him for if not himself?*

It seemed as if she was trying to convince herself of her love for her late boyfriend rather than me. I'd have to consider that aspect later, however. I had listened politely, but knew my time was running short so I needed to veer her off this topic. I had turned the flames under the fish fillet down low so I'd have more time to pull potential clues out of the mourning wanna-be chef. Archie could stick his "chop, chop, need it yesterday" demand where even the oven light don't shine.

As far as I was concerned, solving a violent crime would always trump whether or not some silly broad thinks there's enough salt on her stupid fish. As I turned the fillets over on the grill, I asked innocently, "You're ex the jealous type, maybe hot-headed with a hair-trigger temper kind of guy?"

"Very. He's practically stalking me now, determined to win me back. But when I finally walked out the door, it was 'adios amigo' as far as I was concerned," she replied.

I wanted more, so I gasped dramatically and prompted her with, "Oh, my! You don't reckon he whacked Cooper in a jealous rage, do you?"

"Nah," she said, shaking her head. "I don't really think

he'd be capable of taking another human being's life. He's a doctor. Pat's in the business of saving lives, not ending them. He may harass and annoy someone half to death, but I don't think he could actually kill anyone."

"Who do you reckon would kill your boyfriend?"

"I don't know anyone who'd want to do something like that to Cooper. Everyone liked him, as far as I know. Well, except maybe my ex and this Julio Sarcova dude Cooper talked about," she replied.

Bingo! I thought. *Now I'm getting somewhere.* I continued to grill her in a friendly chat while I grilled the fish in a very unfriendly kind of fashion. "Who's Julio Sarcova?"

"Oh, some guy in town who's ram-rodding the protest in front of city hall tomorrow morning. Pardon my language, ma'am, but he's a real shit-stirrer, if you know what I mean. He'd been harassing Cooper relentlessly, threatening to file some lawsuit."

"A lawsuit?" I asked. "Why would anyone sue Cooper?"

"He said he'd sue MC Hammerheads, not Cooper specifically. It was about some settlement involving one of the houses they flipped a few months ago. Didn't make no sense to me to get so riled up over a little black mold."

"Hey!" Archie bellowed, looking over the top of the swinging doors into the kitchen. "What part of 'yesterday' didn't you ladies understand? The columnist is beginning to fidget and look at her watch. Chop, chop, I told you! I need it *now*!"

"Chop, chop? Really? Give it a rest, dude. It'll be out in a second! Did you want it quick or delicious? 'Cause you can't have it both ways!" I hollered back. *Actually*, I wanted to add, *you ain't getting it either way*. I wasn't in fear of losing my cooking job, so I added, "Take a chill pill, buster!"

It was evident by Avery's wide-eyed reaction she *was* in fear of losing *her* job, and worried my comments might reflect badly on her. "Relax, dear. Archie needs you more than you need him right now. Put some sides on a plate so we can get this fish out to the dining area before the boss wets his pants."

"Thanks for covering for me, um...I just realized I don't know your name."

"Mabel. Mabel Hicks, dear. Now we better build a fire under our bums and get this out to the food critic."

I looked down at the fillet as Avery piled a small mound of rice pilaf on the plate and added three measly stalks of asparagus. The barramundi was on the verge of burning to a crisp. I'd been so focused on garnering beneficial information from Avery I'd forgotten all about the fish I was grilling. *Oh well, at least the asparagus looks good*, I thought. *There just ain't enough of it.*

"Oh, no!" Avery gasped in panic, staring down at the crispy fish filet. "What are we going to do?"

Like I said before, I had nothing to lose. I wasn't out to please anyone. Nor did I plan to be around when the pile of poo-poo hit the fan. But I thought I should at least try to quell the nearly hysterical gal's fears. "Do about what, honey? This barramundi turned out splendidly. Just look at it! It's a real beauty, by George. I believe I've actually outdone myself."

Her "Really?" reply was accompanied by that same "Are you nuts?" expression she'd worn earlier.

"It's blackened perfectly, just like this closely guarded secret recipe calls for. You'll be amazed at how the critic will respond to this dish. Now you get working on that new order for three Mug's combo baskets while I see that this masterpiece is delivered to the critic. Trust me, dear. It's fit for the finickiest of appetites."

"Okay, great." Avery appeared to be relieved, but still dubious. She was no doubt praying that if a student of the renowned culinary school in Paris—and a close personal friend of Wolfgang Puck, I might add—thought it had turned out flawlessly, it must be so.

As Avery grabbed several frozen hamburger patties

out of the freezer, she said, "I want to get the combos out fast so I can spend a few minutes discussing a delicate subject with my ex. I couldn't locate Pat last night, so I stopped by his office this afternoon and asked him to meet me here at five-thirty. I'd like to speak with him while no one else is back here in the kitchen."

Who's stalking whom? I wanted to ask. "You go, girl. Give it to him good! I'll give you all the time you need with him before I return to the kitchen." *Literally, my dear. All the time you need, and more.*

I didn't take the time to wait for a response. I was rushing out of the kitchen, anxious to pass off the plate and get the heck out of Dodge, and didn't notice the bare-chested waitress behind the right swinging door carrying four glasses of ice tea. And, unfortunately for Patrick O'Keefe's sake, he'd arrived a moment too early for the rendezvous with his ex-wife. The door hit the backside of the waitress, who tumbled forward as the tray of teas tilted to the right.

My first thought was that Patrick O'Keefe had the potential of getting drafted by the Texas Rangers if the doctoring thing didn't work out. He made a golden glove catch of one of the glasses without spilling a single drop. However, his golden glove catch didn't prevent the other three glasses from spilling all over him. He caught those glasses with the front of his crisp, wrinkle-free breeches. Every bone-chilling drop.

He looked up at me, studying my face for about two seconds before exclaiming, "Aha! Now I remember where I'd seen you before!"

I didn't have time to reply, apologize, or even look back at the soaked man. A second waitress had taken the Blooming Barrmundi out of my hands and was setting it down in front of a very proper-looking woman with spectacles balanced on the end of her nose.

I ran right past Rip, who stood next to the portal leading into the bar, obviously trying to get a better view of the hubbub going on in the dining section. As I passed him, I hissed, "Run! Run!"

I flew out of that joint like there was a bomb about to go off inside. But the only explosion apt to occur in Jugs 'n Mugs was going to be at table seven when the unsuspecting food critic took her first bite of her recently delivered meal.

CHAPTER 10

I arrived at the bunko party being hosted by Mabel Hicks promptly at seven-thirty. We had ended up only having a short time to eat in order for me to get to Mabel's house on time so had decided to pick up a couple of six-inch meatball sandwiches at Subway. We ate them while sitting on the steps of the beautiful Bayfront, along Shoreline Boulevard in Corpus, before returning to Rockport.

I had planned to segue into a discussion about the murder of Cooper Claypool once the bunko party got into full swing. That proved unnecessary, however. Instead, I was eagerly met at the door by Gracie Parker who greeted me with, "Are your ears burning, Rapella? The girls and I were just talking about how they threw your son-in-law in the slammer for brutally executing his best friend."

I really should have anticipated being hit with this upon arrival. Naturally, everyone had heard about it and knew of my family's connection to the victim. A murder in a town this size was front-page news, and usually continued to be for the next fifteen to twenty issues of the newspaper.

I debated about how to respond for a few seconds and

decided a straight-forward approach was the best option. I told them about the hot mess my son-in-law had landed himself in, due to his relationship with Claypool and the battering Milo had given his friend the night before his death. I stressed that Rip, a seasoned lawman, and I, believed Milo to be innocent of the crime and had launched our own private investigation to prove it.

I probably should have given more thought to what would happen after I shared the particulars with the bunko club members. Most of the ladies there gossiped incessantly, exaggerating and twisting details as they passed the news on to anyone who'd listen. I was certain that by morning Milo would be infamous for being Rockport's first serial killer, and was soon to be on death row after being caught red-handed harpooning his most recent victim.

Too late now, though. I thought ruefully. I'd already let the irresistibly juicy cat out of the bag that I should have kept closed. *Might as well make the most of it.*

"Does anyone here know a Julio Sarcova?" I asked the group.

"Isn't he that hothead who organized a protest to take place in front of City Hall tomorrow?" Gracie Parker asked. Several women nodded their heads. I asked Gracie what the man was upset about.

"It's to protest the newly proposed ordinance that would ban smoking in every public building in the city of Rockport, including every establishment that serves food and beverages," she replied. "Also beaches, parks, and anywhere else the public gathers."

"Oh, curses!" I said in disappointment. "This is not going to be an easy rally to attend, but I'll have to do it, I'm afraid."

"And why is that, Rapella? I thought you'd be all for an ordinance like that."

"I am, Gracie. In fact, I couldn't be any more pleased about the proposal. But attending the rally is the only way I'll have any believable excuse to speak to Julio

Sarcova. And that's only if I get lucky. Unless any of you gals have a better idea," I added, hoping one of them would come up with an easier way to gain an audience with the man.

"I have the perfect solution," Adelaide Hall, our newest member, exclaimed. "He owns the Brass Button Barber Shop on Cactus Street. Barbers hear about everything that goes on in town from their customers. Sarcova may know something useful regarding another suspect no one else has even considered. Send Rip in for a haircut. You can tag along and engage Sarcova in a conversation while he works on Rip."

"Good idea, Adelaide. Unfortunately, it'd take Sarcova about six seconds to cut Rip's hair. He only has about seventeen hairs left, and he's very attached to every single one of them. In more ways than one."

"What could you possibly want to speak to that belligerent fool about, anyway?" Mabel Hicks asked, as she placed her cocoa and caramel cookies on the refreshment table. I'd have bet she'd already locked the coveted recipe back up in her husband's fireproof gun cabinet.

I explained what I'd learned from the victim's girlfriend earlier in the evening. I told the group I needed an opportunity to feel the man out on just how angry he'd been at Cooper, and how far he might have gone to wreak havoc on the guy. "Besides, I've always enjoyed being part of a zealous mob involved in a rowdy demonstration, even if it's not a cause I'm passionate about. Or in this case, one I'm not even in favor of. Don't you girls agree?"

There was a lively debate following my question, and it was at least half-an-hour before the chit-chat at the various tables returned to the usual topics, like, how could Claire Higgins not see that her new hairdo made her look like a skanky call girl; why the teller at the credit union didn't have that hideous growth removed from her hand; and why did Mona Ray put up with that no-good drunken husband of hers when everyone in town knew he was running around on her with the mayor's cousin. As always, it was a fun and enlightening evening with friends.

And just in case you're wondering, I'm happy to report I won the prize for most losses at the end of the game. The "booby prize" it's called. It's not really a category to brag about unless, as in my case, you win a bobble-head doll depicting George Strait. Strait had a vacation home on Key Allegro Island, just blocks from Regina and Milo's place, which he and Norma had owned for years. He'd been one of Rockport's most notable residents, and it was a safe bet there was not one woman in my bunko club who wouldn't risk their marriage for one evening with George.

"Second-hand smoke is a joke! Second-hand smoke is a joke!" I chanted along with everyone, including Gracie, Mabel, Adelaide, and four other members of my bunko club who'd decided to join me in my quest to converse with Julio Sarcova. When it came to meting out justice, us bunko-mates were thick as thieves.

Naturally, we had to look as if we were earnestly contesting the new ordinance so as not to blow our cover. The dark-skinned, very slender, Hispanic man in question was leading the chant from his location behind the podium on a makeshift stage someone had haphazardly thrown together.

One thing that hadn't occurred to me was that the people most apt to oppose a smoking ban were smokers. I could barely bellow out the chant about the "ridiculous" premise of second-hand smoke being harmful due to the overabundance of second-hand smoke I was inhaling.

My eyes were burning and my throat was irritated. I had at least two burn holes in my new sweater before the demonstration even commenced, from mingling with the dense crowd. I'd have been more upset about the sweater had I not already realized the poor stinky thing would reek so badly by the time I returned to the trailer, I'd probably have to abandon it in the dumpster near the entrance of the RV park. I had a blouse on underneath that hopefully would avoid at least some of the overwhelming stench.

As the crowd repeated the mantra, another chant started up. It seemed to me to be an attempt to drown out the original chant. I noticed the crowd had suddenly swelled in size. Sarcova was chanting "We have the right to light," when an influx of people began to answer with, "We have the right to breathe." They carried signs that read "smokers are a public nuisance" and "don't kill my children with your nasty habit." It was then I understood the new arrivals, clearly in favor of the proposed ordinance, were protesting against the protesters who were opposed to it.

This could get ugly very quickly, I thought. We've now created the perfect storm for turning a peaceful protest into a frenzied riot.

Before I could round up my friends, rocks and shoes began to fly. It quickly escalated into an exchange of anything that could be turned into an airborne weapon. I swear I saw someone's dentures zip right by my left ear. If I wasn't mistaken, it was Gracie Parker's upper plate. I looked for her in the crowd but my searching ceased when I saw Mabel Hicks pull a bulky compact out of her purse and heave it at Julio Sarcova, the focal point of the mayhem. Clearly, Mabel had no clue which side of the dispute she was on. The uprising had a vacuum-like effect; it sucked a person, unwittingly, right into the eye of the storm.

I could hear sirens in the distance closing in on the bedlam on East Market Street. Someone had set fire to the stage and the podium was beginning to smolder as Sarcova beat on it with his jacket. I knew it was a preview of coming attractions with which I had no *burning* desire to be involved.

I knew it would be impossible to extract myself from the mob of rebellious citizens, so I concentrated on trying to avoid being beaned in the head by some unidentified flying object. I was ducking and bobbing while I attempted to remove myself from the chaotic scene. However, I'm ashamed to admit, I was no exception to the aforementioned vacuum effect.

When I was hit in the shoulder by a penny loafer, I felt compelled to throw my tennis shoes back at my assailant. I missed on both throws, but at least I felt a slight bit of vindication. What I failed to notice was where my right twelve-year-old Adidas inadvertently made contact.

CHAPTER 11

"What's up, buttercup?" Rip inquired jovially when he answered my call. I felt bad, knowing Rip's cheery mood was about to disappear like David Copperfield's lovely assistant.

"Now don't get mad," I began.

"Oh, no!" I heard him say. "Nothing good ever follows those four words."

"I'll explain it all later and why it wasn't my fault. But right now, it's like this, honey. I need you to come bail me out of jail."

"What?" He was obviously floored by my remark. "Good Lord, Rapella! Have you been arrested—again?"

"Yes. But like I said, this time it's not my fault. You see—"

"I know, Rapella. It's never your fault," Rip cut me off with a long-suffering sigh. "Let me guess. You participated in the demonstration at City Hall this afternoon that we heard about on the news last night? I noticed you appeared intent on the details of the protest, which should have raised a red flag with me."

"Yes. But I only—"

"I had a bad feeling when Adelaide Hall picked you up this morning. She's a rabble-rouser if there ever was one. I should have put my foot down right then."

"Put your foot down?" I asked. His remark hit a raw nerve. I didn't like the implication I needed to be told what I could and couldn't do, and would, without question, submissively adhere to my husband's stipulations. In a different situation I might have challenged his overbearing attitude, but I quickly backed down. As I alluded to earlier, in the course of life one has to pick her fights, and I knew this wasn't one that would end well for me.

"Why do you have to insert yourself into every protest, no matter how ludicrous the cause? For instance, the time you got arrested for marching in front of that little clothing shop, carrying a sign demanding the store offer a senior citizen discount. I still can't believe it. Arrested for disturbing the peace in Ten Sleep, Wyoming, a town of less than three-hundred residents." Rip's voice was beginning to rise. "Not to mention, it was elk and moose hunting season. You were lucky the owners even showed up to open the store."

"They should have realized the customer always comes first."

"Seriously, Rapella? Have you lost your grip on reality?"

"Well, I—"

"And why would you even care about the new smoking ordinance?" Rip was practically yelling into the phone.

"It just isn't right that I can't light up a cigarette in—"

"You don't smoke, Rapella!" He bellowed, drawing each word out for an uncomfortable amount of time to make a point. I'm guessing that angry retort hit 110 on the decibel scale. I had to pull the phone away from my head for fear my eardrum might burst. "I should think you'd be dancing in the street about the new smoking ban."

"Yes, I know, but, you see—" It might have been better if I'd mentioned to Rip that Avery had told me the demonstration's leader might be a suspect in her boyfriend's death. I'd kept that one under my hat to share with Rip after I had more concrete evidence that Julio Sarcova might have had had a motive to kill Claypool. And now I had evidence of a motive, unlikely as it might be.

"I've heard you complain about second-hand smoke a thousand times. And, besides, what have I told you about getting involved in protests in the first place?"

"This was different, Rip. It was absolutely necessary in order to—"

"Absolutely necessary?" Rip asked in a cutting tone. "Really? How do you describe—"

This time I interrupted him with a loud, "Stop! Stop, already! How can I speak in my own defense if you never let me get a word in edgewise?"

"Okay, fine. Speak!" He grew silent, reluctantly giving me an opportunity to describe the situation. But looking around the room, I saw a dozen other protestors anxiously waiting to use the only available phone from which to place their one allotted call. So I said, "Listen, Rip, I really can't go into it right now. I'll explain it all after you come to the station and bail me out."

"Oh, all right. Could I possibly go at least one day this week without having to bail someone out of jail? I can just imagine what the police department is going to say about this. At this rate, we're both going to be run out of town on a rail."

"Please, honey. I'm sorry, babe. I really am, darling. It won't happen again. I promise, sweetheart." If I used any more terms of endearment in my effort to soften up my irate husband, I was going to have to puke. My sucking-up routine was nauseating, but at least it was successful.

"Oh, all right," he repeated. "I'll be up there in ten minutes. Please tell me you didn't burn your bra this time!"

"I didn't, I promise. But I can't say the same for a few of the girls in my bunko club. Who'd have ever thought that at seventy-three, Evelyn would still have such perky little—?"

Click! The call abruptly ended as Rip hung up on me. Now how rude was that?

As expected, I received a lecture on the way home to the campground. I let Rip drone on without responding. I nodded at appropriate intervals, all the while concentrating on what to do next regarding the murder case. It's not like this was the first time I'd been subjected to a dressing down. In an emergency, I could give the speech in his place.

"You have got to quit plunging headfirst into dangerous situations as if you have backup at your beck and call. I'm not a cop anymore. I'm not a sheriff, either. I'm nothing but an old, broken-down retired citizen. I can't come rushing in to rescue you every time you land yourself in the middle of some asinine situation."

"Well, I wouldn't go so far as to say 'broken-down'. After all, you're still able to walk with me in the evenings, albeit not nearly as far as you used to," I finally said, mainly because it was hard to contradict any of his other comments. I wanted to convince him I'd been focusing intently on his sermon, as well. And a little booster dose of buttering up might prove worthwhile.

As if I hadn't even spoken, Rip went right into phase two of his lecture, otherwise known as the "am I going to have to keep my eye on you every second of the day" segment. I eventually sighed theatrically and leaned back in the passenger seat to settle in for the final phase, which was about to commence. It was his favorite part, by the way. I affectionately refer to this section of the lecture as the "it's just a matter of time before you end up dead or serving a life sentence" chapter.

And you thought *I* was dramatic?

When we'd returned to the RV park, Rip studied the Chartreuse Caboose as he stepped out of the truck. He shook his head in disgust and mumbled, "I can't believe you talked me into painting this trailer such a God-awful color, and with the ridiculous sunflowers, to boot."

I had hoped his temper would have mellowed by now so I could tell him some of the information I'd uncovered. But it was apparent I'd have to give Rip a little more time to cool down. He plopped down on the couch, and purely out of habit, picked up the remote to turn on the boob tube. I knew he was still simmering when he sat staring at the television for ten minutes as an old re-run of *Hannah Montana* aired.

I fixed us each our customary afternoon cocktail and silently walked over to hand him his Crown and Coke. I used quart-sized Ball canning jars for this ritual, primarily so I didn't have to get up and refill martini glasses three or four times. I knew a shot of alcohol would likely help put out the fire still smoldering inside my husband's head.

I let him down at least half of his drink before asking, "Would you like to hear why this morning's events were not entirely in vain? I did manage to get some useful info from the instigator of the protest, Julio Sarcova."

"What about him?" Rip asked. I sensed there were still a few ashes not entirely extinguished, so I proceeded carefully. I explained what Avery had said about Sarcova the night before in the Jugs 'n Mugs kitchen. Still, Rip shook his head in disbelief when I finished my next comment.

"I was very fortunate to be stuffed into the same paddy wagon as Sarcova."

"You must be blessed to have such amazing good luck."

I ignored his smart-aleck remark and continued with my recollection of the conversation I'd had with Sarcova. "To initiate a tête-à-tête, I told him I was sorry how the demonstration turned out, because it clearly did not go according to plan."

"No shit?" Rip asked sarcastically. "Getting thrown in the pokey wasn't part of the plan?"

"Actually, according to him, it was. He gleefully

informed me the rowdy protest would surely make the evening news and the front page of the *Rockport Pilot* with so many protesters on both sides of the conflict getting arrested in front of the city hall. All of us getting carted off to jail was advantageous. In fact, our arrests were his greatest hope, Sarcova said."

"You don't say." Rip was unmoved by my explanation.

"You see, he was delighted about the attention his cause would receive due to the riot that erupted. He was quite pleased with himself, to tell the truth. I think he actually encouraged people to protest against the protestors."

"Good for him. So how does this moron's unwarranted narcissism benefit us in this murder case?"

Okay, I thought. *At least he's listening to me now. It's not the supportive attitude I had in mind, but it's a start.*

"Our exchange was not strictly about the protest. I didn't waste any time delving into the murder and his relationship with the victim. It went something like this," I said, before reiterating the entire dialogue between Julio Sarcova and me, as best as I could recall.

After Sarcova had boasted about the fact we'd been busted for disturbing the peace, I had replied, "I'm glad it worked out so well for you, but it's not a good time for me to be locked up. You see, we're moving into our new place this week. Not like brand new, but it's new to us."

Sarcova didn't respond. So I continued. "It's one of those so-called flipped houses. Silly name, don't you think? Kind of sounds like turning a home upside down on its—"

"Who'd you buy it from?" His head swiveled my way, and he suddenly seemed intensely interested in my nervous jabbering.

"Oh, it's some outfit named MC Hammerheads. Cute name, huh?"

"Yeah, real cute," he replied derisively. "I feel sorry for you, lady."

"Oh, now I get it. It's 'M' for 'Milo' and 'Moore' and 'C'

for 'Cooper' and—"

"And 'Hammerheads' for what I'd like to do to both of their noggins."

Ignoring Julio's interjection, I said, "Now that I think about it, isn't there some rapper dude named MC Ham—?"

"Oh, boy! Good luck, lady!" Julio said. I'd been using the irrelevant banter to get him talking, and it seemed to work. "I bought a house from them, too. It's been nothing but a nightmare ever since."

"Oh, dear. Why is that?"

"It started about a week after we moved in. My four-year-old son started having more difficulty in breathing than usual. He's asthmatic, by the way. He was also running a dangerously high fever. After waiting to be seen for over an hour at that walk-in clinic on Third Street, his symptoms subsided. We took him home, assuming it was just a coincidence, until his temperature skyrocketed in the middle of the night and he was struggling to breathe again. We were scared because he has severe reactions to a number of allergens."

"Poor little guy," I sympathized. "Go on."

"On a hunch, I cut out a section of sheetrock right near the head of Hunter's bed. As I suspected, there was a huge amount of black mold that should have been taken care of before the house was sold. The sheetrock was new, so it had obviously been put up to hide all the hazardous mold when it was detected by Claypool and his business partner, Milo Moore."

"My, my. That's just unbelievable, ain't it?" I wasn't just pretending to be dismayed by that kind of unprofessional, unscrupulous practice. What kind of men would do such a disreputable thing, especially with a vulnerable young boy in the home?

"Unbelievable ain't the word for it!"

"What happened next?" I asked. Everyone in the van was listening to our conversation at this point. My bunko-mates acted as if they had no prior insight into the construction company or its owners.

"I confronted Cooper Claypool about it, of course. He agreed to correct the problem immediately and reimburse us for Hunter's medical bills." At this stage in the story, I'd have expected Sarcova to appear at least a little satisfied. Instead, he was livid. As he continued speaking, his ire rose until the officer driving the van had to order him to lower his voice.

"Wasn't that what you had hoped to accomplish when you confronted Claypool?"

"Absolutely! Thing is, the jerk's not fulfilled either promise. I ran into him at Crabby's Bar and Grill Saturday and threatened to sue him if the work wasn't done by this weekend. I haven't heard from the sleezeball yet, and I'd wager he won't have the work done or the medical bills paid by next Sunday, either."

I wondered if he'd witnessed the parking lot brawl between the business partners, but was afraid inquiring about it might make him realize I knew more than I was letting on. I had to tread lightly so it wasn't obvious I was fishing for clues that might implicate him in the murder. His next remark answered my question without me even having to ask it. "The two nincompoops got into it after I'd already approached Claypool in the bar. And, man, speak of hammering someone on the head. I'll bet Claypool's still seeing double."

He was talking as if he didn't know Claypool had been killed, which surprised me. So, with sadness in my tone, I replied, "I doubt that. I'm thinking it's a safe bet Claypool won't get much done by Sunday either. Hard to get much done when you're six feet under."

"Excuse me?" Sarcova asked, obviously confused by my comment.

"He's dead."

"What? What'd you say?"

"Claypool's dead, as in deceased, pushing up daisies, bit the big one, went out with his flippers on, kicked the buc—"

"What are you talking about, lady?" Now Sarcova

looked as if someone had filched his last cigarette. In fact, seconds later he asked the officers up front if he could have a smoke, and the answer was a hearty laugh. He flipped the driver off in the rearview mirror and turned back to me as he asked, "Did something happen to Cooper Claypool?"

"Duh," I replied, probably a tad too insensitively. "Hey, dude. I thought you told me you were living in a flipped home."

"I did. I am." He was staring at me in distrust, probably wondering if I'd been smoking hashish instead of tobacco at the protest.

"Whew. For a second there, I thought you might be living under a rock. How could you not have heard about it? Everyone in the county is abuzz over Claypool's death. It's all over the TV and newspapers, and it's most likely the main topic of discussion in every barber shop in town." I tried not to appear as if I knew he was a barber himself.

"Damn! Lady, I just got back from a couple of days in Las Vegas late last night. In fact, I stopped by Crabby's on the way to the airport in Corpus when I recognized Claypool's truck in their parking lot. I had no idea he was killed after our encounter there. Man, that's a bad deal." His words indicated he was sorry to hear the news, but his sly grin said otherwise. "I guess Moore finished the job after I left."

"No, Milo Moore was cleared. According to the authorities, he wasn't the perpetrator." To my knowledge, Milo hadn't actually been cleared, but I figured it didn't hurt to make Sarcova think he had been.

The van had pulled up to the station, and the officers were preparing to lead us all in for processing. As an officer guided Julio Sarcova away, Sarcova turned toward me and said, "In that case, if I were the homicide detectives, I'd take a look at Maxwell. I know he had a very pissed-off bone to pick with the guy, too."

CHAPTER 12

Rip's blue funk had evaporated by the time I finished with my recital. He leaned forward, and asked, "You surely asked Sarcova who Maxwell was, didn't you?"

"I wanted to, naturally. But they led him to a different room, and I never had an opportunity to speak with him again."

"Do you know where he works or lives?"

"Maxwell?"

"No, Rapella," Rip said impatiently. "Focus now, darling. I'm referring to Julio Sarcova."

"No, but wouldn't Milo know where Sarcova lives since he purchased one of MC Hammerheads' flipped homes?"

"Oh, yeah. I guess you're right. I should have thought of that."

"Focus, darling," I said, in a touché fashion.

Rip flashed me one of his most endearing smiles. I was relieved to see he hadn't taken my sarcastic jab to heart when he continued. "Let's try this again. Did Sarcova give any clues about where we might locate this Maxwell individual he referred to? I'd hate to have to drive to Sarcova's house and ask him."

I shook my head, and asked, "Shouldn't Milo know who Maxwell is?"

After Rip shrugged his shoulders, I placed a quick call to the Moores. Reggie answered the phone and shouted my question to her husband, who was repairing an electrical outlet in another room. She returned to the phone and reported that Milo knew nothing about a man named Maxwell. I informed Rip of Milo's negative response, and he said, "We don't know if Maxwell is a first name or last, but fortunately it's not an extremely common name like Smith or Johnson, and this is a small community. We can ask around. For that matter, I could look at the police department's databases."

"You think they'll let you do that?" I asked.

"Good point, dear. You're much smarter than your average jailbird," Rip joked. "After Detective Reeves informed me Sheriff Peabody had banned me from interfering with the case, I'm kind of hesitant to ask."

"You don't have to, honey," I volunteered. "That's why God created the Internet."

"Oh. And here all this time I thought that was Al Gore's brainstorm."

I chuckled at his remark. Rip swallowed the last sip of his Crown and Coke and then asked me why I was barefoot when he bailed me out of jail. I had hoped this topic wouldn't come up in our conversation. "Well, you see, I threw one of my tennis shoes, and it just so happened that this police officer's head was in the wrong place at the wrong—"

Rip put both of his hands up to stop me in mid-sentence. "I just decided I don't want to know any more about it. This embarrassing incident is going to be hard enough to live down as it is."

"Sorry, dear. Would you like a refill?'

The question went without asking.

"I struck out," I said the next morning when Rip returned from the police station.

"No luck here either," he replied. "I asked everyone I know and no one's heard of a Maxwell around here. You couldn't find anything on the Internet?"

"I found three Maxwells in Aransas County. Mildred Maxwell is ninety-four and living in a nursing home in Aransas Pass. However, according to the nursing staff, on any given day she thinks she's forty and performing on Broadway, or twenty-one and eight months pregnant. Just yesterday she insisted she was one of Shirley Maclaine's former incarnations. A touch on the senile side, you understand."

"Yes, I got the gist. Don't get sidetracked."

"Oh, sorry. Then there's Rowena Maxwell, who's a nun living at the Sisters of Schoenstatt Convent on Live Oak Peninsula."

"Okay, not much potential in those two," Rip said. "So, what's behind door number three?"

"The dearly departed," I replied. "Maxwell Short, former harbor master who passed away with lung cancer in October. He's buried in the Rockport Cemetery, according to a website called *findagrave.com*."

"And that's it?"

"Yes. Unless you want to count Max Wells, a seven-year-old attending Sacred Heart Elementary."

"Not really. I think we can safely mark him off the suspect list," Rip said. With an amused grin, he added, "If Max is anything like Regina was at that age, his alibi could well be that at the time of the murder he was having a jelly bean extracted from his left nostril."

I chuckled at the memory of that traumatic day with Regina in the Corpus Christi Spohn Hospital's emergency room . Then I said, "Or, more likely in this kid's case, he was memorizing words like logorrhea and vivisepulture, because he has the honor of being this year's second-grade spelling bee champion. But, seriously, that's all I could come up with online."

"Hmm, then I guess our best bet is to talk to Milo and get the address of the house Sarcova bought from them. We can feel him out about Sarcova and Cooper's relationship, too. Maybe Milo can shed a light on how volatile their conflict was, and whether or not he thinks Sarcova would resort to violence."

"Good idea, even though he'll realize that I was playing him like a fiddle in the paddy wagon." Reluctantly, I agreed. "Then we can visit Julio Sarcova at his home and see if we can wrangle more information out of him. Find out who Maxwell is and why he feels this person might have a motive to want Cooper dead."

"Sounds like a plan to me!" Rip agreed. And with a chuckle he asked, "By the way, what does logorrhea mean and how do you spell it?"

"I spell it wrong, most likely, and it means the act of talking incessantly. For example, what you were doing on the way home from bailing me out."

"Hmm. I see. And vivisepulture?"

"What I was contemplating doing to you at that same time."

"Do I really want to know what that would have been?"

"Probably not."

"Want to go to Bealls and Wal-Mart with me?" I heard Regina ask when I answered Rip's cell phone. I'd been filling time crossing out addresses in my organizer book that were no longer valid, or that belonged to someone like Cooper Claypool, who was no longer among the living. It had me feeling melancholy while I reminisced about the many friends and family who had already passed.

One begins to think about death a bit more when one's approaching seventy and has to read the obituaries every day to see whose funeral or memorial to notate on their social calendar. Meanwhile, on this Thursday morning, Rip was crisscrossing town looking for someone who knew of a Maxwell in the area. Earlier he'd discussed Julio Sarcova with Milo and discovered very little useful information. Milo hadn't had much contact with the man, and from what Cooper had told him about his interactions with Sarcova, the guy was more bark than bite.

"So? Wanna go?" Reggie repeated over the phone.

"Sure, sweetheart. I'd love to go shopping with you."

I'd been wanting to find a couple pairs of reasonably-priced shorts that didn't begin right below my boobs or end right below my rear end. I wanted to look chic and fashionable, not like a prostitute—or worse, a centenarian. There was a fine line between the two that made it difficult to locate the perfect fit. As for Wal-Mart, there were always things there I needed, but didn't realize I needed until I saw them on the shelves.

"Cool. I'll pick you up in ten."

Seconds before Reggie pulled up to the curb behind our trailer, Rip returned home, irritated and discouraged. He had gathered the nerve to walk into the police station and enter the office of lead detective, Branson Reeves. Although Reeves swore he'd never admit speaking with Rip about the case, he shared what little information the investigators had obtained. Many people had been interviewed, including Milo, Avery Curry, Patrick O'Keefe, Julio Sarcova, a fellow named Lee Gordon, and a few other peripheral individuals.

"Most had hard-to-verify alibis, and only moderate motives, Branson told me. No evidence has surfaced yet proving any of the suspects were involved. This morning the detectives were taking a closer look at the boat, spear, and photos of the victim, trying to come up with any clue or trace evidence that could point them in the right direction."

"Who's Lee Gordon?" I asked.

"Some real estate guy who was a competitor of Cooper and Milo's. He apparently attended some of the same AA meetings that Cooper did, too. The two men had been embroiled in a nasty confrontation during a meeting about a month ago, which is why the detectives brought Gordon in to question. But his alibi checked out easily enough."

"How's that?"

"He was arrested on DUI charges in Galveston Friday night and not released from the drunk tank until late Sunday morning. It's too bad the murder weapon was never recovered."

"But they have the spear that killed Claypool," I said.

"Yes, but like someone who's killed with a handgun, it's the gun that is considered the murder weapon, not the bullet that actually killed the victim. In this case, the murder weapon is the spear gun itself, which was detached from the spear when the cord that connects them was severed by the shooter."

"I see. Well, it sounds like the investigating team has gotten no further than we have in determining who the killer was," I said, now sharing Rip's disheartened mood.

"Did you ask him about a possible suspect named Maxwell?"

"Yeah. Struck out there too. Branson didn't know of anybody named Maxwell in the area. Are you sure that's what Sarcova said?"

"Yes, I'm certain. You're the one wearing hearing aids, not me," I replied defensively.

"Doesn't mean you don't *need* to be wearing them. You make me repeat things almost as often as I do you."

"True. But I'd almost swear that he said, 'Check out Maxwell'. Well, dear, Reggie's here and I'm going shopping with her."

"Pick me up a large bottle of Crown Royal at Spanky's. I have a feeling I'm going to need it."

I was able to find one pair of red shorts that were ideal, and a white pair that were questionable. I'd bought the latter pair with the idea I could always return them. They felt a bit snug in the waist, but had enough extra room in the legs to squeeze in another person my size. There was also a risk with the color. Just wearing white made me so apprehensive and jittery, I tended to spill everything I touched.

"You get everything you needed, Mom?"

"Yes, and a few things I didn't," I replied.

"Like that quart of churned vanilla ice cream?" Reggie asked me with a teasing smile as she glanced at the items in my section of our shared cart.

"That's for your father, Regina. I've landed myself in one of those long-term sucking-up situations, and ice cream usually helps turn the tide."

"What's stuck in his craw? You getting arrested at a protest again? He should be used to it by now. This was what, your third time?"

I merely shrugged my shoulders. It was actually the fourth time, but who's counting? *Besides you, that is,* I wanted to say. *And probably your grouchy father.*

Instead, I said, "If you're ready, dear, let's go check out."

We scrutinized the three open lanes. One lane had a man and woman, each with a loaded cart, and three young children trying to talk their parents into letting them have one of the candy bars offered along the check-out lines. Store owners must not have young children or they wouldn't do this to parents, who are merely trying to get out of the store without an embarrassing meltdown scene by Junior. The last thing these poor folks needed was a trio of even more hyped-up kids to deal with. Most juveniles these days have already been diagnosed with attention disorders. Back in my day, this disorder was called "sugar overload."

Line two had five people with only a few items each. The turn-off was that the last lady in line had a baby who was screeching, not happy about being strapped in a car seat attached to the front of the cart. Her shrieks were approaching ear-drum-splitting level.

Line three was the hands-down winner. There were two ladies in my age bracket with one half-full cart between them. We waited as the blue-haired lady sifted through the items in the basket, picking out her purchases from a mound of intermingled products, which was a time-consuming ordeal. I wanted to tell the ladies that two carts might have been a wiser choice, but

I held my tongue. This was a good thing, considering it'd have been a "pot calling the kettle black" sort of thing, with Reggie and I sharing a basket, too.

When the lady dug in her purse and came out with a fistful of coupons, I quickly backed up to take another gander at the other two lines, only to find they'd both grown tremendously in the interim. Reggie and I had no option but to wait it out in the line we'd chosen.

"Can you believe the price of bacon these days?" The lady being served asked the young check-out boy, who looked as if he spent the majority of his free time picking at his acne. He shook his head and kept scanning the UPC codes on each item as it moved down the conveyor belt.

"Son, are you sure $2.97 is the correct price on the asparagus? I recall the sign saying $2.79 per pound. By the looks of those scrawny stalks, you should be charging even less than that. I have half a mind to return them to the bin. You know, at that ridiculous price, and all."

I had to give the young man credit for the way he handled the situation. "Okay, ma'am. I'll just set them aside and have the sacker return them to the produce department."

The customer quickly changed her tune. "No, that's okay, young man. I'll go ahead and bite the bullet. I just asked in case you suffered from dyslexia. But I guess asparagus is out of season, and produce is always higher then."

The insensitive woman proceeded to argue about an expired coupon, and then another one that wasn't valid on a smaller-sized box than required. The check-out boy held his ground and refused to cave in to the old biddy's demands. I was to the point I wanted to tell him to give her the blasted discount and I'd pay the difference, even if it went against my grain. We all needed to get out of the store before they turned out the lights at closing time.

Reggie leaned toward me, and asked, "What's that I hear?"

"Probably the sound of Rip's ice cream melting." I replied much louder than necessary.

"Yeah, no lie! But what I meant was I believe it's starting to rain."

"Naturally," I replied, growing more and more impatient. If our luck held true, it would be pouring by the time we carried our bags to the parking lot. I watched as the family of five marched out of the store, each kid with a mouthful of chocolate. "Dang it! I knew we should have chosen that line."

After "blue hair" wrote out a check, painstakingly slow, the second lady began to place her items on the belt. She stopped after four or five products and turned to her friend, flipping her long, bleached-blond hair over her shoulder.

"I hope she doesn't think she's fooling anyone with that amateurish dye job," I whispered to Reggie. She shushed me, which is usually a wasted effort.

"Gladys, I need to drop a check by Mack's place on the way home. I hope you don't have anything that will melt in the next twenty minutes."

Gladys shook her head, as I said, "Well I do! If it hasn't liquefied already."

Gladys shot me a withering glance as Reggie elbowed me in the ribs. Blondie had still not resumed placing items on the belt as she commented to her friend, "Our well went dry again, so we just had a new one dug, you see."

As the checker stood behind the counter and frowned, eager to keep the process going, the second lady asked lady number one, "Do you see this mole beside my nose?"

"Of course," her friend responded. "Everyone sees it. That mole's the size of a pencil eraser, for goodness' sakes."

"Humph!" Clearly miffed, the blond woman replied,

"Well, Gladys, I was aware of that without you pointing it out. In fact, I saw my dermatologist yesterday and he assured me it was not malignant. Still, one has to worry."

When the blond-haired lady with the mole sprouting Billy goat hairs opened her purse to dig out her stash of coupons, I lost it. "Come on, you self-absorbed chinwags! Get a move on! Can you not see this growing line of customers behind you? Have the doctor freeze that butt-ugly thing off your face with liquid nitrogen and be done with it."

There was an audible group gasp by the two ladies, the check-out boy, the other customers in line behind us, and, of course, my horrified daughter. Still, my sense of propriety would not let me back off. So I continued to berate the two stunned women. "I'm sure all of us who are being delayed by your gabbing have other things we need to do today. As it is, I'll be lucky to get my groceries loaded in the trunk before my milk expires."

Customer number two stuffed her coupons back into her purse, threw some money at the check-out dude, and exited the store as quickly as she possibly could. When it was my turn to check out, the young man said, "Thanks." I gave Reggie a smug look and had my purchases lined up on the conveyor belt like little soldiers in no time at all.

"Really, mother?" Reggie asked, as we sloshed through the parking lot with our bags. "I can't believe you just called the president of the Rockport Chamber of Commerce and a teller at my bank self-absorbed chinwags, whatever the hell a chinwag is! I have to do business with both of them. Couldn't you have just kept your opinion to yourself for once?"

"I don't care if they are Mother Teresa and Helen Keller. It's rude and inconsiderate to hold up an entire line of customers to discuss some unsightly growth on your face. They needed to be given a courteous nudge."

"A courteous nudge? That might qualify as the understatement of the year. Seriously, Mom? A courteous nudge?" Regina repeated in a disgusted tone. She sighed dramatically as she unlocked the trunk of her car. "And, by the way, Mother. Helen Keller was deaf and blind. She wouldn't be talking about moles and dropping off checks at Mack's well-digging shop while checking out at Wal-Mart."

"Good. Then at least she wouldn't be holding up the line like those two chatterboxes, would she?"

Reggie practically slammed the car door after she climbed into the driver's seat. As she began to drive home, a light bulb went off in my head. "Hey! You just made a remark about Mack's well digging shop. 'Mack's well' sounds a lot like 'Maxwell'. What are the chances Julio Sarcova was referring to the Mack's Well Company?"

CHAPTER 13

Regina tried to contact Milo but he failed to answer her call. So, instead, she used her smart phone to find the address of Mack's Wells, Inc. She didn't hesitate to turn around and head toward Sixteenth Street on the south side of town, which surprised me. Even though Reggie had more invested in this quest to discover the truth behind Cooper Claypool's death than I did, she was by nature less inclined to go to the extent I would to solve the riddle. As long as the identity of the killer was up in the air, my daughter's life would be topsy-turvy and I didn't see how she'd get a decent night's sleep. I knew I wouldn't.

The well company was across the street from a large, fenced-in boat storage facility. The sign on the door was faded and the building was old and in ill-repair. It appeared to me as if Mack was in dire need of an influx of business. And we were about to pretend to be a couple of those much-needed customers.

"Can I help you, ladies?" A gruff, raspy voice asked from behind a pile of metal pipe. A solidly built man who stood well over six-and-a-half feet looked up from a wooden chair when we walked around the pipe. He snuffed his cigarette out in a tin can half-filled with sand. Sand was a plentiful resource in this neck of the woods, but to degrade it with cigarette butts just seemed wrong to me. But he did show concern for our well-being when he cautioned us, "You might want to step away from those well casings, ladies. They've been known to become dislodged and avalanche down to the floor. And, excuse my French, ladies, but it's one hell of a hassle to restack them."

"Yes, sir," I replied as both Regina and I moved away from the pile. I could see his point as the pile didn't look particularly stable. In fact, it looked as if it was on the verge of cascading toward Reggie and me. But I pushed the notion aside, and asked, "Is Mack here, by any chance?"

"You're looking at him. Mack Schilling here." As he introduced himself, he shook both of our hands. Without a doubt, Mack Schilling had once been the picture of physical fitness. But aging had made his six-pack look more like a keg.

He was a bear of a man but his handshake said otherwise. His grip was surprisingly lame, but it might have been out of gentlemanly respect. Had we not been ladies, Mack's clench might have crushed walnuts.

I started to respond, but Reggie beat me to it. "Nice to meet you, Mr. Schilling. I'm Regina, and this is my mother, Rapella."

"It's a pleasure to meet you ladies, as well. What can I do for you today?"

Before either of us could reply, a strapping middle-aged fellow stepped from behind a wall dividing the small office area from the larger public area where we were located. He had that ripped appearance indicating he spent a lot of time in a gym. However, I could see where his body might mature into that of his father's if he gave up whatever intense work-outs he was engaging in. He glanced over to see his father speaking with the two of us gals, and asked, "Got it, Papa?"

"Yeah, son. I can take care of these nice ladies. You need to get the men lined up for the job in Portland, anyway. I told the Strykers you'd be there by now. Give them a ring, Trey. Let them know you're on the way.'

"All right. I'll tell them we'll be on the road in ten minutes." Mack resembled the younger man enough that I knew calling him "son" was not just a habitual moniker. Mack's Wells, Inc. was a family business, it seemed. Like a lot of ma and pa operations in this area, it probably passed down from one generation to the next, until the next successor in line had no desire or ambition to take over the company. Mack turned back to Reggie and me, and asked, "Now what brings you two lovely ladies in here today?"

"Well—" I began. I paused when I realized I hadn't thought of a credible ruse before walking in the shop. Before I could come up with one, he cut in.

"That's a deep subject, ma'am. And it also happens to be what we do best around here." He laughed heartily at his own play on words. I could tell it wasn't the first time he'd used that one, and he no doubt cracked himself up every time he pulled it out of the hat.

After a few more gritty guffaws, Mack choked and began to cough. As soon as he was able to quell his cough, he reached in his front pocket for a cigarette and a tarnished Zippo. I tried to recall if I'd seen this dedicated smoker at the protest the previous morning. If he hadn't attended, he'd missed a golden opportunity to support his habit. And best of luck to the city of Rockport in forcing this massive man to go outside his own business to light up.

I laughed politely, and said, "Yes, a well is exactly what we need."

"Where do you want us to drill this well?"

"Um, you know, out in a rural area, west of town." I didn't think telling him I wanted him to dig a well next to my travel trailer in the RV park would fly very far. "Although I'm really not ready to commit yet. I just stopped by to get an estimate."

"I need you to be more specific, ma'am, because the location could greatly affect the cost. I wouldn't want to

give a nice lady like you a bid that's way over-blown."
Mack was built like a giant Sequoia, or a man who could
handily chop one down. But despite his easy-going, teddy-
bear demeanor, I felt uncomfortable around him. It was as
if there was a barely concealed fuse lit just below the
surface of his smile. I was glad my daughter had
accompanied me.

"Okay. It's out on, er, I should say, it's by a road. No, I
meant to say—"

Aware I was floundering for words, Reggie stepped in.
"It's just west of Holiday Beach off 35 N. Highway, Mr.
Schilling. It's fairly sandy ground, barely above sea level. I
don't think you'd have to drill very deep to find water." I'd
discover later she'd described an area where Milo's younger
brother lived.

"We never have to drill very deep," he replied with a
wink. "But I'd still have to see the—"

"Maybe it'd help you narrow it down if I told you I
recently moved into one of those flipped houses out—"

"Did you say flipped houses?"

"Yes, but I just—"

"Who'd you buy it from?" Mack interrupted, suddenly
very serious, as if his reaction rested on my response. "Not
those Hammerhead buffoons, I hope."

"Why, yes. As a matter of fact, that's exactly who sold it
to me. A couple of extremely delightful men own the
business and were a real pleasure to deal with."

"Yeah, right. Sorry, lady. Can't help you." His reply was
practically venomous. He immediately spun around to
return to the chair he'd been sitting on when we had first
entered the building. It was obvious that, as far as he was
concerned, the conversation was over and we were not to
let the door hit us in our rear ends on our way out.

"Why not?" I asked in stunned disbelief. I was sincerely
alarmed by the man's abrupt mood change.

"Yes, why can't you help her?" Regina added with
rugged tenacity. After all, her husband was one of the
buffoons Mack clearly had no use for.

"All I can say is, you better watch your back with that no-account outfit. I haven't been paid for the last three jobs I've completed for those charlatans. And I don't see any sign of that changing any time soon." Mack was worked up now. Just the mention of Milo and Cooper's company had transformed the gentle giant into a nail-spitting monster of a man. My uneasiness increased. I could smell the acrid odor of the man's fuse smoldering.

"Why not?" I asked for the second time.

"You tell me, lady! It ain't from not trying. I've had more than one go-round with those guys. Claypool paid me to fill up a dry well, and then advertised the property as having a well with a constant supply of water. The well was dry again before the ink on the purchase agreement was. Now the couple have to have water delivered regularly or go to the expense of having a new well drilled. The MC Boneheads are involved in a law suit over that deal now, too, which serves them right."

I could tell by Reggie's body language she wanted to tear this guy a new one. She clearly didn't take kindly to having her husband referred to as a "buffoon," much less a "bonehead." I didn't want to split hairs, but if it weren't for my allegiance to my only child, I'd have agreed with Mack. I hadn't known Milo very well, or for very long, but I had detected a measurable amount of boneheadedness in his character. And before you look up "boneheadedness," if it's not recognized by Funk and Wagnall, it should be. In fact, it should be found frequently on every politician's Wikipedia page.

I turned to my daughter and could almost visualize tiny puffs of steam escaping from her ears as she moved a couple of steps closer to Mack Schilling. Before she could ask to borrow a step stool from Mack so she could bitch-slap him, I said, "I'm sorry to hear you've had such disturbing issues with Cooper and my son-in-law, Milo."

Mack took a step backward as his eyes blinked rapidly several times. He stared at Reggie and me before glancing over at a forklift sitting next to the delicately balanced pile of well casings. It was as if the idea of using the piece of equipment to manually remove us from the building was flitting through his mind. Before the opportunity was lost, I needed to get him talking, even if it took provoking him to do it.

"Actually, Mack, I thought you looked like one of their spear-fishing buddies Milo introduced us to the day we were signing the paperwork in his office. Have you ever gone out spear-fishing with him and Cooper? Are you the buddy they introduced us to?"

"No, definitely not. You must be referring to Pinto, who I can't believe even associates with those two blowhards. Pinto's way out of their league, as am I. Those two are definitely not buddies of mine. I've never stepped foot in their office, nor do I ever plan to."

"Out of their league? Really? And just what league are you in?" Reggie was fuming. When Mack didn't respond, Reggie asked, "I'm curious. Exactly what league *does* pond scum fall into?"

"Listen lady. I not only don't enjoy fishing of any kind, I also don't take any pleasure in being in the company of those two bast—"

"Gee, can you think of any more insulting B-words to call my husband and Cooper? Buffoons? Boneheads? Blowhards? And now bast—"

I decided it was time to step in before the two came to blows. It'd be like watching a full-grown fox wrestle with a baby bunny. Not that my next remarks were any less provoking than Reggie's. "I doubt they were too fond of your presence either. Nor would they want to take you out fishing with them. It's not like you're much of a prize, you know."

My cutting remark flew over his head like a paper airplane. Mack said, "However, I did see them when I took my wife, son, and daughter-in-law out for an evening cruise on my new ultra-expensive yacht," he boasted. His vanity left a bad taste in my mouth. "They were standing next to Cooper's boat, hiding their spear-guns and trying to pretend they were working on the motor. But I'd already spotted them with binoculars before they even realized we were in the vicinity. They were bailing off the boat with their guns when I first saw them."

"Why would they hide their spear-guns?" I asked. I was baffled by why Mack would consider their actions shifty.

"Why else? Spear-fishing season wasn't open at the time. If a game warden had been anywhere in the area, I'd have turned them in. Poachers are a plague to sportsmen everywhere, but Moore and Claypool are the two most despicable offenders around. And Cooper Claypool was the worst of the worst when it came to being unprincipled."

"Oh, my. Your hatred of the man obviously runs very deep. You didn't have anything to do with his recent death, did you?" I don't know what made me ask him point-blank if he was involved with Cooper's gruesome death. Out of the corner of my eye, I saw Reggie's mouth drop open as she rapidly scanned the room. Looking for the nearest exit, I'd guess.

With bugged-out eyes, Mack Schilling pointed to the door and bellowed, "Get out! Both of you! What are you two, anyway? Undercover cops? I had nothing to do with that jerk's death, and that's exactly what I'll tell the investigators if they hassle me about it. The way I see it, he got what he had coming. Karma's a bitch, you know. Now get off my property before I throw you off."

We believed him and high-stepped it out of the building. I swear it was an accident when my foot caught the edge of a well casing on the bottom of the delicately-balanced stack, causing the entire pile to begin cascading down, one by one rolling across the large concrete floor. Restacking them would keep this boorish man busy for quite awhile, I thought spitefully. And, I admit, gleefully.

Back in the car, with Mack standing on the doorstep of his shop, meaty hands on his hips, glaring at us, Reggie peeled out of the parking lot. It took several long seconds for her wheels to get traction in the muddy puddle the recent rain had created. The ensuing spray of dirty water coated the front window of the irate man's shop and turned his light blue sweatshirt a speckled brown. He lifted his arm to shake a fist at us before extending his middle finger just as we reached the asphalt pavement.

"By his reaction, I'd say if he wasn't the perpetrator, he knows who was," I remarked. "My question sure put a burr under his saddle, didn't it?"

"You have any doubt it wouldn't?" Regina replied incredulously. "Could you possibly have been any brasher when you pointed your finger at him and practically accused him of being a murderer?"

"I know I could have been a bit more tactful, but I think—"

"Tact is not in your DNA, Mom. I'm just relieved we didn't get filled with lead on our way out. Didn't you see the little snub-nosed revolver lying behind his butt can on the desk?"

"No, actually I didn't. But, I suppose you're right," I agreed. "I should have been more discreet. I have to ask you, honey. Did you know Milo and Cooper were spear-fishing illegally?"

Her face flushed at the question and she remained silent.

"Okay, that's all the answer I need, Regina. I have to say I'm not very proud of your new husband. Or you, for that matter. What I don't understand is why Milo would toss my redfish overboard like it was nuclear waste for being a fraction of an inch too short, but think nothing of poaching fish with a spear-gun."

"It was always Cooper's idea, Mom. He pressured Milo to go until Milo caved in and joined him. Cooper was ticketed by a game warden twice, by the way. Thankfully, Milo was not with him either time. Cooper was out alone and probably had his back to the game warden's boat and didn't see or hear him approach. I'm pretty sure the second time, he was banned indefinitely from spear-fishing in the entire state of Texas. Not that something like that kept him from doing it anyway. He tried several times to get Milo to go flounder-gigging out of season too, but Milo always refused."

"I'm beginning to question Milo's choice in both friends and business partners. So, how about these lawsuits I'm hearing about? Were you aware they existed?"

This time Reggie vehemently denied knowing anything about them. She said, "But that might explain why in the last couple of months Milo's been turning every nickel over a dozen times before he spends it."

Although I didn't say anything about their financial woes to my already distraught daughter, I thought, It also explains why since the day we arrived in town, we've had to pick up every tab when out with Milo and Reggie, no matter how small the bill. I didn't want Reggie to feel bad when it wasn't of her doing, so out loud I said, "At least our visit with Mack provided some very intriguing information. We have a few new leads I think we should follow."

"If you say so, Mother."

"I do." I sat back in my seat with a satisfied smile on my face.

"Oh, no!" Regina gasped. "We forgot you had ice cream in one of your grocery bags. That's going to be a mess."

"It'll clean up. It's not having the ice cream on hand to appease your father that concerns me. In fact, let's stop back by the store, after I pick him up some Crown at Spanky's, so I can purchase another carton of Blue Bell."

"All right," Regina agreed. "But for both our sakes, why don't you just stay in the car and let me run in and buy the ice cream."

My daughter can be so uptight and fussy at times.

CHAPTER 14

"Fine detective work, my dear Watson," Rip remarked after I'd told him about our encounter with Mack Schilling. Naturally, my description of our interaction with him was abbreviated, omitting the part of being ordered off his property following my rash accusation and the ensuing accidental well-casing avalanche. What Rip didn't know wouldn't hurt me. He flashed me an endearing smile and added, "Now I remember why I love you so much."

"Oh? So it's not my penchant for getting thrown in the slammer?"

"Not hardly. You spent too much time with Lexie Starr, and her impulsiveness rubbed off on you, I'm afraid. But despite your aggravating habit of being over-the-top lackadaisical about the risky situations you get in the middle of, and being too set in your ways, there's still no other woman in the world I'd rather share the rest of my life with."

"Same here, honey." I leaned over to kiss Rip, convinced Regina had not already spilled the beans. I was thankful Rip had gotten over his little snit. He'd always been the type of person who couldn't stay mad at someone for very long. He certainly never held a grudge, as I have been known to do.

Rip and I were sprawled out on the couch in front of the television with my head nestled into the crook of his arm. On TV was an old rerun of *Family Feud*, from back when Richard Dawson was the host. We'd finally upgraded to a thirty-two inch flat screen the previous winter, even though I was reluctant to spend money on a new one when the old twenty-inch model still had a pixilated, but visible, display. Rip's persuasive pitch for a better television finally won me over. He'd hung it on the wall, and I had to admit it was nice to have the extra room in the living area. A crystal clear picture with which I could actually distinguish between John Wayne and Betty White was handy too.

Deep in thought, Rip caressed my back for a few moments before saying, "It certainly sounds like Mack Schilling had a motive and the temper to go along with it. You didn't happen to get a chance to ask him about his whereabouts Saturday afternoon, did you?"

"No. It was the next question I'd hoped to ask. But something came up and we weren't able to continue the conversation. And I'm sure he'd have clammed up and refused to respond even if I had."

"Hmmm. Is the iPad handy?"

"Yes it really is. Very handy, in fact. I find myself using it all the time now to research information about something, or someone. You wouldn't believe how many times I've been able to find out—" I shut up when I realized he was staring at me like three or four marbles had just escaped my head via my right ear. "Oh! Did you mean, 'Is it where I can retrieve it easily'?"

At Rip's nod and disrespectful, "Duh," I stood to pick it up off the kitchen table. "What do you want me to search?"

"See what you can find out about Mack Schilling. Now that we have a name, there might be something on the Internet that's revealing."

"Good idea. Mack called Trey, the younger man, 'son,'

and Trey called Mack 'Papa,' so it's clearly a family business." When I searched Mack's name, I found many sites mentioning his well-digging business. He seemed to be highly respected in the community and had received many positive reviews from former customers. The only less-than-flattering comments were that Mack needed to wash his overalls more frequently, and his help should watch their language around impressionable children and ladies. Nothing too earth-shattering.

Then I happened upon a Mack Schilling in the society pages of a previous edition of the *Rockport Pilot*. "This is odd, Rip. It's a birth announcement for a baby named Chandler, born to a Joyce and Mack Schilling, III. Mack was too old to have a baby unless he'd divorced Trey's mother and married a woman young enough to be his daughter."

"Think about it, though. The father of this baby has to be Trey. Trey's not an uncommon nickname for the third in line to be called when three generations in a row share the same name. It could get confusing if you don't give at least one of them a nickname. It's quite possible Trey had a bone to pick with Claypool and Milo, too."

"You're right. Possibly even more provoking than his father's 'pissed-off bone', as Julio Sarcova put it. Now that I think about it, Trey would be in the same age bracket as the two boys. Let me Google 'Trey Schilling' and see what pops up."

It didn't take long to discover Mack Schilling, III, was a twelve-year veteran of the Texas Parks and Wildlife Department. An Aransas County game warden, to be more exact. Trey had been married to a Joyce Chriswall-Schilling for four years, after divorcing a Peggy (Adcoff) Claypool sixteen years prior. Coincidence? Hard to tell at this point. At the time the newspaper was printed, Trey and Peggy had a three-year-old son named Adrian Claypool, who would now be twenty-one. They also had a son named Chandler, as confirmed by the birth announcement I'd just discovered. Chandler would now be seventeen.

In a separate article about Trey's father, Mack, Jr., who owned the well service company Regina and I visited, it was mentioned that his son was a part-time employee.

"Being a game warden might have given Trey a second reason to be infuriated with the murder victim. I'm surprised Mack didn't mention his son worked for the Parks and Wildlife Department. What are the chances Trey was aware of Claypool and Milo's poaching? Mack told us he caught the two fishing out of season one day, but he didn't have the authority to arrest them like his son would have. What are the chances it was Trey Schilling who got Cooper banned for life from spear-fishing?"

"Quite good, I'd guess. Between the fact MC Hammerheads stiffed his father on a number of occasions, and the likelihood Trey arrested Cooper for poaching, I'd say there was plenty of bad blood between the two men, and possibly Milo, as well."

"I hadn't thought of that, Rip. Could Trey be our killer? And could he be gunning for Milo now? Is it possible one or both of the Schillings have their sights on Milo?"

"Of course it is. Anything's possible. Even if Trey's not our killer, whoever is could want retribution against Milo just as badly as he did Cooper if the perp's anger is based on a business deal with the MC Hammerheads company that soured. And, let's face it, darling. It's still not totally out of the question Milo was somehow involved in Cooper's death. I'm still teetering on the fence about that possibility. My gut tells me he's not, but my mind tells me I shouldn't disregard him as the perpetrator, or an accomplice, only because I have a personal interest in the outcome."

"That's true. He still seems to have the most incriminating evidence and opportune circumstances of anyone." I agreed with Rip's assessment, even though I prayed those factors were entirely coincidental. "We can't totally believe anything Milo tells us. After all, he lied to us about knowing anything about the cut on the back of Cooper's head immediately after we discovered the body."

I was shocked by the direction the case had suddenly taken. We couldn't burn daylight dillydallying when a killer was on the loose, and Milo might have a target on his back, regardless of the fact we didn't know for certain he wasn't personally involved in the murder. No more lolling on the couch wasting precious time, not that we'd wasted all that much in the last few days. "We need to get our rears in gear, my dear!"

Then Rip said, "I agree! Let's invite Regina and Milo to join us for supper at Paradise Key. I'd like to delve into the financial status of MC Hammerheads Construction Company and discuss the lawsuits they're involved in and/or being threatened with. I'd also like to get a better idea of Milo and Cooper's past interactions with the Schillings. That will help me determine if Milo needs police protection."

"Will Detective Reeves and/or Sheriff Peabody cooperate if you request the department assign officers to keep an eye out for Milo? I know Joe wasn't sold on having you involved in this case to begin with."

"If the department resists, I'll hire a couple of security guards to protect him myself. I still have a few in my back pocket. And, they're not just wanna-be cops, as some call them. They're skilled, top-notch individuals."

"Oh, good. That's a relief. I'd like to ask Milo what he knows that he's not sharing with us. It's obvious he's not being completely forthright. We can't help him if he isn't up-front and honest with us. I'll be tactful, of course."

"Ha! That's funny, Rapella. Tact is just not in your DNA, so let me do the talking. Okay?"

That was twice in one afternoon I'd been told the exact same thing. And by the two people dearest to my heart, at that. There appeared to be a consensus that I couldn't be counted on to use diplomacy when discussing critical matters. It hurt my feelings and put a big fat bumble bee in my bonnet, but I decided it probably was best to let Rip handle the situation. At least somewhere, buried deep in that DNA the two were talking so disparagingly about, was the ability to recognize when even my most persuasive arguments were not going to influence Rip, a former law enforcement officer with a butt-load of experience in manipulating suspects.

I picked up the phone and rang my daughter to make dinner plans for the evening. I wouldn't be taking "no" for an answer, either.

We had reservations for four at five o'clock. Regina had argued it was too early for supper, and informed me her bummed-out husband just wasn't up to going out. So I, in turn, informed her that her father was not issuing an invitation, he was issuing an order. She finally agreed when it dawned on her she and Milo had no choice but to join us for supper whether they liked it or not.

We were seated by the window overlooking the shallow water of Cove Harbor. Paradise Key was located right on the water and we watched an aerodynamically-designed "cigarette" boat glide up and tie off to the dock alongside the restaurant. Two young couples disembarked, climbed the steps, and took a table on the outside deck, where an exceptionally talented one-man band was entertaining the customers. Paradise Key was one of the most popular eating and drinking establishments in the area, and for good reason.

We all placed our orders for adult beverages. I ordered my customary tequila sunrise, Rip requested Jack and Coke, and the kids settled on fruit-flavored margaritas. I debated over what to eat and decided on a meal I rarely ordered anywhere else because of the expense; a surf and turf combo. That delectable entree at Paradise Key was worth bending the budget a bit.

As expected, Milo's mood was subdued, Reggie's was apprehensive, and Rip's and mine were inquisitive.

Reggie exchanged an anxious smile with us, but Milo was finding it difficult to make eye contact with any of his dining companions. After a long, uncomfortable silence, I asked, "So, kids. What's up with you two? What have you been doing today? Milo?"

Rip flashed me an expression that I deciphered as, "What part of 'let me do the talking' didn't you understand?" I ignored him and turned to hear Reggie reply to my question after waiting several long moments for a response from Milo. "He was working on finishing up a job Cooper had been overseeing."

Rip flashed me another look that clearly meant "Put a lid on it!" And trust me; I can expertly interpret every facial expression in Rip's repertoire. I realized he'd hoped to have a few slugs of whiskey under his belt before he launched into an intense discussion regarding the murder case, and wasn't pleased I'd tossed him into the middle of the ring before he was prepared to throw a punch. But he recovered well from the abrupt change in ambiance amongst our foursome. In a no-nonsense voice, he asked his daughter, "Can your husband no longer speak for himself, Regina Louise?"

Nervously, she turned to Milo and said, "Um, yes, Daddy, of course he can. He's just worn out. Tell them about your project, babe."

"Just removing some drywall to replace some studs and insulation. That's all." Milo explained as briefly as he could without looking up from the table and the napkin he was mindlessly toying with.

"Would that be at the Sarcova home, by any chance?" Rip asked. Milo's head jerked up and he looked Rip in the eyes for the first time that evening.

"Possibly to eradicate black mold from inside the walls?" Rip added, staring at Milo as he waited for a response to his inquiry. With another remark spoken in question-like fashion, he continued. "Black mold that was intentionally covered up to save on the expense to fix an issue you both knew wasn't honest or ethical to conceal?"

When Milo spoke again, his voice was loud and edgy, "That was Cooper's fault, not mine! I was trying my best to convince him we needed to correct a wrong he'd knowingly committed."

"How's that?" Rip asked. "And lower your voice, son. We don't need to cause a scene in a public venue."

"Okay," Milo replied. You could visibly see his manner change into one of resignation. "The company has been in dire straits financially, I'll admit."

As if a light bulb went on over her head, Regina addressed her husband. "Is that why you wouldn't agree to let me get a new car?"

Rip turned to Regina and spoke sternly. "Sit back and keep quiet, Regina. This conversation doesn't concern you. And it's of no consequence why Milo didn't want you to replace a perfectly good vehicle with an unnecessary and exorbitantly priced car you wanted for nothing more than to flaunt as a status symbol. It was a ludicrous idea on your part even if he could afford it. But right now we have more important things to concentrate on. Your husband is still a prime suspect in a murder investigation. We're trying to get to the bottom of it before it adversely affects both of your lives."

Reggie sat back in her chair, her mouth gaping open in shock. As far as I could recall, her father had never spoken so harshly to her before. I reached under the table to pat her knee consolingly. I could feel her pain.

Just then the chair behind me tapped the back of mine as our waitress seated customers at the adjoining table. I glanced over my shoulder to determine if I should reposition my chair to allow more space for the diners behind us. I heard a loud gasp as I looked into the disgruntled eyes of Dr. Patrick O'Keefe. My jaw dropped even lower in shocked surprise than Regina's just had after the tongue-lashing from her father. It wasn't just the Irishman who'd shocked me, but his dining partner, Avery Curry, as well. Considering she'd complained he was stalking her, she seemed to be very accommodating to her ex-husband.

Avery smiled and waved at me in greeting. She started to address me by saying, "You wouldn't believe what happened after you left Jugs—"

"Oh, no! I'm not sitting at this table, miss!" Avery hadn't had time to complete her sentence before her infuriated dinner date exclaimed loudly. "This table won't work for me."

Confused, the waitress said, "But I thought you requested this table next to the water-front window?"

"That was before I noticed who was sitting at the table next to it!"

Avery looked befuddled, as did our waitress, who stumbled over her next words. "Um, I'm sorry, sir. I, uh, didn't realize, uh, there was a problem with, um—"

"I don't want to be soaking wet for a third time this week. And with that lady behind me, the likelihood of it happening is extremely high." The redheaded doctor was too wound up to let anyone else finish a sentence. He ordered the waitress to take them to a different location. "Move us to a table out on the deck so we can enjoy ourselves and listen to the music."

The clearly confused waitress led O'Keefe and his equally baffled ex-wife across the large room toward the door to the outside patio. "I'm so sorry, sir," I heard her mumble before the din of the other customers swallowed up her voice.

"Well, so much for my wish not to make a spectacle of ourselves," Rip said with a roll of his eyes. "Let's wait to continue our discussion until all the other patrons stop gawking at us."

Our drinks arrived, and Rip downed half of his in one long swallow. It seemed to bolster his resolve as he turned back to his son-in-law and said, "Continue with your explanation about the company's financial situation, son."

I could tell by the look on the younger man's face he had hoped the disruption would put an end to the inquisition. He took a deep breath, and said, "The renovation of the Sarcova house was Cooper's responsibility. I was trying to get a duplex ready to sell and had run into a few major complications. It wasn't until after the contract was signed on the project that Cooper told me he'd covered up black mold inside the walls of several rooms with fresh sheetrock and paint. Eradicating the mold properly would have severely cut into our profits, he said. I was livid, but I didn't know how to approach the buyer and admit he'd been screwed over. Neither of us had anticipated a medical emergency would occur involving their young son."

"So you're telling us you didn't agree with your partner's cover-up scheme?" Rip asked.

"You're damn right I didn't agree!" Milo's response was spoken with sincere abomination. "You may not think very highly of me, sir, but I am not a monster. I would never put the life of a child at risk just to save a few bucks. That's one of the things Cooper and I had been arguing about for several weeks before his death. When we were approached by Julio Sarcova about his son's illness, I was appalled. I insisted Cooper immediately correct the matter and make good on Hunter's medical bills, but he balked at the idea."

"Why?" Rip inquired.

For a guy who had very little to say, Milo suddenly couldn't stop talking. He spoke directly to Rip as he replied, "Cooper was in charge of all the finances regarding the MC Hammerheads Construction Company. I was more the hands-on partner who supervised the projects, dealt with suppliers, and lined out the subcontractors. We'd recently taken on a number of projects, and had been paid for two large renovations we'd already completed. I assumed we were in great shape, money-wise, and had hopes of expanding the business. When I told Cooper I wanted to purchase several more duplexes to flip, he tried to convince me it wasn't a good move on the part of the company. I persisted and finally got him to admit we were nearly bankrupt. He eventually told me he'd borrowed money from the company account to pay off some gambling debts."

"In Texas, gaming is illegal. Where was he gambling?" Rip asked.

"Online. He got hooked on some poker site that costs real money to play, and it was real money you had to pay when you lost. He was also into some loan shark for a lot of money he'd lost when he went to Vegas with his girlfriend the first week of September."

"You are referring to the woman accompanying Dr. O'Keefe this evening?" Rip asked, pointing to the couple now dining out on the deck.

"Yes, sir. O'Keefe and his ex-wife out there split right before Cooper took Avery to Vegas on a gambling vacation. I'm surprised to see O'Keefe and Avery dining together tonight, considering the bitter custody battle they've been engaged in."

"Oh!" I said. "So you know about Liz?"

Regina looked at me in bewilderment as her equally bewildered husband nodded in agreement. Milo stopped for a few seconds to regroup and remember where he'd been going with his response to Rip's inquiry about Avery Curry. "So, anyway, he was being badgered and harassed by some dude to pay up. The demands became increasingly threatening."

"Is the loan shark local?" Rip wanted to know. He swallowed the last bit of his drink and signaled to our waitress to bring him another. Reggie was still nursing hers, as was I. However, I noticed the Vodka Collins Milo had ordered after he'd drained his margarita was already half-finished. He quaffed the remainder down in one long swallow and asked the waitress for a refill when she arrived with Rip's drink.

"No. If I remember right, the loan shark lives in El Paso. But he has this thug working for him who's been putting so much pressure on Coop that he started drinking heavier and heavier. The goon was leaving threatening messages on his cell phone using a voice-modulator like you see on TV when someone's being held for ransom."

When Rip briefly glanced at me in perplexity, I said, "There's probably an app for that."

Milo nodded his head, and agreed. "Like everything else, there *is* an app for that, and I'm sure that's what this guy was using to bully Cooper. I tried to get Coop to take the matter to the police, but he wouldn't listen. Said the caller was all talk. I listened to a few of the messages and I thought the voice was British, but I couldn't be certain because of the way it was altered by the modulator."

Rip nodded but didn't respond. He motioned for Milo to continue.

"Eventually, to get this thug off his back, Cooper borrowed money from our business account without telling me. He acted like he wasn't bothered by this guy's terrifying messages, but I knew he was worried. I know I was concerned about what this thug might do to him. So I can't say I totally blame him for tapping our business account. He'd originally planned to get it paid back quickly, no doubt hoping I'd never have to know about it. With his recent out-of-control drinking binges, and all, I wasn't convinced he hadn't accumulated new debt in the meantime. This same dude with the British-sounding voice left a voice-mail on our office phone about a week ago. I discovered the threatening message Friday afternoon when I stopped by our shop to get some time-sensitive documents. On the taped message his eerie-sounding voice said, 'This is your final warning.' Coop had been on the verge of alcoholism for twenty years, but even at his worst, he was at least a functioning drunk. I'm sure that's why he was already blitzed by noon Saturday when I ran into him at Crabby's."

That was quite likely the most words I'd ever heard

Milo speak in a row. And every single one of them was spoken in a trembling and panicky manner, which made me feel for Milo. The agony in his voice reassured me he was telling us the absolute truth.

"And you didn't think to tell all this to the investigators when they interviewed you Monday morning? Couldn't you have at least clued me in about it?" Rip asked. There was resentment in his tone. "What's up with you, Milo? I hate to say it, but in the detective's eyes, you're behaving like a guilty man trying to cover his tracks, bud. What else do you know that you haven't told anyone?"

"I swear I had nothing to do with my friend's murder, Rip! Please believe me. I wouldn't do something like that to my worst enemy." Turning a bit green around the gills, Milo pushed away the appetizer plate next to his glass of water that the waitress had recently delivered.

"Was Cooper your worst enemy at the time of his death, Milo?" Rip asked, clearly not yet won over by his son-in-law's declaration of innocence.

"No, of course not. I loved him like a brother, Rip. I really did. Ask Regina."

Regina nodded woodenly. She'd made it clear earlier she wasn't all that fond of Cooper, but I'm sure she understood the two business partners had a long-standing friendship.

Milo resumed explaining his relationship with the victim. "We've had our squabbles over the years, naturally, but it never affected our friendship. We'd have forgotten and forgiven the Friday afternoon brawl in the bar's parking lot within days, I assure you."

The greenish tint to Milo's complexion made him appear as if the shrimp he'd eaten off the appetizer platter were rancid from being out in the sun too long. But despite any queasiness he might have been experiencing, he continued to defend himself.

"I'm scared to death, sir. Those messages for Cooper have me really shook up, and I'm afraid of what this dude might do to me if I mention him to the cops. You should have heard some of the things he threatened—no, actually promised—to do. Not just to Cooper, but to me and my family, too. He even knew Dusty and Tiffany's names and where they lived. I had hoped the homicide detectives would arrest the killer without me having to put my family's well-being in jeopardy."

It shook me to the core to hear Milo say this bully had even threatened to do harm to my grandchildren. Tiffany was Regina's twenty-eight year-old daughter who lived with her husband in Albuquerque. Dusty, who was named after my late brother, was twenty-six and living in Myrtle Beach, South Carolina, with his male partner. We didn't get to see our grandchildren often, but I spoke with each of them nearly every week on the phone.

"I understand your concern. But you still need to come clean with the crime scene investigators, son. Keeping important information to yourself is not going to help the police force get this killer arrested and off the street." Rip was obviously exasperated with Milo. He tried to reassure Milo and ease his fears. "I'll see to it you have police protection until this murder case is closed."

"Yeah?" Milo's appeared unmoved. He evidently needed more convincing than Rip could offer. I knew I would. "So, what about your daughter, Rip? For that matter, what about you and Rapella? Are we all going to be followed by cops at all times of the day and night? It's Regina I'm most worried about."

"You and me, both, son. No offense." This was clearly a catch-22 situation for Rip. He desperately wanted Cooper Claypool's killer caught and brought to justice. After all, the focus of his life for many years had been putting bad guys behind bars and protecting good guys from being victimized by them. But just as adamantly, he wanted to keep his family safe and sound. Could he really put his only child in harm's way, even if it was his best hope of exonerating her husband?

I felt a light tap on my shoulder. I leaned toward Reggie as she quietly whispered to me. "By 'police protection,' is Daddy referring to that witness protection program where we'd have to move away from everyone we know and assume new identities?"

"No, sweetheart. Nothing near that life-altering. Just police officers keeping an eye out for your personal safety around the clock until this crime is solved and the real killer has been apprehended. Relax, honey. Your dad knows what he's doing, and he'll make sure you're never in any kind of danger." Even as I tried to assure her with my comforting words, I was praying for my daughter's safety. I leaned back in my chair as Rip questioned Milo about the threatening calls.

"Please tell me you saved those messages sent to Cooper by the thug, or thugs."

"No, sir. I'm sorry. I never imagined they'd end up being important in a murder investigation."

"None of them? Seriously, Milo? Not even this last one you just discovered Friday?"

Milo shook his head apologetically for the second time, and Rip slammed his drink down with a thud. It made a hard enough impact that water jumped out of several of the glasses on the table. Then Rip exploded with a few profanities I wouldn't have wanted to repeat. Finally, he settled down and asked wearily, "What in the tarnation were you thinking, boy?"

Half of the people in the restaurant turned to scrutinize us once again. I wanted to tell them all to mind their own business, particularly that nosy Bertha Snow who I'd recognized from across the room. She'd been shoveling it in like she was dead set on acquiring a third, or was it fourth, chin. But as sure as I'm telling you this story, Bertha would be the first to pass on her rendition of the disturbance at our table to every gossip hound in her 'Purple Hat' club.

I restrained myself from making a scene to avoid a disgusted look from Rip, even though he'd prompted the situation himself with his exceedingly loud cursing.

"I guess I wasn't thinking, sir," Milo responded. In alarm, he'd pushed himself a foot or two away from the table when Rip had laid into him. Under normal circumstances, Rip would have requested Milo refer to him by his first name, but I sensed he intentionally didn't in this case so to maintain the upper hand. He wanted to keep Milo on the defensive, where he was more apt to leak any knowledge regarding the murder he'd previously held back. Rip was impatient, wanting this canary to sing with no further delay.

"What's the loan shark's name, Milo?"

"I don't know, sir. Neither Coop nor I had a clue to his true identity."

"Okay. So what *do* you know about this local goon who works for the El Paso loan shark and was pressuring Cooper?" Rip asked.

"Not much. Never met him or heard his real voice. As I told you already, even the British accent might have been a result of the voice disguiser's distortion capabilities. I don't know his actual name, but Coop referred to him as Captain Hook. He must have introduced himself to Cooper with that nickname," Milo replied, before swallowing as if his throat was filling with bile. The poor guy looked miserable, and I felt for him. I knew he was being more open and honest than Rip could have hoped, but it wasn't nearly enough to satisfy the former detective.

"Okay," Rip said. He took a long, deep breath to keep himself calm. He was usually a very mild-mannered man. But if you ignited his fuse, you'd better jump when and exactly how high he demanded. With annoyance, he asked, "So let me ask you this. What have you done about the financial quagmire the company had found itself in? Have you personally done anything to try and appease Julio Sarcova?"

"I tried. Coop knew MC Hammerheads was in the red already and didn't want to borrow the money to satisfy the buyer. I appealed to him to let me loan the company some capital, interest-free, until things turned around. I'd been putting excess funds away for a rainy day and felt it was in Reg's and my best interest to use our personal savings to get the company back into the black." Milo paused to turn toward Regina, shrug, and whisper, "I'm sorry." Then he turned his attention back to Rip and continued. "After all, MC Hammerheads provides a major portion of our livelihood, and taxes on Key Allegro don't come cheap, you know."

"Yes, I *do* know. If you remember right, I tried to talk you two out of buying a pricey home on the island until you had accumulated enough money in savings to put down a substantial down payment. But, instead you—"

I interrupted Rip before he veered off course just when we were gathering crucial information. "Honey, that's water under the bridge. Let's stay on topic and let Milo continue with his story."

Rip nodded after a short hesitation and encouraged Milo to continue.

"So, I knew we had several lucrative contracts on the horizon if we bid the jobs conservatively. If we'd tried to make it all back on one project, we'd never be the lowest bidder. But I couldn't convince the hard-headed guy to let me help bid the jobs, or fix the issue and prevent a lawsuit. I mean, don't get me wrong. I loved the dude like a brother, but he could be very obstinate and hard to deal with at times. I was concerned about his drinking and gambling, but I couldn't get him to talk it over with me. That's basically what started the fight in Crabby's parking lot. I found him drinking there after he'd told me he'd be visiting his dying uncle. He'd promised to complete a project we were coming down to the wire on before he left for San Antonio. I was counting on him to make good on his word, you know. But he accomplished nothing on either Thursday or Friday, and the job was left to me to finish, which I managed to do Saturday morning before I headed over to Crabby's. We had enough to deal with as it was, without one partner bailing out on the other and leaving him in a tight spot."

"I see. So it sounds like he had his own demons to deal with," Rip replied, thoughtfully. "I assume you knew about the company's ever-increasing debt to Mack's Well Company, also. Correct?"

"What? What debt?" It was clear by the way Milo's face instinctively flushed, he knew nothing of the impending lawsuit threatened by Mack Schilling to recover the money due the well-digging company. I totally believed him when he said, "I have no idea what debt you're referring to."

Rip asked me to explain to Milo what we'd learned earlier that day at Mack's Wells, Inc. Afterward, Milo turned to Reggie and asked, "Why didn't you tell me about that before we headed over here for supper?"

Regina had been silent like I had, still brooding about the dressing-down she'd received from her father, I'd guess. She looked as if the bartender had slipped a mickey in her peach margarita and I had to nudge her to bring her out of her stupor. She recovered quickly and replied, "For one thing, Milo, I thought you surely knew about it, and I was angry you hadn't discussed it with me. This morning was the first I'd heard about it, too. And I didn't have time to say anything about it earlier today. You got home ten minutes before we had to leave to arrive here by five."

"I'm sorry, Reg. I was kept in the dark about our blossoming financial woes. Cooper never said much to me about the bills and payments. I knew very little about the money side of the business. That was Coop's wheelhouse and I trusted him. Foolishly, of course, but I didn't realize it at the time. I was more of the hands-on partner. Cooper was rarely on site, unless I needed a helping hand to get a project finished. Just like I needed on Saturday morning, but I assumed Coop was with Uncle Charlie."

As Milo spoke, our waitress was passing out plates of

delectable-looking food. The aroma had my stomach growling. We spent the next forty minutes lingering over our supper. Milo looked drained and emotional, so I was relieved when Rip chose not to continue the conversation after we'd finished our meals. Instead he hugged Regina, and put his arm around Milo as he said, "Let's talk tomorrow, son. We'll drop by after breakfast. Keep your head up, Milo. We're here for you and Regina and will do whatever it takes to help."

As I got in the truck and fastened my seatbelt, I wondered how much "whatever it takes" was going to cost us. Not only in money, but in blood, sweat, and tears, as well.

CHAPTER 15

I got up with the chickens the following morning. After a cup of coffee, I walked over to the campground pool to swim a few laps and get some much-needed exercise. While I'd been over-working my brain, I'd been under-working my body. I left a note next to the coffeemaker so Rip wouldn't be concerned at my absence when he crawled out of bed. I knew he'd tossed and turned half the night and was, at last, dead asleep when I quietly slipped out from under the covers. Under normal circumstances, Rip beat me up nearly every day. (And that's something you want to be careful saying lest you get your husband arrested for spousal abuse.)

After an hour of water aerobics and laps, I returned to the Chartreuse Caboose to find Rip reading the *Corpus Christi Times*. He had walked to the campground office and bought one from the paper machine out front. He glanced up at me, and said, "This article I just read says despite the best efforts of the investigating team, no perpetrator has been arrested in the murder case of the fifty-two year-old Rockport construction worker. It goes on to say the DNA report on some skin found under the victim's fingernail came back matching that of the victim's. My guess, Claypool probably scratched a mosquito bite or something."

"Does the article say if they found any useful trace evidence at all?" I asked.

"No, what little trace evidence they'd been able to recover was all attributed to Claypool, so the results were of no benefit to the case, according to Sheriff Peabody. Then the article states the only suspect under investigation at this time was the victim's business partner, but so far they'd been unable to discover any non-circumstantial evidence against him. Didn't mention Milo's name, but everyone in town knows who they're referring to. Real subtle, huh?"

Rip's aggravation with the media was apparent, and I wasn't happy with them either. The evening news the night before had also indicated Milo was the main suspect. The reporters obviously had no credible information to share, so they threw Milo under the bus, probably in order to appease the public with some kind of update and make their assignment newsworthy. If the evidence against Milo was as overwhelming as the media had been implying, he'd already be under arrest for first-degree murder."

"That's not fair! It's just plain wrong to drag someone's character through the mud when there's no concrete evidence to prove they're guilty of the crime. They should have to wait until they have substantial proof against a suspect before they can denigrate him in newspaper articles and television broadcasts," I said indignantly. "It's no different than when some kid accuses a teacher of some form of abuse; physical, verbal, sexual or otherwise. The media never seems to take into account the child might have just wanted to get back at the teacher for giving their pathetic book report a failing grade. The poor teacher's life is turned upside down and his integrity and character are irreparably destroyed before his innocence can be verified."

"Calm down, sweetheart. I totally agree with you, but I'm not awake enough yet to be up in arms about it, or anything else," Rip said. He pulled out the chair across from where he'd been sitting at the kitchen table and urged me to take a seat while he poured me a glass of orange juice. He must have instinctively known I had far exceeded my morning quota of caffeine. Perhaps the only clues he needed were my bugged-out eyes, flailing arms, and the incensed exclamations erupting from my mouth during my rant against the media.

We sipped on our juice as we exchanged sections of the newspaper. I read an article about the diminishing amount of oysters being harvested in Aransas Bay. The oystermen were only averaging fifteen to twenty bags full per commercial boat. The article stated the season was November first to April thirtieth coast-wide in Texas. "Aransas Bay, once a plentiful source of oysters, has been over-harvested for so long, the beds are about gone. A poor oyster harvest isn't only tough on me, it's hard on the local economy too," a local boat owner named Philip Bean was quoted as saying.

There was a black and white photo of the oysterman but the sun was behind him, silhouetting Mr. Bean's body and making his features hard to distinguish. More of his statements were included in the article. "I've been working my crew hard, trying to dredge up enough oysters to keep the operation running. But between the fuel and the help, I'm barely breaking even this season. I'm about to the point of begging a few adventuresome tourists to go out with me just for the experience of harvesting oysters."

I sat back and thought about this article for a few minutes. My mind wasn't nearly as sharp as it'd been fifteen to twenty years ago. Or, more honestly, even fifteen or twenty days ago; my memory seemed a tad bit fuzzier with each and every revolution of the sun. But I knew the name Philip sounded familiar. I thought perhaps Rip might have a lot more brain cells left than I did, so I asked, "Honey, do you remember the name Milo gave us for that third fishing buddy of his and

Cooper's? Wasn't it Philip?"

"What third fishing buddy?"

"Never mind." So much for Rip having an overabundance of brain cells to throw around. Granted, we both were holding on to a corpse at the time Milo was talking about this friend of his. Still, the name Philip rang a bell with me. I recalled Milo telling us that he and Cooper had a friend who bought a spear-gun at the same sporting expo as they had. They called this man Pinto, as in pinto *beans*, and Philip's last name was indeed Bean, according to the article I'd just read. And now I realized that when Milo said Pinto didn't have time to fish this time of year because he was "out in his boat working from daybreak to dusk," he almost certainly was saying Pinto was a commercial oyster harvester.

What are the odds this Philip Bean is the third of the three stooges? For that matter, what are the odds this so-called friend of Milo and Cooper's called Pinto was involved in Cooper Claypool's murder? I wondered. And was this fellow in the newspaper article serious when he said he'd like tourists to help him in exchange for the experience of harvesting oysters?

Suddenly there was nothing I wanted to do more than experience firsthand the art of harvesting oysters!

Needless to say, Rip was less enthusiastic than I about the opportunity to learn how oyster boats operated. When I explained my reasoning, he rolled his eyes and asked, "Have you lost what few marbles you had left? There's an impressive fleet of oyster and shrimp boats moored in Fulton Marina. It's beyond me how you came to the conclusion that the Philip Bean in that newspaper article is the third friend the boys called Pinto. Have you been into the cooking sherry again, sweetheart? Sniffing the crazy glue? I'm serious, Rapella. You're grasping at straws now."

"What?" I couldn't believe Rip had said that after all

the leads I had uncovered in our private investigation of Claypool's death. He acted as if he thought I'd become a Loony Tune; Cuckoo for Cocoa Puffs. He quickly endorsed that impression with, "I'm afraid you're losing it, sister."

The fact Rip had the habit of calling any man who was younger than him "boy" usually tickled my funny bone, but none of my bones were laughing this time. And whenever he referred to me as "sister," I knew he was annoyed. But it didn't shut me up this time because I was now more annoyed at him than he was at me.

"Listen, buster. You may think I'm being ridiculous, but I think it's worth looking in to. The detectives have made no breakthroughs in their investigation. Sometimes checking out a hunch pays off, you know. Remember that case you had involving the elderly woman working as a greeter at Wal-Mart? She was so old and frail the store manager should have held a mirror under her nose every hour or so just to make sure she was still alive. And do you remember what your gut told you? You had a hunch she was behind the rash of thefts. Sure enough, she was caught shoplifting jewelry on her breaks and hiding the loot in her under—"

Rip cut me off with an offensive expletive. He then said, "Mrs. Primrose's kleptomania is hardly on the same level as this murder case. We haven't got the luxury or time to chase down every wild goose in the county. I'm going to the station today to discuss the potential suspects we've tracked down and see if they've been given thorough-enough scrutinizing. I might have to tear down walls to get in to see Detective Reeves again, but I'm going to give it my best shot."

"Okay, fine. But not before I drop a dime on my new son-in-law," I replied, resentfully. I reached for the cell phone and found Milo's name on the contact list. He picked up on the fourth ring as I was thinking about the voice mail message I might have to leave.

"Quick question, Milo," I said, pleasantly after greeting

him. "By any chance, is Philip Bean the friend you referred to on Sunday as Pinto?"

"Yeah. Why do you ask?"

Before I responded, I turned and nodded at Rip with a smug smile I couldn't resist. Then I asked Milo, "Do you know if he's been interviewed by the homicide detectives?"

"Yeah, he called me from the police station yesterday morning. He'd been totally shocked at the news of Coop's murder. Pinto said he heard about it from a fisherman when he was delivering some table shrimp to a bait stand in Rockport Harbor. Did you know you can buy table shrimp to cook at some of—?"

"I'm interested in any motive Pinto might have had to kill your friend, not boiling shrimp for supper. Please stay on point, Milo."

"Yeah, okay. So he drove straight to the police station to see if there was anything he could do to help out with the investigation. The detectives interviewed Pinto, of course. But he was cleared right away and Detective Reeves took down his cell number in case they needed to contact him later," Milo replied. "Which, as far as I know, they haven't."

"Rip and I were just discussing how often a premonition turns out to be right on target. So, what's your gut feeling about Pinto? Could he be putting on a front? Any chance he had a 'pissed-off bone' to pick with Cooper and lied about it to the detectives?"

"Nah. He thought the world of Coop. We met Philip at the same bait shop I was just talking about, only a short time after he moved here from Galveston about four or five years ago. He supplies a number of stands with shrimp, mullet, crabs, and even sea lice, to sell as bait. He told me once he makes more money supplying bait stands than he does harvesting oysters."

Milo was straying off topic again, but this explained to me why neither Rip nor I had ever heard of Philip Bean before. Being an officer of the law here for so many years, there were very few Rockport residents Rip wasn't at least somewhat familiar with. But Philip Bean had relocated here after we'd already left the area to become full-time RVers. He most likely wouldn't realize we were Milo's in-laws. Not recognizing Rip as the former sheriff of this county would be to our advantage, too, if we got the opportunity to speak with the oysterman. "Where might we locate Mr. Bean to speak with him?"

"Why would you want to speak to Pinto? He already spoke to the detectives and was cleared. He wouldn't have any clue what happened to Coop, I'm sure."

"You're no doubt correct," I replied. "But just for the pure heck of it, tell me a little more about him."

"Well, all right. Not that it's going to help any. Trust me!" Milo seemed very reluctant to talk about Pinto. It was almost as if he felt he was ratting out a close friend.

Why does it seem to me that every time Milo opens his mouth, my faith in him gets a little more uncertain? I wondered. And why, whenever he says "Trust me," does my trust in him plummet even further?

I was suddenly aware our premise of vindicating Milo was on shaky ground. How could we persuade an entire team of investigators our son-in-law was in no way, shape, or form connected to Cooper Claypool's death when we weren't convinced ourselves? I listened closely when Milo finally began to explain his and Cooper's relationship to Philip Bean.

"Pinto's an older dude who probably shouldn't even still be oystering at his age, but he goes spear-fishing with us on occasion too. Never out of season, though. Pinto seems to be in excellent condition. He's always treated us both as if we were his own sons. The old man shared a lot of interesting stories with us, and on occasion, a rare nugget of wisdom."

"That's nice," I said, not swayed one bit. I was certain Ted Bundy and Jack the Ripper could have spun fascinating tales too, and even once in awhile come up with some drivel a guy like Milo would consider wisdom. "How *old* is this buddy of yours?"

`"Well, um, I didn't mean to say he was old, you know, just um, you see, I meant just older than us," Milo stammered.

"How much older?"

"Well, you know, a few years."

"Exactly how old is Pinto, Milo?" I felt like I was trying to pull a rolling pin through a keyhole.

"Pinto's like sixty-seven, I think."

"Okay. I'll give you a pass on that one, even though I don't consider Rip and me old at sixty-eight. When you're Pinto's age, in a mere fifteen years, I guarantee you won't consider sixty-seven old, either. So, anyway, had there been any ill will at all between him and Cooper recently?"

"I dunno. I don't think so. Why? You aren't seriously thinking Pinto might have killed Coop, are you?"

"You never know. As my pal, Lexie Starr, told me, you never want to leave any stone unturned when you're investigating a crime. Do you think he'd let us help out on his oyster boat? You know, just for the experience and all. He made a comment to that effect in an article in this morning's paper."

"Yeah, I read that too. But I doubt he meant it literally. Pinto surely knew Cooper and I would give him a hand whenever he seriously needed some free labor. So, are you saying you want to feel him out?"

"Of course we do. Got a problem with that? We're trying to prove you're innocent, you realize. And if that takes incriminating a good friend of yours, then so be it."

"I know. And I appreciate your help. I really do," Milo sounded sad. After a brief silence, he added, "Let me give him a call and I'll get back—"

"No! Wait! I don't want him to know of our connection to Cooper, or to you. And, I certainly don't want him forewarned of our intention to question him.

Understand?"

Silence.

"Understand?" I repeated.

Sustained silence. I looked at the phone to ensure the seconds were still clicking off. We hadn't been disconnected.

"I asked you, Milo, if you understood what I told you and agree not to give him advance notice of our desire to meet with him." I wasn't going to take no for an answer. Nor was I going to except a non-response as an affirmative one.

"Okay. I promise I won't contact him," he finally said.

"Where can we find him? We'll arrange an accidental meeting, so to speak." As I spoke with Milo, Rip was shaking his head and groaning. If he rolled his eyes one more time, I hoped they'd get stuck in that position, like my momma used to say would happen to me when I'd crossed mine just for fun.

"He hangs out on his boat most of the time, even when he's not out in the bay working. He's kind of a lonely old, er, I mean mature, man. That's why we invite him out fishing with us now and then. Sometimes Coop and I would stop by the marina just to visit with him. Share a beer, and shoot the shit, you know." I could detect a fondness for Philip Bean in Milo's voice. He confirmed my deduction when he added, "He didn't kill Coop. Pinto loved him, and I'm pretty sure he would have given his own life to save Cooper's. He's a real decent and straight-shooting kind of guy."

"I agree he's an unlikely suspect, Milo. We'll in no way insinuate we believe he's capable of murder. But conversing with him might lead to some clue we've overlooked that'd help nail down the real killer. So, what's his boat look like?"

"Pretty much like every other oyster boat in the marina. It's white with a faded orange stripe down the sides. Only real distinguishing feature is the boat's name, 'Hook 'em,' painted on the stern."

"Hook 'em?"

"Yeah. He spent most of his life in Austin, you see."

"Oh, sure. I get it. 'Hook'em Longhorns' is the motto of the University of Texas, which is located in Austin. Right?" As a long-time Texan, I knew how devoted Longhorn fans were.

"Yeah."

"Okay, then. Pinto's boat should be easy to locate," I said. "And I think it's worth a shot, don't you?"

"Whatever," Milo said. He sounded like a man who had resigned himself to let the chips fall where they may. I wasn't about to let that happen. I've heard of many a prisoner who's been exonerated after being falsely incarcerated for several decades. I was determined my daughter's new husband wasn't going to be one of them.

I ended the call and looked into Rip's eyes. Without saying a word, he knew what I was asking. With a deep sigh, and a shake of his head, he echoed Milo's halfhearted reply. "Whatever."

"You do realize I think you're barking up the wrong tree thinking this Philip Bean had anything to do with the murder, don't you?" Rip asked me before he took a cautious sip from his cup of steaming "Jumping Red Fish" espresso. I was already over-caffeinated so had ordered "Copano Sunset," a Nicaraguan decaf.

We'd decided to grab a quick bite to eat at the Rockport Daily Grind on South Austin Street where the best coffee in town could be found. Their daily quiche specials were favorites of ours, too. We didn't linger over breakfast as we usually did; chatting with the gregarious owner or getting acquainted with newcomers visiting Rockport and/or the coffee shop for the first time. It was already almost eight and we didn't have time to dawdle. Before ending the call with Milo, he'd warned me Pinto liked to head out of the marina at straight-up nine.

Twenty minutes later, Rip and I were strolling down the parking lot next to the bulkhead at Fulton Marina. As expected, it didn't take long to find Philip Bean's boat. The captain of the "Hook 'em" stood in the hull of the boat stacking empty burlap bags in a neat pile when we walked up. Darkly tanned, his face was weathered and wrinkled from too many hours in the sun. He seemed to personify the *Old Man and the Sea* character, Santiago. In Hemingway's story, Santiago killed a large Mako shark with a harpoon, much in the same way Cooper had been speared. For some odd reason I felt sad, just as I had when I'd read the classic novel.

Dressed in old but clean denim overalls, Philip Bean looked older than most of us sexagenarians. I'm not sure why they call a person in their sixties a *sex*agenarian because, at least in our case, it had become somewhat of a rare occasion when sex entered the picture.

The scene before us now, of a fellow working aboard his old boat with its veneer as weathered as the fisherman's face, was so peaceful and serene that my first instinct was to snap a photo with our cell phone. It reminded me of an old painting I'd admired in one of Rockport's many art galleries. It made me wish for a moment that I, too, had the talent to capture this scene on a canvas.

"Good morning, sir. Beautiful day, isn't it?" I asked to catch Philip Bean's attention.

With a friendly smile, he tilted his head up, nodded, and replied, "Aye-aye, my lady. Morning to you folks, too."

He immediately resumed stacking bags. He didn't seem anxious to be distracted from his task. That didn't stop me from trying to start a conversation with him, however. "Say, you look familiar. Aren't you that fellow I read about in the *Times* this morning?"

"That I am." His response was short and given without a pause in his work. Rip gave me a "let's not bother the guy" look, which I naturally ignored.

"If I recall correctly, you mentioned the possibility of taking tourists out on an oyster run and letting them work in exchange for the unique experience. Were you serious?" I asked.

He set down the empty burlap bag he was holding and turned toward us. After giving us the once over and apparently deciding we didn't look like productive oystering material, he replied. "Nah, just joking with the kind lady who writes for the paper. It's been a rough season so far. Hard on the bones. Harder on the wallet, though."

"Oh, dear. That's not good. Too bad you were just kidding. My husband and I would love to go out with you and learn how an oyster boat functions. It would be a memorable adventure for the two of us. It really does sound like a lot of fun."

"Aye. It is that," the man agreed. "For about five minutes. After that it's just hard, backbreaking labor."

Rip spoke up then. "I can only imagine. Have you thought about retiring? Men our age should be kicking back, enjoying life while we still have any of it left."

"Then what would I do?" Pinto asked, wearily. "This ol' bloke's gotta keep eating. This season's even worse than when we had the red tide a few years back. So, you see, I ain't exactly rolling in it. No retirement fund to fall back on in this bloody business. And my Social Security check won't even pay for the fuel to operate this hunk of junk."

Rip nodded solemnly; obviously sorry he'd asked the man such a personal question.

"Yeah, I hear ya." I shook my head as I commiserated with the poor fellow. I wanted to appear humble, as if we were in the same boat he was. Truth was, if we hung around Milo and Regina much longer, we really *would* be sharing Pinto's financial woes.

"At least I don't sail outta here at first light like I did in previous years. I'm getting too old to get motivated that bloody early in the morn."

"Yeah, I hear ya," I repeated.

I could feel the door closing on our chance to question him about Cooper Claypool and started to turn to walk away when I was surprised by the craggy man's next words.

"If you folks would like to tag along on our run today, I'll be happy to welcome you aboard. My crew should be here shortly. I don't want you involved in the work, though. It can be a dangerous job if you're not used to it."

"I'll bet!" Rip said cheerfully. His attitude had suddenly improved dramatically, now that he knew he wouldn't be expected to earn his way.

"Oh, my goodness!" I exclaimed. I jumped an inch or two off the pavement in exhilaration, then placed a hand on each cheek and gushed. "That would be wonderful, sir. Thank you so much. Are you sure you don't mind? We wouldn't want to be in your way while you're trying to earn a living."

My exaggerated giddiness was not lost on Rip, who muttered under his breath, "Easy, girl."

"No worries. I'd enjoy the company; someone new to converse with 'sides the crew who talk about nothing but hot women and their next drunk fest." With a laugh the seaman leaned over the side of his boat and reached across the span between the stern of his boat and the bulkhead to shake my hand. "My name's Philip Bean, as you already know from the newspaper article. But I'd prefer you call me Pinto like everyone else does."

"Aye, aye, Captain Pinto," I playfully replied with a salute. "And you can call me Rapella."

He then turned to Rip and the two men introduced themselves. Pinto must have noticed Rip's "God help me" expression. He asked, "You sure you're up for it, my friend?"

"I guess so. You know how it is. Gotta keep the old lady happy." In response to Rip's smart aleck remark, the oysterman flashed Rip a knowing smile. When Rip quit grinning like the Cheshire Cat, I punched him in the shoulder in retaliation for being dubbed his "old lady."

Pinto laughed and told us he was planning a short run that day because two of his three deck hands had to attend a court-ordered AA meeting that afternoon. With a shrug, Pinto added, "Can't keep the Willis boys off the hooch, if you know what I mean. They're both one DUI away from hoofing it. But help's hard to find these days. You gotta take what you can get. If I pay the Willis boys just enough clams to buy a couple of six-packs, they're happy as a clam at high tide."

Pinto chuckled at his own clever double entendre, which I thought was a fitting analogy for a guy in his line of work.

Rip laughed along with Pinto, and then said, "Yeah, I know what you mean. Things just aren't like they were back in our day, are they?"

"For sure." Pinto agreed before he motioned for us to walk down the pier next to his boat. He reached out his hand to assist each of us in turn as we boarded his boat. Even though I had an ulterior motive for wanting to be there, I truly was eager to watch an oyster boat in operating mode. Rip's disposition was rather subdued, more resigned than anything.

I was ready to set sail, looking forward to a new adventure. I didn't realize it at the time, but I'd soon be looking forward even more to getting my feet back on solid ground.

CHAPTER 16

We watched as a faded green vehicle pulled into the marina's parking lot. Two sketchy looking men in their mid to upper twenties wearing stained, tattered jeans crawled out of the cab. Both were of medium height and didn't have a spare ounce of fat between them. One of them, the crustier of the two, opened the tool box alongside the bed of the El Camino and brought out two pair of thick rubber gloves. The other one reached in and grabbed a couple of pairs of rubber boots.

A newer model Jeep Wrangler with no top pulled up beside the El Camino, and a middle-aged man built like a WWE wrestler joined the other two fellows. I was surprised to see his right arm was a prosthetic, with a stainless steel claw on the end where his fingers should have been. *Maybe he's a lumberjack who had a rough go-round with his ax*, I thought. *If so, at least he left his blue ox at home.*

"There's my motley crew now," Pinto said. "Billy, Bob, and Spider."

"Spider?" Rip asked.

"Aye. Don't know why he's called Spider, and don't want to know. But that's what he asked me to call him."

"What happened to the big dude's arm?" I asked, even

though it was none of my concern.

"Bob's never said and I've never asked." Obviously, Pinto was not inflicted with my inquisitive nature. He went on to say, "But he uses that hook so efficiently, you'd never know he wasn't using two real hands like everyone else. He opens and closes it using the muscles of his back. I ran into him at Tackle Town one day and instead of the hook, he had on a prosthetic arm and hand that looked so authentic it was difficult to tell it wasn't real."

"Yeah, it's remarkable what they can do these days, isn't it?"

"For sure."

Watching the three men walk toward the boat, I had second thoughts about tagging along on the abbreviated oyster run. If I'd happened upon this trio in a dark alley, I'd die of heart failure before they had the opportunity to mug me. I glanced at Rip, who didn't look any less skeptical than I was.

After they came aboard, Pinto introduced the guys to us. The brothers, Spider and Billy Willis, looked as if they hadn't invested more than two bucks in laundry detergent their entire adult lives. They both had a fishy smell to them, as well. I was glad the fish stench was nearly masked by the overwhelming odor of liquor. They were already into the "hooch" and it wasn't even nine yet. When the taller and rattier one extended his hand to shake, I waved him off, "Sorry. Sore finger. But it's nice to meet you, Spider."

I tried hard not to gag at the nasty aroma radiating from the man. It was on par with a bag of rotten potatoes I'd once found in a plastic tub in an under-carriage storage compartment. After a few unbearable seconds, I had to turn away from Spider in pretense of being startled by the squawking sound of a blue heron chasing a snowy egret away from his territory. It was a sound I'd heard many, many times before, but one I thought might alarm a tourist from up north.

I waved at Spider's brother, and said, "You must be Billy. Nice to meet you two."

Rip was apparently able to ignore the smell and greeted the two men with a warm handshake. Was this the same man who frequently informed me I had too much perfume on?

Rip looked up as Pinto introduced him to Bob who, by my estimation, stood about six-foot-five, and weighed around three-hundred pounds. His build and stature reminded me of Mack Schilling. Bob was massive, but not slovenly or tubby. Clean shaven, appropriately clothed, and solid muscle. He even emitted a nice scent I recognized as Jovan Musk.

"Nice guns," Rip said admiringly, as he shook the dude's right hand. At least his deformity didn't affect his handshake, or most likely, his writing. Bob had a ninety-six percent chance of having been born right-handed. His missing left arm could have been a birth defect, which would have automatically made him right-handed, even if by default.

"Hello, I'm Rapella," I said politely with a wave.

When he opened his mouth to respond, I noticed his two front teeth were absent. He had a jagged chip on his bottom left incisor, and his first bicuspid on the bottom right was missing entirely. His gap-toothed smile seemed out of place because all of his remaining teeth appeared straight and bright. His gums below the missing teeth were red and inflamed, as if he'd had them knocked out recently.

His parents had probably drained their nest egg to get their boy braces and wouldn't be too pleased with his smile today. Growing up on fluoride-free well water, I'd had bad teeth when I was the Willis boys' age. But I'd nipped the potential of an ever-expanding expense in the bud and had them all pulled and replaced with dentures when I was only twenty-eight. I'm too money conscious to pay for new choppers more than once.

Perhaps my curious expression was telling, because

after introducing himself to both of us, Bob remarked with a touch of a lisp. "Excuse my missing teeth, folks. I've got a dentist appointment scheduled to get them taken care of."

"I'd hate to see the other guy," Rip quipped jokingly.

Bob just grinned and began to put his rubber boots on, evidently not interested in explaining what had occurred to cause his jack-o-lantern smile.

At straight-up nine we set sail, departing the marina through an opening in the jetty. We tracked north for several minutes before we turned west to cross under the long Copano Bay Bridge, which was under construction. A new bridge was being built east of the current bridge, which was east of the original bridge. The three bridges stood side-by-side, spanning the open water. The oldest bridge had been utilized as a fishing pier for years. It had a wide gap in the center to let vessels enter into Copano Bay. The one under construction was lofty enough to allow future passageway for sailboats and other taller vessels.

Standing at the helm, Pinto turned to Rip and me and hollered, "There's a reef over there I want to try first. If it's not productive, we'll head over to the island where we usually go. Oysters have become so few and far between, it's hardly worth the effort anymore. They really should close both bays for a couple of years to give the oysters time to spawn and replenish the beds. Of course, I'd die of starvation in the interim."

Pinto's smile indicated he'd been kidding, but the grim expression that quickly replaced the grin said otherwise. The din from the motor and wind made conversation difficult, so Rip and I just nodded in response. Before long, we arrived at the area our captain had pointed toward. As the men worked to get the dredge ready, the boat gently rocked back and forth. The undulating motion felt soothing.

Rip and I had come to the marina prepared for the possibility of going out on the water that day; we ate a light breakfast at the Daily Grind, donned comfortable clothing, sunscreen, deck shoes and sunglasses, and put on headwear for protection from the sun. Rip had chosen a cheesy ball cap he'd purchased at Yellowstone National Park when we'd worked at a campground there one summer for free rent and a little cash. I wore a large-brimmed straw hat with a chin strap. It made me look like I should be on my hands and knees planting petunias in a flower garden. But I was glad we'd thought to bring them, even though the sun was only rarely peeking out from behind the clouds. The worse sunburn I'd ever sustained had been on a mostly cloudy day and it was not an experience I wanted to repeat.

The swells caused the boat to bob up and down, so Rip and I looked around for a safer, more comfortable place to observe the harvesting procedure. Aware of our concern, Pinto motioned for us to sit on top of a large padded cooler. It was stable, out of the wind, and provided us a good view of the operation. We'd have to play it by ear on how and when to initiate a conversation with Pinto about the homicide case.

The men began lowering the dredge, a strong wire mesh basket-looking contraption. After it had dropped to the bottom of the bay, Pinto began steering the boat in a circular pattern, dragging the basket along the sea floor. He appeared delighted after they hoisted up the dredge on a pulley and spilled its contents out onto a large and severely scratched-up wooden table. The platform had a railing constructed with two-by-fours around its perimeter that prevented any spillage.

Pinto walked back to the stern and all four men began sorting through the pile, tossing sea weed overboard first. They picked out a few clams and a large blue crab, depositing them in two separate plastic containers that resembled webbed laundry baskets. After all the other odds and ends were removed from the pile, they began sorting through the oysters, culling out the larger ones and pitching the smaller ones, and dead shells, back into the water. I observed how they used mallets to break apart the clusters.

Pinto had not exaggerated about Bob's abilities. Even with a prosthetic arm that employed a metal hook in lieu of a hand, he was as quick and nimble as the other three men working alongside him who had full use of both their natural upper limbs. Because of his bulk, I dubbed him Big Bob. He showed no sign of being disabled at all. But then I've always considered "disabled" and "handicapped" to be a frame of mind more than a physical condition. Earlier I had wondered if the missing limb was a birth defect, and now that seemed quite likely, because Big Bob utilized the hook as if he'd been doing it his entire life. Pinto had never inquired about what had necessitated Bob's need for a prosthetic, so I decided not to be nosy and ask, either.

This dredge-dragging, basket-dumping routine was repeated numerous times as multiple burlap sacks were filled with oysters and stacked off to the side. The three men worked at a rapid, but harmonious, pace. Bob remained silent for the most part while the Willis brothers chatted about a "blond bombshell" who worked at the local Dairy Queen, and a party they were attending that evening at Redfish Willie's.

I hadn't gotten my sea legs yet, but I wanted to get a closer look at the variety of stuff they were acquiring from off the sea floor. They'd already found two marine batteries, a rusty spinning reel, and a hard plastic chunk from the shroud of an Evinrude boat motor. They'd dragged up enough tangled fishing line to wrap around the bay twice and cussed the anglers who'd thoughtlessly deposited it in the bay.

When an anchor was dredged up along with a bucket full of oysters, I was happy to discover I wasn't the only person to toss one overboard without tying it to the boat first. Now perhaps Rip would quit teasing me about the mishap.

I wobbled over toward the table like a drunken bum and asked the men, "How big do they have to be?"

Billy held an oyster up and said, "Like this one. At least three inches wide."

"Then it looks like you got a lot of keepers there," I said, happy for Pinto. It appeared to me to have been a productive day so far. Out of pure politeness, I said, "They look delicious."

"Here you go, lady," Spider said, splitting open an oyster and tossing it my way. "Try one."

Naturally, I fumbled the catch. I nearly lost my balance trying to juggle the oyster, but it fell to the deck anyway. I retrieved the shell and opened it completely, staring down at my worst nightmare. I was revolted at the idea of eating the raw oyster but didn't want to seem unappreciative. "Thanks, Spider."

"Yeah, okay, lady."

I hadn't really expected the oldest Willis boy to remember my name for longer than a few seconds, and he looked surprised I'd remembered his. Even with my ever-increasing number of senior moments, a name like "Spider" was hard to forget.

Spider reached around Bob and handed me another oyster, clearly not wanting to watch an instant replay of my first clumsy attempt to catch one. I was relieved when he said, "Give this to Rip."

"Okay. Thanks again!"

Raw oysters are one of those things you either love or you hate. Rip loved them. Me, not so much. But I felt obligated to somehow get the one Spider gave me down with four pairs of eyes staring at me, waiting for my opinion of the coveted delicacy. Knowing I detested oysters, Rip watched me with an ornery grin plastered across his face as I nearly gagged trying to swallow the despicable thing. The oyster felt like a raw egg slithering down my throat. I badly wanted to run to the side of the boat and spit it out, but I suffered through it. I nodded at the men, and said, "Um, yeah. Very good. Quite salty though."

And disgustingly slimy, I thought.

"Wouldn't you like another one, dear, seeing how you enjoyed that first one so much?" Rip asked. I gave him a look that would make a grizzly race back into his den.

I turned back toward the Willis brothers, and Billy, having heard my husband's remark, handed me yet another oyster. And the boy, God bless him, had hand-picked the largest damned oyster he could find. "Here you go, grandma. Bottom's up!"

I wasn't sure I appreciated being called "grandma" by a scuzzball like Billy Willis but felt I had no other choice but to down the second ghastly ball of goo. The next look I shot Rip, after I managed to choke it down, would have killed that grizzly before it'd even have a chance to turn and run.

I wanted to slap the smirk right off his face. He glanced over at Pinto and asked, "Mind if I have one more too?"

"Absobloodylootely! Have all you want, bub. You too, my lady."

When I didn't enthusiastically lunge for another oyster, Pinto cheerfully encouraged us both to partake. "Help yourself, folks. There's plenty to go around. We've happened upon a generous bed this morning. So generous, in fact, I'm surprised it isn't in a restricted area. Have all you want, folks."

"I think I'd better limit myself to two. Unfortunately, too much sodium's not good for my hypertension," I replied, pasting on my most convincing expression of disappointment.

Rip, however, couldn't eat enough of them. After I reclaimed my perch on the cooler, he wandered over to an open bag of oysters and began gobbling them down. I was relieved he seemed to be enjoying himself, but not totally surprised. Food always had been the shortest route to Rip's heart. Joking and chatting with the crew, he'd eventually had his fill of the little goobers. After utilizing the head, he elbowed his way in at the table and began picking out crabs, clams, and other bits and pieces out of the spoils, as the other men culled through the oysters.

"You best put some gloves on, bub. There's an extra pair in the steering cabin," Pinto advised.

"Nah, I'm fine. Just picking out the riff-raff. I'll leave the oysters to you guys," Rip said, brushing off Pinto's offer. He then began chattering like he was a talk radio host.

I waited impatiently for him to stop jabbering about inconsequential topics like his inability to whistle, the asinine idea of putting buttons in lieu of zippers in a man's fly, and how nothing tasted better than a good 'ol fried Spam sandwich. Just the thought of Spam made me want to upchuck the repulsive oysters I'd eaten. When it became clear to me that Rip was never going to segue into a conversation about the murder of Pinto's buddy, I reluctantly joined the fast and furious commotion at the sorting table.

I still hadn't gotten my "sea legs" yet and was beginning to think I never would with the seas rougher than normal. I had to keep one hand clamped to the railing of the table just to remain upright. With the other hand, I practiced the art of culling through creepy, gooey things without actually ever laying a hand on any one of them. If any of the men noticed I was accomplishing nothing, they didn't mention it.

When there was a brief pause in the action, I asked nonchalantly, "Wasn't that something about that fellow who got killed with his own spear-gun?"

Pinto's head spun so fast toward me, I don't know what kept it from snapping in two and flinging its way out into the water. The look on his face was alarming.

"Why do you ask?" He was staring at me as if I were a never-before-seen sea creature they'd just dredged up from the floor of the bay. "What have you heard? Has there been a break in the case? Have you heard something about a suspect being apprehended or identified?"

"Why, no," I replied, taken aback by his sudden

anxiousness. "I doubt I know anymore than you do about the murder. I just thought maybe you'd heard something while speaking with other fishermen around the marina."

Due to his reaction, I wondered for a second if Pinto really might know more than I did about Claypool's death. Perhaps a lot more than *anyone* else knew about it. From his accent and some of the terms he'd used, it was apparent he was originally from England. Milo had commented about the British accent of the man named Captain Hook. Was it possible he had any connection to the murder? It didn't seem likely to me. Milo had sworn there was no way Pinto was involved, and I had a tendency to agree with him. He appeared to be too laid back, too easy-going – or at least until I mentioned Claypool's murder.

After a long breath and an even longer exhale, Pinto replied, "No, haven't heard much. Nothing at all, really. Crying shame though, isn't it?"

"Very much so," I agreed.

Rip's attention had been piqued and he joined the conversation. He glanced from one man to the next, all around the table before asking, "Was he an acquaintance of yours, Pinto? Or any of the rest of you men?"

Without looking up, the man I'd dubbed Big Bob answered first. "Nope, never heard of the guy."

Spider was next and only a touch more helpful than Bob. "Billy and I seen him at a few of our AA meetings. I remember Claypool introducing himself and saying his drinking had escalated in recent months due to money problems. Saw him with his lady at a bar one day too. For an older broad, she wasn't half bad. She could do better than Claypool, for sure. I know I'd be happy to take her for a ride, if you know what I mean."

I *did* know what Spider meant and had half a mind to pick up one of the mallets lying on the table and wallop him over the head. The Willis brothers were laughing so hard at Spider's wisecracks that a thimbleful of the tobacco Billy had been chewing shot out of his left nostril and onto the wooden table. I had to look away or risk having one of the snotty-looking oysters I'd eaten erupt from one of the orifices on my face, too.

When he'd gained control again, Billy swiped a grimy, slimy and now briny, sleeve across his face, pointed at Pinto, and said. "Captain Bean was pretty tight with Claypool, I know."

I'd expected Pinto to be irked by Billy's offhand remark, but instead he became emotional. With a tear in his eye, Pinto nodded, and agreed with the deck hand, "That's right. Cooper was like a son to me. He and his buddy used to take me fishing with them and would come sit in the boat and pop a few tops with me once in a while. News of his death broke my heart. I still can't bear to even think about it, much less talk about it."

He was clearly devastated about Cooper's murder, and I knew the buddy he'd referred to was Milo. I told him I was really sorry for his loss. Rip shook his head at me, but I felt compelled to inquire anyway. After all, when would we ever have another opportunity to question him? I think Rip nearly swallowed his tongue when I said, "We heard he was into a loan shark for quite a bit of money. Did you know anything about that, Pinto?"

The Willis boys had resumed working, but Big Bob took a short break from his labor to gaze at Pinto as the captain responded. "Yeah, I did, actually. I begged him to let me float him a loan, but he refused. Our other buddy tried to get him to accept a loan too. We both knew how brutal those goons can get to entice a bloke to pay up, and we were afraid of what might happen to Cooper. Now I wonder if his life might have been spared if I had tried harder to get him to take me up on the loan. I'm sure Cooper knew my funds were a little dried up too and didn't want to put me in a bind. But I'd have gotten by somehow. I'd been down and out before and will no doubt be down and out again. But I'm still here, ain't I?"

Relieved to hear Milo's claims about the rejected loan corroborated, I caught Rip's eye. He winked to let me know he shared my sentiment. I turned back to Pinto when I heard him blow his nose on a handkerchief he'd extracted from a front pocket in the rubber apron he wore. He was upset. Big Bob spoke up to comfort him. "Don't blame yourself, boss. Most likely his death had to do with an issue regarding his business, not his unpaid debts. There was probably nothing you could have done about it, no matter how hard you tried."

"Probably not. But, still, I gotta wonder. Now boys, get the bucket ready to drop again." Pinto and the crew resumed concentrating on the task at hand. Pinto's mood was somber and withdrawn for the next twenty minutes. He'd sounded convinced the murder had been perpetrated by the loan shark or one of the shark's men. He put his hand on Rip's shoulder and suggested again that he grab the extra pair of gloves in the steering cabin.

"Trust me, I'll be all right." Rip spoke with great self-assurance. The man may exhibit the common sense of a lemming at times, but he was never short on confidence.

I had ceased even pretending to be helping out. I was convinced there'd be no more information coming from any of the men that day. I stood alongside my husband, while holding on to the table with both hands. The waves and swells had increased slightly and it had become more difficult to remain afoot. Suddenly, Rip yelped in pain. I looked down to see blood gushing from a deep cut in his left hand. As the boat had scaled an enormous rogue wave, the unexpected jolt had caused Rip to slice his palm on the sharp edge of an oyster shell while trying to drag out a crab that was nestled below it.

Big Bob glanced at Rip's hand, and said, "Yep! Been there, done that. You should have listened to the boss."

"Yes, I see that now," Rip replied dryly. He groaned and moaned in pain as the blood flowed. He had a lower threshold of pain than I did, and was more dramatic when ill or injured. In other words, Rip was a typical male. And like most men, he liked to be babied and fussed over in situations like this one.

As the rest of the crew continued to toil, Pinto grabbed an old, and no doubt bacteria-laden, towel and wrapped it around Rip's wounded hand. Instead of spouting an "I told you so" remark, as I'd have been tempted to do, Pinto said, "You might need to get that hand stitched up, bub. We'll be heading back shortly anyway. Looks like the cold front is going to hit several hours earlier than forecast. We need to get back before the wind picks up and it gets too rough out here. And 'sides that, it's after two. By law we gotta quit harvesting by three-thirty, anyway."

The choppy water was already too rough for my liking. The rocking motion of the boat was no longer soothing. It was making those horrid oysters I'd swallowed want to return to the sea. And I had a sneaking suspicion they would soon get their wish.

After a drenching splash of water spraying over the bow of the boat slapped all of our faces, Pinto ordered the crew to swiftly finish up with the pile they were working on, and secure the dredge and sacks of oysters. He motioned for Rip and me to return to our positions on the padded cooler where there was a bar in front of us we could hold on to. I presume he wanted to avoid an impending "man (or woman) overboard" distress call as much as we did. With one hand wrapped, and still hobbling around a bit with his new hip replacement, I'd have put my money on Rip being the subject of such an incident.

Just as the crew was getting everything ready to make the trip back to the marina, I felt my stomach roil and Rip looked at me with concern. "You're looking a little green around the gills, Rapella."

There was no time to respond. I'd noticed earlier a sign on the door of the boat's small bathroom that read "No chumming in head" so I bolted to the side of the boat and immediately lost my cookies, a.k.a. the nasty oysters. After I threw up everything in my stomach, I began to dry heave. I had never felt so sick in my entire life. If you've never been seasick, it's not something you ever want to experience. Worst of all, I suddenly realized somewhere in the midst of my projectile vomiting, I had lost my upper plate of dentures. I'd puked my teeth overboard and they now resided somewhere on the bottom of the drink, probably next to an anchor some other fool had pitched out prematurely. So much for only paying for a new set of choppers once.

Still nauseated beyond belief, I made my way back to the cooler to sit beside my husband, who was holding his wrapped left hand with his right one. I was upset, and after I told Rip my upper plate was lost at sea, he patted my thigh with his good hand and tried to comfort me. "It's okay, sweetheart. I'm relatively certain Dr. Shaft is still practicing here in town. He made your first set and can surely make you a replacement plate. We'll get you in as soon as we can. Don't worry. It could have happened to anyone."

Big Bob hoisted the boat's large cast iron anchor as if it weighed almost nothing. There seemed to be very little he couldn't handle with just the hook on the end of his prosthetic arm. Soon we were tacking home. Pinto changed the boat's angle periodically to enable him to ride the swells smoothly and not capsize the vessel. He was a seasoned sailor, but there was only so much he could do to protect us against Mother Nature. The ride was anything but smooth.

I was trying to keep my mind off the queasiness in my belly. I was thinking about how lucky I was to have such an understanding husband. I couldn't have found a better partner than Rip. He was always there to comfort me when I needed consoling and quick to forgive when I stomped all over his last nerve. I leaned over and kissed his cheek. I spoke loudly so he could make out my words. "We'll head straight for the Urgent Care facility when we get back to the marina, honey. Thank you for always being so good to me."

"My pleasure, Rapella. And I could say the same thing about you. What do you say we go to that new restaurant in Portland after I get my hand sewn up? I think a nice juicy Porterhouse sounds like just the thing for supper. Don't you?"

I playfully punched Rip in the arm. He was well aware that I would be gumming my food until I got my upper dentures replaced. "Yeah, right, buster. You couldn't cut a steak tonight any better than I could chew one."

Once I'd thanked Captain Bean profusely and gotten my feet back on solid ground, my nausea had abated. I stepped into the truck on the driver's side, with Rip cradling his hand in the passenger seat. I was backing out of the parking spot when Big Bob walked up to his Jeep, parked right beside us. I rolled down my window and said, "It was nice meeting you, Bob. Good luck with the teeth. Looks like I'll be seeing my dentist soon too."

"Yeah, guess so," Bob said as he swung himself into the topless Jeep.

"Hey, Bob. I was wondering—"

"Enough small talk, Rapella," Rip said impatiently. "Let's go."

"Yeah?" Bob asked, with a quizzical expression.

"Come, on. Quit gabbing. My hand's throbbing. There's nothing Bob can tell you that would be of any significance in the murder investigation." Rip was agitated and cranky, and I didn't blame him. Still, I had a question I needed to ask. So I shouted over the roar of the Jeep's motor as the huge man fired it up.

"How did you know Cooper Claypool owned a business if you'd never heard of the guy?" Big Bob graced me with a stone-cold glare before slamming his gearshift into reverse. Gravel flew as he backed out of his spot and peeled out of the parking lot. I coughed twice to quell the irritation of dust in my throat, and had to blink several times to clear the grit out of my eyes.

After I'd blotted the grime off my face with a wad of

used tissue I'd stuffed in my jeans pocket, I turned to Rip. He wore a blank expression. I was certain he was reflecting back to the earlier conversation about Claypool and wondering how he'd missed the inconsistency in Bob's remarks. Despite the fact he was in pain and not in the best of moods, I had to get my licks in when I could. "Nothing of significance, huh?"

Shaking his head in bewilderment, he replied, "I stand corrected."

CHAPTER 17

"Doctor Shaft will be with you in a jiff." The young dental assistant clipped a drool bib around my neck before leaving the room, shutting the door behind her. I glanced at my watch. It was two minutes after nine. I'd been lucky to get an appointment early the following morning due to a last minute cancellation.

I didn't want to waste a lot of time getting my dentures replaced because it took precious time away from our personal investigation and added twenty years to my appearance. I also wasn't fond of gumming every morsel of food and wanted to limit that aspect of it as much as possible.

To pass the time, I studied the posters affixed to the walls. But looking at diagrams of impacted wisdom teeth, abscesses, and gingivitis only entertained me for a short spell. I began fidgeting in the chair, getting more incensed as the minutes ticked by. *When will a few of these doctors and dentists who are habitually behind schedule learn their patients' time was just as valuable as their own?* I wondered, irritably.

When I checked my watch for the fortieth time, it was nine thirty-three. At that point, I exited the room and tracked down the dental assistant. She was busily pecking around on her cell phone, texting her boyfriend, no doubt.

"Miss, could you please tell me when I can expect Dr. Shaft to see me? I have a busy schedule today and I've been waiting more than a half-hour already." The assistant finished her text and sent it before she looked up at me with an annoyed expression.

"I already told you he'd be with you in a jiff."

"Then I reckon I don't understand dental jargon, young lady."

"Huh?"

"Exactly how long is a 'jiff'? Forty-two minutes? Four-and-a-half hours? Three days? Give me some kind of estimate so I can juggle my schedule accordingly."

"Don't ask me," she replied, as if I were interrupting an extremely important texting session. Was she informing her boyfriend he was going to be a "baby daddy"? Letting her parents know of the devastating news she'd just received about her recent liver biopsy? In my opinion, anything less crucial should be delayed until she clocked out. Apparently, even the dental assistant's time was worth more than the patient's in Dr. Shaft's office. The unprofessional young lady turned her attention back to her phone when a beep indicated she'd received an incoming text. She read the text first, then took an abbreviated call on the office phone. She was neither elated nor devastated by the text, so I knew it wasn't critical. I felt like grabbing her cell phone and tossing it into the trashcan. With an insincere apology, she said, "Sorry, but Doctor Shaft had to run to the bank to make a deposit."

"He *ran* to the bank? Maybe if he had taken his car instead of running it wouldn't have taken so long." I began to walk away in a huff. But I stopped mid-way and turned back to face the assistant because I couldn't refrain from adding one more jab. "And maybe if he didn't charge such exorbitant prices, he wouldn't feel it necessary to make trips to the bank during office hours."

Just then, Dr. Shaft walked in the front door and down the hall toward me and his assistant. "Good morning, Mrs. Ripple. Haven't seen you in a while. What brings you here today?"

"I lost my upper plate." I smiled in case he thought I was kidding.

"And you don't know where you left it?" His tone indicated losing one's dentures was virtually impossible. *This old bird must be mistaken.* I could almost read his mind. *After all, she is at that full-blown dementia age.*

"Of course I know where I left them," I replied indignantly. My mood was sliding downhill like a kid riding a trash can lid down a snowy slope. "I left them on the bottom of Copano Bay."

"All right. Let's go take a look." He guided me back to the dental chair. I opened my mouth to once again show him the empty void that false teeth once occupied.

"All we should need to do is have another plate made from the mold they used to create the original one," I informed Doctor Shaft.

"Oh, if it were only that easy." He chuckled in amusement at my apparently inane remark.

"What do you mean by that?"

"I would need a warehouse to store all the molds we've made for my patient's dentures over the years."

"So, are you saying they no longer exist?" I asked.

"Yes, that's what I'm saying. Molds are never retained after the dentures have been made. People's jaws and mouths are in the process of changing throughout their entire lives. Storing old molds would serve no purpose, you see."

"Not to mention, less profitable for dentists, I'm guessing." I may seem as if I'm intolerant of dentists, and I don't mean to sound disparaging. But we've spent more money on Rip's teeth through the years than we did on the home we sold when we retired. He was determined to keep his own teeth as long as he possibly could. But then, he always was more extravagant with money than I was. I wouldn't even be replacing my dentures now if not for the fact I truly do prefer chewing my food. I turned my attention back to Dr. Shaft who'd just instructed his assistant to take an impression of my gums.

Uh-oh, I thought. Hope she didn't take any of my spiteful remarks personally. If so, I'll be lucky if she doesn't let me gag to death before yanking the tray full of what feels like Sakrete out of my mouth.

"So, I'm afraid we'll need to start from scratch and make a new set of molds. But first, we'll need to take x-rays to ensure there are no underlying problems," he said, with a self-satisfied smile.

"Of course you will," I replied. I wasn't proud of my foul mood, or my malicious retorts, but I had a good reason to feel as if I was being taken advantage of. "Whatever it takes to keep the lights on."

With a wink, he countered with, "I guess this is what one gets when one doesn't take every precaution with their dentures."

Dr. Shaft is a very appropriate name for you, smart ass.

I was standing at the check-out counter in the lobby, which had numerous people sitting around in hard, uncomfortable chairs awaiting their turn to be given the *shaft*. I paid no attention to the faces of the unfortunate people occupying those seats. However, I was not surprised to discover the dentist was behind schedule, inconveniencing six or seven members of his faithful clientele.

I was writing a check for the over-padded amount I was being charged when the snobby assistant opened the door into the lobby and motioned for the next patient to follow her to the room I'd just exited.

More out of habit than anything, I looked over my shoulder and saw Big Bob unfold his tall frame from a wooden chair. I turned to him and said, "Small world, isn't it? I had no idea we used the same dentist."

Big Bob showed no sign of wanting to converse with me. In fact, he walked past me as if I were a life-sized cardboard cut-out depicting a dental hygienist holding a container of some dental floss being advertised. As he silently passed by me, I sarcastically said, "It was nice to see you again, too."

I'd always thought there was no such thing as coincidences, and that things happened for a reason. The receptionist was hanging up the office phone, after notating a name in her appointment scheduling book, when I nonchalantly said, "Don't you just hate when you run into someone you've known for ages and can't recall their name? Just like that fellow. His last name is on the tip of my tongue. Johns, Jones, Johnson, or is it—"

"Chrisman," the receptionist politely volunteered. She could give lessons to Dr. Shaft's dental assistant on how to deal courteously with the public. "And I know what you mean, Mrs. Ripple. That happens to me all the time, too."

"Oh, yes, of course. Bob Chrisman. Silly of me to forget." I thumped the side of my hand with my palm to emphasize my charade of a memory lapse.

"Bob?"

"Yes. Wasn't that Bob?" I asked, mystified by the receptionist's confusion.

"Well, I can't say for positive, but I don't think so. It says Royce Chrisman here in my scheduling book." She turned the book around and pointed to the name, as if she thought I might not take her word for it.

"Oh, of course," I said, with a laugh. I thumped my temple again." I'm sure he uses his legal name for situations like business contracts, utility bills, and, of course, dental appointments. But all of his friends call him by his nickname. Which is Bob, of course." Even as I lied through my missing teeth, I had to wonder if he'd been using an alias for nefarious reasons. Because, seriously, who would give a guy named Royce a nickname like Bob? Did Philip Bean know Big Bob's real name was Royce Chrisman? Or, on the other hand, had Bob given an assumed name to the office receptionist? On the third hand, was his given name something else entirely?

I could have left it at that and exited the medical building without uttering another word. But, as you surely realize by now, that would have gone against every grain in my body. I wanted more information if I could figure a way to weasel it out of the receptionist. I spoke with a nostalgic tone to appear as if I was reflecting back to an earlier time. "Rip and I have known Bob, I mean Royce, for ages. After all, we used to live across the street from him on Harbor Oaks Drive. No wait, that wasn't it. It was actually when we lived on Spruce, I believe."

"He lives on South Pearl Street now," the kind-hearted, unsuspecting lady replied after briefly scanning her computer screen. "He must have moved since then."

"Yes, he apparently has." I returned her smile. If Dr. Shaft could overhear this conversation, he'd be convinced I really did suffer from full-blown dementia.

"I'm surprised he didn't let us know he'd relocated. Must have been tied up at work, or something. I assume he still works at the marina?" I asked.

"I don't know about him working at a marina. I didn't realize he'd worked anywhere but the DMV office. In fact, he's the one who assisted me last month when I went in to get my license renewed."

"Oh goodness," I said, as if something important had just occurred to me. "Thanks for the reminder. I need to get my driver's license renewed too, before it expires on Saturday. Well, have a nice day, dear. I'll be back on the twenty-fourth to pick up my new choppers."

The receptionist advised me to go to the DMV in a neighboring town, which just happened to be the office where Royce worked. See what I mean about things happening for a reason? The DMV in Aransas Pass was always so busy that people would often have to get there at the crack of dawn to get their license the same day. And I didn't have that much time to wait in line. As I walked away, the receptionist gleefully remarked, "Plus, it'll give you and Mr. Chrisman a chance to catch up."

We're going to catch up, all right, I thought, as I stepped up into the truck. Driving back to the RV park, I was trying to devise my next move. Due to his evasive actions, I felt confident that Royce Chrisman, a.k.a. Big Bob, was involved in Claypool's murder, if he hadn't actually done the dirty deed himself. My driver's license actually *was* set to expire on my birthday, December eighteenth. I had several weeks to have it renewed, but there was something to be said about not letting grass grow under one's feet. Especially when time was of the essence and one had an ulterior motive not to waste it.

My new plan was to visit the DMV office that very afternoon rather than put it off until a later date. According to Dr. Shaft's receptionist, even though the DMV where Bob worked was farther away, it'd still be more time-efficient than going to the closer one. And, even if it wasn't, my only reason for renewing my license this early was to get a face-to-face meeting with Royce Chrisman. We needed to "catch up", you see.

Given the fact driver's license photos were notoriously hideous, and also that Texas driver's licenses were now good for seven years, I'd have to remember to avoid flashing my usual toothy smile when the picture was taken. The gaunt appearance from being toothless made me look old enough as it was. Lord knows when it came to photos, I didn't have much to work with even in the best of times.

When I returned to the campground, Rip was fast asleep on the couch. I knew this before I even opened the trailer door because his snoring was vibrating the blinds. On the way home from the dentist, I'd been thinking about how I'd ever convince Rip to accompany me to the DMV office and hadn't come up with a feasible plan yet. I wasn't likely to convince him this man named Royce, and/or Bob, and/or any other possible alias, was a viable suspect to begin with.

I could explain what had taken place at the dentist's office a hundred times, embellishing the story more and more with each telling if I had to, and Rip would still never believe confronting this huge, cagey fellow was a good idea. As usual, he'd tell me I was chasing my own tail, barking up the wrong tree, acting like a dog with a bone, turning our investigation into a dog and pony show, or any of a dozen other canine clichés. But, frankly, I wasn't quite ready to let sleeping dogs lie.

I don't know if you'd call it woman's intuition, or just a wild-ass hunch, but something told me I was finally on the right trail. I had to act on a gut feeling this overwhelming, or I'd get no sleep that night.

As my Pappy used to say, "It's easier to ask for forgiveness than permission," and that's especially true when you're fairly certain permission wouldn't be granted. So I grabbed a memo pad off the counter and penned "Out and about, be back in a few hours." I placed it underneath the remote control, where I knew he'd find it because the remote would be the first thing he'd reach for when he opened his eyes. At least if the half-finished Crown and Coke on the table next to him had already warmed up to room temperature and the ice had melted.

I quietly gathered up the items I'd need to renew my license. I knew from experience it was usually on the third attempt you'd finally brought all the miscellaneous documents that the DMV clerk would demand to see. I'm sure there are few people who relish the idea of going to their local DMV. It had the reputation of being one of the most disliked public offices in nearly every county in the country. But I found myself looking forward to the opportunity to speak with Big Bob where he couldn't just race off in his Jeep when he recognized me in the crowd. At least not if he valued his job or needed the income it provided.

Little did I know at the time, my enthusiasm would evaporate like morning dew on a pumpkin as soon as I reached my destination.

CHAPTER 18

"Number seventeen."

As I walked into the building, I heard a nasally female voice call out from her position behind the counter. I recognized it from the call I'd made to the DMV on my way home from the dental office to collect the necessary documents.

I pulled a paper tag off the roll—number thirty-four. Every chair in the room was occupied, and there were at least a dozen people standing or sitting on the floor. A couple of younger men looked as if they'd been camped out all night. It reminded me of the *Best Buy* parking lot the evening before Black Friday

I knew I was in for a long wait. I don't normally suffer from claustrophobia, but in this small room, filled to the gills with people, I experienced an overwhelming sense of not having enough oxygen to breathe. I considered standing outside where I could at least breathe in clean, fresh air. *One rogue germ in here could potentially launch an influenza outbreak in all of south Texas,* I thought. *And I don't have time to lounge around in bed for several days while I recuperate.*

On the other hand, I didn't want to miss my chance when number thirty-four was called. There were only two clerks working behind the counter. Royce Chrisman and an older woman with snow white hair, who looked to be at least twenty years beyond retirement. It was clear she wasn't still working because she loved her job or enjoyed dealing with the public. Her face was frozen in a petulant frown. Her raspy voice carried across the room as she harshly snapped at each person she assisted. To make matters worse, like a sleeping sloth, she moved so slowly you'd have to place a pole beside her to determine if she was moving at all.

Scanning the room for a place to sit, I saw only one decent spot left on the floor to park myself for a long spell without being trampled on. I decided I better claim it before the portly man with a sunburned bald spot on the top of his head snatched it up. He had walked in the building just seconds after I had, letting me go inside ahead of him as he'd gentlemanly held the door open for me. I had assured him I was most appreciative before two other people entered directly behind us. It seemed as if two people were walking in the door for every one that was walking out.

A sense of impatience and disgust filled the room like a cloud, as if it'd been fogged for termites. Every few seconds, I could make out an audible sigh from someone in the room. When a man with a low-timbered voice spoke to an elderly gentleman, who was no doubt his aging father, the white-haired clerk squawked. "Quiet down over there. If you folks have something you need to say, take it outside."

Wow, I thought. What a ray of sunshine that old bat is.

This wasn't my first rodeo, and I was thankful I'd thought to bring my iPad with me just in case I'd need something to while away the time. When our daughter had gifted us with the tablet the previous Christmas, Rip and I had been outwardly enthusiastic, but inwardly skeptical. As I mentioned earlier, after serving as an over-sized coaster on the end table for eight months, I had learned enough about the device while staying at the

Alexandria Inn to render it useful. Not only that, but I was now on the verge of needing an intervention for my *Candy Crush* and *Boggle* addictions.

"Eighteen," Royce Chrisman called out. He looked up to scan the crowd for his next customer, then stopped abruptly when his eyes locked with mine. The expression on his face was priceless. I could almost read his thoughts. *Is that old lady stalking me, or what?* I wanted to tell him I was his bad penny and would keep showing up until I was convinced he had nothing to do with Cooper Claypool's murder.

That thought made me turn on the iPad and Google his name. Royce isn't a common name, so I wasn't surprised when only four Royce Chrismans popped up. Two were already deceased and had resided in Alaska and North Carolina, and another one was starring as Chantilly in a drag queen production on the Las Vegas strip. The only other hit I got was a Bar Mitzvah announcement. Considering this Jewish Royce Chrisman was most likely around the customary age of thirteen, I disregarded him, too. But congratulations and Mazal Tov to the young man, just the same.

I found nothing of interest on the list of sites my search produced other than a few articles about the late Alaskan who had won a number of dog-sled races and at the age of sixty-two had fallen just short of being a contestant in the inaugural Iditarod competition in 1973. Sounded like a remarkably fascinating fellow, but he obviously wasn't making threatening phone calls from the great beyond.

Could Royce Chrisman be just one of a number of aliases this man used? I wondered again. Could one of his monikers be Captain Hook?

He did have a prosthetic with a "hook" of sorts in lieu of a hand. I glanced up at him and noticed he was wearing a different prosthetic today. As Pinto had noted the previous day, it was almost undistinguishable from his other, natural arm and hand.

Mr. Chrisman was holding a small boy around a year old while the boy's mother filled out some paperwork. I saw the boy laugh joyfully at something Royce had said or done in an effort to entertain him until the mother was able to reclaim him. Royce Chrisman had to look like a gigantic monster to such a tiny child, but the boy appeared very much as ease in his arms. He giggled, babbled blissfully, and grasped the thumb on Royce's prosthetic hand with his tiny fingers. It was a touching scene, I had to admit.

I've always heard that dogs and children were good judges of character and wondered if this young Hispanic child had judged Royce correctly. Despite my inclination to dislike everything about the fellow, I was truly impressed with his resilience, tenderness, and "can do" attitude.

To help fill the time as I waited for my number to come up, I played a few games of Scrabble against my cyber opponent. The computer had the benefit of unlimited knowledge at its disposal, yet still I managed to beat it on my fifth attempt. Out of desperation I'd made up the word "bezique," using all seven tiles including my "Z" and "Q" and landing on a triple-word-score space. Unlike the "quizbee" I'd tried my previous turn, it turned out "bezique" really was a word, defined as a card game resembling whist, and the lofty score it generated was enough to put me over the top on my final play.

I decided to quit playing Scrabble while I was ahead. Instead, I read a note from my niece in Buffalo, Wyoming, and deleted spam messages, which encompassed at least seventy-five percent of my email folder. I then tucked my iPad away in my purse and withdrew a small spiral-bound notebook.

Anxious to make at least some measure of progress in the murder investigation, I was going over everything we'd learned to this point, ruminating about who might have had the most provoking motive and greatest desire to kill Cooper Claypool. I began creating a list of the suspects I still believed were potential perpetrators.

Under Philip Bean's name on the list, I penned in "a.k.a. Pinto." The oyster boat captain seemed genuinely fond of both Cooper and Milo. However, it was always conceivable he'd been pulling the wool over our eyes. And, I suddenly realized, Cooper and Milo's eyes, as well.

After all, how often do they interview neighbors of serial killers on television who describe them as the "nicest neighbor I've ever had." I'm sure the men who flew hijacked planes into the World Trade Center had made a few American friends while they were infiltrating themselves into our society. American citizens who'd never have suspected one of their Muslim friends could carry out an act of brutal terrorism that would result in the death of almost three thousand human beings.

The 9/11 attack also killed nineteen hijackers, whom I considered sub-human and destined for hell anyway. If not for convincingly portraying a perfectly normal and rational citizen, the terrorists would have been apprehended and awarded a free trip to Guantanamo Bay before they could pull off such a devastating act of violence. My point is you really couldn't count anyone out until you could crawl inside their head and see for yourself what made them tick. And that was exactly the reason I was sitting in the crowded DMV office that afternoon. I wanted to crawl inside Royce Chrisman's gigantic head and have a look around.

Percolating in my mind since meeting Philip Bean was his slight British accent and some of the terms he'd used; bloody, bloke, and so forth. Milo had told Rip and me he was almost positive he'd recognized an English accent in the voice mail message he'd come across: Captain Hook threatening great bodily harm to Cooper, Milo, and their families if Claypool didn't make good on his loan soon.

And looking back, I also recalled that the name of

Pinto's oyster boat was "Hook 'em." At the time, like Milo had inferred, I'd taken for granted the name was derived from the fact he was a fan of the University of Texas, as in their motto, "Hook 'em Longhorns." Could "Hook 'em" actually be derived from his own nickname, Captain Hook? Or even vice-versa, perhaps?

Just who was this intimidating man who referred to himself as Captain Hook and had threatened Claypool numerous times? Figuring that out was my main focus at this point, particularly since in his last threatening message, Captain Hook had increased his pool of possible targets to include Milo, Regina, and my grandkids. As these thoughts crossed my mind, I scribbled annotations in my little notebook, as Lexie Starr had taught me to do.

"Twenty-three," the old gal called out. When the rickety gentleman she'd shushed earlier took a few seconds to grab his cane and stand up unsteadily from his chair, with the assistance of the younger man sitting next to him, the irritable clerk, who was snail-like herself, harshly chastised him. "Step it up, mister. I ain't got all day, you know."

Meanwhile, in the last few minutes, seven more customers had entered the room. Fortunately, five of them took one glimpse at the crowd and returned to their vehicles, no doubt thinking the next time they showed up they'd be waited on instantly. Silly fools.

As Royce Chrisman, or whatever his real name was, called for number twenty-four, I went back to concentrating on my list.

Julio Sarcova: I considered him a highly unlikely suspect. Granted, he was irate about the mold issue in the home he'd purchased from MC Hammerheads. Who wouldn't be? He wanted the problem resolved, and once again, who wouldn't?

But would Sarcova kill the man he was counting on to eventually complete the job? It seemed to me to be a flimsy, illogical motive to commit cold-blooded murder.

And, according to Detective Reeves, Sarcova's alibi had been verified, placing the barber in a Las Vegas hotel on the day of the murder. But that hadn't necessarily prevented him from putting a hit out on his nemesis.

Murder for hire was an option any one of the suspects on my list could have chosen, for that matter. I didn't think the mob still had a stronghold in Las Vegas, or much affiliation there whatsoever, but it was always possible the true reason behind Julio Sarcova's Vegas trip was to make arrangements or pay for services rendered.

Dr. Patrick O'Keefe was still on my list even though the detectives had cleared him as a viable suspect. It would not be a far-fetched notion that he might want to exact revenge on the man who stole his wife. A wife he still seemed to be carrying a torch for, at least in my opinion. And then there was the woman in the middle of the three-ring-circus, Avery Curry. What motive might she have to want her boyfriend dead? She seemed to be a very sweet lady when I interacted with her at Jugs 'n Mugs. But that takes us right back to Ted Bundy, who could charm the pants off one beautiful woman after another.

Could this feasibly be a crime involving more than one perpetrator? I wondered. After all, there are several possible scenarios involving twosomes.

Lexie Starr had taught me to never overlook any conceivable possibility. I felt a tag-team type killing was one of those possibilities that shouldn't be overlooked.

Could Pinto and Royce Chrisman, who I still preferred to call Big Bob, have planned Cooper Claypool's murder together? Could it have been part of a devious scheme created by O'Keefe and Avery Curry to execute Cooper for personal, or even monetary, benefit?

And what were the odds that Mack Schilling, and/or his son, Trey, might have killed Cooper out of revenge for not being paid for their work? They'd been stiffed not once, but three times. Both Schillings also loathed the victim for his illegal and immoral fishing practices. When I had questioned Milo the previous evening, he'd told me Trey only helped out on odd jobs for his father when his work schedule as a game warden allowed. Milo also admitted that indeed it had been Trey who'd been responsible for the arrest that earned Cooper his lifetime ban from spear-fishing in Texas. Milo also stated he'd never personally been arrested or even ticketed by Trey.

Mack had said he would have turned Milo and Cooper in to a game warden if one had been in the vicinity when he spotted them poaching with his binoculars. So why did he not mention to Regina and me that his own son was a game warden and had arrested Claypool for serious offenses in the past?

I found it hard to believe either of the Schillings hated Cooper enough to kill him with his own spear-gun. A spear-gun, turned murder weapon, which had never been located despite, according to Detective Reeves, numerous attempts by the Coast Guard, homicide detectives, and scuba divers the police department had contracted. Branson Reeves had informed Rip that the spear itself, which had been extracted from Claypool's chest, had produced no clues to whom might have fired it.

But if killing Claypool out of anger at his penchant for poaching game fish *was* true, could Milo be next on either Schilling's list?

It was questions like the last one that convinced me we needed to find a way to get to the bottom of this "who killed Cooper?" conundrum as quickly as possible. We didn't want to give the other shoe the opportunity to drop. For if it did, it just might kill Milo and crush Regina in the process. And who knew for certain whether or not our grandchildren could be in danger, as well?

"Thirty-three," Chrisman said.

Oh dear, I thought. I'd been concentrating on my

suspect list and hadn't realized my number was coming up. I was the next to be called and it seemed clear I was going to be waited on by the older clerk who was just finishing up with her current customer. Thinking fast, I scanned the room for the chubby gentleman who had entered the building just after I had. His number would have to be thirty-five, I reasoned. If I could convince him to trade numbered tags, Chrisman would have to wait on me.

I darted across the floor, making the target of my sprint a bit uneasy. Seeing me hurdle two fussy toddlers and a decrepit old man was probably his first clue I was someone to be leery of. As I drew near, the man took a step back in a defensive manner. It didn't help I was having one of my bad hair days, which usually fall on Monday, Wednesday, Thursday, and/or random weekend days, with an occasional Tuesday or Friday thrown in for good measure. My curly salt and pepper hair was even more of a mess today than usual because I hadn't taken the time to check it out in a mirror, much less comb it.

Just as I reached the gentleman, I tripped over an invisible obstacle on the tile floor. At this stage, I'm reasonably certain I appeared to be a lunatic who'd managed to escape from an institute for the mentally insane by crawling through the drainage pipes of the local sewer system. Breathlessly, I said, "Excuse me, sir. Could you do me a teeny, weenie favor?"

The overweight man opened his mouth but did not respond. Fixated on me, his eyes never blinked or lost contact with mine. Trying to act less panicky, I took a deep breath to calm my nerves, and said, "I'm sorry. I just realized I left a document in my vehicle that I'll need if I'm to get my license renewed today. Would you mind trading numbers with me? It'll give me time to retrieve the item and will put you next in line to be called up, which I'm sure you'll be grateful for after such a lengthy wait."

His mouth still agape, he silently extended his arm, offering me his number thirty-five paper tag. He'd yet to bat an eyelash. With a trembling hand, I took the tag from his fingers and handed him mine.

"Thirty four," a familiar deep male voice called out from behind the counter.

Crap, I thought. Customers were being sent home right and left to obtain required, but missing, documents. Chrisman's last customer must have fallen into that category and been quickly dismissed. Many irate customers had left the room in varying degrees of wrath. One Vietnamese gentleman cussed the elderly female clerk all the way to the door, causing quite a stir among the waiting crowd that was growing more restless and infuriated with each minute that passed.

Although the man spoke in his native language, his message had been clear to everyone in the room. The angry fellow switched over to broken English as he hollered over his shoulder, "Why you no tell me I need 'official' birth *carnificate*, not 'record cf *borthe*' last time I here?"

"Because you didn't ask!" The lady hollered back. Who'd have thought the geriatric employee would be so feisty? I would have applauded her spunk had I not been more in favor of knocking her off her stool.

I can't repeat what the Asian said as the door was closing behind him. Suffice it to say, it was a graphic expletive, pronounced perfectly, that had all the women in the room blushing. Despite the nature of his remark, the agitated crowd cheered in response. And now I was on the verge of losing my opportunity to speak to Royce Chrisman. I didn't have a moment to waste.

"Changed my mind," I said, snatching my original tag out of the portly man's hand and dropping his on the floor in my haste to reach the counter before another number was called. As I turned to race to the counter, I apologized to the dumbfounded man, "Oops! Sorry. Just realized I have everything I need, after all."

Royce Chrisman was angry when he looked up to observe my face. He asked, "What's up with you, anyway?"

"Small world, huh?"

"It ain't *that* small, lady. You got a problem with me or something?"

"No, of course not. I need to renew my driver's license and you pulled my number. It was purely the luck of the draw. As a matter of fact, I was quite surprised to discover you worked here." I set my documents down on the counter to validate the reason I was standing in front of him at that moment.

"Yeah, lucky me. And even luckier for the gentleman you nearly bowled over to make sure I called your number. Purely the luck of the draw, of course." His sarcasm was uncalled for as he picked the documents up off the counter in front of him. And as if spotting the ghost of his late grandmother in the back of the room, he blanched at my next remarks.

"However, now that I think of it, I *do* have something I wanted to ask you, Bob. Or should I say, Royce?"

The solidly built man, whose hairline had receded prematurely, nodded in obvious disbelief. When he didn't reply verbally, I preceded to grill him like a slab of ribs.

"You aren't fooling me, Mr. Chrisman. I'm not the airhead you may think I am. I know you were involved in Cooper Claypool's death. So, exactly what part did you play in the murder of the man? My son-in-law is being unfairly scrutinized by the detectives and had absolutely nothing to do with his partner's death. I want to put an end to that nonsense and see the real killer brought to justice."

"I had nothing to do with his death either, lady. And I'm under no obligation to answer to you, anyhow. You're no more in law enforcement than I am."

"Uh. Well, I was, uh..." I was at a loss for words, uncertain how to respond to a statement that was unarguable. Then, an inspiration hit me and I played my ace in the hole. "Are you aware my husband was better known in these parts for years as Sheriff Ripple?"

"Lady, I don't care if your husband was better known as Queen Latifah. Did you happen to notice how many people are waiting in line behind you? I have no time to chat with you about a crime I know nothing about. And my supervisor is already upset with me for being two hours late to work. Dental appointment delayed me this morning, as you are keenly aware."

"Yeah. Did they gouge you as blatantly as they did me? The cost of dental work these days is atrocious." I was getting off track and needed to veer back toward the subject at hand before I was tossed out on my behind.

"Man, you can say that again." Unconsciously, Royce flashed a quick smile as he picked up my little pile of paperwork and handed it to me. "Now take your stuff and go so I can wait on people who sincerely do need to be assisted."

"I really do need to renew my license, Mr. Chrisman. These are my actual documents to take care of that matter." I grabbed my fistful of paperwork from his outstretched hand and waved them in his face. "I spoke to Ms. Congeniality over there on the phone before I drove over here, to see what I needed to bring with me. So, while you're assisting me with the matter, you can explain your involvement with Cooper Claypool."

Chrisman shook his head in disgust. His increasing displeasure with me was reaching the boiling point. "Ain't happening, lady. I've got a job to do. This room is full to the rafters already, and I don't need to make the situation worse by spending all day talking to someone to whom I have nothing to say."

"Hey now. It's plum rude and unprofessional for a civic employee to speak to a customer that way!"

"Good. Glad you noticed. Listen, lady. I couldn't have killed Claypool. I spent my entire Saturday at the Sunset Acres nursing home visiting my grandmother. Every nurse in the facility could vouch for me."

"So did they?"

With a sheepish expression, Royce lowered his head and replied. "It hasn't been necessary. I haven't been questioned by the police and don't feel as if I have much to offer that'd help them in their investigation. I'm practically as clueless as you are, ma'am."

Not thrilled about being labeled "clueless", I asked, "So why didn't you volunteer a statement and your easy-to-verify alibi just in case it might prove beneficial in some way?"

"Let me briefly explain what happened. Cooper and I were classmates in high school. In fact, we were good friends until he stole my girl right before the senior prom. Our relationship has been very contentious ever since." Royce stopped talking and glanced over at the old lady who was busy spitting nails at her current customer and oblivious of Royce's conversation with me.

"Go on," I prompted.

"I ran into him at the boat launch the evening before he was killed. He sucker-punched me in the mouth when I made a comment about his girlfriend, Avery Curry. Incidentally, she was the homecoming queen our senior year."

"You made a disparaging comment, I assume?"

"Yeah, I guess so. Not disparaging enough to knock my teeth out, though."

"So, what about the name 'Bob'? Why the alias?"

"Listen, lady. I have to get to work before I get fired and have another problem to deal with."

A couple of minutes later it was my turn to complain as I was departing, "Why didn't anyone tell me I needed *two* items to serve as proof of residency when I called this morning to see what I needed to bring?"

"You probably didn't ask," the white-haired spitfire replied, while the entire crowd watched the door hit me in the rear end as I was storming out.

CHAPTER 19

"Yikes!" I hollered out when I opened the driver's side door of the truck and saw a large body in the passenger seat. I'd used the public bathroom before I'd left the building, delaying my departure. I certainly hadn't expected a low-resonating voice to say, "Hurry up and get in," when I opened the drivers-side door. I was relieved, and I'll admit, a bit terrified when I realized it was Royce Chrisman in the passenger seat.

"What the—" I screeched.

"I haven't got much time, lady," Royce said, cutting me off. "I told my boss I felt nauseated from the Novocain I'd been injected with this morning and needed to use the restroom. I don't want her to find me out here talking to you. I had to beg to use the restroom as it was."

"How'd you get in my truck?"

His raised eyebrows clearly indicated I should have already known he could break into Fort Knox if he so chose.

"Okay. Whatever. Why did you sneak out here to talk to me? Not that I'm not happy that you did."

"Because I knew you would dog me until I did. That's why!" he exclaimed, before exhaling in a heavy extended sigh. "You're an exasperatingly determined woman, Rapella."

I merely nodded, knowing there was no way I could dispute his assessment of me. I was surprised when he called me Rapella. I'd begun to think Royce thought my actual given name was "lady."

"So, listen, lady." Royce looked around anxiously, clearly uneasy about being seen in my truck. "I realize your husband is the former sheriff. And I know Cooper Claypool was your son-in-law's best friend and co-owner of MC Hammerheads. So I understand why you want to find out who killed the guy. But if you think I had anything to do with his death, you are barking up the wrong tree."

"I assume that's the same wrong tree my husband keeps accusing me of barking up."

"Huh?" He asked, clearly confused by my remark.

"Never mind. Go on with what you wanted to tell me."

"Okay, look. Cooper and I were classmates in high school like I told you earlier. And, of course, Milo, too. They were a lot tighter back then than I think they've been lately."

I wondered at his last statement. Did he have reason to believe they were at odds enough for Milo to want Cooper dead? Was Royce aware of MC Hammerhead's financial situation and the rift it had caused between the two long-time friends? I would have dug deeper, but I didn't want to interrupt Royce while he was on a roll.

"As I was telling you, the three of us had a rather contentious relationship after Cooper started sniffing around my high school sweetheart while I was confined at home for two weeks with a highly infectious case of mono."

"Did your girlfriend cheat on you with Cooper, then?" I asked.

"No. And she and I broke up a month later over a totally different issue. But that's not the point!" He spoke indignantly as he explained. "Cooper never scored with her, or anything. But, it's the principle of the thing, you see."

"Oh, yes," I replied, nodding my head. "That dreaded old 'principle of the thing'. More feuds have been ignited by that pesky 'principle' thing than anything else. So, how does this tie into Cooper's death? '

"That's what I'm trying to tell you, lady. It doesn't!"

"Huh?" Now it was my turn to be confused.

"Cooper and I have pretty much avoided each other in the years following high school. We'd see each other around on occasion. But we never approached or spoke to one another. I've had very little contact with Milo since high school, either."

"What's all this got to do with you using an alias? I was beginning to think you also went by the nickname, Captain Hook."

"Captain Hook? What in the world are you talking about?" He'd used a very explicit word in place of "world" which I won't repeat. "Excuse my language, ma'am, but I don't have a clue where you got that name."

As if a light bulb flicked on in his mind, he suddenly looked down at his left arm, and asked, "Is this what you're talking about? The metal-claw prosthetic I used on the boat yesterday?"

"No, not exactly. Long story, but I'll try to be brief. Someone who calls himself Captain Hook had been making threatening calls to Cooper regarding some money he owed a loan shark. And, I'm not proud to admit this, but I thought someone might have nicknamed you that because of the hook attachment on your other prosthetic."

I was afraid I'd tick the guy off so was taken aback when he laughed loudly. "I have to say, Captain Hook would have been preferable to some of the names I was called back in my school years. Kids can be brutal, you know."

"Do you mind sharing with me how you lost it?" Royce shook his head, so I asked, "Was it a birth defect?"

"I wish. I was in a helicopter accident when I was

young." His eyes misted over and I knew it was an emotional subject for him. "I'm lucky my arm is all I lost."

"I'm so sorry, Royce. So, have you any idea who this Captain Hook might be?"

"I can't say for certain, but my guess is Paulie Winterkorn who works in some capacity for a loan shark down in El Paso. I'd bet he's the dude who'd been hounding Cooper."

"Yes, I agree. Milo told me he thought Captain Hook's boss lived in El Paso. Is this man, Paulie Winterkorn, as dangerous and scary as he sounds? I'm a little afraid for my entire family's sake."

Royce laughed again. "Hardly. That weasel-faced little dweeb might sound threatening on the phone, but in person he looks less Hulk Hogan, and more Pee-wee Herman's crazy uncle after a sex change operation gone bad. Trust me. He couldn't whip a girl scout selling thin mint cookies on his front porch."

I chuckled along with Royce at his depiction of the man he believed was dubbed Captain Hook. "That's really funny, and quite a relief, I might add."

"I'm sure it is. And, by the way, Pinto doesn't know my real name is Royce Chrisman. I didn't want him to mention my real name to Cooper or Milo, who I knew were good friends of his. You see, I really need the extra cash I earn working on his boat on the side, and I didn't want to give him a reason for not hiring me, or firing me after he'd spoken to Cooper and/or Milo about me. I'm trying to save up to buy myself a small house. I'm tired of renting and want to settle down and have a family one of these days."

"I'd never mention your real name to Pinto. The man doesn't seem to have an inquisitive bone in his body."

Royce laughed. "Yeah, I guess you're right about that. He's never asked me one thing about my personal life. Not even how I lost my arm."

"So, what does Pinto think your name is?"

"I introduced myself to him as Bob Valentine."

"Valentine?" I asked, in amusement. "With a zillion and seven surnames to choose from, you of all people picked Valentine?"

"Hey, I'm a romantic. What can I say?" Unexpectedly, Royce's demeanor relaxed and he looked at me with a broad smile. He was quite handsome with the temporary teeth Dr. Shaft had given him. *Maybe the dentist is worth his salt, after all.* I thought. However, I remained silent because I wanted to hear all Royce had to say but not get him in trouble with his boss.

"So, anyway, I have to make this quick so I can get back to my station before 'Ballbusteria' comes looking for me. You met the cantankerous old broad, so you ought to be able to relate."

"Absolutely! Please continue." I smiled back at Royce, amused at the unflattering, but fitting, moniker he'd created for his boss.

"The weekend before Cooper's death, I ran into him at the boat launch at Cove Harbor Marina. When he recognized me, he cut right in front of me with his boat trailer so he could utilize the only available boat ramp before I did. Naturally, I insulted his mother."

"You insulted his mother?"

"I called him a son-of-a—"

"Got it. Carry on."

"I got out of my truck and walked over to the ramp and like I told you earlier, the big prick sucker-punched me in the mouth after I told him Avery was crazy to want to hang out with a guy like him."

"Sounds to me like you were intentionally trying to provoke him into a fight."

"Well, I wasn't, although I can see now why it might have appeared that way to him, too. But, truly, I had no intention of getting into a physical confrontation with him. Just wanted to ask him why he was in such a hellfire hurry to launch his boat that he had to cut me off the way he did."

"Aha!" I said as something dawned on me. "That

explains your missing teeth, and the abrasions on Cooper's knuckles that were already beginning to heal over when we found his body."

"Yeah," Royce agreed, hanging his head. I sensed a touch of humiliation in his response. I'm sure it was because he was embarrassed his opponent had gotten the better of him, despite the fact he outweighed Cooper by a good fifty pounds. Then as if my last comment had just registered in his mind, he asked, "You and Sheriff Ripple found Cooper's body? Holy crap! I had no idea."

"*Former* Sheriff Ripple. And yes, my husband and I were out on a fishing excursion with Milo when we found him dead and floating on top of the water."

"With a spear in his chest, I heard."

"Yeah. Awful, isn't it?"

Royce nodded in agreement and said, "I guess I shouldn't have been so surprised. Cooper always was an impulsive, reckless kind of guy. No telling who he ticked off."

"So you weren't questioned by the police, huh?" I asked, Royce's last remarks echoing in my head. Everyone seemed to have formed the same impression of the victim: reckless and impetuous. What kind of situation had Cooper Claypool's risky and impulsive behavior gotten him involved in? Obviously it was something that had placed him in grave danger.

"No, the police never contacted me. Cooper and I were the only two in the vicinity when that incident at the boat launch occurred. No one witnessed the confrontation, so no one had any reason to suspect me of committing the murder," Royce explained. "And, believe me, ma'am. I would never kill another human being no matter how big the temptation. I just don't have it in me to take another person's life."

"I believe you, Royce." And I truly did. "That explains why you didn't want to admit you even knew him when we mentioned him on Pinto's boat. You didn't want to give anyone the idea you might be a likely suspect when you had nothing to do with the victim's death. And you feared if you willingly waltzed into the police station to offer a statement about the boat launch episode, you'd suddenly be relegated to the investigating team's radar, guilty or not, and put under intense scrutiny as a potential suspect. Am I correct? "

Royce nodded his head. "Exactly. I don't need that complication in my life right now."

"Yes. I totally see your point." I knew instinctively Royce Chrisman was telling me the truth, and I could understand his reluctance to get involved in the investigation in any way. I actually felt sorry for the guy and didn't want to be the person responsible for bringing the wrath of God down on his head when he didn't deserve it. I was getting ready to tell him I wouldn't repeat a word of what he'd told me, but Royce was not finished explaining his circumstances. Now that I'd tapped the well, it didn't want to stop flowing. And, as you could probably guess by now, that was just fine by me!

"I was afraid I might lose my job even though I was not responsible for the guy's death. And I didn't want my reputation tarnished by being a suspect for a murder I didn't commit. Even after an accused person is exonerated, the negative vibes hang over them like a fog that never seems to dissipate."

"Yeah, I know what you mean," I said in agreement. "It's like a teacher who is falsely accused of molesting a student. Rip and I were just discussing that very subject. Even after being proven innocent, their careers are adversely affected, along with their personal lives, for the rest of their existence. Definitely not fair to the wrongly accused individual, but reality just the same. I can understand why you'd want to avoid that at any cost."

"Worst of all, Rapella, I didn't want my grandmother to think I might have done something that unchristian-like. I'm not scared of much, but I'm terrified of

Grammy Webb. Grammy's four-foot-nine and one-hundred pounds of pure badass when she's teed off. I walk the chalk when I'm around her, let me tell you."

I had to laugh at his admission of being scared spitless of his diminutive grandmother. But he wasn't fooling me. This man loved her above all others, and feared disappointing her more than angering her. "Grammy Webb means the world to you, doesn't she?"

"Yeah, she does," he replied, blushing at the admission. "Grammy raised me after my parents were killed in the same helicopter crash that took my arm. I was seven at the time and don't know where I'd be now if not for her."

I was enjoying the illuminating exchange with Royce, but I didn't want him to put his job on the line by spending any more time talking to me. I'm sure Ballbusteria's grandchildren were scared spitless of her, just like Royce claimed to be of his much-beloved Grammy Webb. I told him he better get back inside and assured him his story was safe, and would go no farther than me, him, and the lamppost—or the DMV parking lot, in this case.

As he opened the truck door, I asked one last question, "Before you go, do you know anything about Julio Sarcova or Dr. Patrick O'Keefe? Both are on my personal suspect list, you see."

"Working here at the DMV, I know a lot of people in the area, ma'am. I worked in the Aransas Pass office for a few years before I was transferred to this one, and that's where the majority of Rockport citizens go to renew their licenses. Believe it or not, that office usually has a longer wait time than we do here. So, anyway, Sarcova is a well-respected barber in Rockport, and known for being a mouthpiece for every cause one can imagine. I think he files lawsuits more frequently than I change underwear. But Julio has good morals and is basically harmless. And O'Keefe? He's just a full-of-himself doctor who thinks he's God's gift to the medical profession. But regardless of his overwhelming ego, and underwhelming bedside manner, I'd bet big money that, in line with the Hippocratic Oath he pledged, he'd never actually harm anyone. And, frankly, everyone in town thinks he's still in love with his ex-wife, Avery Curry, and also that Avery was only using Claypool to make O'Keefe jealous. Cooper was nothing more than a rebound boyfriend, according to a few of Avery's friends."

"I think I'd have to agree with you on that score. Now get back to your post before you land yourself in the unemployment line."

"Thank you, ma'am. You're actually an all-right kind of gal." He flashed me a beguiling smile as he shut the passenger door.

I unrolled my window and hollered out as he walked toward the back door of the DMV building, "You're a fine man, Royce. I watched you interacting with that young boy earlier. You'll make a great father someday when you've settled down with that family you're longing for. I appreciate you being open and honest with me."

Royce Chrisman smiled one last time and waved as he disappeared inside the building. I felt extremely satisfied with the outcome of my spur-of-the-moment decision to come to the DMV and speak to the man I now knew was one-hundred-percent innocent of the malicious killing of Cooper Claypool. I could hardly wait to get back to the trailer and tell Rip all about my revealing and rewarding day. Unfortunately, however, I was going to have to make another trip to the DMV before my license expired in mid December.

CHAPTER 20

"I've been thinking, Rip."

"Did it give you a headache, my dear?" He asked, as he placed my chosen afternoon highball on the table; equal amounts of tequila and orange juice with a splash of Grenadine.

"Watch it, buster!" I replied playfully before continuing. "I'm being serious, Rip."

Rip sat down across the table from me with his own drink. In a teasing manner, he leaned forward, put his elbows on the kitchen table, and dramatically placed his chin in his cupped hands. Looking directly into my eyes and with a mischievous smirk, he said, "Talk to me, girl."

He was in a light-hearted mood, and that's when I most enjoyed his company. But there was no time to engage in joyful banter with him. "You made a comment about how it was unfortunate the murder weapon had not been recovered."

"Yes, I remember," Rip replied, leaning back against his chair and crossing his arms in front of his chest. I was almost sad to watch his cheerful frame of mind disappear like money in a slot machine. With a more somber tone, he replied, "Sometimes the murder weapon can speak louder for the victim than any witness or trace evidence ever could. Where are you going with this?"

"I've just got this niggling notion about Claypool's death."

"And what would that be?"

"I really don't want to tell anyone yet."

"Then what was the point of bringing it up if you don't want to share what this "niggling notion" of yours is about?" Rip reacted almost angrily, as if I was purposely dangling a glazed doughnut in front of him that he couldn't quite reach.

"It's just that I feel so strongly inclined to pursue this idea, even though it sounds preposterous, highly unlikely, and ridiculously absurd even to me. I guess I'm just curious if you could get Milo to take us back out to where we discovered Cooper's body."

"Yes, of course I could. And then?" Rip still sounded as if he were peeved. "I know you well enough to know there's more to your inquiry than you've shared with me so far."

"I want to try to find the spear-gun that was used to kill Cooper."

"Seriously?" Rip asked, now appearing skeptical. "And while we're at it, shouldn't we search for that needle someone lost in a haystack somewhere?"

I tried to suppress my frustration, knowing patience would fare better than snippiness in this situation. "It might actually turn out to be not as difficult as you'd think. Milo sounded confident the spear came from Cooper's own gun because he recognized it as the same, or at least similar, model he and Cooper used to spear red snapper and occasionally sharks. Remember?"

"Yes, I recall him making that comment. But that doesn't mean others didn't purchase the exact same models at the show as they did."

I was glad I hadn't overreacted to his caustic remark as I took in the fact he was now settling into our discourse with more enthusiasm. The idea of Cooper being killed by some other suspect, using an identical spear-gun as the victim's, was really not the suspicion I'd had in mind. But if that's what it took to get Rip to go along with me, I'd latch on to it. So I switched gears and continued.

"I realize, given the law of averages, the possibility of the spear, itself, belonging to some other individual is not great. But, don't you agree it's still within the realm of possibility? The boys purchased the new-fangled spears at the same expo where they bought the guns. Correct?"

"Yes," Rip consented. "And I see exactly where you're going with this now."

You do? I wanted to ask. *I don't even know where I'm going with this yet.*

I listened intently as Rip went on to explain where I was supposedly going with my niggling notion. "It goes without saying those three were not the only local men who attended the gun show in Corpus Christi. The Coastal Bend is home to many hunters and anglers. And spear-guns, along with the necessary spears, were likely hot-selling items at the show."

"My thoughts exactly, Rip!" Not really, but I had him right where I wanted him and had every intention of taking advantage of it. "Do you know if the investigating team has looked beyond the same individuals we've targeted? Or have they cast their net wider and discovered possible suspects we're not privy to yet?"

"As you know, I'm not exactly being kept in the loop. But I haven't heard any suspect mentioned that we haven't considered. In fact, I spoke to Detective Reeves, and he was more informative today than he's been to date. He indicated in a round-about way that every one of them has been cleared. Their alibis checked out, or there were other factors making them virtually incapable of committing the murder."

"Including Sarcova, O'Keefe, and Avery Curry?"

"Yep."

"The Schillings? Both Mack and Trey?"

"Yep."

"And dare I ask? Does that also take in Milo?"

"Sorry. That I don't know. For obvious reasons, he didn't even bring up Milo's name when we spoke earlier. I assumed Branson would have told me if he'd been cleared, however."

"I was afraid of that. You didn't mention Royce to Detective Reeves, did you?" I knew my voice sounded edgy, but I had promised Royce his story would be safe with me. When I told him it'd go no farther than him, me and the DMV parking lot, I'd forgotten to mention I'd be singing like a canary in a gas-filled coal mine the second I saw my husband, the former county sheriff.

"Of course not, honey. I promised you I wouldn't say anything about him to anybody, not even Milo and Reggie, and I haven't. You told me you didn't believe Royce could commit such an atrocity. After hearing your recital of the conversation you had with him, I agree." Dolly had leapt up onto Rip's lap and he'd been absentmindedly scratching her behind her ears as he spoke. At any moment she could reach her daily allowance of human contact and turn to embed her needle-sharp teeth into Rip's hand. "Trust me, sweetheart. I don't want to complicate Chrisman's life without good reason any more than you do."

"Thank you. I'm going to call Milo and see if he'll take us out into the Gulf where he told us he and Cooper often fished. They hunted for red snapper around the oil rigs with their spear-guns, he said. He also mentioned some island with an oyster reef near it."

"Yes, I remember that. And, believe it or not, I agree it's worth a shot," Rip said with a satisfied wink. He was getting more and more enthusiastic with every thought he voiced. "If by some chance we do locate the spear-gun, it might provide the clue that sews up the entire investigation. After all, solving a crime often rests on one small discovery that blows the entire case wide open. We could take it to the seller the three men bought their spear guns from and ask him if he remembers, or had a record of, any other buyers who purchased the same model of gun and/or spears. As you inferred, the spear may not have been fired by Claypool's own gun as everyone's been presuming. His spear-gun could have fallen to the sea floor when he was shot by someone else's, and still be where it landed. After that, and only after that, I'll turn the murder weapon over to the investigating team. Good detective work, Miss Marple!"

Even though I hadn't meant to infer what Rip thought I had, just hearing him agree to my suggestion to take a trip out to search for the murder weapon took a load off my shoulders. Not only that, I was impressed he could so casually drop the name of one of Agatha Christie's main characters, Miss Jane Marple. For that matter, I wouldn't have wagered he could pull *any* classical literary character's name out of his hat other than the Pink Panther and Rhett Butler. He'd always enjoyed watching Peter Sellers movies and what little he knew about Rhett Butler was only due to the amusement he got from saying, "Frankly, my dear Rapella, I don't give a damn."

While I'd reiterated my interactions with Royce Chrisman, Rip had been seasoning two tiny chuck-eye steaks he planned to barbecue on the small gas grill that slid out on a shelf from inside one of the outside storage compartments. I'm certain it had been the main feature that had put Rip over the edge when deciding which trailer he'd wanted to purchase almost six years ago, even though I'm also certain he'd never confess to it.

He'd always been drawn to cleverly designed gadgets and flashy widgets when purchasing vehicles. The man in Rip attributes his choices to things like horsepower, torque, and handling. But the little boy in him buys the truck with the shiny dual exhaust pipes because the growling roar they emit when he stomps on the gas pedal sounds so incredibly awesome.

A few minutes later, while Rip lounged in a lawn chair with his daily cocktail, refilled four times already, he was keeping an eye on the sizzling steaks. As he relaxed and enjoyed the beautiful sunset on the west horizon, I mulled over every entry I'd made in my notebook since our impromptu investigation had commenced. It wasn't a complete accounting by any means, so I tried to recall other details I'd committed only to memory—a risky and ill-advised practice at my age.

I desperately did want to locate the murder weapon, but my "niggling notion" was not exactly what I'd led Rip to believe. I still believed the actual concept running amok in my mind was almost too far beyond probability to share with anyone, even my often cynical, and always bullheaded, husband.

CHAPTER 21

"Who just pulled out of your driveway?" I asked Regina when she opened her front door the following morning. While we'd been driving down Flamingo Road, a faded green Chevy S-10 pickup had been backing out of the kids' driveway. When the vehicle passed by, we'd tried to make out its occupant, but the windows were too darkly tinted to identify the driver. As Reggie responded to my question, she was plainly shaken up by whatever had just taken place.

"That whack job just told me to tell Milo he knew what had happened to Cooper. He also said if Milo doesn't pay what Cooper owes his boss, he may be in mortal danger, along with the rest of his family. I didn't know what to do or say to him, but I was ticked off, so I just kind of freaked out on him." Reggie turned to her father as she added, "I'm so relieved you're here now, Daddy."

Rip gave her a quick one-armed hug, and asked, "Did the man tell you his name?"

"No, but he was really creepy. Would never make eye contact with me, which gave me the willies."

"Can you recall the exact words he used?"

"No, not exactly. But, fortunately, I have most of it recorded."

"You do?" Rip's eyebrows arched as he spoke. "That's my girl! I taught you well."

"Yeah, you did. I had my phone in my hand when I answered the door. As soon as he told me to give Milo a message, I hit the record button so I wouldn't forget what the message was. Since he never looked directly at me, the weirdo had no clue he was being taped."

"Can you describe him for me?" Rip inquired.

"Um, let me see. Kind of a hard description to put into words, actually."

When Regina hesitated, I asked, "Does 'weasel-faced little dweeb' seem to fit the bill?"

Reggie thought about it for a second before nodding enthusiastically. "Yes, it does, Mom. That description fits him to a tee! Skinny geek with a bad complexion and gnarly teeth. As you'll notice in the recording, he had a slight British accent. Kind of like he'd moved here to the states years ago but still retained a touch of his native brogue."

I turned and spoke directly to Rip. "I bet it was Paulie Winterkorn, the man Royce told me about."

Then I turned back to Reggie and explained, "Winterkorn works for a loan shark out of El Paso. He's probably afraid he'll lose his job if he doesn't produce the money Cooper owed him. Royce is certain he's the one who called himself Captain Hook in those threatening phone calls and messages to Cooper."

"Who's Royce?" Reggie asked. I merely shrugged. "Loose lips sink ships" was a phrase that came to mind. There was no reason to test how loose my daughter's lips were at this stage of the game. I'd made a vow to keep my conversation with Royce Chrisman to myself, after all, and I intended to keep my word.

"Let's go sit at the kitchen table and listen to the recording," Rip suggested after I'd neglected to answer our daughter's inquiry.

The transcript of that recording went as follows.

"Tell him I know what happened to Claypool, and I'm not going to let up until I get my boss's money back. I can't afford to lose this part-time job, because working at my regular job ain't cutting it and I got bills to pay." We listened to the high-pitched, nasally voice emanating from Reggie's cell phone. I'd been right about Paulie's insecurity regarding his part-time job. As Reggie had said, there was definitely a hint of an English accent to Winterkorn's voice.

"What kind of full-time profession are you in?" Regina had asked him. I could sense by her voice she was frightened but doing her best to appear calm and collected.

"Well, it's um, I'm a uh—"

"Yes?"

"Let's just say I'm in advertising and leave it at that," the annoyingly effeminate voice replied.

"You're the dude who was leaving those nasty messages on Cooper Claypool's phone, aren't you?"

Silent pause. Reggie's voice is then heard again. "Call yourself Captain Hook, don't you? Does calling yourself that cartoonish name make you feel more intimidating? If so, it's not working. Very childish, if you ask me."

"Well, I, um, it's just that I, uh—"

"Spit it out, numb-nuts. I ain't got all day to talk to some idiot who showed up uninvited on my doorstep."

I was relieved to hear the fear in Reggie's voice disappear and an assertive, almost aggressive tone replace it. It's clear the guy she was speaking to was stymied by this sassy broad he'd encountered. It took him awhile to counter her jab.

"Listen up, sweetheart. I'm not Captain Hook. Captain Hook's a great big muscular guy. A body-builder, you know. Real scary dude. Eats guys like your husband for lunch."

There was no response from Reggie other than a scathing snicker, and the man began to sound desperate to convince her it wasn't he who left the messages. He was realistic enough to know his appearance made it evident that any eighty-year-old female librarian could take him out if she so chose and his wimpy physique wasn't going to induce anyone to cave in to his demands. "Captain Hook competes in cage-fighting on the weekends. You're surely familiar with those fights where the competitors beat each other half to death? Look at me. Now, do I look like the kind of guy who'd compete in something as barbaric as that?"

"Not at all. You look more like the kind of guy who'd aspire to be the hop-scotch champion on the neighborhood playground."

After I heard her response on the recording, I reached across the table with my hand up to give her a high-five. I couldn't recall the last time I'd been so proud of her. I enjoyed seeing her exhibit this seldom-revealed spunky side.

"Listen," the man said defensively. "You can think what you want about me. It's Captain Hook you should worry about. Unless, of course, you don't mind if your husband suffers a similar fate as his friend. Captain Hook shows no mercy to guys like those two. Nor does he go easy on the wives and children of men who won't pay him back the money he loaned them in good faith. You better see to it Claypool's debt is covered for Tiffany and Dusty's well-being, if nothing else."

"Oh, really?" It was clear by the cynicism in Reggie's voice she was not convinced this cage-fighting fiend existed.

"You better believe me, Regina. I work for the loan shark, all right, but more as a consultant. I am not the animal who left those messages, I assure you. That dude's a mean son-of-a—"

"Methinks thou dost protest too much." Reggie cut the man off, but not before I winced at the idea this creep not only knew my daughter's name, but my grandkids' names, as well. *Watch it, girl*, I thought. *Don't let your mouth write checks your cheeky behind can't cash.*

Milo had claimed Captain Hook had also mentioned all three names in his latest threatening voice message, which made me even more convinced Paulie Winterkorn was the man who'd made those calls.

Apparently, this guy was not in Reggie's college Shakespearian Literature class. In response to her "methinks" remark, he uttered, "Huh?"

"That's a line from—"

"Whatever. Just give Milo the message. 'I know exactly what happened to Cooper Claypool and he better be careful how he—'"

"Just give me the dude's number and I'll have Milo get in touch with him." Regina was clearly disgusted with the creep at this point. It was obvious she just wanted this slime-ball off her property as fast as possible.

"Milo doesn't need to get in touch with Captain Hook, or my boss. I can promise you, they'll be in touch with him if a cashier's check for seventy-five grand isn't delivered to this address in the next five days." This last remark was spoken in an intimidating tone. Regina told us he'd written down a P.O. box number in El Paso on a frozen burrito wrapper he'd pulled out of his back pocket and handed it to her. The last thing we heard before the recording ended was the slamming of the wooden front door.

Rip and Regina hashed over her encounter with the man I was sure was the Paulie Winterkorn who Royce had told me about. I sat back and took in the discussion without adding my input to their exchange.

"Can't we track the loan shark through the post office box?" Reggie asked her father.

"I doubt it, honey. These kinds of dude are pretty slick and know how to play the system. They operate on a need-to-know basis. The mail box was probably rented under an assumed name and is checked for mail about once a week by someone different every time before being closed after a month or two. Do you remember anything uniquely specific about this guy; identifying tattoos or other remarkable physical features?"

"Not really. Didn't notice any tattoos, but he did have an unusual odor. I recognized the scent but haven't been able to place it yet."

While the two chatted, I flitted around the kitchen, using a dishrag to wipe off a small coffee spill on the granite countertop, placing several dirty utensils in the dishwasher, wrapping a twist tie around the neck of a overflowing bag of trash and replacing the bag with a new one I'd found in the walk-in pantry. The fact the size of the kids' pantry exceeded the entire square footage of our trailer did not escape me.

I listened to Rip and Reggie's discourse with one ear while I listened for Milo to get home with the other. Reggie had said he was on the way home from his office.

When Milo finally walked into the kitchen, his first words were, "Anything to eat? I'm starving."

"That's it!" Reggie exclaimed. "The dude smelled like Canadian bacon."

"Canadian bacon?" Rip asked, as Milo simultaneously asked, "What dude?"

As Rip and Reggie were filling Milo in on what had occurred earlier, I was thinking to myself, Where does one usually find Canadian bacon? I can think of no more likely place than a pizza parlor.

CHAPTER 22

Milo had left his boat in the water after we'd handed over Cooper's body at the boat launch Sunday evening. While I had driven his truck and trailer home from the boat launch parking lot, he and Rip had taken the boat home and left it on the electronic lift attached to the kids' dock. There was also a Jet Ski lift, and I was a bit surprised Reggie hadn't made sure there was a brand new shiny Sea-Doo proudly displayed on it. I don't imagine either she or Milo would have used it very often. But, just adding the illusion of its owners being affluent would no doubt have served Regina's purpose in purchasing it.

I don't know from where she got this spend-thrift trait. Was it an act of rebellion from growing up with a mother who'd scour through Good Will stores and flea markets rather than buy her child a closet full of new school clothes every year? My reasoning was there seemed no point in spending a lot of money on clothes Reggie would outgrow within months anyway.

However, I do remember feeling bad—in fact remorseful enough to apologize the afternoon she'd exited the school bus sobbing uncontrollably. A boy one grade ahead of her had pointed at her attractive, but well-worn t-shirt in front of the entire class, and exclaimed, "Hey, that's one of my old shirts! My mom sold it in our garage sale last month for a dime!" I learned my lesson that day. Saving a buck here and there was not worth causing your child to be humiliated at school.

After that incident, I always bought Regina inexpensive, but brand new outfits she could wear unabashedly to school. Not an over-abundance of outfits, but an adequate supply. We weren't vagrants, after all, and I didn't want her classmates to treat her as if we were.

As I rested on a chaise lounge on the kids' back deck, I was surprised when Regina hollered out the kitchen window, "Mom! Let's go! The men are going to load the boat with everything we'll need while we're gone."

We took Regina's car to town and I had her drive by every dining establishment she could think of that offered pizza. We were looking for the faded green S-10 pickup. There were not many of them still on the road, so I figured it'd be easy to track down.

Regina could only think of a few places likely to serve pizza. There were no S-10 pickups in the parking lots of the first two restaurants, but parked next to a dumpster behind the third one, Pirate's Cove Pizza Parlor, was a vehicle matching the description. I was pretty certain it was the one we'd seen that morning pulling out of the kids' driveway. Regina recognized it immediately.

"That's it!" She exclaimed. I motioned for her to pull into the parking lot.

"Milo expressed the desire to squelch his hunger, and there's still plenty of daylight left. We all should get a bite to eat before we head out on what might well be a long day on the water. How does a Canadian bacon pizza sound?" I asked.

"Pizza sounds perfect, Mom! But make it pepperoni, please. I'm afraid I'll never be able to choke down Canadian bacon again without seeing that jerk's face in my mind."

We took a seat on a bench inside after we'd placed our

order for an extra-large hand-tossed pepperoni pizza to go. When I spotted an older gal who pranced around as if she owned the place, I walked over to her and asked her if a Paulie Winterkorn was an employee there.

"Captain Hook?" She asked with an amused lilt to her voice. "Sure does. He's right up the street."

Puzzled, I followed her to the window next to the bench where Reggie still sat. The jovial lady pointed to an intersection almost a block further down Market Street. Pacing back and forth was a guy in a pirate costume depicting Captain James Bartholomew Hook, the Disney character who antagonized Peter Pan after Peter cut off his hand and fed it to the crocodiles. The costume, complete with a humongous fishing hook duck-taped to his left hand, and a toy-like steel sword in his other hand, was comical and had to be embarrassing for a grown man to be seen wearing. Just standing at an intersection wearing a pizza banner was degrading enough.

There were cardboard signs draped over Paulie's shoulders; one across his chest that read, "Ahoy there, Mates! Now serving lunch at Pirate's Cove," and another spanning his backside that read, "Offering large three-topping pizzas for only $10."

Laughing almost uncontrollably, I thanked the lady for pointing Paulie out to us. After she had returned to her station, I sat back down beside Reggie, who couldn't quite wrap her head around the fact the comically dressed guy on the corner was the same guy who'd threatened her husband on his own doorstep a couple of hours earlier. "If Cooper knew he'd been intimidated all that time by, well, that 'little weasel-faced dweeb' peddling pizza in a pirate costume, he'd turn over in his grave!"

I had to giggle along with Reggie at her remark. Our quiet giggling turned to out-right laughter again after I quipped, "Well, 'Captain Hook' might be all of that, but he did tell you he was in advertising, didn't he?"

* * *

The guys were sitting on the back deck with Miller Lite bottles in their hands. After I explained what we'd just discovered, we all went inside and polished off the pizza.

"You all ready to go?" Milo asked after Regina and I had cleared off the table and put the saucers and silverware in the dishwasher. I was delighted to see Milo acting almost giddy about our decision to try to locate the murder weapon. He'd told us he had several very possible locations to check out where we might just get lucky and stumble across Cooper's spear-gun. He said, "The Coast Guard and detectives probably searched all the standard places where most guys go spear-fishing, but Cooper, Pinto, and I had some great spots no one else seemed to know about, and like most fisherman, we kept their locations close to our vests. Of course, when we came in the other night it was almost dark, so we'll have to swing by the marina first to fill up."

Rip reached for his wallet instinctively.

If Earth spun as rapidly as the numbers on this gas pump dial, our planet would be flinging people off it right and left, I thought, watching the price increasing in leaps and bounds as Milo held the nozzle while filling the fuel tank. I was shocked, but pleased, he hadn't asked us to cover the cost this time. After all, it was his neck we were trying to drag off the chopping block.

"That comes to $98.27," the attendant said casually. Of course, the price sounded nominal to the attendant, no doubt. He probably filled up fuel tanks on the large yachts moored in the marina frequently and was accustomed to totals in the thousands, making our tab sound like chump change.

"Dang it!" Milo exclaimed, reaching into his back pocket.

"What?" Regina, Rip, and I asked in unison.

"I must have left my wallet at the house."

"Of course you did," Rip replied, without even trying to disguise the skepticism in his voice. He turned to give me a look of disbelief as he pulled his wallet out and extracted a credit card that was still warm to the touch from the scorching it had endured the last time Milo stopped for fuel.

Finally, we were underway. Rip sat silently for a good fifteen minutes, still simmering from being screwed over once again by his son-in-law. I leaned over and spoke quietly enough so Milo and Regina couldn't hear me, but loud enough for Rip to make out my words over the roaring of the motor. As usual, he wasn't wearing his hearing aids.

"Might as well let it go, dear. He admitted they were in financial trouble, and the cost of fuel and maintenance on a boat adds up quickly. We both wanted to come out today to look for the spear-gun, and renting a boat to take us out would have cost a great deal more than the fuel did." Under normal circumstances my ears would be emitting more steam than Rip's in a situation like this. But at that crucial stage in our investigation, I was intent on finding the spear-gun and needed Rip to be focused on the prize, as well.

He nodded reluctantly, but his mood lightened up and soon he was back in the moment, directing Milo to start at the most likely locations Cooper might have been fishing the Saturday morning of his death.

As we left Aransas Bay and sailed out into the Gulf, Milo said, "First I want to try the place where we had good luck the last two times we fished there. I know the detectives probably searched around every oil rig between here and Florida, but they may not have known about this other special place of ours. It's off a remote island, not much more than a decent-sized sand bar that has a small oyster reef on its east side."

About ten minutes later, Milo appeared startled as he pointed and exclaimed, "What the heck?"

With our older and less efficient eyes, Rip and I gazed

in the direction Milo had indicated. When it became apparent neither of us could make out anything but a far-away apparition that could have been anything from a barge being propelled by a tug boat to a Styrofoam cooler that had flown off the deck of a boat while it was in motion, Milo elaborated, "There's a boat out there."

"Boat?" Rip asked.

"What boat?" I added.

Clearly exasperated, Milo raised his voice as if hearing loss was the reason we were stupefied. Of course, in Rip's case, it very well may have played a part. "The boat! Over by the shore line of that island."

"And?" Rip asked. I still couldn't make it out, and I doubt Rip could either. It was unclear to both of us why seeing a boat would have caused Milo's exclamation to begin with, so Rip added, "Is that a problem?"

"It's an oyster boat!" Milo replied, as if that would clear up our confusion about why the boat was even worthy of pointing out. But for me, anyway, it didn't clear up anything.

"Why wouldn't an oyster boat be a normal sighting over there? I can see a sandy island beyond the boat now. Isn't that the one you just mentioned with the oyster reef by it?" I asked.

"Yes, but the reef is nowhere near the size a commercial boat would harvest oysters from. Besides, the reef is right up by the shore, not accessible with an oyster boat to begin with."

"Okay," Rip responded, making it obvious he still had no clue either as to why Milo was so animated by the boat's presence.

"It looks like Pinto's boat." We had gotten a little closer to it by this stage, and Rip, who hadn't put off obtaining new eyeglasses because of the expense as I had, held his hand over his eyes to shade them from the sun. He stared a few seconds longer, and agreed with Milo.

"Yes, I think you're right. It does look like his boat. I

can almost make out the 'e' and 'm' at the end of the boat's name on the aft."

As the vessel in the distance rocked in the waves, Milo said, "Yes, I can read it clearly now. That's definitely Pinto's boat, but what worries me is that it looks like it might be adrift. Maybe not, though, because the direction of the wind has the boat at an angle that would block our view of the anchor rope if it's out."

"Can you call Pinto on your phone? Maybe he needs assistance," Rip asked. There was trepidation in both Milo and Rip's voices as they spoke. Were they thinking what I was thinking? Had the killer struck again? Had Philip Bean suffered the same fate as Cooper Claypool? Had he been on the killer's hit list too?

We hadn't had a cell phone long enough to know much about them. Teaching us about new-fangled electronics was a bit like trying to train a cat to shake hands and fetch Frisbees. I repeated Rip's question to Milo. "Can you call him?"

"I have no signal out here and I'm sure he doesn't either. But I might be able to contact him on the marine radio," Milo explained.

All this time, Regina had been sitting silently in one of the aft chairs located on each side of an aerated live well, which, according to Milo, was in need of repair. Reggie appeared more interested in acquiring a suntan than locating a weapon or identifying oyster boats. It became apparent the ramifications of another one of Milo's friends' boats being adrift at sea had not occurred to her when, without even opening her eyes, she asked, "Can somebody hand me a bottle of water out of the cooler?"

I handed her the water and wondered for the four thousand and eighteenth time if she and my *real* daughter hadn't been accidentally switched in the hospital nursery after their births.

After much finagling with the knobs to control the squelch and tune in to frequencies by Milo, we finally heard Pinto's voice. It came over as a crackling sound, cutting out more often than not. "Is ____you____? Can you____me? I can't ____out what____ __ing."

"Yes, yes! It's Milo! Can you read me?" The relief in his voice and on all of our faces was evident. Not including Reggie's face, that is, which was busy having another round of sunscreen slathered on it. But the important thing was that Pinto was okay. Or alive, anyway.

"Crackle, crackle, crackle. What____ ____ doing ____here?"

"What are *you* doing? Why are *you* out here?" Milo spoke loudly into the hand-held microphone.

Crackle, crackle, ____ thought ____ low humming sound, so that ____ could____ , loud startling squelch sound, and now ____ crackle, crackle, screech, heading ____ ____ ____ ina ____ silence, high-pitched squawk, and then more silence, is what we heard emitting from the radio.

"Must have lost the freaking signal," Milo muttered, pounding on the radio as if that might help in some way. It was the same technique Rip used when he tried to repair the television, refrigerator, and pretty much every other electronic apparatus that had stopped functioning properly. It wasn't working for Milo any better than it'd ever worked for Rip.

While Rip stood at the helm steering the boat, Milo tried several more times to contact Pinto, to no avail. So we could make out his words, Milo shouted, "I have a signal now. Don't know why he can't hear me. But I think he might have been saying he was heading back to the Fulton Marina where he moors the boat. I'd still like to know what he's doing out here in the first place."

"Me too," Rip hollered back. Where Milo had sounded concerned, Rip sounded suspicious. I was apprehensive, as well, wondering if this might turn out to be one of those cases where a perpetrator returns to the scene of his crime for whatever reason.

"I'm going to try to cut him off if he heads this way."

"Okay. Good! I'll turn the helm back over to you."

It was several minutes later before our paths converged. When Pinto realized we were trying to stop him, he brought his boat to a halt. His motor was still running in neutral when we pulled up alongside the *Hook 'em*. Looking up at Pinto in the taller vessel, Milo yelled out, "Whatcha doing out here, Pinto?"

"Well. I, um, just wanted..." Pinto paused to gain control of his emotions. He appeared both embarrassed and distraught. There were dark circles under his eyes and he appeared ten years older than he had when we joined him on the oyster run just a couple of days earlier. Finally, he spoke again. "I didn't get a chance to say goodbye to Cooper and it's been bothering me more than I'd anticipated. Haven't slept well since I heard about his death. I just can't believe someone would do such a thing to a guy like him. He has always—"

Choked up, Pinto couldn't continue. He shut off the motor of his boat and sat down wearily on the edge of the hull. Milo had trouble speaking, too, as he replied, "I know. I know, buddy. I can't believe it either. I'd introduce you to my in-laws, but I heard you've already met."

"Hello, Pinto," I said. Rip also greeted the oysterman before Milo continued speaking. "As you may know, I was one of the prime suspects in his murder because of our friendship and business association. Also, I'm sorry to say, we had a bit of a dust-up in Crabby's parking lot the night before his death."

Pinto shrugged, unconcerned, and as was his nature, didn't ask for any of the juicy details. "Boys will be boys."

"Yeah, I know," Milo replied. He hung his head and swiped at a tear making its way down his cheek. "But I went way, way too far that day, Pinto. I acted so foolishly, so over-the-top violently, and, well, I hurt my best friend. I hurt him bad. More than anything, I wish I could turn back the time and tell him I loved him that night in the bar, and just left the fact he'd lied to me go unmentioned. I knew he was having a tough go of it, fighting demons he couldn't beat. I should have offered to help him, not lashed out at him."

"You couldn't have predicted he'd be killed hours later, son." Even as Pinto mourned the loss of a close pal, he tried to console his other friend who was grieving just as deeply.

"I know, buddy. I just wish that stupid fight in the parking lot had never happened. I was upset and over-reacted to being lied to by my best bud. Knowing that it's the last memory I'll have of our friendship is killing me. It's something I'll have to live with the rest of my life, I guess, but I deserve to suffer. In fact, considering what I did to my best friend, I deserve to suffer a lot."

Rip had winced at Milo's use of the term "dust-up" again to describe the donnybrook that had taken place outside the bar and grill on Saturday. But I saw his expression change to one of empathy when Milo admitted he'd been wrong to injure his friend and partner, and hitting Cooper with a beer bottle was totally uncalled for. The memory of their last time together was eating Milo up, like a cancer he couldn't rid himself of. It hit me then that neither of us had taken in to account the devastation and remorse Milo had to be struggling with since the death of his closest friend. We both should have shown more compassion; offered more solace and support this last week instead of hounding him for answers.

The same realization must have occurred to Rip. He put his arm over Milo's shoulder and pulled him toward him for a warm and lengthy embrace. "You're going to have to let that go, son. Cooper would want you to. You had no way of knowing that'd be your last interaction with your friend. Don't you imagine he felt he had that angry reaction from you coming, for deceiving you? In his shoes, wouldn't you have understood your partner's anger? I guarantee you he felt guilty and remorseful when you ran into him at Crabby's. He loved you as you loved him and wouldn't want you to carry that guilt around on your shoulders. What you're doing now to help find justice for his death is what's important. I believe he is watching over you now and knows you've got his back."

Rip's comforting words helped. I was relieved to see our daughter get up and hold her grieving husband in her arms, consoling him. Not even trying to stem the flow of tears streaming down his cheek, Milo looked up and said, "Thanks, Pop. I needed that."

Little did we realize then, but "Pop" would be Milo's term of endearment for Rip from that moment on.

Pinto volunteered to help us search for Cooper's spear-gun. He anchored his oyster boat out in the deeper water and climbed aboard Milo's fishing boat. We beached the fishing boat on the sandy shore of the island Milo had thought was our best hope of finding the spear-gun. Rip and I scoured the sand and scant foliage on the east side of the island. Milo had described the west side as primarily a marshy wetland and we could hear the unique trumpeting sound of sand hill cranes resonating from the area.

Meanwhile, Regina polished her fingernails as she waited in the boat and Milo and Pinto searched the surf and out farther in the water, clothed only in denim jeans and cotton shirts. Intensely focused on their mission, they both seemed unaware they were shivering from the chilling affect of the cool water. Disappointment was evident on their faces, as I'm sure it was on mine too.

Later, after checking numerous other spots, Milo and Pinto trembled as they discussed whether or not to continue their search or admit defeat and head in. Overhearing their debate, the niggling thought that had been plaguing my mind for the last couple of days made a return, demanding to be heard. So I complied. "I know you two are half frozen, but could I ask you boys for one more little favor?"

"Sure," Milo replied.

Pinto concurred. "Of course you can."

"Can we return to that very first place we searched, just for another hour or so? I feel driven to take another look around the island with the oyster reef."

The men were happy to oblige. I think they both believed they hadn't given the area a thorough enough search. They seemed almost as anxious as I was to return for another scouring. Twenty minutes later we had returned to the site. This time Rip and I followed the men into the water. Only Regina remained in the boat, not anxious to risk chipping the polish on one of her newly manicured nails. Not pleased with her self-absorption and shallowness, I would have dragged her butt out of the boat myself if not for the fact I knew she'd only be in the way.

We spread out, each covering a different section. I headed straight to the oyster reef. The shells were sharp, but I had thick-soled tennis shoes on to protect the bottoms of my feet.

Convinced frostbite was responsible for my numb toes, I was about to call it quits and return to the boat to wrap my feet in a dry towel, when I spotted a glint of light about twenty feet away, on the base of the thigh-high water. I got increasingly excited the closer I got to the object reflecting light from the sun, which would be setting in the west in another hour or so.

I reached down and grasped the object to lift it out of the water. With great enthusiasm, I hollered out, "I found it! I found it! I've got the spear-gun!"

Everyone quickly gathered together in a cluster close to shore. Regina had even exited the boat to join us in the surf along the bank. Milo took the gun from me and turned it over and over in his hands. There were a few feet of the cord that had been severed still attached to the gun. "Yep! This is Coop's short-barreled gun. And here's where the killer cut the cord so the murder weapon wouldn't be found trailing from his victim's body." He was pointing to the frazzled end of the cord that had connected the spear to the spear-gun.

"No so fast," I said breathlessly.

Everyone turned to look at me with concerned expressions, as if worried my mind was being affected by too many hours in the sun.

"I recall Rip's hand being sliced open by an oyster shell," I explained. Then, glancing at Milo, I continued. "And also you losing what you thought was probably a stingray when the fish swam into a small oyster bed the day we went fishing. Instead of being cut by the killer, couldn't the cord have been severed by an oyster shell? Look where I found it? Directly on top of the reef you told us about."

Milo and Pinto both nodded simultaneously. Pinto asked, "Yeah, that's possible, I guess. What are you getting at?"

"I really don't know, precisely. But check out the gun and see if anything looks amiss about it." I don't know why I felt so strongly that we'd overlooked a possible cause of death, but I did. I imagine it was due to the fact that every single suspect we, as well as the investigating team, had come up with had been cleared by the detectives, and nothing in the way of motive or evidence implicated any other individual.

"You know, now that you mention it, Rapella," Milo said, clearly astonished by something on the spear-gun he'd just noticed. "There is a lot of gunk around the trigger mechanism, which happens when you don't clean the gun after every use. Cooper was never very good about maintaining his equipment."

"That's an understatement if I ever heard one," Pinto said, with a touch of amusement in his tone. He reached out to take the gun from Milo's outstretched hand and said, "This model is bad about jamming to begin with, and that gunk can cause the trigger to malfunction, too."

"That's what my gut was telling me. I recalled you explaining the issues with Cooper's less-expensive model, and have also noted that everyone I've talked to who knew Cooper personally, described him as reckless and impulsive. So, tell me fellows. Is it possible the gun could have jammed and then accidentally discharged when he was trying to get it working properly again?" I asked. My mind was whirring as my hunch appeared to be heading toward a satisfying fruition.

I could tell Milo and Pinto's minds were racing with possibilities, as well. Rip asked, "But, wouldn't it fire the spear away from him if that happened?"

"Well, sure. Unless—" Milo paused, deep in thought.

"Oh, yeah. I hadn't thought of that," Pinto said.

"And you know how he was," Milo added.

"You're right," Pinto agreed, as if the two were tapping into the same wavelength and no words were required for them to reach the same conclusion. "I bet that's exactly what happened."

"What? What happened?" Rip asked impatiently.

Pinto looked at Milo, and in unspoken agreement, directed our attention toward the spear-gun in his hands and began to explain. "Rapella hit the nail head-on. Cooper was not only negligent when it came to taking care of his equipment, he was also lackadaisical about safety practices. Like I was just saying, this trigger mechanism is not only prone to jamming, the accumulating gunk you see here is a result of bypassing the recommended cleanings. Along with the gun's inclination to jam in the best of circumstances, this build-up of gunk could have greatly exacerbated the issue."

When Pinto paused, Milo took over, "In the event of a malfunction, you should always work on it with the barrel facing away from you, purely for the sake of safety. And I mean absolutely always! I caught Cooper turning this gun inward one time after it jammed, because at only nineteen-inches long, it can be tempting to work on it that way. He actually had the spear resting up against his chest while messing with the trigger mechanism. I warned him about how dangerous it was, even wearing a loading pad to protect his chest from bruising by the powerful recoil of the gun when fired. As per usual, Cooper just blew me off."

"I caught him doing that twice," Pinto added. "Naturally I warned him about it, too. Because, you know I loved Cooper, and my man, Milo here, as if they were my own sons. In fact, I practically got down on my hands and knees and begged Cooper to not take such a risk. Offered to work on his gun myself, in fact. He just laughed it off. Looking back, I should have insisted he turn the gun around, facing away from him as it should've been. If I'd been insistent enough, Coop would have complied, if for no other reason than to humor me."

Rip shook his head in sorrow. "Captain Bean, as I told Milo, you can't hold yourself responsible for someone else's foolish decisions. You both tried to dissuade him, but I promise you, nothing either of you could have done or said would have prevented Cooper from holding the gun facing toward himself when he was out here alone that day. People are creatures of habit by nature. As you just alluded to, Pinto, had he turned that gun the correct way when you asked him to on those earlier occasions, it would have only been to appease you and get you off his back."

Pinto nodded. "You're probably right, Rip. Like most men, I suppose, Cooper *was* hard-headed. I have no doubt now that's exactly what happened. I hate knowing that such a tragic and preventable mishap caused my friend to lose his life, but also relieved that someone else didn't take it from him."

"Me too," Milo chimed in. "I don't know why that possibility never occurred to me, knowing his habit of taking crazy risks. Particularly after I'd learned the coroner said he'd been shot at extremely close range.

That alone should have been a clue."

"Yeah, I should have thought of that too," Pinto said.

"You two lost a close friend. You were too emotionally invested in the situation to dwell over every potential occurrence. Fortunately, Rapella was thinking more clearly than the rest of us, looking at the situation from every perceivable angle," Rip said, smiling at me. He reached out and pulled me toward him in a warm embrace and kissed me on the forehead. "Good job, sweetheart. Your intuition or niggling notion as you referred to it, paid off!"

I felt my chest expand in pride, so thankful my hunch had been proven to have merit. I could have been left looking like a fool had it turned out I was totally off base. We'd been trying to track down a killer who never existed. Cooper Claypool's death had not been a murder, after all, but rather an unfortunate blunder. He'd fallen victim to a careless mistake. Cooper's demise had been an accidental death of his own making, a determination I hoped would make it easier for Milo and Philip Bean to forgive themselves for their friend's untimely, and self-induced, passing.

Just as Pinto had maintained, despite the overwhelming sorrow and heartache we were all experiencing, I had mixed emotions; sad my son-in-law's friend and business partner had suffered an avoidable death, but happy we'd discovered the truth behind his passing.

And to be perfectly honest, I'd have felt rather silly if today's efforts had amounted to nothing more than an unsuccessful hunt for that "needle somebody had lost in a haystack somewhere."

EPILOGUE

Life settled down after the county coroner and investigating team had agreed the cause of Cooper Claypool's death was accidental, not homicidal. His body was released to the family for burial, and we all attended the somber and emotional memorial service at the Duncan Cemetery in Flour Bluff, Texas, where his parents were also entombed.

Regina and I had been busy decorating for the holidays. In my daughter's home, that task entailed hanging lights across the front and back decks, as well as every tree or shrub on their property, and finding places to display box after box of figurines and knick-knacks, including a dozen pine-scented candles, none of which were we allowed to light.

There were way too many decorations for the eight-foot tree in the family room; ornaments of every shape and size, tinsel, pine cones and satin bows to tie to the branches, and numerous odds and ends with a seasonal vibe to them. The weight and over-abundance of unnecessary crap hanging on their Christmas tree made it look as though it might topple over at any given moment. If that were to happen, the ensuing crash would also take down the "damned flamingo" statue in the corner of the room. *And what a crying shame that would be*, I thought mockingly.

Decorating the Chartreuse Caboose, on the other hand, consisted of hanging a holiday-themed dish towel from our oven handle, and taking our ceramic Christmas tree out of the storage compartment under our bed to place on the kitchen counter. That small decoration alone effectively reduced the available working space for meal preparation to about the width of my hand. We didn't have space to spare for a second holiday decoration.

Our twelve-inch Christmas tree had colored lights that shone through little holes in the ceramic which represented ornaments. It had been a trailer-warming gift from my Bunko club when we'd sold our home and become full-time RVers nearly six years ago. With limited space in our thirty-foot home on wheels, it had been the ideal gift.

After a refreshing dip in the kids' pool, we were relaxing on the back deck overlooking Milo and Reggie's dock and boat lifts, enjoying our customary afternoon cocktails. I was drained from the seven-and-a-half hours of decorating Regina's home, followed by the minute and thirty-seven seconds spent decorating my own. I actually could have knocked our place out in less than a minute if I hadn't had to sweep up a half-filled box worth of pasta shells. Dolly had knocked the opened box over when she'd tried to jump up on the counter to quell her curiosity about the new holiday addition. She should have realized by now she'd devoured one kitty treat too many to successfully clear the height of the counter, and quit trying.

Reggie was sitting at the patio table with its umbrella opened up. She was addressing envelopes in order to mail their Christmas cards out the following day. I kept my mouth shut when she put a stamp on an envelope addressed to Rip and me. Good grief! Couldn't she see I was sitting right next to her and saved the forty-nine cents?

Rip was relaxing in the shade, holding his afternoon highball, as he told the kids about Sheriff Peabody stopping by the campground to speak to him early that morning. I'd been so relieved when Joe apologized to Rip for hurting his feelings and explained his reasoning for banning him from getting involved in the case. I had listened as the contrite sheriff talked to his former boss.

"You were always my hero, Rip. Choosing me to take under your wing and promote meant more to me than you could imagine. I didn't want you to think that all the hours and hard work you put into grooming me to take over your position had been a royal waste of time. I knew ignoring standard procedures would have looked like unprofessional and sloppy police work to you. Looking in your eyes, Rip, and seeing you were disappointed in me would have broken my heart."

"I totally understand, Joe," Rip had assured his protégée before the man continued.

"But if we'd discovered any concrete evidence to arrest a perpetrator, trust me, you'd have been the first person I called. But, as you guys know, there was no perp to arrest in this case. Many thanks from the entire department for the work and time you put in on your own to solve the case for us. And, my friend, if a detective position opens up, I might be offering Rapella a job." Rip and I had both laughed, but knowing Joe appreciated our uninvited meddling was a relief to both of us. I was particularly proud Sheriff Peabody had singled me out for my efforts in resolving the puzzling case.

Rip had shown the younger man a great deal of warmth and consideration, and assured Joe Peabody of his pride in the exceptional manner in which he handled the responsibility of such a demanding position. Rip's mood had lightened dramatically after the current sheriff's visit, as if a heavy load had been lifted off his shoulders.

"Tell the kids what else Joe told you," I prompted.

"Oh, yes, of course. Joe had to have his ankle X-rayed yesterday after he thought he might have broken it stepping off a curb awkwardly—"

"And where exactly was that curb?" I asked mischievously.

"In front of Rockport Donuts." Rip grimaced dramatically and then turned to look at me. He jokingly cautioned me. "And there best be no more wisecracks about cops eating doughnuts."

The kids and I laughed before Rip continued. "Fortunately, Joe's ankle was only sprained. However, while he was at the health clinic, Dr. O'Keefe told him that he and his ex-wife, Avery Curry, were getting back together, putting their divorce on hold for now, and trying to repair their marriage. Avery had told Patrick she'd only taken up with Cooper Claypool to elevate her poor self-image following their separation. And Avery admitted she'd hoped to make her ex a little jealous too, which it seems to me she accomplished in spades."

Then I related to the kids more of what the sheriff had said. "And Rip forgot to mention that Dr. O'Keefe has also agreed to let Avery enroll in a culinary trade school so she can pursue her dream of becoming a chef. She's a nice lady, so I was really happy to hear that news, especially considering that, just out of the blue, Jugs 'n Mugs let her go a couple of days ago." I didn't even have to look at Rip to know that once again his eyes were in danger of becoming stuck in the "rolling" position. It would serve him right if they did.

Before Rip could make a smart-aleck remark, I prompted him again. "Don't forget to tell them what Joe told you about Paulie Winterkorn and the loan shark in El Paso."

"Oh, yeah. Joe said they brought Paulie Winterkorn in for questioning but decided not to charge him with harassment since the defendant was already deceased and there seemed to be no purpose in spending taxpayer money on a case against him. He told the detectives he'd read about Cooper's murder in the paper and was afraid for his own well-being for not having collected the money owed his boss."

Rip took a sip of his drink and turned to Milo. "Winterkorn decided to take advantage of the situation and try to manipulate you into paying off Cooper's debt, which explains why he showed up on your doorstep. Joe assured me that Paulie Winterkorn will never agree to work for a loan shark again, judging by how terrified he'd been of retribution by his merciless boss in El Paso when he failed to collect Cooper's debt. And, by the way, Winterkorn told Detective Reeves he hadn't expected to be met at the door by Milo's new wife, 'Bridezilla'."

"What *should* I do about that unpaid loan, Pop?" Milo asked after we all stopped chuckling.

"Nothing, son. It wasn't your loan to begin with, and the El Paso Police Department informed Joe that the loan shark was currently incarcerated for some unrelated crime and his goons would never harass you again. And the best news of all is that Peabody assured me the assault charges against you would be dropped too, Milo, for the same reason no charges were filed against Winterkorn. Cooper's death was self-inflicted and it would serve no point to fine you, or waste taxpayer money keeping you behind bars for the conflict at Crabby's."

"Oh, thank God," Milo and Regina said in unison. The overwhelming sense of relief was palpable on the Moores' back deck that afternoon.

"I have a bit of good news, too," Milo said with a joyfulness we'd never had the pleasure of witnessing before. "Coop had inherited his parent's paid-off home. With no family left to speak of, he left it to Pinto in his will. And Pinto has decided to sell his boat and retire, which is perfect timing because the Parks and Wildlife Department has just announced they're closing Copano and Aransas Bays to commercial oyster harvesting for awhile to let the beds replenish and become healthy once again."

"We'll he be able to make it financially?" I asked, recalling the conversation we'd had with him about retiring.

"With no mortgage payment and his new part-time job with MC Hammerheads, he'll get by all right. I'll make sure of it." Milo winked and smiled, genuinely delighted for Pinto. And I'm sure he was equally pleased at the idea of having his respected friend work with him in the future. Rip and I shared his happiness.

"Tell your folks your good news, babe," Milo said as he patted Regina's thigh. Reggie had closed a deal for a client purchasing a multi-million dollar bayfront home on Finisterre, the costliest and most prestigious street on Key Allegro Island. "Location, location, location" was a very apt phrase for homes on the coast. We congratulated our daughter on the hefty commission she was going to receive from the sale; it would go a long way in helping the couple get back on a good financial footing.

Regina went inside and fixed us all another round of drinks while Rip tried to help Milo devise a workable financial plan for both Milo and Regina, personally, and for the MC Hammerheads Construction Company. He was determined to help get the kids back on their feet before they lost their house to the bank and watched their business go belly-up.

Rip offered to float the kids a loan to properly take care of the mold issue in the Sarcova's home and reimburse them for their son's medical bills, settle the outstanding debt to Mack's Wells, Inc., and take care of a few other obligations hanging over their heads. I was surprised to hear Milo graciously turn down the offer.

"I want to do this on my own, Pop. I sincerely appreciate the offer, and will keep it in mind if worse comes to worse. But I think I can cover all those things if I sell my new BMW and all but a couple of guns in my firearms collection, a few of which are worth a mint. I don't need such an expensive truck to drive, either. I plan to sell it, too, and lease a truck without all the bells and whistles I never use anyway. And who needs three dozen guns and enough ammo to blow this entire end of the island off the map?"

Rip smiled, clearly impressed and surprised with Milo's response. "If you're sure, son, but—"

"No 'buts' about it. I need to work this mess out myself, and with Regina's help, we can save our home *and* our business. She's agreed to cut back on spending money for anything that's not absolutely necessary."

Good luck with that, I thought. I eavesdropped as Milo continued.

"As sole owner of MC Hammerheads now, I need to learn better business skills. I handle the bills at home, but as I said before, the financial end of the business was part of Cooper's responsibilities. It's a whole different ball of wax than our personal finances, but it's all up to me now. I'll never remove the "C" in the company's name, though. Cooper and I built MC Hammerheads together, and I want to make him proud of how well our business does in the future," Milo said.

Not to mention, I thought, "M Hammerheads" sounds rather bizarre.

I was happy to see Rip's opinion of his new son-in-law had softened in the last few days. I think knowing for certain Milo hadn't had a hand in the gruesome death of his partner had taken a load off Rip's mind, as it had mine. With affection in his voice, he reassured Milo.

"I'm sure you'll make him proud. I know I'm proud of you. Rapella and I will be in Rockport for another three or four months before heading north to Montana. I'll help you line out the finances, and do whatever I can to assist in keeping the business going forward. You may want to think about hiring an accountant to take the pressure off you. You probably need to be out in the field overseeing the actual construction process instead of spending a lot of time in the office."

"Yeah, I do. Good idea. I appreciate your offer to help me get lined out. And that's one offer I *will* accept. Sorry I didn't make your efforts to exonerate me any easier when the detectives were convinced I'd killed my best friend. Cooper's death totally rocked my world, and I was too shaken up to think clearly. I was even a little pissed off that anyone would seriously believe I'd do something that atrocious."

I'd been listening half-heartedly to the men discussing the future success of Milo's house-flipping business, praying his plan would prove to be successful. However, I was skeptical about how much help Regina would be in Milo's quest to cut back on expenditures. Just that morning she'd purchased a gazing ball for their front yard. A gazing ball, for goodness' sakes! And no gazing ball would be complete without the dolphin statue the ball had been displayed on, she'd insisted. The ball with the reflective patina nestled securely into the space between Flipper's opened jaws. 'A must for the landscaped island in the center of our circle driveway," Reggie had stated, as I was trying to figure out what purpose it would serve.

Milo and Reggie's back deck was a great location to watch the hustle and bustle of life on the waterfront: the passing of boating vessels of every variety, from kayaks to million-dollar yachts. There were blue herons, snowy egrets, pelicans, osprey and cormorants all vying for the best post to perch on to soak in the sun and dry off their wings. And often, there were *real* dolphins frolicking in the water, right next to the deck on occasion. Best of all, the Moores' deck offered the most awe-inspiring view of the late afternoon sun setting on the horizon, reflecting a host of beautiful colors across the often tranquil waters of the bay.

At the moment, my mind was on what we could do tomorrow for fun, now that all of our time and energy wouldn't be spent on trying to track down a non-existent killer. Looking back, I realized Milo had been correct. Fishing really had gotten into my blood. Hooking the scarcely undersized redfish had been so exhilarating; it had unwittingly made me anxious to try again in hopes of catching a keeper. A legal-sized one I could hold up for a photo to show off at my next Bunko club meeting. When there was a pause in the men's conversation, I asked, "How about going wade-fishing tomorrow?"

"No way!" Rip, Milo, and Regina exclaimed in harmony.

"The Christmas boat parade is tomorrow night. Let's grill hamburgers and sit out here to watch it," Reggie suggested as an alternative. Her idea was met with much enthusiasm. It stands to reason it would take the fellows a while to shake the memories of our last fishing trip. And watching the interesting array of boats circling Little Bay, all decorated and lit up like a—well, like a Christmas tree—sounded fun to me, too.

The ripple effect always amazed me. Cooper Claypool's single bad decision had instigated a wave, followed by a week's worth of wrinkles that had us chasing our tails and barking up a lot of wrong trees. But all that was behind us now, and we could finally settle down and enjoy the holidays with Regina and Milo in our own hometown.

Even though I felt a bit miffled that no one had agreed to my fishing suggestion, and only a bang-up boat parade would change my miffedness to miffaliciousness, I was still proud to be the person who was most responsible for solving the perplexing riddle of Cooper Claypool's death and stemming the tide—a rip tide of sorts.

Turn the page for an

excerpt from

RIPPED

TO

SHREDS

A Ripple Effect Cozy Mystery
Book Three

Jeanne Glidewell

"Screech! Screech! Screech!"

"What the——?" I started to ask Boonie Whetstone, the owner of the Rest 'n Peace RV Park, which was nestled amid the tall pines in the Bighorn National Forest. He was in the laundry room with me, emptying quarters out of the machines into a three-pound coffee can. He'd wrap and resell them to customers to use to do their laundry, he'd said. Now that was a recycling plan I could appreciate.

"Screech!"

"What in the world was that?" I asked. I'd dropped my basket of clean clothes, startled by the eerie noise. "It sounds like a woman screaming out there in the, um, out there in the——"

"Boonies?" Boonie chuckled at his pun after finishing my sentence for me. As I bent over to collect my clothes, many of which would have to be refolded, he replied, "Could be a number of things. A screech owl, perhaps. Maybe even a female mountain lion."

"Screech! Screech!" We heard emanating from within the not-so-distant forest again.

"Yeah, my guess is a lion," Boonie said with a knowing nod, as if telling me there was a wild baby bunny running amok in the woods. If there *was* a bunny running out there, it was probably because a mountain lion was chasing it, intent on devouring the poor thing for lunch.

"There are mountain lions that close to us? Couldn't they come right into the campground?" I asked nervously.

"Yes, of course. The elevation's eighty-nine hundred feet here, and I don't have an electric fence around this RV Park, you know." He laughed and winked, not at all concerned about the possibility of having feral, customer-eating cats in the vicinity.

"Maybe you should invest in one."

As if he hadn't heard me, Boonie went on to explain. "Female mountain lions, or cougars, will scream like that when they're calling out for a mate. Their mating season usually runs from December through March. It's mid-April, but they'll mate at other times of the year sometimes."

"Well, there goes the 'Rest 'n Peace' aspect of your park, Mr. Whetstone," I said with a shudder. When we'd first arrived, I'd thought the RV Park's name was a clever idea for such a quiet, serene campground, but now I found it more ironic than cute.

"Don't worry. They're not apt to bother you. Wouldn't hurt to carry a can of pepper spray when you're out and about on the grounds, though. We sell some in the office for just that reason. Probably not all that effective, but it gives our customers a little peace of mind, anyway."

"I'd settle for a little peace of mind at the moment. I'll go buy a can right now while my last load is drying."

"Sorry, ma'am. The store's closed on Sundays. Only the check-in desk is open."

Swell. "Not apt to bother you" and "not all that effective" were not comforting phrases to me. I didn't have pepper spray to carry on my way back to the Chartreuse Caboose, our thirty-foot travel trailer. What I had was a spray bottle of *Shout*; a stain remover, not a cougar remover.

"Screech!" I heard again as I took a step outside twenty minutes later. Its source appeared to be eerily close. I quickly stepped back inside and closed the door, giving myself a few extra minutes to bolster some courage. Leave it to Rip to request the site at the farthest end of the campground. "Closer to nature," he'd said. *Closer to wild, dangerous animals, too*, I thought. *And, at the moment, too blasted far from the laundry room for my liking.*

I can't stay in here forever. I told myself. When I'd left the trailer, my husband had been watching our team, the Dallas Cowboys, getting routed by the Patriots, and was no doubt snoozing on the couch by now. I'd have to move as briskly as possible returning to the trailer. *If I come face to face with a cougar, my only option will be to try to 'Shout' it out'! Not a very reassuring concept!*

I made it back to the trailer in record time. And that's taking into account I had to stop once to pick my clean clothes up off the gravel and shove them all back into the basket in one big wad. When a toddler I'd just passed shrieked for her mother, I'd come completely unglued. I'd flung the basket, armed myself with the bottle of Shout, and assumed a defensive posture, all in the space of a second-and-a-half. The young child, now terrified of me, was a cute little girl, and I prayed she wouldn't become an hors d'oeuvre before "me-ma" took her back inside.

When I entered the trailer we'd painted chartreuse, with yellow and brown sunflowers to give it even more style, my husband of nearly fifty years, Clyde Ripple, better known as Rip, was just waking up from his nap. There were four or five cheese puffs scattered across his chest as if he'd fallen asleep mid-snack. He was intrigued, but not all that apprehensive about having big cats in the area. "We'll pick up a couple cans of that pepper spray tomorrow if it makes you feel better. Are you still planning to go garage-sale shopping with Cora?"

"Yes. She's picking me up in about an hour. Willie will hang out here with you while we're gone. In the meantime, I need to fold these clothes for the third time and put something in the slow cooker for supper. Rump roast sound okay?"

"You bet! My rump's about to waste away to nothing, you know." We both laughed. Rip had put on fifteen pounds since retiring from law enforcement six years ago, and he wasn't exactly emaciated back then. Following his retirement, we'd sold our home, gotten rid of most of our belongings, bought the Chartreuse Caboose, and hit the road as full-time RVers.

At the present, we were in northern Wyoming. My late brother's daughter, Cora Beaufont, and her husband, Dirk, lived in Buffalo, just east of the Bighorn mountain range.

Cora's father, Dusty, the youngest of my four brothers, died ten years ago when Cora was twenty-nine. She and I had always been close. Dirk, an engineer for a large oil company, was spending three months in Ingleside, Texas, overseeing the construction of a large oil rig. We decided it'd be a good time to visit Cora and our great-nephew, twelve-year-old William, or "Slick Willie" as we called him. We'd keep them company while Dirk was away on business. I was looking forward to a fun month in Wyoming with my favorite niece.

"Hey, Aunt Rappie! Over here!' Cora called out across the crowded garage. Story, Wyoming, a town north of Buffalo that fewer than a thousand folks called home, was having a city-wide garage sale all weekend. We'd already been to three places and found nothing of interest. Many of the same people we'd seen at the other sales were now shopping at this one, as well. Clearly, we were all on the same circuit. When I approached Cora, she was holding up a camouflaged box the size of a brick. "Here's what you need!"

"What is it?" I asked.

"A game camera!" She'd been told on the way to town about the screeching I'd heard in the forest. "You can attach it to a tree in the woods and get photos of any kind of critter that passes by. It's motion-activated, and takes color photos during the day and infra-red ones at night. Cool, huh?"

"Yeah, *real* cool. Except that'd involve actually walking into the woods where a mountain lion might be waiting to stalk me like a baby moose. No thanks, sweetheart!"

I had to admit, though, the possibility of capturing a photo of the critter making the spooky sounds was enticing. Unfortunately, at times, my curiosity was stronger than that of our fifteen-pound cat, Dolly. And I was more apt to be killed by it, too, I realized.

"Take Uncle Rip with you to set the camera up and check it for photos occasionally. He does own a gun, doesn't he? After all, he was a county sheriff for six or seven years."

"Ten, actually. But I'd never let him shoot an animal," I said. "Except maybe with his pellet gun just to scare it off."

After much debate with Cora, and even more with myself, I decided to invest in a like-new "critter cam". I hadn't planned on spending my entire twenty-dollar wad on only one item, but it was exciting to think about what kind of critters I might get photos of in the forest. I could feel my enthusiasm mounting.

Little did I know at the time that my new critter cam would snap a photo of a critter of the two-legged variety; even more menacing and lethal than a mountain lion.

———◆———

RIPPED TO SHREDS
available in print and ebook

THE RIPPLE EFFECT COZY MYSTERIES

A Rip Roaring Good Time
Rip Tide
Ripped to Shreds

Also by Jeanne Glidewell

The Lexie Star Mystery Series
Leave No Stone Unturned
Extinguished Guest
Haunted
With This Ring
Just Ducky
Cozy Camping
The Spirit of the Season (A Novella)

Jeanne Glidewell, lives with her husband, Bob, and chubby cat, Dolly, in Bonner Springs, Kansas. In the winter the three of them travel to their waterfront condo in Rockport, Texas, to spend time with friends, enjoy the milder climate, and wade-fish the bays off the Gulf Coast. In Dolly's case, she does less wade-fishing and more napping, but is a "coastal kitty" nonetheless. Dolly gets her exercise by guarding the condo from being overtaken by an  army of the small lizards that frequent the back deck.

Besides writing and fishing, Jeanne enjoys wildlife photography, traveling both here and abroad, and spending time with her four grandchildren. She and Bob owned and operated a large RV park in Cheyenne, Wyoming, for twelve years. It was that enjoyable period in Jeanne's life that inspired her to write a mystery series involving a full-time RVing couple - The Ripple Effect series.

As a 2006 pancreas and kidney transplant recipient, Jeanne now volunteers as a mentor for the Gift of Life of KC program, helping future transplant recipients prepare mentally and emotionally for their upcoming transplants. She's an avid advocate for tissue and organ donation and encourages everyone to make their decision to become a donor known to their family and friends. Marking "organ donor" on a driver's license is not enough to ensure your final wishes are adhered to. Please consider giving the ultimate gift - the gift of life - when you no longer have a need for your organs.

Jeanne is the author of a romance/suspense novel, Soul Survivor, six novels and one novella in her Lexie Starr cozy mystery series, and two novels in her new Ripple Effect cozy mystery series. She is currently writing book three in this series, Ripped to Shreds, and hopes to have it released in the late spring or early summer of 2016.

Jeanne loves hearing from readers. Contact her at: JeanneGlidewell@epublishingworks.com